SLAVE QUEEN

ALSO BY H.B. MOORE

The Omar Zagouri Thrillers:

Lost King
Finding Sheba
Beneath: An Omar Zagouri Short Story
First Heist: An Omar Zagouri Short Story

Esther the Queen
Daughters of Jared
Eve: In the Beginning
The Out of Jerusalem series
The Moses Chronicles series

WRITING AS HEATHER B. MOORE

Power of the Matchmaker
Love is Come
Heart of the Ocean
The Fortune Café
The Boardwalk Antiques Shop
The Mariposa Hotel
Falling for June
The Aliso Creek series
The Newport Ladies Book Club series
A Timeless Romance Anthology series

SLAVE QUEEN

AN OMAR ZAGOURI THRILLER

H.B. MOORE

Text copyright © 2016 by H.B. Moore
All rights reserved.

Published by Thomas & Mercer, Seattle

www.apub.com

Amazon, the Amazon logo, and Thomas & Mercer are trademarks of Amazon.com, Inc., or its affiliates.

ISBN-13: 9781503938830
ISBN-10: 1503938832

Map Credit: Don Larson

Cover design by M.S. Corley

Map illustrated by Don Larson

For my critique group members:
Michele Holmes, Jeff Savage, Annette Lyon,
Sarah Eden,
and Rob Wells.
It really does take a village to raise a writer.

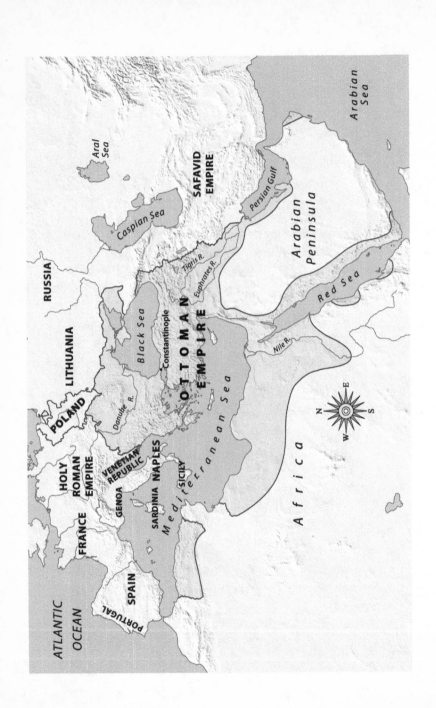

SULTAN SÜLEYMAN

LINEAGE

Sultan Süleyman the Magnificent: November 6, 1494 – September 7, 1566

Father: Sultan Selim I
Mother: Ayşe Hafsa Sultan

Consorts:
Mahidevran Sultan
Children: Mustafa, Raziya
Gülfem Hatun
Children: Murad
Roxelane Hürrem Sultan
Children: Mehmed, Mihrimah Sultan, Abdullah, Selim II (successor to Süleyman),
Bayezid, Cihangir

*"My woman of the beautiful hair, my love of the slanted brow,
my love of eyes full of mischief . . .
I'll sing your praises always. I, lover of the tormented heart."*

—*Poem written by Sultan Süleyman
to Roxelane*

❖ CHAPTER ONE ❖

IZMIR, TURKEY

Baris Uzuner turned the bolt in the lock for the second time, double-checking that the front door was secure. Not that it would keep anyone out who really wanted to break into his Antiques & Gold Shoppe situated on Anafartalar Street in the heart of Izmir. Baris was no stranger to break-ins. It went with the business of dealing in antiques, a commitment he'd made when accepting the position of Director of the Turkish Royalists. While the organization worked to recruit other Royalists faithful to the mission of restoring the monarchy, Baris spent his days seeking evidence of the true royal lineage of the Ottoman Empire.

It was no easy feat, but it was Baris's passion; and now, millions of dollars spent and many high-risk endeavors later, he had a healthy collection of artifacts from the early sixteenth century purchased on the black market. He smiled every time he thought about this growing collection. As a descendant of the sultan Süleyman the Magnificent, Baris felt a strong connection to the empire. This had led to his becoming director of the underground organization.

Baris rattled the door knob just to make sure it was secured. It was.

Although Baris had installed a first-rate security system when he'd opened the shop, within weeks a thief had disarmed it and walked right in, helping himself to merchandise worth thousands of Turkish lira. The missing merchandise hadn't exactly broken Baris's heart, since it'd all been purchased with campaign money, but one particular painting had been stolen—a portrait of the sultan. Because Süleyman was an icon to Baris and the Royalists' cause, this theft felt personal.

Since his high tech system had failed him completely, he'd installed good, solid dead bolts. He'd left the alarm system on the front store window. A rock or brick through the glass would sound an earsplitting alarm. Baris had canceled his security contract, so no security team would be dispatched in the event of a breach. But a thief wouldn't know that. A thief also couldn't know that Baris had just received a shipment of pottery discovered beneath one of the sixteenth-century mosques built by Süleyman's famous architect Sinan.

Baris had tapped into one of the oldest, most secretive black market antique businesses, and it was like Christmas morning each time he got approval for a purchase. Well, Christmas morning if he'd been Christian.

Ten years before when he'd become the director of the Turkish Royalists, they'd unanimously decided that members had to be Muslim. It was the only way to fully respect the sultan line. When the Turkish Royalists once again established a monarchy in Turkey, they would declare the country Muslim. The nation would be unified in one purpose of mind and become true defenders of Islam.

Now, satisfied he'd secured the front entrance, Baris made his way through his store, walking around the high-tabled displays, designed to bring goods closer to customers' eyes. His store wasn't lit with common overhead fluorescents, but rather strategically placed floor lamps which cast an ethereal and even ancient glow about the shop. The lighting created a powerful ambience, especially when used in conjunction with subtle incense and low music. He'd perfected becoming a shopkeeper.

Baris turned off the lamps as he made his way to the back of the shop and stopped before his small storage room. He kept the storage room door covered with a dusty Byzantine Empire tapestry. Each night before leaving, he made one final check on this space where he kept his growing Ottoman collection. And tonight, he couldn't wait to inspect the new shipment. He'd hidden it as soon as it had been delivered by an unidentified courier.

As he swept aside the tapestry, dust bloomed from the fibers. Baris ignored the tickling in his nose and typed the code into the keypad by the door. It clicked open immediately, and Baris stepped inside. Two lights turned on, triggered by motion, and Baris closed the door behind him, ignoring the prickling sensation from standing in such a small, closed room.

Baris eagerly crossed to the crate and used a screwdriver to loosen the screws. There was no label or other identification, just the simple wooden construction that marked all the black market deliveries Baris received.

The lid lifted easily, and Baris removed the metal case inside. As expected, there was a combination lock built into the metal case, and he entered his assigned combination. The case unlatched, and as Baris lifted the lid, his quick breaths mirroring his racing heart.

There, nestled inside the padded case, were three jars. Baris's eyes burned with emotion. Judging by the indicators on the pottery, Baris guessed they were Ottoman Empire, mid-1550s. The jars were beautifully glazed and painted with battle scenes between Turkish warriors and Mongols. The Turks were depicted as winning with their short bows and yataghans, and the Ottoman flag showed it was a royal battle. *Royal,* Baris thought. This was a very good sign. These jars had been used in the royal chambers, possibly for wine or water, or even coffee. His ancestors' hands and lips may have touched these very vessels.

His pulse pounding, and his hands starting to perspire, he picked up the first vessel, knowing he might be the first person to touch the pottery with bare hands in hundreds of years. In a few moments, he'd put on gloves, but for now, he wanted to feel the slick, dry thickness of the pottery connecting him to the sultan's court.

Baris brought his nose to the narrow opening of the jar and inhaled. He breathed in a musky, spicy scent. Coffee? Tea? Incense? With one hand Baris reached for his cell phone and turned on the flashlight. He shined it into the opening, looking to see if there were any coffee bean remnants. The fine hairs on his neck stood on end as he spotted a rolled piece of parchment inside.

For a moment he stared, disbelieving. Had the excavators not seen the parchment inside? If so, that meant Baris would be the first human to possess the parchment since it was placed there four hundred years ago.

He reached inside and drew out the rolled parchment. It could be anything, he told himself—a poem written by the sultan or a letter sent to one of his wives. Dozens of those had been recovered already. The few that they sold had fetched a nice price from private collectors, which in turn Baris had funneled back into the Royalist organization, but the ones they didn't sell were stored in the Royalist archive warehouse.

Baris spread out the parchment and knew instantly it wasn't a piece of ancient literature. It was an official letter or record of sorts. The waxed seal had been broken at some point, but by lining it up, the seal was plainly that of the sultan.

Taking a deep breath, Baris started to read the text from the beginning. It was beautifully written old Turkish, the lettering an art form by itself.

The date was the first thing that alerted Baris to the significance of the parchment—1552. A year before Mustafa had been executed, the oldest son of the sultan's first wife Mahidevran. The sultan had ordered Mustafa put to death when he discovered Mustafa had committed treason. Some historians believed that Mustafa was set up—that the sultan's favorite wife Roxelane arranged for the deceit so that the sultan would have him put to death and make room for Roxelane's own son to inherit. Which he did. Selim II became the next sultan, and his son Murad III followed after.

Baris's attention was riveted the moment he spotted Mustafa's name in the text. Slow chills crept along his neck, and he read every word carefully once, twice, and finally a third time. He wasn't even sure he'd breathed for several moments. This was a letter written by the sultan to his favorite wife, instructing her to falsify records that would demonstrate Mustafa's guilt of treason.

We must clear the way for our sons to inherit the throne. I feel that my good fortune in battle may not last many more years. This matter is urgent, and I leave it in your capable hands, my good wife. Your ever loving Süleyman.

If the words had been shouted in a market square over a loudspeaker, they couldn't have been more clear.

In Baris's hands, he held evidence that Mustafa had been wrongfully executed, that Roxelane and the sultan had plotted to kill the rightful heir to the throne. That the esteemed sultan and first lady of the Ottoman Empire were, in fact, cold-blooded murderers. This meant that Mustafa's line could finally be recognized as the true and living heirs of the sultan. A line that still had living descendants today.

Including me.

Roxelane's line through her son Selim II had spread all over the world, but Mustafa's line had stayed in Turkey. Yes.

Baris held a document that would bring thousands more flocking to the Royalist organization. He imagined the men who would join their organization, donate money and resources, infiltrate various levels of the Turkish government, and ready themselves to rise up when the time was right. Rise up and defeat the Turkish government and install the true descendant of the sultan through the line of his true heir, Mustafa.

Me. I am the descendant of Mustafa.

An e-mail alert pinged from his phone, pulling Baris from his frenzied thoughts. He looked at his phone. It was his black market contact. Surprise shot through him. He'd never been contacted before without himself first contacting Bata Enterprises.

He opened the e-mail immediately: *Shipment sent by mistake. Do not open. Courier will arrive within the hour to retrieve shipment. Confirm you've received this notice.*

Baris stared at the message for several moments before replying. Then he typed: *Confirmed.*

He didn't bother to close up the metal case or reaffix the top of the crate. Instead, he left the storage room, shut the door firmly, crossed to the cash register, and opened the drawer below it. He deftly removed a pistol and twisted on a silencer.

There was no way Baris was letting these letters go. With this revelation, their recruits would skyrocket. Within a year, they'd be poised to take over the government. True order would be restored to their homeland.

Even though the e-mail had said the courier would return in an hour, Baris didn't have long to wait. A soft knock sounded on the back door, and Baris called out, "It's open."

A tall figure stepped inside, and Baris noted the man wore brown trousers and a shirt. No identifying feature stood out, except for a pepper of gray in the man's dark hair.

There would be no words between the two men; that was how Bata Enterprises worked. All communication was electronic. But even if the courier had intended to greet Baris, he'd never know. Baris lifted the pistol and aimed at the man's forehead. There would be less blood that way. One shot, and the courier's knees buckled.

As the courier collapsed to the floor, Baris walked forward and stood over the dying body.

He did a quick search of the man's pockets. Inside the jacket, Baris found what he was looking for—the man's cell phone. It would take Baris only moments to open the settings and figure out where the courier had traveled from.

◆ CHAPTER TWO ◆

TEL AVIV

SIX MONTHS LATER

A ringing phone wasn't something that Omar Zagouri ever wanted to wake up to in the middle of the night, especially when the caller had a 212 country code. *Morocco.* Adrenaline shot through him, fully waking him up. He gripped the phone with its glowing screen and strode from his bedroom before answering the call. If the news wasn't terrible, then there was no need to wake Mia, who was, miraculously, sleeping in his bed, although they hadn't been speaking much for the past week.

"Rahim?" Omar answered, his voice scratched from sleep.

"Your mother's ill." His father's voice sounded far away, as if the technology of cell phones hadn't advanced for a decade.

Omar exhaled, letting the adrenaline settle to a low hum. "What's going on?" For his father to call him in the middle of the night, Omar knew this wasn't an ordinary illness.

"Pneumonia," his father said, his weariness coming through the connection. "She was just released from the hospital, after being pumped full of more than one antibiotic."

Omar hadn't even known she'd been in the hospital. He let the annoyance at his father fade so that he could focus on getting the more important information out of the man. "Should I come out?"

His father paused, and in that pause, Omar heard everything his father wasn't telling him. There was a reason that Omar wouldn't ever be able to call him "father" over a live connection—it would give away their relationship if anyone had tapped his father's phone. It would be too easy for one of Omar's enemies to use his family against him. And the Arab nation of Morocco would not be too pleased to learn that one of their trusted government employees had a son who worked for the Israeli government. When his father had moved from Canada back to his home country and went to work for the Moroccan government ten years ago, he'd given up much of his privacy.

Omar worked for one of the exclusive departments of the Israeli government as an undercover agent, his official title Special Agent for the Preservation of Cultural Heritage and Ancient Artifacts. And although a few months ago he'd been appointed director, an assignment that continued to cause him angst, he found his best days were those in the field, not sitting behind the cracked cypress wood desk in the stuffy Tel Aviv office.

His father, Rahim Zagouri, was not a man of many words–unlike Omar, who had the habit of getting into trouble with almost everything he said. Perhaps he should have taken lessons from his father.

With his father still not speaking on the other end of the line, Omar made up his mind. "I'll catch the next flight out of Tel Aviv." He might have said too much already, true to form, but he couldn't take the words back now. If his father's employer discovered who Omar was, his father would have a lot to answer for.

"See you tomorrow," his father said. Then the line went dead. It seemed his father had accomplished what he'd set out to do.

Omar was going to Morocco to visit his extremely ill mother, but as he sat on the couch in the dark living room and listened to the silence of the night, he wondered if his mother was truly the one who was ill. Perhaps nothing his father said had been true. But he'd only needed to give Omar a reason to come to Morocco. Omar could only afford to become lost in thought for about thirty seconds before he powered on his laptop and looked up flights from Tel Aviv to Casablanca.

Omar would be taking Mia with him. It was about time she met his parents. Once he had two first class tickets booked, he sent a cryptic text to his boss, Simon Greif.

Going off grid for a few days. Will be in touch.

He didn't expect his phone to stay silent for long. Omar wasn't even sure Greif slept, and if he did, he accomplished it with his eyes open.

The reply came twenty seconds later. *What am I supposed to tell Italy?*

Eat more pasta? Omar texted back. One of his talents was quick repentance. *Send Sol. He'll get the job done.*

Greif wasn't giving up. *Italy first. Then go off the grid. I'll throw in a bonus.*

In Omar's world, money talked. Loudly. But if he were to scroll through his cell phone log, it would tell him that the last time his father had called was nearly three months ago. And that was to see if he was still alive after hearing about an explosion Omar had narrowly escaped.

Omar typed: *Mia's coming with me too.* Then he turned his phone off, not interested in whatever hailstorm Greif might throw with the new information.

Now, all Omar had to do was convince Mia, who was much more loyal to her job than he was, to travel to Morocco with him and meet his family.

He walked into the bedroom and stood in the doorway for a moment, watching Mia sleep. She was turned on her side, her dark curly hair framing her face, her long lashes resting peacefully. When those eyes were open, there was nothing peaceful about them—at least not lately. They'd been through a lot together while working for the same undercover department. They'd broken up, gotten back together, moved in together, nearly lost each other, and now . . .

Omar didn't know what to think. He loved her, but apparently when he'd proposed to her last week, that had been a game changer. Mia had taken a bag stuffed with a few essentials and had disappeared for two days. She was good at that. When she returned, she said she wasn't ready to talk. And it had been like that for five straight days now.

He exhaled slowly, not sure how he was going to break the ice between them and get her to go meet his parents, of all things. The timing couldn't be worse. But he had to try. Omar walked around the bed and sat next to her. He almost regretted having to wake her since she seemed to sleep so little anyway. She woke up immediately with the movement of the bed. He often woke in the middle of the night to see the glow of her computer screen coming from the front room as she typed away at another infernal report.

At least, he told himself as a sort of consolation, she was in *his* apartment. Not hiding somewhere, not out on a dangerous job, and not with another man. He took comfort in that.

"What is it?" she said, her dark eyes flashing in the dimness as every part of her became aware. Those three words were the most she'd spoken to him since her pronouncement upon her return.

"My father called."

Her eyes shifted from wariness to concern.

"My mother has been in the hospital with pneumonia," he said. "She's home now, but her health is fragile. My father wouldn't have called if he wasn't very worried."

Mia was sitting up now, leaning against the headboard. "I'm sorry." Her words were simple, generic even, but they were genuine coming from Mia.

Omar looked away then, unprepared for the emotions swirling inside of him. His mother was Jewish, which technically made him Jewish as well, although he'd never declared his religious beliefs one way or another. But it had felt natural to live in Israel, become employed there, and to dedicate his time to a country built on myriad faiths.

"I've made a plane reservation, and—" He stopped. His voice was trembling, and the tightening in his chest was making it difficult to catch a full breath. Maybe this was what people called delayed shock. While speaking to his father and then texting his boss, his mind had been clear, rational, and his heart hadn't felt like it was being squeezed into a tiny ball.

Mia's arms slipped around his neck, pulling him toward her, and habit made him move his hands to her waist and bury his face in her neck. She smelled of vanilla soap and warm sleep, and Omar was lost.

She spoke into his ear, sending shivers along his skin. "Do you want me to come with you?"

"Yes," he whispered. "I booked two tickets."

Her laughter was soft, and she drew him closer. He knew this was an olive branch, not the whole tree. It might last for hours or days, but then they would be back to her original rejection of his marriage proposal.

Regardless, he wanted this woman to be his forever, even when she wasn't speaking to him for days, and even when every undercover assignment she accepted had increasingly filled him with dread. That was how he knew he was in love with her. In a line of work where agents risked their lives on a regular basis, life had to take on a passive quality. Before Mia, he'd never let himself truly care about another agent or let a friendship deepen below the surface.

Somewhere along the way he and Mia had fallen in love, apparently he more so than she. Just as his father had warned him in their brief talks over the years, once he let his heart into the picture, his life would change. The more he fell in love with Mia, the more he understood his parents and their sacrifices. Both his mother and father had abandoned their countries to start fresh in Canada, where no one knew them, and no one could relegate them to a cultural box. In some societies, it was still considered a mortal sin for a Jewish woman to marry a Muslim man. Omar had been a product of their mixed marriage.

And irony of all ironies, Omar had proposed to a Christian. Mia was Christian and the love child of a man who had forsaken his pedestrian life and risen to be elected the Coptic Pope.

But here, now, Omar held Mia in his arms, as she ran her fingers through his hair, like a mother would a young child. And he didn't want to be anywhere else and couldn't imagine anything better—well, except if she'd say *yes*.

Until then, he'd take this moment.

"What time is the flight?" she asked, drawing away from him, gazing into his eyes.

He felt himself falling again. And he hoped the spiral would never stop. "The flight is at five thirty a.m."

Her eyes flickered to the iHome on the dresser on the other side of the room. It was just past 3:00 a.m. "We don't have much time to pack," she said, ever the practical one with her reports and lists. "So you'd better hurry and kiss me."

Omar didn't need to be asked twice. He kissed her as if she were the only pool of water left in the Rub' al-Khali Desert. Tomorrow, he'd be with his parents, with Mia at his side. Come what may, for better or worse they'd be together as he faced the true reason his father had summoned him to Morocco.

❖ CHAPTER THREE ❖

ISTANBUL

The job interview was not exactly what Leyla Kaplan had hoped for, but she needed something to use as an excuse so that she didn't have to go home for the summer and be courted by Ruslan. Even the idea of being courted in the twenty-first century sounded ridiculous. But her parents and her grandparents had lived in the small village of Mengen their whole lives, where arranged marriages were still held in high esteem. For practical purposes, of course. Which might have made sense in the fifteenth century after the Mongols had ravaged the coastal villages, killing the men, raping the women, and enslaving the children. The community had been forced to marry their pregnant daughters to the few remaining men, starting a chain of polygamous marriages and many children, who then all grew up and had to marry.

By the middle of the sixteenth century, the Ottoman Empire had taken its land back from the Mongols. Villages and cities had grown and prospered, bringing wealth to Leyla's village, since it was a stopping point in the Bolu province between Ankara and Istanbul. Her village was famous for its cooking schools and cuisine. And famous for being the home village of one of the concubines in Sultan Süleyman the Magnificent's court. The Ottoman sultan had found Leyla's ancestor beautiful, when he had passed through the village, and had ordered her to the palace.

Leyla's ancestor went willingly, of course, a great privilege to serve the almighty sultan. It seemed the village of Mengen hadn't progressed much by the twenty-first century, though, because the tradition of arranged marriages persisted, and the head families of the village intermarried to redefine property lines. If Leyla married Ruslan, then his inherited property, which used to be Leyla's great-uncle's, who died without a direct heir, would come back into the family.

The genealogical charts of the Mengen village would confuse any expert.

And the fact that Leyla had earned a scholarship to Istanbul University was almost unprecedented in her village. "What will you do with a university degree?" her mother had asked, more than once. Leyla's degree was in political science, with an emphasis in Ottoman studies.

Leyla couldn't blame her mother—the woman wanted her three sons and one daughter surrounding her, as any Muslim mother would. She spent her days taking care of everyone, bossing them around, and falling into bed completely content. What could be more important than family gathered around a table piled with food?

But Leyla had wanted something different, and fortunately her father had felt a rush of pride when the scholarship offer arrived from the university.

"It will only be four years, and then she'll be home to marry," he'd told her mother.

Still, her mother wept. And she'd be weeping now if she knew that Leyla was taking a summer job instead of returning home, and that she wouldn't be coming home at the end of summer, either. She'd already accepted the adjunct professor position in the university's political science department, starting in the fall.

Leyla checked the bathroom mirror once more in her tiny one-bedroom apartment a few blocks from campus. She wore her killer red lipstick, had her dark hair pulled back and tied with a red and black scarf, and had donned her black pantsuit with a bright cherry blouse.

She'd splurge on a taxi to take her to the campus where the interview would be so that she didn't arrive a sweaty mess.

By the time she stepped out of the apartment building and hailed a taxi, the heat of the morning had already permeated her suit. She took a sip from her water bottle as she settled into the back seat.

"Leyla?" the taxi driver turned, looking at her.

She blinked in astonishment at the driver. "Naim? You're driving taxis?"

"Just for the summer," Naim said.

They'd been in a couple of level four history classes together last year on the Beyazit campus of Istanbul University. But Naim had graduated and Leyla thought he'd found a job in Izmir working for a museum. It was a shock to see him now . . . and she was a bit pleased as well. She knew she looked good today. Her university student clothing mainly consisted of a pair of jeans and a plain knit top. She never bothered with makeup, let alone lipstick.

The Leyla that Naim was seeing now wasn't the woman he was familiar with, and she noticed that his gaze was definitely appreciating her. She tried to offer a nonchalant smile, while her pulse raced. "What are you doing back in Istanbul?" she asked.

"Going back to the university for my graduate degree," Naim said.

Leyla wasn't surprised. He'd always been the top student in her classes. He'd also been the popular man among the ladies. Rumor had it that he was promised to someone in his hometown, but he'd never spoken of her, and he'd hung out with plenty of girls on campus. Leyla remembered with a pang that he'd asked her out once, but then had to cancel for some reason. He never fully explained, and she never pestered him to find out. She figured that if he liked her, he'd ask her again. But he never did, and she'd tried to forget about him, only being friendly when they crossed paths.

It was impossible to forget him now. Naim's hair had grown to the edges of his collar and his hazel eyes were nearly gold in the morning light. His height seemed to dwarf the midsize taxi.

"That's great you're back," Leyla said. "I'm working as an adjunct professor on campus this fall while I begin work on my graduate degree as well."

His dark brows lifted, and a smile spread across his face. A smile that used to make her heart flutter. It might be fluttering now, but she refused to pay attention. "Congratulations, Leyla."

"Thank you. And congratulations to you as well."

He nodded. "Where to, princess?"

He'd started calling her that over two years ago when he found out that one of her ancestors had been a concubine in Süleyman's court. "I can't very well call you concubine," Naim had teased, "so princess it is."

"Illegitimate princess, you mean," Leyla had teased right back.

The name had stuck, and although it brought a rush of heat to Leyla's cheeks each time he'd spoken it, she found it endearing as well. "I've got an interview for a summer job," she said. "We're meeting on campus in the political science department conference room."

"What kind of job?" Naim asked, as he pulled into stalling traffic.

"It's actually for an antique shop in Izmir, but apparently there's a lot of work to be done in Istanbul. I'll be working out of my apartment on my laptop unless I need to travel to an antiques auction."

"Wow," Naim said, turning at the next corner. "That sounds interesting . . . you'd be good at that—with all those history classes you took."

"I hope so," Leyla said. "It will only be a short-term summer job, but it will at least get me through until fall semester starts." She said nothing to him about her parents waiting for her back home. She would have to make that phone call eventually.

All too soon, Naim was pulling up to campus. As he slowed to a stop, he turned and said, "Let me see your phone, I'll put my number in it. When you get out, text me. I'll drive you back."

"Oh, I can walk," Leyla said in a rush of air. "I don't usually splurge like this, but I didn't want to arrive hot and out of breath for the interview."

"It's on me, no charge," Naim said. "I'd like to catch up more."

Leyla was stunned. So stunned that she agreed, then climbed out of the taxi into the hot air, wondering what had just happened.

She walked to the campus building, her thoughts tumbling against each other, far away from the upcoming interview. What did Naim mean? Would he ask her on a date? Ironic that they were both finished with their undergraduate degrees now, but still on the same colliding path.

Leyla stepped into the cool interior of the building, and her thoughts leapt from running into Naim to the impending job interview. As she approached the conference room, she could see another student sitting at the table across from an older gentleman.

The man must be the antiques store owner. Although he was wearing a modern suit, he also wore a traditional turban which surprised Leyla and made her hesitate for a moment. She came from a village of very traditional people, and she was a bit wary of working for someone with the same mindset. In fact, he probably wouldn't hire her because she was a woman.

Before she could turn around, the man had seen her through the window and motioned her inside. Surprised at his boldness, she walked to the door. The student who'd been sitting across from the man turned and waved.

Leyla slowed her step. What was Ender doing here? He was a sophomore at the university and had worked as her assistant on her final research project on the rise of Istanbul.

Ender rose and opened the door. "You can thank me later when you get the job," Ender announced with a crooked smile.

It was no secret that Ender liked Leyla a little too much for her comfort. He was a sweet kid, but he reminded her of one of her brothers with his moppy hair and soulful eyes. There was no romantic interest on her part.

"Are you interviewing for the job too?" she asked Ender in a low voice, hoping she didn't sound too brazen in front of the antiques dealer.

"No, he called me in to tell him all about you." He leaned forward with one of his signature winks. "Don't worry, I told him only the good stuff."

The man at the table laughed, then rose to his feet. He was tall but his shoulders were stooped, as if he was older than his years. His dark eyes appraised her. "Welcome, Leyla Kaplan. I've been looking forward to meeting you."

Leyla was dumbfounded. Had he already talked to her professors about her?

Ender slipped out the door, and it shut softly behind Leyla. She stuck out her hand, as a test of sorts, and the antiques dealer shook her hand with a firm grip.

"I'm Baris Uzuner. Thank you for your interest in this job." He motioned for her to take a seat, and then he sat down. "I've been looking forward to meeting you for some weeks now."

Leyla's mind raced. One of her professors had notified her about the job opening, but she hadn't realized that this antiques dealer was specifically interested in *her*. She had assumed he'd be interviewing others for the position as well.

"I have surprised you, I can see that," Baris continued. "Let me explain. A friend of mine is a professor on campus, and I often talk to him about some of my antiquity finds. When he mentioned he had a particularly bright student who'd done a unique study on Sultan Süleyman's dynasty, I was immediately intrigued. When he told me you also read older Turkish forms, I was sold."

Leyla didn't know how to react or what to say, but she was flattered. "Thank you," she finally said.

"I'm an avid collector of artifacts from his era, and recently I've come across pieces that have never been seen. I need an assistant to help me track down the remaining artifacts of what I think will be a stunning collection." His gaze was intense, in fact, a bit unnerving.

She couldn't quite place his eye color. Dark brown mixed with gray, she decided. When Leyla realized he wanted her to respond, she said, "I'm definitely interested."

Baris removed a set of papers from a folder on the table and slid them in her direction. "You must understand that everything you work on for me must be strictly confidential. I wouldn't want any information to get out before it's been properly prepared."

Leyla took the papers and glanced through them. It looked like a standard nondisclosure document. She paused as she read the final paragraph. "I can't use my real name when working with your clients?"

"It's just a safety precaution, as well as a way to provide continuity," Baris said. "Whether you're my assistant or some other fellow down the road, the name will stay the same and my clients won't be bothered with a change in employees."

It made a strange sort of sense. "But what if I'm talking to someone on the phone? Won't they know your employee has changed when I leave at the end of the summer?"

"There will be no phone calls, only e-mails and texts," Baris said. "Many of the artifacts pass through very delicate channels, and the utmost privacy is required."

Leyla wasn't sure how an e-mail was more secure than a phone call, but she didn't specialize in security tactics.

Baris slid another piece of paper in her direction. "This is your pay for the first week. When you are trained, I will increase it."

Leyla stared at the numbers. They were higher than she had first been told. In fact, she'd make more this summer than the next nine months of teaching. How could she say no? The alternative was to return home and face turning down Ruslan.

"I accept the position."

Baris smiled, displaying a couple of gold-capped teeth. "Excellent." He pulled a pen from his jacket and handed it to her. She tugged off the cap and signed the contract.

Baris checked her signature, added his own to the document, then reached under the table and brought out a computer bag. He unzipped both sides and lifted the top canvas; inside rested a sleek sliver laptop.

"For your use with work only," Baris said. "This laptop's IP can't be traced."

"I didn't realize security was so tight for antique dealers."

He simply smiled. "For the best of us, it can never be too tight."

❖ CHAPTER FOUR ❖

MOROCCO

Apparently Morocco was having a heat wave, but Omar didn't think twice about the perspiration soaking his neck as he hurried through the airport with Mia and caught a taxi.

He hadn't realized how tense he was until he slid into the back seat of the taxi and inhaled the stale cigarette smoke. His stomach clenched with anticipation—he was glad he'd given up smoking, but right now one cigarette would be nice.

"We'll be there soon," Mia said, sliding close to him and grasping his hand.

Omar was grateful for her affection. With the recent strain between them, he welcomed it. If only he weren't rushing to his mother's deathbed.

The taxi couldn't have moved slower if the engine had been off. The morning traffic downtown had to be at an all-time record of congestion. Finally, when the government flags of the city hall building came into view, Omar felt some of the tension leave his body. They were almost there. His parents' government apartment was only a block from city hall.

Mia paid the driver as Omar grabbed their bags from the trunk, then he strode to the entrance of the apartment building. When he showed his ID, the security guard buzzed them in. No words needed to be spoken as they both bypassed the elevator and took the stairs to the second-floor apartment. Omar had only been to this location once before. The twice-painted stairs, the mosaic tiled floor in the corridor, the tall potted plants at each end, situated below grated windows, were all familiar.

He exhaled heavily before knocking on the door. Almost immediately it swung open, and his father stood there, thinner and grayer than Omar ever remembered seeing him.

"Omar," his father said, a hitch in his deep voice. And then he stepped forward and pulled Omar into his arms.

Omar had no complaints about his upbringing, but his father had never been an affectionate man. Yet this man now gripped him like a lifeline. His father's shoulders began to tremble.

Mia stepped quietly past them with the bags and set them down inside the foyer.

When his father released him, Omar had to wipe his own eyes. He cleared his throat, willing the emotion to stay down, then said, "Father, I'd like you to meet Mia Golding."

He fully expected her to stick out her hand and shake his father's, but instead she hugged him, then kissed him on each cheek.

Omar was grateful she was so caring toward his father.

"Come in, come in," his father said. He grasped Mia's hand and didn't let go as he led her into the living room.

Omar closed the front door then turned to follow. The apartment was as he remembered it. Gold and green couches, glass tables, silk flower arrangements, a large brass clock on the wall. Elegant and simple.

"Would you like tea or coffee?" his father asked.

Mia squeezed his father's hand. "Let me get it. You and Omar sit and talk. I know you've been apart for a long time."

His father hesitated, then sat in the armchair; Omar took the couch. Mia moved to the adjoining kitchen separated from the living room by a half wall.

"Your mother's in the bedroom," his father said in a low voice. "She is very much looking forward to seeing you, but she's asleep right now."

"How is she doing?" Omar asked. "If she's out of the hospital, she's doing better, right?"

His father's eyes shifted away from Omar's for a moment. "I haven't told you everything."

Omar stiffened. "What do you mean?"

Mia went still in the kitchen, looking from father to son.

"She . . . she was cornered at her office when she was working late," his father said in a slow voice. "The man who confronted her wanted information—information she refused to give him. So, the man . . ." His father's voice cracked.

Omar jumped to his feet. "What happened to her?" Without waiting for an answer, he crossed the living room, passed the kitchen, and strode down the hallway to his parents' bedroom.

"Wait, Omar! I need to explain—"

Omar stopped in the doorway of the bedroom. His mother Shira lay in bed, covered up to her chest with a blanket. She wore an oxygen mask, and an IV was hooked up to one of her arms. She didn't look like a woman who'd been through something as simple as pneumonia.

A deep cut ran along her neck, and another across her cheek. Both had been stitched, but the surrounding skin was red and swollen. One of her eyes was swollen shut, and the other had a deep bruise beneath. Her arms and hands were scored with smaller cuts.

"Holy shit," Omar said. In his thirty-four years, he'd never seen anything more upsetting. His own mother lying in bed after being beaten. Everything inside him felt sick, and he vacillated between want-ing to throw up and yelling at his father for not telling him. He crossed to his mother's bedside and grasped her hand. He watched her chest rise and fall with shallow breaths, her bruised eyelids twitch. The oxygen tank clicked on with a slow hiss.

A gasp came from the direction of the door, and Omar knew Mia had followed him.

He couldn't speak, couldn't move. One part of him sensed that Mia had crossed to the other side of the bed and had taken his mother's other hand in hers. Omar thought of the beautiful, vibrant woman that his mother was. Of how she'd married a man against her parents' wishes and then followed him to Canada, where Omar was born a year later.

She'd faithfully supported her husband in his career. Wherever he landed, she adjusted and created a home. Recently she'd been doing secretarial work in the same department his father worked in.

Was this attack connected to his father's work? Omar didn't know any of the specifics of his father's duties, except that he worked in the Ministry of Foreign Affairs and Cooperation.

He turned to see his father hovering in the doorway. He looked like a broken man, but that didn't quell the fury building inside Omar. He crossed to his father and gripped his arm.

"How could you let this happen?" he said. "You're supposed to be protecting her."

His father's mouth opened, but no words came out.

Omar grabbed his father's arm, leaning close. "I don't care about the privacy laws in the Moroccan government, I want information. Now!"

"Omar," Mia said behind him, in a warning tone.

He ignored her and kept his gaze on his father's pitiful face. How dare his father crumple into weakness. Someone was responsible for his mother's injuries, and Omar wasn't going to play the gentleman to find out who.

"Tell me the man's name," Omar ground out. "Tell me who's responsible for this."

"I . . . I don't know," his father stuttered.

"You think I believe that? Someone did this to Mother to get at *you*." He released his father's arm and stepped away before he did something he'd regret.

"You don't understand!" his father said in a shaky voice.

"There's only one thing I understand, and that's someone has to pay," Omar said, anger surging through him. "I'll start with your boss if I have to."

"Omar." Mia was at his side, grabbing his arm. "Give your father a chance to explain."

A tear dripped down his father's face. "I brought you here to see your mother because I couldn't explain any of this over the phone."

Omar gritted his teeth. "Explain. Now."

Another breath, and his father raised his hands and said, "The man who attacked your mother was trying to force information from her about . . . *you*."

If Omar had been slammed in the stomach, he couldn't have felt the impact more. He wanted to double over and throw up. The room was silent except for the hissing from the oxygen tank.

Mia gripped his shoulder as if she were trying to anchor him into one place. Omar closed his eyes and said in a measured voice, "What do you mean?"

When he opened his eyes again, his father had lowered his hands. "Come into the living room where we can talk, and I'll tell you everything I've been able to piece together. It's not much yet, but you might be able to shed more light."

"Omar?" A whisper touched the back of his neck. His mother. He turned to see her better eye fluttering open. She lifted her hand, and without any further thought, he was at her side. He leaned over and kissed the cheek without a row of stitches.

"I'm here, Mother," he said.

Her mouth twisted into a grimace, which Omar realized was supposed to be a smile. "Yes . . . you're here."

Omar waited, holding her hand, his emotions battling furiously. Her eyes slid closed again, and her breathing evened out. He continued to sit next to her for a while and simply held her hand until the questions burned too hot in his mind. Finally, he stood and faced his father. The man was slumped against the wall, Mia next to him.

"I want to know everything," Omar said in a flat voice.

His father nodded and straightened. Then Omar followed him into the living room. They sat across from each other, Mia at the far end of the room, her arms folded as she watched both men.

"She does secretarial work in my department, as you know," his father began in a hushed voice. "I was in meetings most of the day, and at the end of our meetings, she said she'd stay longer to type up the minutes." He took a breath and clasped his hands in front of him. "I told her I'd buy something from a restaurant to take home for dinner so it would be ready to eat when she arrived."

He gazed down at his hands. "When I returned home with a couple of sacks of hot food, she still wasn't there. I waited another thirty minutes and called, but she didn't answer the office phone. And you know how she won't use a cell phone."

Omar knew. He'd sent his mother various cell phones over the years, but she had yet to reply to one of his texts.

"Since it was getting dark, I decided to walk back to the office and escort her home." His father stopped talking and visibly swallowed. "I knew something was wrong when I found the security system compromised. It was shut off. I hurried up the stairs and into the office. She was . . ." His voice broke. "She was behind the reception desk. I could see her feet. I thought . . ." He buried his face in his hands, breathing heavily.

Mia crossed the room and sat next to him on the couch. She rested her hand on his shoulder, and eventually he raised his head and spoke again.

"She was breathing. I called the ambulance, and then I called my boss. He told me to not give the paramedics any information; he didn't want anything to get to the press. Said he'd investigate the security system and watch the surveillance footage." His father rubbed his face with his hands. "I still haven't seen the footage or received a report."

Omar clenched his jaw. That would all change now that he was here. He couldn't wait to storm into the man's office and make his demands.

"She was at the hospital for a couple of days, but when all the tests came back fine, other than her injuries that would take time to heal, she was released."

"What about the IV?"

"Just a precaution so that none of her lacerations become infected," his father clarified. "It's also easier to give her pain medication through the IV. And the oxygen is something she's probably needed for a while. Her energy has been depleted over the last several months. She wouldn't let me tell you."

Omar scrubbed his hands against his pants, itching to physically get hold of his father's boss.

"There's been no identification made yet?" he asked.

"The description your mother gave could match thousands of men in Morocco."

Mia pulled out her phone. "Tell us what she said."

"She said the intruder was thick set with a mustache. That his lower lip was disproportionately large. That he smelled as if he had been sweating in his shirt." As his father spoke, Mia typed in notes.

"What kind of shirt?"

"A knit polo," his father said.

"Did he have a weapon or did he just start punching her?" Omar asked.

Mia snapped her head up to look at Omar.

"My guess is it was a knife," Mia suggested.

A shudder went through Omar, mirrored by his father.

"Mia's right," his father said. "He . . . he threatened to cut her if she didn't give him the information about where her son lived."

Omar felt the breath leave his body. He knew one thing for certain, just by listening to the short description of the man. "He was a hired thug," Omar concluded. "Nothing more than a knife and a lot of nerve. Didn't even bother with a clean shirt."

His father leaned forward on propped elbows. "That's my guess too. But he asked the strangest questions. Ones that made your mother think he was a lunatic. It wasn't until he slashed at her with the knife that she thought she was in any real danger."

"What—what did he ask?" Omar said.

"He asked about the last time her son had been to Istanbul and if he was ready to face the crimes committed against the son of Süleyman the Magnificent."

Both Omar and Mia stared at his father. "The Turkish sultan from . . . hundreds of years ago?" Omar knew his mother's family lineage extended back to Turkish royalty. But her great-grandmother had married a Jewish man, emigrated to Palestine, and raised all her children in Judaism. Her Muslim-Turkish background had faded with time and a few generations.

Mia looked from Omar to his father. "Are you descended from the sultan?"

"Omar is through his mother, all the way back to the sultan himself and his favorite wife, Roxelane."

Mia typed a few words into her phone.

Omar couldn't fathom why a man would torture Shira to find out information about a man who had been dead for hundreds of years. "Was he some sort of genealogy freak?" he asked. "What else did he say?"

"She said the man repeated himself over and over," his father said, "saying he had to find you and you had to pay for some crime having to do with the hierarchy of the Ottoman Empire."

"I'm guilty of something that happened before I was even born, or my mother was born," Omar said with a shake of his head.

"Did he specify which son of the sultan?" Mia asked, scrolling on her phone. "There are quite a few listed here." She tapped her screen. "Three consorts or wives are listed, and a concubine. All had children. Selim II became the next sultan after Süleyman, but he was not the oldest male child." Another tap. "He was one of Roxelane's sons; Roxelane was his favorite wife. It looks as if Mustafa, another son of the sultan, was the true heir, yet he was executed for treason at the age of thirty-seven."

Omar exhaled. "Mustafa? I think I've heard the story before. Maybe on a BBC special."

Mia raised a brow and met Omar's gaze. "I think we have some research to do."

He gave her a nod then looked at his father. "First, I need to meet with your boss and see the security footage."

❖ CHAPTER FIVE ❖

ISTANBUL

Leyla let her finger hover over the saved cell number for Naim. The walk back to her apartment would only take fifteen minutes, but the day was growing hotter by the minute. She stood at the curb where Naim had dropped her off, but his taxi was nowhere in sight.

Perhaps she'd call; and if he didn't answer, she'd hang up and not bother to leave a message. He might have just been trying to be nice. It wasn't like he'd made any effort to ask her out again after he'd cancelled their first date.

Still. He'd told her he wanted to catch up. *Polite?*

She pressed "Send" and listened to the ring tones on the other end. After the third one he answered, and Leyla cursed her breathlessness as she said, "It's Leyla."

"Leyla!" His voice was warm. "How'd the interview go?"

"Fairly well, considering I got the job."

"That was quick," Naim said. "Can I pick you up?"

As she considered, she saw his taxi turn the corner and head her way. So he hadn't been far. "If it's not inconvenient."

"It's not," he said, clicking off his phone.

Leyla couldn't help but smile as he drove up and slowed the taxi. He jumped out of the driver's seat before she could open the back door. Hurrying around the front of the taxi, he opened the passenger door for her.

"Front seat?" she asked.

"Since you're now my guest, you get first class treatment."

Leyla laughed and glanced away from his hazel eyes. He was standing a bit too close for her heart to maintain a normal beat.

"Want to get some coffee?"

She had a lot of reading to do before she met with her new boss tonight to review her new job. He'd set up her secure e-mail, then showed her a couple of PDFs on the laptop, each over fifty pages long, that detailed the intricacies of Süleyman's court. She knew most of it, but Baris wanted her to study other speculations by historians. Still, if she said no to Naim now, she might not come across this opportunity again. "Sure, I'd love some coffee."

He grinned and shut the passenger door, then walked around the taxi again and climbed into the driver's seat. "I know a great place that will be quiet this time of the morning."

Leyla looked over at him. "I've never been to a quiet coffee shop," she said.

"You're right." He pulled into traffic and steered easily around two motorcycles whose drivers were in some sort of argument. "Did your new boss give you homework already?"

"He did," Leyla said, settling the case she carried between her feet on the floor. "Lots of reading about Süleyman the Magnificent, well, more specifically his consorts." She stopped. "Oh, sorry. I'm not supposed to discuss my job." At least she hadn't said anything about artifacts.

"Really?" Naim threw her a curious glance.

Had she already breached her contract? She released a sigh. It wasn't like Naim was going to call up Baris and report her. The two men would never meet, likely never would. "My boss had me sign a nondisclosure. I guess antiques dealers can be quite competitive."

"Trying to get the highest bidders to buy from them, I guess?" Naim said, seeming nonplussed about her mention of the nondisclosure.

Maybe it was completely normal. She didn't have any experience with antiques dealerships. "The ironic thing is that I've never even been to an antiques shop."

Naim laughed. "You're with the right guy then. I love them."

Leyla wasn't sure why she was so surprised. It wasn't like she knew Naim very well outside of the university. He could have all kinds of hobbies and interests that she knew nothing about. "I didn't know you were so interested. Are you a collector?"

He paused, and Leyla attributed it to him driving through a narrow alley, barely avoiding an overturned trash can. "You might say my father is a collector."

"What does he collect?" Leyla asked.

They exited the alley, and Naim pulled along the curb, stopping in front of a small café. She'd never been in this out-of-the-way neighborhood before and found the flower boxes perched in the shop windows along the road charming.

"He collects whatever he can get the most money for," Naim said in a light voice.

But Leyla sensed a bit of tension in his words. "So he's a dealer too?"

Naim popped his door open and walked around the taxi to open her door before answering. "I guess that's a good way to put it."

Before she could ask him what he meant, someone came out of the café and said, "Naim!"

The man was as wide as he was tall, and he practically shifted the earth as he walked over to greet them. First he shook Naim's hand enthusiastically, then turned to Leyla and kissed her on both cheeks.

"What's the occasion, Naim? You've never brought a beautiful woman here before."

Naim laughed. "Leyla, this is my cousin Volkan." He turned to the man. "Leyla is at the university with me. She's working for an antiques dealer for the summer."

"Very good," Volkan said in a jovial voice, although he threw her a curious look.

Leyla wondered if she should read more into the fact that Naim had brought her to his cousin's café.

Naim had been right. This café was very quiet, and they spent their time talking about their university classes. By the time they left an hour later, the tables had started filling up. On the drive back to her apartment, Naim asked Leyla about her hometown, and she found herself telling him about her family.

"Your family sounds very close, similar to mine," Naim said. "Have they tried to marry you off yet?"

Leyla flushed at the question. "They are very traditional, as is most of Mengen, and they have hinted about a certain man they think I should be interested in."

Naim's gaze held hers for a moment as he pulled to a stop in front of her apartment building. "If they're traditional, they'll arrange a marriage for you, am I right?"

She thought of how different he was from the men in her village. Naim was educated, witty, resourceful, confident . . . "They've mentioned it a time or two."

One of his eyebrows lifted, as if he were waiting for her to tell the complete truth.

"All right," she started. "There's a reason I'm staying in Istanbul for the summer."

"What do they think about your professorship?" he asked.

It was like he could read her mind. "They don't know about that, either."

"I'm guessing a certain man will be brokenhearted," Naim said.

"My mother will be more disappointed than Ruslan will ever be," she said, perhaps sharing too much information. "I don't think Ruslan has once looked me directly in the eye. His shyness is almost crippling, although he's a master at woodwork. If he could just live in the backroom of his father's shop and carve all day, he could probably survive without eating or drinking." She'd definitely shared too much information.

Naim studied her, and she was afraid she'd somehow offended him. He probably thought she was coldhearted. But then he smiled and reached over and lightly squeezed her arm. "I don't blame you for staying in Istanbul. I mean, where else would you get such great coffee?"

She laughed, although it was mixed with a bit of trepidation. She couldn't put off telling her parents for much longer. They'd expect her home by the end of the week. She'd have to tell them she wasn't even planning on packing, let alone planning a wedding for the end of the summer.

"Thanks for the coffee, and thanks for driving me around," Leyla said.

Naim nodded. "Thank you for putting up with me."

"No problem," Leyla said with a laugh.

Then Naim touched her arm again, his hand lingering. "We should do it again, in a couple of days."

"All right," she said, her heart starting a slow pound. He was probably just being polite, nothing more.

"Good, I'll call you later then."

She popped open her door before he could get out to open it. "Sounds great." Then she climbed out and unlocked the main door to her building. The heavy metal door clanged noisily behind her before she allowed herself to turn and look back at the taxi as it was swallowed up in traffic and exhaust fumes. Naim was an intriguing man. She supposed she'd always known that, but she had never thought he might be interested in her.

She took the stairs two at a time to the third floor, forgoing the elevator. Once she changed and settled down before her new laptop, she had time to process her conversations with Naim. She definitely wanted to get to know him better, although the more she thought about it, the more she realized he'd asked most of the questions. She decided the next time she was with him, she'd reverse the roles.

Leyla started to read. Most of the information about Süleyman's court she already knew, but she read with interest the multiple theories of the death of Mustafa, the oldest son who was heir to the throne. A few historians believed that Süleyman's chief wife, Roxelane, had plotted his downfall so that her son would inherit.

According to the PDF, there had been letters exchanged between Roxelane and the sultan, detailing the plot—which meant both of them were in on it.

Leyla sat back in her chair and reread a few of the paragraphs. Unless letters were actually found to prove the plot, it could only be conjecture.

The laptop chimed, and Leyla opened the new e-mail, surprised she was already on someone's contact list. She'd have to ask Baris how to handle it. But when she read the e-mail, her blood stilled.

Urgent! Come right away to the shop. Make sure you aren't followed.

The e-mail had no signature, but it had to be from Baris. He had given her the address of the shop, and even if she were to find a taxi waiting in front of her apartment building, it would take her at least twenty minutes to get there.

Leyla changed back into her pantsuit, grabbed the computer bag, and hurried out of her building. The sun was just sliding behind the western row of apartments, casting most of the street in shadow, as she hurried to the corner of the building lot, keeping her eyes open for a taxi. At the sight of the first empty one, she waved it down. The taxi driver, a thick man in his sixties, hardly paid her any attention as he drove to the shop.

After paying the driver, she nearly stumbled out of the taxi, nervous to see what was going on with Baris. The door of the shop was an elegant gold metal framing glass, and the words *Baris's Antiques* were painted prominently in the center of the door. She found the door locked, though the lights were on inside. Because the windows were tinted, she couldn't see if Baris was nearby. She knocked a few times. After several moments of waiting, she decided to see if there was a back door.

When she saw it, she sighed with relief. She tried the knob, found it locked, so she knocked. A voice answered, "Coming!"

Moments later the door opened, and Baris let her in, wiping at the perspiration shining on his forehead. He barely looked at her as he led the way into the shop. Stepping inside, she was immediately struck with the smell of incense. It would have been soothing except her stomach was a knot of curiosity.

She followed Baris into a storage area. Ahead was a counter with a cash register. To the right was an open door. Baris motioned for her to walk with him into the other room. Inside, he bent over a crate and closed a metal case that was open inside of it.

"Did anyone see you come around the shop?" he said in a rush.

"I . . . I don't think so," she said.

He fitted a lid on the crate and hammered three nails into it. Then he looked up. "Good. Carry this out through the back door, and I'll lock everything up. Load it into the front of my truck, then get in and wait for me."

Leyla shouldered her computer bag and did as she was told even though she had a dozen questions. The crate wasn't heavy, but its sharp edges made it awkward to carry. She propped it against her hip in order to open the back door and step outside. In the rear parking lot was a small truck. It was the only vehicle in the four-stall space, so it had to be Baris's.

She opened the passenger door and set the crate on the floor, barely able to wedge it between the seat and the dashboard.

Then she climbed in, keeping the passenger door propped open with her foot. The cooling night breeze felt good after her mad rush to the shop. She wondered about Baris. Why was he so panicked? And should she really be riding alone with him in a truck to who knew where? She might be his employee but she knew hardly anything about him. Yet she was intrigued why he needed her help so suddenly tonight.

Her breath froze as she saw a man coming along the side of the building. He hadn't seen her yet, and it was clear from his quiet movements that he wasn't an ordinary visitor. He wore a traditional Muslim robe of dark gray, but no turban. Both his hair and beard were long, and Leyla estimated him to be in his forties.

Was he looking for Baris? Should she say something to him? The fear pumping through her veins kept her quiet. She wished she could shut the passenger door and hide below the window, but shutting the door would make too much noise.

She watched the man approach the back door and place his hand on the knob, then turn it. Horror shot through her as he drew a gun from inside his robe.

She had to warn Baris, but how? She slowly pulled out her phone, her hands shaking. He'd told her never to call him, only e-mail, but she hadn't programmed the strange series of numbers of his e-mail address into her phone yet. She stared at the man once again, feeling helpless, although Baris was only paces away inside the shop.

Then everything moved at warp speed. The door flew open and Baris appeared, holding a gun of his own. And as Leyla watched in disbelief, Baris aimed and fired at the man several times. The man's body jerked as he slammed to the ground and went still. There was no doubt he was mortally wounded.

Leyla wanted to scream, then throw up, then run until she was home, but she couldn't do any of it because Baris was racing toward the truck, gun still in his hand.

❖ CHAPTER SIX ❖

KINGDOM OF POLAND

AD 1521

"You are the most beautiful woman in Rohatyn," Tashi whispered, his breath hot against Aleksandra's neck. "Perhaps in all the Kingdom of Poland."

Aleksandra sighed and took another step away from Tashi—a man of pretty words. He was handsome, and he'd been pursuing her for months. Perhaps she should make her choice of husband, please her family, and put an end to the village gossip.

"You flatter me, Tashi, but it will be years before you can afford a wife such as me." Aleksandra was mostly teasing, but she also wanted him to know that she would not live in a hovel and work in the field as a donkey the rest of her days. She would not be like her mother, left widowed and poor. Aleksandra had tried to remain humble in the beauty she possessed, but also intended to use her gift from God to her best advantage. If she had to settle for one of the men of her village, she wanted her husband to be smart and ambitious.

"Months," Tashi corrected. "I have joined the militia and will prove myself in battle. In no time at all, I'll be made a captain. I'll be joining the Polish defense against the Turks in a few days. The Turks have advanced on the south border already, and I mean to stop them before they reach our village."

In previous battles, the Turks had never bothered with the small villages—who wanted a few carts of vegetables and women with calloused hands? They saved their brawn for the larger cities. With a main city controlled, the surrounding villages immediately fell into subservience. But seeing the fiery determination in Tashi's deep brown eyes was almost enough to convince Aleksandra to consider him for a husband. Though she knew better. Her father had died years ago in a battle against the Turks. It seemed the Ottoman Empire wasn't large enough, and the Kingdom of Poland continued to be a target. After her father's death, Aleksandra had watched her mother try to feed four children, doing anything and everything. Some of her jobs were visible as she worked in the neighbors' fields. Her other ways of earning money were not visible as she shooed the children outside and disappeared behind the damask curtain with a visiting man.

Aleksandra would not be like her mother. She would not be a slave to the earth nor to men offering money to visit her bed. Like Aleksandra, her mother had been gifted with great beauty, but her mother had chosen a man whose crops had failed and had ended up joining the militia.

As Tashi continued to make his promises, Aleksandra's gaze slid across the market square where the harvest festivities were at their height beneath the evening sky. Two other men watched her: Portan and Sabu. Portan was a widower with two young children. Aleksandra would be well taken care of in his home, although the days would be filled with watching his children, and the nights lonely while he traveled as a merchant.

Sabu was interesting, but something about him put off Aleksandra. His eyes wandered far too often for her comfort. She'd even caught him watching her mother once. But Sabu was one of the wealthiest men in the village of Rohatyn, and Aleksandra wondered why, at the age of thirty he'd never married. Gossip about Sabu ranged from his impotency to his preference for other men.

Aleksandra didn't believe any of the gossip. Yet behind his finely featured face was a darkness. And that unsettled Aleksandra.

Perhaps the widower was the best option. At least she'd have a home of marble and stone, and if the marriage bed was distasteful, she'd have plenty of solace when he traveled.

She tuned back into Tashi's epithets. He truly was handsome with his wavy brown hair and square chin. But she couldn't overlook his destitute status. If she married him, she could be a widow before she reached the age of eighteen. And she might find herself laboring in a field before long.

"You are a brave man," Aleksandra said, reaching up and touching Tashi's face.

His cheeks reddened, and it thrilled Aleksandra to see the effect she had on him. His gaze dipped to the fitted bodice of her dress, then rose and lingered on her lips. She had let him kiss her once already, and perhaps that was a mistake, but Aleksandra hadn't seen any harm in allowing herself a moment or two of pleasure.

"If we were betrothed before I left, I would fight in your name," Tashi said.

Charming. He was charming as well.

"I will not make any promises," Aleksandra said, this time stepping close to him and tilting up her face so that his eyes became mesmerized by hers. "But I will not make a decision about the man I'll marry for several more moons."

"That is all I can ask then," Tashi said, his voice a rushed whisper. He leaned down, and Aleksandra knew he intended to kiss her—to claim her in front of the entire village.

Although Aleksandra's skin anticipated his heated touch, she could not be so foolish. She stepped out of his reach once again, gave him her most brilliant smile, then turned and walked away.

She felt his gaze heating every part of her as she moved through the crowd. It was time for her to grace the other men of the village with her presence. She knew Tashi would be watching her intently; if it gave him more motivation to stay alive in battle and become a captain, then he'd return to her alive. And perhaps there would be a reward waiting for him.

But tonight she wasn't leaving anything to fate.

"Aleksandra," Sabu said with a bow as she passed by him.

She'd intended to speak with him, but wanted it to seem as if he were capturing her attention. She slowed and turned, raising her brows in mild surprise. "It's nice to see you at the festival," she said in a demure tone.

Her act did not fool Sabu for one moment, but she could see in his appreciative gaze that he was willing to play her game. His narrow face and deep green eyes were in shadow beneath a trimmed alder tree. The torchlights in the market square gave off just enough light to make everyone seem mysterious.

"It is nice to be here," he said. "I've been watching you enjoy yourself." His eyes seemed to bore straight into her, and her face warmed at the intensity.

"It seems that most of your laborers are here, celebrating."

His smile widened. "It is, after all, their accomplishment."

"With some help from the landowner?" she said in a light voice.

He gave a small shrug, his eyes glittering. "A little help."

Sabu was the most prominent landowner of Rohatyn, and most of his employees were at the festival, celebrating another successful harvest. Sabu was no stranger to celebrating and encouraged it among his employees when it was due. He could also be a harsh taskmaster.

Punishments might be rare, but they were swift. Disloyalty or thievery was punished by the loss of a hand or an eye or a foot.

But here, now, Sabu was all charm. His narrow face tilted. "I'm having a private dinner at my home after the festival. Would you like to be my guest?"

Sabu's private dinners were legendary, and although neither Aleksandra nor anyone she knew personally had ever been to one, she knew well enough to decline the succinct invitation.

"I've made a promise to another," she said, deciding not to lie outright. She and her closest friend, Bethany, were going to join in the harvest moon dance at the lake tonight. Women age seventeen and up were invited to the female-only event, and this would be both Aleksandra and Bethany's first year eligible to attend.

Of course, she assumed Sabu's dinner engagement would be over before the midnight dance, but he didn't have to know that.

"Ah, well," Sabu said, stepping toward her until he was merely a hand span away.

The intensity of his gaze as it trailed down the length of her body, then up again, told Aleksandra that this man did not favor other men. She found she'd stopped breathing as she waited for him to finish his perusal.

"Perhaps you'll join me in the knife-throwing game then," Sabu said, motioning to the far side of the marketplace where a sackcloth dummy had been constructed, filled with straw, and used as a target. Young children were lined up, eager to take their turn.

"The game is for children," she said with a laugh.

"Yes, but it might be fun to compete with each other, just for sport," Sabu said. "I hear you are an expert."

Aleksandra laughed again. "Who told you that?"

"Your brother Reese—he told me your father taught you all, and that you always beat out the boys in the village," he said, his eyes lit with amusement.

She was flattered, but it had been years since she'd tried her skill in any serious form. Glancing over at the group of boys throwing the knives and cheering each other on, she said, "All right, but just one throw. I don't want to take over what the children are doing."

Sabu grinned, and Aleksandra was surprised at how much the smile softened his linear features. He motioned for her to go ahead of him, and she led the way to the game.

When the young boys saw Sabu coming their way, they immediately quieted and looked up at him in awe. One of them even held out his dirty, bent knife.

"I have my own," Sabu said, "but tonight, we'll let the lady throw first."

The boys' attention snapped to Aleksandra, their eyes wide. She just smiled, and pulled out the knife she always kept tucked into her waistband. With the boys and Sabu watching her intently, she closed her eyes for a few moments, breathing in and out. Then she was ready. She opened her eyes, focused on the center of the stuffed target, and threw.

The knife sailed through the air, straight and true, as if she'd been throwing for years. Her muscles and limbs had remembered the perfect arc to send the knife on. It landed in the center of the sackcloth head.

"There goes its nose," Sabu said, a laugh in his voice.

The boys cheered, and heat crept to Aleksandra's face as she accepted their praise. One of the boys scrambled to retrieve her knife and returned it to her.

She thanked the boy, then turned to Sabu. "Your turn."

He gave her a slow wink, then pulled a curved dagger from a leather thong tied around his calf. Aleksandra didn't say anything, curious to see how he'd throw a knife with a curved blade. It reminded her of the yataghan knives that warriors used, except this was smaller.

He threw it well, but the knife didn't sail straight. It clipped the shoulder of the sackcloth form and clattered to the stone pavement.

The young boys groaned in good humor, and Sabu retrieved his knife. Striding toward Aleksandra, he held out his empty hand. She grasped his hand, and he brought her hand to his lips and pressed the softest kiss on the back of her fingers. "Well done," he said. "You win this round. You know where my home is if you change your mind." And then he was gone, moving through the crowd. Visible one moment, gone the next.

Aleksandra stared after him until she was no longer able to pick out his tall form. She ignored the young boys begging her to throw again. How was it possible that her heart could pump hot blood for such a man, a man she knew was dangerous? She said goodbye to the boys, then walked to a quiet area beneath the alders, where she stopped and scanned the crowd.

Tashi was watching her, which meant he had probably seen the entire knife-throwing competition. He stood by a long table piled with food and drink. Although another man spoke to him, Tashi's gaze was riveted to Aleksandra. She lifted her hand in a wave, and his lips curved upward.

But she couldn't stand there all night, making eyes at Tashi. She had another man to connect with. Her gaze soon found Portan. He was standing on the outskirts of the market square, his eyes focused on his children who were playing in a group. He was a good father, Aleksandra admitted to herself. His children were always clean and wearing quality clothing. Of course that might be due to his housekeeper. But a man ruled the home, so Aleksandra could credit Portan.

She started to make her way toward him, and when he noticed her advance, he straightened, as much as a short man could straighten. His height didn't bother her since Aleksandra was tall for a woman anyway.

Portan nodded to her as she neared him. He was a man of few words, and Aleksandra didn't have to worry about seductive invitations from him. His wide set eyes studied her, and Aleksandra could almost see him realize that she was now of an age to marry.

"I am looking for my mother, have you seen her?" Aleksandra asked. She knew that Portan would think her forward if she talked of something else. But asking after a family member was perfectly appropriate. Even at the harvest festival, when many traditions of men and women interacting went by the wayside.

"Not since the start of the festival," he said.

In truth, Aleksandra was surprised he'd remember such a thing. "Are your children enjoying the evening?"

His gaze strayed to them for an instant, then darted back to Aleksandra. "They are. Thank you for asking."

Aleksandra wanted to laugh at the formality of their conversation. Instead, she nodded. "I'm pleased to hear it. I must continue looking for my mother." She left him then, to watch her leave and to wonder. She'd accomplished her goal. Speak with the man and get him to think of her and his children in the same few moments.

She walked away from the main crowd and climbed up the hillside until she had an overview of the market square. Once out of the noise and commotion, she sat on the hill among the grasses, drew her knees up, and was able to look across the entire valley.

The sun had set well over an hour ago, but there were still splashes of orange against the violet horizon. She rarely missed watching the sun set; it was the only thing left that still connected her to her father. From the time she was a young girl, her father would hoist her on his shoulders and point out the vibrant colors of the sky.

"Look, Aleksandra," she imagined him saying. "Watch how the colors shift as the sun sinks in the sky. What do you think makes the colors change?"

No matter how she answered, her father said she wasn't quite right. And then he'd left for battle, never to return, never to tell her what made the colors of the sky change. Aleksandra kept her gaze on the horizon that she and her father had spent so much time studying.

The movement was small at first, and Aleksandra wouldn't have noticed if she hadn't been staring at the exact spot. But as the seconds passed, the movement became a series of movements, then divided into solid shapes. A man on a horse with a flag. Three men. Five men. Dozens of men.

Aleksandra's blood chilled.

Riding down the ridge, heading straight for the valley, came a legion of soldiers. Swords raised. Eyes filled with war.

Then the screams started, and the people in the market began to flee. Men grabbed whatever they could to fight with. Women sobbed. Children were trampled.

The Turks had arrived.

❖ CHAPTER SEVEN ❖

MOROCCO

Omar hunched over the small screen, replaying for the third time the footage of the man entering the building. The description his father had given him was accurate, but Omar also noticed the man had a slight limp. Another indicator that he was a hired thug. A professional operator wouldn't have been able to get away with such a handicap.

The video cut out when the man entered the office. Conveniently. Omar played the loop again, trying to see if the video really had ended or if his father's boss had shortened it on purpose. How deep did the deception go?

He sat back in the squeaky chair in his father's office. It had been a process just to get clearance to enter the building, let alone sit at his father's desk. How had an intruder gotten through? Omar touched "Play" again and watched as the intruder effortlessly scanned in his ID and the door clicked open.

Omar paused the video and squinted. Something had caught his eye that he hadn't noticed before. The man had a marking on his right hand. A tattoo maybe. Omar took a picture with his phone of the screen image, then expanded the image. The tattoo was a curved shape, thicker at one end, which should have been familiar to Omar since he'd studied ancient languages and symbols. But this one he didn't recognize.

He saved the picture to his phone, then uploaded it into Google search. Nothing came up that matched the tattoo, which meant the picture was too pixelated.

The office door opened behind him, and without turning, he knew it was Mia. Her light, flowered scent preceded her. Her hand rested on his shoulder and she leaned over him. Her hair tickled the side of his face as she peered at the image.

"What's that on his hand?" she asked.

"A tattoo." Omar lifted his phone. "Google images can't identify it."

She slipped into his lap, and he wrapped his arms about her. "Why do you need Google when you have me? That's a yataghan."

"The knife?" He pulled her closer, while staring at the image. "I think you're right."

"I know I'm right." Mia looped her arms about his neck. "We'll find him, Omar," she said, looking directly into his eyes.

"I sure hope so," he breathed. He wanted to believe Mia more than anything. "I just need a starting place."

"I think you've found it." She leaned away from him and powered on the computer at the desk. "Let's hope the Internet is high speed."

"Nothing's too good for government employees." He watched as she selected the Internet icon and let it load.

When she stood from his lap, he tried to pull her back down, but she only said, "I need to get serious here. Move out of the chair."

So he did. He leaned against the desk as she typed in several searches. Moments later myriad pictures popped up with various depictions of yataghans. Some were in paintings, others, sketches.

"See?" Mia said, comparing the blurry image on his phone to the images on the computer. "Now let's do another search." She typed in a string of words including yataghan, Sultan Süleyman, Roxelane, and Ottoman Empire.

"Wow, look at this," Mia said, looking at one of the search findings. "Roxelane was an expert knife thrower. She often used the yataghan symbol as part of her signature in letters."

Now Omar was definitely paying attention.

"Let's find out if there are tattoo parlors in Morocco that ink this symbol," Mia continued.

She typed in another search and a group of tattoo parlor phone numbers popped up. Ten minutes later, she had several texts to her phone that the tattoo artists had sent her of their work. Out of the five Mia received, one was a near match.

"It's hard to say if it's exact, but we'll find out," Mia said, rising to her feet. "Come on, they close in thirty minutes."

Omar hurried with her out of the office building, and they grabbed a taxi to ride the few blocks to the tattoo shop. Teens lounged in front, inked and pierced in places Omar didn't think were possible. A glowing fluorescent sign flashed pink behind the teens' heads, making them look like part of a garish billboard.

Mia pushed the front door open, and Omar stepped in after her, quickly taking inventory of the shop. A man sat in a vinyl chair while a woman with two thick black braids inked his arm.

A tall man with a shaved head approached them from a curtained hallway, wiping his hands on a towel. "Are you Mia?" he asked, gazing at her in an appreciative way.

"Yes, can you show us your design book?"

The man gave Omar an unimpressed once-over, then turned toward a cluttered counter. He picked up a tattered plastic binder and handed it to Mia. "The knife designs start about halfway through."

"Do you keep a record of the tattoos you ink?" she asked in a very sweet voice.

The man huffed, his gaze narrowing for a moment. "In a way. We have receipts, and I can usually guess which group the tattoo is from by the price."

Omar leaned against the counter, trying to appear friendly. "Just the two of you working here?"

The man glanced over at the dark-braided woman. "Yeah." She'd turned off the tattoo machine gun and was dabbing the customer's arm.

"I'd like to talk to you after this customer leaves," Omar said in a low voice. "I'll make it worth your time."

"How much?"

Omar took out a billfold from his jacket, and the man's eyes popped. "This is part of it," Omar said. "If the information is useful, you'll get more."

The man crossed to the customer, checked over the ink handiwork, hurried him through the process of explaining how to care for the wound, and then had him pay.

Mia followed the customer out, glanced down the street, then came back in and locked the door.

"All right," Omar said, placing the billfold on the counter, then opening the picture icon on his phone. "Do either of you recognize this guy? We're looking for any information at all."

The man shook his head, but the woman's eyes shifted away before she said, "No."

"Can you get your receipts and sort out the ones with any of the knife tattoos?" Omar asked, directing his request toward the man. He cast a glance at his employee, then set off toward the curtained door.

Once they were alone with the woman, Mia said, "You're Saida, right?"

The woman's eyes narrowed. "How did you know my name?" She was a large woman and probably used to intimidating instead of the other way around. But she hadn't met Mia yet.

"I *always* do my research," Mia said, stepping toward her. "We know you recognize the man we're looking for. We can promise you that you'll regret not telling us who he is."

Saida folded her arms, her bright acrylic nails flashing red as they settled on her thick flesh. It was a challenge, and Omar knew that Mia wouldn't like it.

"I know you live on Avenue Lalla Yacout, and I know you got in a fight with your boyfriend last night."

Saida's eyes widened.

"I also know that you have a kid who your mom is raising, while you go through men like whiskey," Mia said, taking another step closer. "I know your mom lives on Boulevard d'Anfa with your son, and I don't think you want to risk him growing up with a mom in prison, do you? I mean, a deadbeat mom who works in a tattoo parlor is bad enough."

The woman's mouth fell open. "Why would I go to prison? I've done nothing."

Mia took one more step, which put her nearly chest to chest with Saida. "Because of what I planted in your apartment twenty minutes ago. Is this one loser really worth the price of your freedom?"

"What did you plant?" Saida asked.

"One phone call to the police, and they can inform you later."

Saida backed away, shaking her head and looking toward the hallway where her boss had disappeared. "You can't do that."

"It's your choice," Mia said.

Someone from the outside rattled the door, trying to open it. Omar crossed to the window, and one glare from him sent the potential customer on his way.

The boss stepped through the curtain, carrying a cardboard file box.

Saida lifted her hand. "Those won't be necessary. I know who they're looking for."

The boss stopped and set the box down.

Saida turned back to Omar and Mia. "His name is Deniz. He came in about two months ago and got the tattoo."

Omar nodded. The name Deniz was Turkish.

Saida glanced at her boss, then looked down, her face flushing. "We went out a few times after that. Just for drinks."

Mia stepped forward again, and this time Saida didn't back away. "Number, please."

With a shaking hand, Saida reached into the neckline of her shirt and pulled out her cell phone nestled beneath her bra strap. She scrolled through her contacts, then selected a name and rotated the phone so Mia could see it.

Mia quickly typed the number into her own phone. "When's the last time you saw him?" she asked.

Saida swallowed. "Three days ago."

"Do you know where he lives?" Omar asked.

"We never hooked up at . . . his place," Saida said.

"Anything else?" Mia asked in a steady tone.

Saida took a deep breath. "The tattoo," she whispered. "At first I thought he just liked knives, but one night he told me it was a symbol for a Turkish queen who planned the death of her own stepson. He got the tattoo so he could remember his own vengeance against her descendants." Saida slipped her phone back in its place and looked away. "I was creeped out, and I started avoiding his phone calls. The last time he texted me was to tell me he was going out of town for a couple of weeks."

Mia and Omar left the shop, and by the time Mia had hailed a taxi, Omar had connected the phone number with a street address. He copied it into the map feature and stared at the location. "This isn't a neighborhood."

Mia peered at the screen. "It looks like a shopping center, but that doesn't make sense."

"Unless his number is registered to a shop he works for?"

They climbed into the taxi, and Omar gave the driver the address. As the taxi navigated the streets, Omar leaned back and looked over at Mia. "Nice work in there. It seems you're becoming indispensable."

She nudged his shoulder. "I've always been indispensable."

"That's true." He reached for her hand and tugged her toward him, attempting to kiss her, but she pushed at his chest. "Not here. You'll distract the driver."

Omar didn't care, so he moved in again, but Mia hadn't been kidding.

"All right," he said, straightening. But just as she relaxed, he leaned over and kissed her anyway.

She swatted him, but then she laughed.

"The driver is watching us," Omar whispered.

She slid her hand into his, and despite the unknowns before him, Omar felt peace for a moment.

❖ CHAPTER EIGHT ❖

KINGDOM OF POLAND

AD 1521

Aleksandra ran toward the chaos. The screaming women. The helpless children. But the Turkish soldiers reached the festival crowd first. Aleksandra jerked to a stop as she saw one of the soldiers hack into a village man with his sword. The villager tried to defend himself with a knife no larger than his own hand.

She knew the Turks were merciless in battle, her own father had died at their hand, but these villagers were unarmed, unprepared. They wore no armor, had no weapons, and the Turks didn't differentiate between men, women, or children.

"Oh, dear Lord," she whispered, as her knees trembled and her breath stuttered. She could only stare in disbelief at the sight before her. She hoped her mother was at their home, earning her money on her back. It might very well save her life this time.

But what about her three younger brothers? They were at the festival. She studied the moving mass beneath her, frantically searching for her brothers. But there was too much confusion. Too much blood. All the warmth drained from her body as she watched a Turk grab a young girl by the hair and hoist her onto his horse. The young girl screamed, but no one could help her.

And then two soldiers were looking Aleksandra's way, pointing.

Her heart nearly stopped. She turned then, away from the horror, and started to run up the hill. She clutched at her skirts, not caring that her best slippers were getting filthy. She pushed through trees and bushes, trying to stay out of sight of the soldiers who'd seen her. She refused to look back, to see if they were following. She ran around smaller houses as the screams behind her faded.

The scent of smoke reached her and a new fear arose. Were the Turks torching the market? Images of death raced through her mind, propelling her forward even faster.

She passed the smaller homes, and dashed up the long, winding steps toward Sabu's elegant two-story home. Just a short time ago, she'd confidently turned down an invitation to have dinner with him. How she wished she were that woman again and that all she had to worry about was a village man's interest in her.

If she survived tonight, she'd never be the same woman again. What would the Turks do if they found her? Breathing hard, she at last reached the front entrance to Sabu's home. She pushed against the doors, surprised at how easily they opened. Apparently he had no fear of thieves on festival night. Perhaps because no one dared steal from the wealthiest man in the village.

The grand hallway was dim and smelled of orange and lemon oil, likely rubbed into the wooden floor and the staircase rail leading up to the second floor. Aleksandra had to make an instant decision. Up the stairs? Or should she hurry to the back of the house?

Shouts coming from outside pushed her into action. She ran for the stairs, then made a left until she reached what she hoped would be there. A storage space behind the stairs. She crouched and tucked herself as far back into the dark corner as she could, gathering her skirts tightly about her. Now, if she could only stop her rapid breathing from making a sound.

The front doors crashed open, and Aleksandra had to stop herself from screaming. Every part of her body pulsed in fear. She didn't allow herself to move, to breathe, even to blink. Male voices pierced the dimness, their words rich and foreign. A new shudder seized her. They'd seen her, they'd followed her, and now they were searching for her.

Aleksandra had heard of women in other cities who'd pierced their own hearts with a knife when captured by the Turks. Now she understood why. The fear had driven them to madness . . . or was it sanity? Her hands trembled as she released her skirts and reached for the small dagger she kept tucked in her waistband.

Her fingers closed around the solid hilt, and she took in the smallest bit of comfort. That comfort was stripped from her when a hand closed around her ankle and she was dragged from her hiding spot.

Aleksandra screamed and kicked, trying to release the hold. Laughter sounded above her, and she looked up to see two soldiers looming over her, their eyes greedy as they stared. The tallest one bent down and gripped her arm painfully. Aleksandra twisted away, but his grip only tightened.

The taller soldier twisted her arms behind her back so she dropped her knife. He held her in place, facing the second man, who shouted at her in Turkish.

Unbeknownst to the soldier, Aleksandra understood every word.

She'd always prided herself on studying other languages, but she'd never imagined it would be a curse. She understood every insult the man was throwing at her, every command, yet she kept her face turned away, and let the tears fall. Let them believe she was a helpless, hysterical female.

"Where is the man who lives in this house?" the soldier asked, grabbing her chin and forcing her to look at him.

She jerked her head away and said something in her own language. The soldier gestured as he spoke, trying to make her understand. She just continued in her ruse of acting confused and kept shaking her head, that no, she didn't understand.

"Take us to him," the soldier stepped closer and grabbed her shoulders.

She was practically pinned between the two men. She couldn't move, and she knew there was no way she could overpower them. She had no doubt that once they gave up trying to find Sabu, they'd turn on her and use her, then leave her broken.

A commotion came from outside, and two more soldiers entered the house. Aleksandra used the distraction to her advantage. She lunged forward and down, pulling away from the tall soldier, then she dove for her knife. Grasping it with both hands, she rolled away from the soldiers, then scooted against the stairs and pressed the knife against her chest.

The newly arrived soldiers started shouting, and all four men advanced on her.

Aleksandra cried out for them to stop. In Turkish.

They all stopped, surprised that she'd spoken in their language.

"I would rather die than tell you where the master of this house is," she spat out.

"He is your husband?" one of the newly arrived soldiers asked, crouching so that he was eye level.

This soldier was different somehow. He wore an embroidered over-tunic, and his silver belt with inlaid jewels was clearly the mark of a captain or even a commander. He was several years older than she, yet he didn't have the hardened look of his comrades. His brown-green eyes were bright with intelligence. His beard had been trimmed close to his face, sculpting his jaw, and his mustache was scant, a mere shadow above his top lip.

For some reason, she felt compelled to tell him the truth. "I am not married."

"Ah, you are protecting your lover, then," the man said.

"No," she whispered, feeling calmer. Something about the presence of this man made her feel like control had come back into the room. His eyes didn't have the greed and wildness of the other soldiers.

His mouth curved upward. "We are not here to harm you. We've come to resupply."

A bitter laugh escaped Aleksandra. "By killing innocent people, you resupply the blood on your swords?"

His gaze was steady. "Ah. You are clever." He tilted his head. "If we had walked in and asked politely, would your village have fed and clothed us?"

"You do not even know the name of the village you raid?"

"Rohatyn," the soldier said in a quiet voice.

Aleksandra should not have been impressed with a Turk, but she was. "Now what is your name?"

She hesitated. Her name would mean nothing to him, she meant nothing to him. Why did he even ask? He must have taken her hesitation for refusal.

"I am Süleyman," he said, his tone even.

She stared at him. "Süleyman . . . Süleyman, the sultan?"

He nodded, a smile touching his lips. And then he was reaching out to her, and his fingers wrapped around her hand, the hand that held her knife. He slowly, gently prodded the hilt out of her fingers as his gaze held hers. "I don't want any harm to come to you," he said.

And despite all the chaos reigning outside, she believed him, although it was nearly impossible to consider.

"We found the master," a man's voice sounded from outside. More soldiers entered the house, a wide-eyed Sabu in their custody.

He immediately saw Aleksandra.

Süleyman rose to his feet and turned. "We need you to act as a spokesperson and interpreter for us. If your people obey us, then lives will be spared."

Sabu's gaze shifted from Aleksandra to the sultan.

"How long will your army stay here?" Sabu asked in Turkish.

She shouldn't have been surprised that he spoke the language because he was known to travel to other kingdoms. Aleksandra assessed the men in the room. The nearest soldier was several feet away. The sultan was the closest, but she guessed the other soldiers would work to protect him. Now that they had Sabu, they had no need of her.

She wondered how fast she could make it up the stairs. And then where would she go from there?

"A few weeks," the sultan said, then he listed the things he expected Sabu to comply with as his army's men used the village to feed themselves and rest. Aleksandra slowly moved up a step, then another.

Sabu agreed to the sultan's demands. She froze as Sabu said, "The woman stays here."

Süleyman shifted his weight and looked from Sabu to Aleksandra, as if considering.

What did Sabu mean? Of course she was going to stay here.

"She comes with us," the sultan said.

"No." Sabu strained against the men holding him. "I told you which night to come. I offered my home and my food to your men. But the woman stays with me."

Offered? Sabu had *offered* the Turks his home and food?

The sultan turned to her again, and she shrank back against the steps as he walked toward her. He stopped and gazed at her. "She is a beautiful woman, and I can see why you want to keep her. But she is more than just beautiful. She is intelligent and clever."

He grasped her arm in a sudden movement, hauling her to her feet. Aleksandra nearly stumbled against him, but righted herself.

"A beautiful woman who speaks the language of the villages we will pass through is a valuable asset," the sultan continued.

"No!" Aleksandra cried out. She tried to escape his grasp, but several of the soldiers immediately surrounded her, and one of them tied her wrists together with a thick rope.

"She's my betrothed," Sabu said, his face reddening. "I have been loyal to you. Would you break an oath between a man and a woman?"

"Loyalty is something I value," Süleyman said. "But there is no such oath. The woman said you are not her husband or her lover. That leads me to believe she is not betrothed to you, either."

If only Aleksandra had lied, but then she wondered if the sultan would really have let her go if she was a married woman. The soldiers propelled her toward the door. "Please!" she cried out. "Please let me go!"

Even if they did suddenly untie her, she wouldn't be able to run more than a few paces. Her adrenaline of the last few minutes had peaked, and she felt ready to collapse with exhaustion. She didn't know what kind of help Sabu had given the Turks, but it was clear that he was a traitor to her people.

"My family," she whispered, as she was gagged with a thick piece of fabric and forced onto a horse. A soldier tied her to the saddle, securing her wrists and ankles until her skin chafed beneath the ropes.

She closed her eyes in defeat as the horse jolted forward, tears coursing down her cheeks.

❖ CHAPTER NINE ❖

MOROCCO

The taxi turned into a deserted strip mall, and Omar told the driver to wait for them. He and Mia walked to the location of the address they'd found and stood in front of a goldsmith shop. Well, it had been. The front window was cracked and the door looked as if it had been broken into at one point. No jewelry was on display and the lights were off.

The surrounding shops had closed for the night, and Omar wondered what had happened to this one.

Mia turned on her cell phone flashlight and jimmied open the door.

"Watch for broken glass," Omar said, just as his foot crunched on some. He tried the light switch, but nothing happened.

Mia swung her light around, scoping out the room, and a slow chill ran along Omar's back. The place had been ransacked, and he doubted that Deniz was anywhere near this place now.

"I don't want to stay here long," Mia said, her voice echoing against the walls.

Omar agreed. He turned on his phone's flashlight and moved to a space in back that looked like it had been a storage room. Or once had been. It was a junk heap now. "I don't even know where to begin."

"We might not have to begin," Mia said from the other room. "Look at this."

He joined her in the main shop. Her light bounced off the wall where a picture had been stripped off to reveal a hole in the plaster. Mia kept the light steady, and Omar moved closer to the wall to peer through the hole.

He nearly jumped back when he realized he was looking at the top of a man's head. And by the looks of it, he'd been wedged between the plasterboard and the framing of the wall.

"Is he alive?" Mia whispered.

Omar reached past the man's head, and felt for a pulse in the neck. The skin was warm and the pulse faint.

"He's alive. Call an ambulance."

While Mia made the call, Omar looked for something to bust the wall. He found a crowbar not far away—probably what had been used to make the hole in the first place. Not wanting to disturb any fingerprints, he pulled off his shirt and used it to grip the crowbar. Then he started to hack away at the wall.

A faint moan came from the man, and Omar said, "Sorry. But we've got to get you out of here. If you're the one who attacked my mother, then you'll be more than moaning."

By the time Omar had the wall opened and the man lying on the glass-littered floor, the ambulance had arrived. Two paramedics rushed in and checked the man's vitals, then fired questions at Omar and Mia.

Omar tugged on his shirt as Mia answered. "He's my brother," she told the paramedics in Arabic. She inserted plenty of emotion in her voice to be convincing. "Will he live?"

One of the paramedics said they wouldn't know anything until they got him checked at the hospital. Mia asked for the hospital's information, and within minutes they were directing the waiting taxi to follow the ambulance.

"Was it Deniz?" Mia asked Omar in a quiet voice in the back seat.

"Yes."

She pulled out her phone and called Omar's father with the information. After she hung up, she grasped Omar's hand. "Don't do anything stupid. The more information we can get out of him, the better."

"When I'm finished with him, he won't be leaving the hospital for a while."

Mia leaned her head on his shoulder and slid her arm through his. "Whatever you do, don't get arrested."

He scoffed. "That hasn't happened for . . . months."

"Exactly."

As the ambulance pulled up to the hospital, and Omar and Mia climbed out of the taxi, sending the driver finally on his way, Omar's heart rate skyrocketed. They'd have to pretend to be family to access Deniz's room, not to mention field a few police questions as well.

Mia led the way, confident in her ability to impersonate Deniz's distraught sister.

They waited in the lobby for nearly an hour before a nurse came and spoke with Mia.

"You may see him, but only for a few moments," the nurse told them in Arabic, glancing from Mia to Omar. "We are still trying to determine if there's internal bleeding, and we need to monitor him closely."

"Thank you," Mia said, standing and pulling Omar with her. "We just want to tell him we're here for him."

They strode down the hall to Deniz's room, and as soon as they entered, Mia shut the door.

Omar was at the man's bedside. Thankfully, he was awake, although Omar wouldn't have minded seeing him dead. It would be harder to get information out of him if that were the case, though.

"You saved my life," Deniz said in scratchy, thickly-accented Arabic.

"You'd better understand how close you still are to dying," Omar replied in Turkish. Omar had dedicated himself to learning the language when he'd been assigned to investigate Bata Enterprises a couple of years ago. He leaned over the bed so that his face was close to Deniz. "Do you know who I am?"

The man's eyes had widened at Omar's use of Turkish, but now he simply stared. "Zagouri."

"Correct. And I'm your worst nightmare."

Deniz lifted his head from the hospital pillow and looked toward the door, but Omar was blocking his line of vision. "It's just us, buddy."

Deniz closed his eyes and exhaled.

Omar gripped Deniz's shoulder, making him wince. "We can make this very difficult or easy. Your choice. Why are you looking for me and who hired you?"

When Deniz still didn't answer, Omar increased his grip. "I can put you back in that wall, and this time no one will find you."

The man visibly shuddered, but his gaze moved to Mia, as if asking for her help.

Mia folded her arms and didn't move.

"We can make this hard, and painful," Omar said, pulling out his gun and pressing it to Deniz's forehead. Mia didn't even flinch, but Deniz's eyes widened and his breathing quickened.

"We're in a hospital," he said in a choked voice.

"We are, but it will be too late for emergency surgery if I have to use this," Omar growled.

"We know what the tattoo on your hand represents," Mia said.

Deniz's face paled even more. "Then you know of the letters that were found," he said in a dead tone. He closed his eyes. "You might as well kill me now. I have failed in my mission, and I'm a disgrace."

Omar knew the man was bluffing. He kept the gun at Deniz's temple as Mia came to stand on the other side of the man. "Are you descended from the sultan too?" she asked.

"Yes," Deniz said after a heavy swallow. He opened his eyes. "We have been wronged for too many centuries."

"Some historians would agree with you," Mia said. "But there's another way to settle this. We can help you."

"No one can help me. Baris knows I didn't kill Omar Zagouri. That's why . . . I was nearly killed."

Mia glanced over at Omar, then back to Deniz. "Who's Baris?"

"He's an antiques dealer," the man said.

Omar almost laughed. An antiques dealer was sending a thug after him?

Deniz looked straight at Omar again. "Baris wants you dead. You're descended from the traitor wife of Sultan Süleyman. Baris has evidence that the sultan's oldest son and heir Mustafa was wrongfully executed. The throne should have passed to him, but the sultan and his chief wife killed him. And now Baris is taking his revenge."

"Four hundred years later?" Mia questioned.

"You don't understand, lady. The passage of time is nothing to Baris. He believes he was born to avenge his ancestors." He held up his tattooed hand. "This is the symbol of restoring the monarchy. By any force necessary, even if we have to battle with the ancient yataghans."

"Baris wants to restore the sultanate government?" Omar asked, lowering the gun but keeping it visible. "Who's behind him?"

"The Turkish Royalists, an organization that's been around for over a hundred years," Deniz said. "His supporters are getting these symbols inked onto their skin, and he's working to get rid of anyone who might stand in his way."

"Where do the Turkish Royalists get their money?" Omar asked. If he knew anything about conspiracies to overthrow a government, it always came down to money. So how was Baris funded? Collecting a few thousand liras here and there wouldn't cut it.

"The donations have always been anonymous."

The man's answer wasn't good enough for Omar, but perhaps Deniz didn't know the inner financial workings of the organization. He'd change tactics for now.

Omar glanced over at Mia, then looked back to Deniz. "What's the proof you were talking about? How can Baris prove the murder of Mustafa?"

Deniz gave a small shake of his head. "I haven't seen them, but Baris claims he has five letters written between the sultan and his wife Roxelane. He claims there are more, and he's working to get his hands on the rest of the collection."

This caught Omar's attention. "Where were these letters found?"

"An excavation somewhere in Istanbul," Deniz said.

Istanbul was only so big of a city, although its borders were smaller than the original scope of Constantinople during the era of Süleyman.

"How did Baris get ahold of these letters?" Omar asked. Baris wasn't a known archaeologist, which meant he was a collector. Logistics told Omar that Baris had purchased the letters from a dealer, perhaps on the black market.

"I . . . don't know exactly," Deniz said.

The look of panic in his eyes told Omar that the man knew more than he was letting on. He shifted closer, keeping his gun steady and his voice hard. "You're not an old man, Deniz. You can live to see a better day, *if* you tell me where Baris gets his artifacts."

Deniz's chest deflated. "He probably has more than one source."

"But?" Mia prompted.

"One of the main dealers he's worked with is Bata Enterprises."

Omar shouldn't have been surprised, but the name sent a jolt into his gut. He'd dealt with Mr. Bata on more than one occasion, and the results had never been pleasant. And the mention of Bata Enterprises also triggered another thought—one he'd discuss with Mia later.

"Your work is finished, Deniz," Omar said, pocketing his gun, then leaning over the man and gripping both of his shoulders. "You won't die today. You *will* go to prison, though." He glanced at Mia, who gave him a nod, then left the room, shutting the door behind her. "My mother is hooked up to an IV and on oxygen. You might think about hiring a lawyer, but believe me, none of them will be able to get you out. This hospital room is your last moment in the free world."

Deniz struggled against Omar's grip, but they both knew it was futile. The door clicked open, and Omar finally released Deniz and straightened. He stayed just long enough for the two policemen to read the charges filed against Deniz. Omar's father had been busy while they were following Deniz to the hospital.

Omar left the room and joined Mia in the corridor. She slipped her hand into his and they walked side by side to the elevator. Neither of them spoke. Omar was already formulating how he'd track down Baris and put a stop to the conspiracy against the Turkish government. And he'd find out who was funding this madness. He planned to start with investigating the possible involvement of his nemesis, Bata Enterprises. Most of all, he wanted to see the letters of the sultan and Roxelane for himself.

⬥ CHAPTER TEN ⬥

KINGDOM OF POLAND

AD 1521

"Take the woman to the main camp," Sultan Süleyman said to the soldiers surrounding Aleksandra.

She had been forced onto a horse, her hands tied in front of her. She had no idea what had happened to her family or the other villagers. Sabu was still inside his home, probably trying to negotiate for his life.

"I don't want us in this village for long," the sultan continued. "Tomorrow we'll start bringing supplies to the camp."

One of the soldiers said, "You're not staying here?"

"I'll be at the main camp, planning our next strategy." The sultan climbed onto the black horse.

Aleksandra watched him mutely, unable to speak or protest with the scarf tied around her mouth. Another soldier came up beside her on his horse and grasped the reins. Her horse started forward, and soon Aleksandra was riding behind the sultan, in the middle of a group of soldiers. They rode down the hill toward the marketplace.

The darkness completely covered the land now, and the only light came from the waxing moon above and the torchlights still burning in the market area. The sultan turned the procession to the right before they reached the main square, but they were close enough that Aleksandra spotted the motionless bodies in the square. Innocent people from her village.

Bile rose in her throat, and she wanted to look away, close her eyes. But she forced herself to study the scene, so she wouldn't forget. The overturned tables, the bleeding men, a dead child who'd probably been trampled, broken instruments that had been jauntily playing music a short time ago . . . the smell of blood and something more rank. Death.

If her mouth hadn't been gagged, Aleksandra might have screamed at the sultan, then screamed for her family. Had her brothers survived? Where was her mother? What would they do when they found she was missing?

It seemed there were those who would fight for their village, and others like Sabu who would do anything for gain. Their party continued to the base of the foothills until they reached the road that led out of the village beneath the mass of velvety sky.

When they reached the wagon road, they rode faster. As they crested the final ridge that led out of the valley, a group of men rushed onto the road, swords and daggers ready.

Aleksandra gasped as her horse lurched to a sudden stop. The Turks didn't hesitate for a moment and charged the men, their own swords drawn.

Beneath the moonlight, Aleksandra recognized them as men from her village . . . "Tashi!" she screamed, although all that came out was a muffled cry.

The village men were sorely outmatched by the Turks' skill and strength. Aleksandra trembled in horror as the Turks cut down one man after another.

She screamed again as Tashi was overpowered by one of the soldiers.

The sultan whipped his head toward Aleksandra. "Is he your brother?"

She nodded, her eyes filling with tears, desperate to save Tashi with any sort of lie. Even if she never saw him again, she had to do whatever she could to spare him.

"Halt!" the sultan called out, just as the soldier who had Tashi in a headlock brought a knife to his throat.

"Spare the man. He's the woman's brother." The sultan looked at Aleksandra as he spoke.

Miraculously, the Turk let Tashi go. He rushed toward Aleksandra's horse, and a soldier grabbed him once more.

"Go!" Aleksandra told Tashi, shaking her head, hoping he at least understood that much.

He must have seen the determination in her eyes, because he turned and ran off into the hills before the Turks could change their minds. All the men he'd come with were dead. Only Tashi had survived. Only one. Aleksandra could hardly breathe through her gag. She hadn't done enough.

The soldiers mounted their horses again, riding hard. The moon offered just enough light for them to continue on the road yet watch for any further ambushes.

It seemed they'd been riding for hours when the Turks finally slowed the horses. They'd reached a ridge that concealed a small valley.

The sultan drew his horse over to Aleksandra and said in a low voice, "That man wasn't your brother, was he?"

How did he know? Would he punish her? A moment later, the sultan pulled his horse ahead of hers again, and she could only stare at his broad shoulders maneuvering the horse down the ridge toward the valley.

Beneath the moonlight, Aleksandra could make out rows of tents, so dark in color that they were barely visible in the night. The closer they drew to the first row, the more rows seemed to appear. Thousands of men were camped here. The sultan had only required a small portion of his army to capture her village. That didn't make sense unless it was staged from within. Aleksandra realized it had been—through Sabu.

She didn't know what would happen to her next, but she fully planned to get the first dagger she could find. She'd use it on a soldier or herself, whichever came first. The sultan rode into the middle of the camp, whereas as Aleksandra's horse was redirected to the south along the edge of the camp. She didn't know which was worse, being separated from the sultan or continuing in his presence. On one hand, he'd shown mercy to Tashi and to her, yet on the other, the sultan had been the one to invade her village in the first place.

When the soldiers riding next to her drew her horse to a stop before a large tent, she inhaled sharply. This was it. This was where she'd meet her fate. All was quiet beneath the dark sky, and Aleksandra dreaded being taken inside any tents.

Her wrists and ankles were untied from the horse, and a strong arm forced her to the ground. Her knees buckled, and she sagged against the soldier. He muttered something that might have been a curse— Aleksandra wasn't so completely versed in the language—and then commanded her to walk ahead of him.

She had no choice. There were four soldiers surrounding her. Next thing she knew, she'd stepped into the absolute blackness of the interior of the tent. She was prodded along and nearly stumbled more than once. As her eyes adjusted to the new dimness, she made out shapes of people sleeping on the floor. All women.

Even though her arrival must have been a disturbance, they continued sleeping through the commotion. One of the soldiers pointed to an open spot on the ground and commanded her to sit down.

She slipped to the ground, grateful to be sitting on firm earth and not riding. When the soldier drew out the dagger tucked into his waist belt, Aleksandra wondered if she'd be executed here among all of these sleeping women. Or worse, if the soldier was going to force himself onto her.

She shrank away when the soldier bent over and grasped her arms. In a single swift motion, he cut the ropes from her wrists. Her skin throbbed and burned where the ropes had been, but she was free. She gazed about the tent, wondering if any of the sleeping women had a dagger beneath their clothing.

"Don't move," he hissed at her, reaching for her ankles.

She tried to scoot back, to resist the soldier's touch at her ankles, but he was quick and strong. She inhaled a ragged breath at the pain darting through her ankles.

The second soldier clamped an iron shackle around each ankle, connected by an iron chain. It was then that Aleksandra noticed the other women were also in shackles. This only meant one thing. The women were all slaves, probably captured and brought from other villages throughout the Kingdom of Poland.

The world grew smaller around her until it was hard to draw in a full breath. She was now a slave. Impossibly, new tears burned her eyes and fell upon her cheeks.

Then a soldier shoved a metal cup toward her. Aleksandra didn't even smell the liquid to see if it was foul. With trembling hands, she gulped down the contents. It was a watery tea, tasting of bitter grass. But she didn't care. If it was poison, then all the better.

Her stomach both tightened and relaxed, absorbing the liquid desperately.

Three of the soldiers left the tent, and the one who'd shackled her ankles took up a position at the tent entrance, his gaze on her.

She sat huddled for a moment, her knees drawn up, her arms wrapped around her legs. The breathing of the women rose and fell around her in an almost musical cadence. Not one of them had stirred in their sleep. It was as if they were dead, and Aleksandra shuddered at the thought. They might as well be—what sort of abuses had they been through?

With the soldier turned guard watching her, she studied the woman sleeping closest to her in the dimness of the tent. She was a small thing, delicate almost. Her features were fine, quite beautiful in the daylight, Aleksandra guessed. And then she noticed that the women were similar—young women like herself, none of them looking older than twenty years of age. They appeared tired and worn, but their beauty shone through their exhaustion.

Aleksandra kept her arms wrapped around her legs, too afraid to lie down. It would be a sort of defeat, she realized . . . to let herself fall into the slumbering world, completely defenseless and unaware.

But when she felt a jab against her leg hours later, she realized she had indeed lay down and fallen asleep. She startled awake and opened her eyes. The soldier was still at his post by the front entrance, but the women were getting to their feet. One of the women must have nudged her awake.

Aleksandra sat up, groaning at the throbbing in her ankles from the shackles. She saw similar skin chafing among the women.

"Where are we?" Aleksandra asked the young woman closest to her.

The woman turned her head to stare at Aleksandra, then brought her finger to her lips.

"We can't speak?" Aleksandra asked in a whisper. She rose to her feet, standing next to the woman who was several inches shorter, but at least a few years older.

The woman shook her head and held up her hand as if to say, *Wait, we'll talk later.*

Then the women formed a ragged line and started to move out of the tent. Aleksandra hurried to follow after them, finding her shackles cumbersome to walk in. She watched the other women as they walked, and tried to mimic their movements. It did make walking easier, but each step brought another surge of pain to her sore ankles.

Dawn burst over the eastern hill as Aleksandra stepped out into the morning air. Although the sun hadn't quite risen, the entire camp was awake. Smoke from dozens of cooking fires rose toward the blue-gray sky, and not far from the women's tent, in an open space, two sets of soldiers were sparring with swords. They were stripped down to their trousers, their torsos bare and gleaming with perspiration.

Aleksandra found herself slowing her step to watch the fighting men. There was a grace about them, a tenacity, and their lean and muscled bodies moved about as if they were in a choreographed fight. She had never seen anything like it. The village men she'd grown up with practiced their fighting with short thrusts and heavy footing. These soldiers were practically prancing like a horse; they were so light on their feet.

The woman behind her pushed Aleksandra forward, and she moved quickly again, following the others as they shuffled past the fighting men. When the women reached a wide trough filled with murky water, they crowded around it and began to wash. Aleksandra stared, unable to comprehend how these women thought they could get clean in such dirty water.

When some of the women had finished, Aleksandra stepped up to the trough. The foul smell made her stomach recoil, and she decided she'd be cleaner by not washing.

"Where you from?" someone next to her whispered.

Aleksandra looked over in surprise. It was the woman who'd told her not to make a sound inside the tent. Aleksandra looked toward the guards. They wouldn't be able to hear her if she whispered.

"Rohatyn," she said. "What about you?"

"Zaliwki," the woman said, dipping her hands into the water. "You've come from one of the farther villages, which means this campaign will be over soon."

"Campaign?"

"*Shhh.*" The woman moved on, passing Aleksandra and bumping her slightly.

Aleksandra took that as a sign to follow and stay close. The group of women walked toward a tent that was open on three sides. Aleksandra could very well guess that it was the food tent. The smell of spices and cooking filled the air, making Aleksandra's stomach tighten with longing.

A short, stocky man bustled between the rough-hewn tables, calling out orders to several men who were dressed no better than the women. They must be servants or slaves, Aleksandra decided. Their tunics were stained and ripped, their beards scraggly, their gazes hollow.

Bowl after bowl was ladled, and the women didn't hesitate snatching one and slurping it down, almost before they'd cleared the tent. Aleksandra tasted hers tentatively. The soup tasted like warm water, but it was sustenance. She gulped it down, determined not to be the last woman out of the tent. The empty bowls were deposited in a large barrel, and then the women turned toward the western hills.

"Where are we going?" Aleksandra whispered to the woman as they moved away from the food tent.

"We're taking care of the horses," the woman said in an equally quiet voice. "What's your name, slave from Rohatyn?

"Slave?"

The woman gave a soft chuckle. "What did you think you were? A harem woman?"

Aleksandra opened her mouth to reply, but she didn't have any words.

"Would we be so lucky," the woman continued. "As members of the sultan's harem, we'd at least be fed more than once a day."

Dread crept into Aleksandra's heart. "Once a day?"

The woman nodded, her arms and neck suddenly seeming too thin, instead of showing the elegance that Aleksandra had first believed. "I'm

Roma," the woman continued. "Not many of us share our names with each other. It's too painful to become friends."

When Aleksandra furrowed her brow in confusion, Roma said, "Death is a common occurrence. We lost two women last week, then you arrived."

"How . . ." She was about to ask how the women died, but then realized she didn't want to know. "My name is Aleksandra."

Roma nodded. "Don't tell anyone. It is the only thing they can't take from you."

❖ CHAPTER ELEVEN ❖

IZMIR

"I didn't know who else to call," Leyla whispered into the phone. She'd watched Baris gun down a man, then experienced a terrifying ride in Baris's truck as he ranted about the Ottoman Empire and the evil wife of Süleyman. Her head pounded, and her stomach felt like it had been turned inside out.

"Where are you?" Naim asked in an urgent tone through the mobile phone.

Leyla didn't know. They'd been driving for six or seven hours. She'd climbed out of Baris's truck when he'd stopped to fill up the gas tank. Now she was sequestered in the ladies' bathroom.

"By the sea," Leyla said, then winced. Much of the country of Turkey was surrounded by the sea. "I'm guessing Izmir. He hasn't told me that, but I know he has a shop in Izmir. He won't stop talking about Süleyman."

"The sultan?"

"Yes." She took a ragged breath. "I don't dare ask him any questions. I mean . . ." Her voice cracked. "He killed a man tonight. I . . . I don't know what to do."

"You need to stay calm," Naim said, his tone more gentle now. "Take deep breaths. I'll find you and get you out of this."

"How? You're hours away." Her voice rose in panic and tears broke out. "I don't know where we're going or what will happen—"

"Leyla," Naim said in a sharp tone. "Stay quiet around Baris. When you have a chance to use your phone, drop a pin and send me the location. I'm already on my way."

And she believed him because she could hear the sounds of traffic coming from his end of the line.

"Remember, don't let him take you out of Turkey," he said.

Her breath stalled. She hadn't considered that. But she hadn't ever thought she'd be kidnapped, or as good as kidnapped. Baris hadn't exactly forced her to come with him, but she hadn't dared to jump out of the truck and run away. The memory of his gun firing still echoed in her mind. Even now, in the ladies' room, she couldn't imagine herself sneaking out and escaping down the road.

She was so confused. What had happened in the alley? Was Baris the good guy or the bad guy? Had he been acting in self-defense?

On the drive, he'd ranted and talked incessantly about an organization called the Turkish Royalists. Leyla had heard of a political movement that wanted to restore the monarchy to Turkey, but she never took it seriously. Every parliament election was shadowed by this group of protestors who made speeches about returning Turkey to its monarchical roots, which had been broken up since World War I. Baris spoke as if he were a member of the Royalist organization and kept banging his fist on the steering wheel to make his various points.

The sleeve of his shirt had become unbuttoned, and Leyla noticed a prominent tattoo on his arm, a curved knife—a yataghan. The type of knife used in the old battles when the Mongols and Byzantines invaded Turkey in the thirteenth and fourteenth centuries. The warrior Ozman had decided to fight back and armed a legion of Islamic holy warriors with yataghans and short bows that shot fast and straight. It was then that the country of Turkey began to repel its invaders.

Leyla had listened to Baris's frantic ramblings, reluctant to interrupt and question him. When her father or brothers were upset, it was best to let them talk it out. In a couple of hours, they'd become reasonable again.

"Leyla, are you okay?" Naim's voice was soft.

"I think so," she said, taking another deep breath and wiping at her eyes. "I'm just scared."

At another time, Naim might have laughed. But his tone was perfectly serious when he said, "I've put a tracer on your phone number. I'll see you before you know it."

He hung up before Leyla could ask him how he knew to put a tracer on her phone. Was he some sort of a technical genius? For all she knew, there was an app for that.

She stared at the dark screen of the phone, it only had half a battery life left, and Leyla didn't know if she could believe that Naim would somehow find her and get her out of this situation. She wasn't even sure why she'd called him, except she couldn't think of anyone else.

She could just imagine her parents' reaction if she were to call home and tell them her new boss had shot a man in front of her. If she did get out of this safely, and her parents found out, they'd blame everything on her desire to go to a university in a big city and her decision to put off marrying.

Leyla pushed through the bathroom door and stopped short.

Baris was standing right outside the restroom, waiting for her.

She was grateful she'd slipped her phone into her waistband and put it on silent.

His gaze shifted behind her, scanning the bathroom, then his eyes were back on her face.

"Did you speak to anyone?" he asked.

"No one is in the restroom," she said.

He gave a quick nod. "We need to get back on the road."

Her heart dropped. But as they walked back to the truck, she said, "How long will we be gone?"

"As long as it takes to get the documents secured." He opened the passenger door for her, and ushered her inside. His stiff demeanor and angry look let her know it wasn't a gentlemanly thing to do, but more to ensure she was staying with him.

She slid into the truck seat and leaned her legs against the crate. Baris tossed over a package of crackers, and she opened it, realizing she was hungrier than she thought. She could have eaten almost anything.

As Baris wove his way through deserted neighborhoods, Leyla read the street signs, trying to keep track of where they were going. When Baris finally pulled up in front of an apartment building, she noticed that the neighborhood was quiet and dark, not run down and not exclusive, either.

Baris drove around behind the building, then turned off the truck's engine. "Don't speak to anyone in the building. Do you have a scarf?"

"No," Leyla said, picking up her computer bag.

"Don't make eye contact," Baris said. "Stay right next to me at all times." He opened his door and came around to her side to pick up the crate. She followed him to a back door that Baris unlocked with a key.

They entered a dimly lit hallway, their footsteps echoing on the hard floor. A door shut down the corridor just as Baris opened the door to the stairwell.

Without a word, he nodded for Leyla to precede him, and she started up the narrow stairs. When they reached the landing for the second floor, Baris said behind her, "Fourth floor."

She continued to climb, her fear increasing with each step as they neared the fourth floor. It had been about thirty minutes since she'd spoken to Naim. She hoped he'd really be able to find her, but then what? Baris still had a gun.

"Here," Baris said, as she approached a thick door. It didn't look like the other doors in the corridor. This one was obviously built for added security, with a metal-grate door in front of it.

Baris handed the crate to Leyla then proceeded to unlock the two doors. He flipped on an overhead light and reached for the crate.

Leyla walked into the apartment. The stench of stale air and sour food greeted her, and she almost backed out. But Baris was already locking the doors.

"Set the crate on the table." He flipped on more lights.

She set down the crate, then slid the computer bag off her shoulder. As the lights came on, Leyla was awed by a massive map on the wall. She moved toward it and realized it was a hand-drawn genealogical chart, the lines and letters extremely neat.

Baris came to stand next to her and pointed to the top of the chart where an elegantly painted name stood out larger than the rest.

Süleyman the Magnificent.

Above his name were the names of his parents, but all of the other names were listed below, branching out like a massive spider web. Birthdates and death dates were carefully listed beneath each name, and even the lineage of the sultan's concubines was included.

The names at eye level were eighteenth-century descendants, and the script continued down the wall in lists of descendants who were still alive.

"Do you see your name?" Baris asked.

A slow chill went through Leyla. "My name?"

He moved down the wall to the far left and pointed. Leyla crossed and looked at the clear lettering: Leyla Kaplan. Beneath her name was a blank expanse of wall. "This is amazing." Indeed, but it sent another shiver through her, one she couldn't quite identify.

And then she noticed that certain names had small red marks and others had small blue marks. Hers contained a blue mark.

"What do the marks mean?"

"Oh," Baris said, with hesitation in his voice. "The blue marks represent those who are from the innocent lines. The red ones are the guilty lines."

"Innocent and guilty? Of what?"

A small smile twitched his mouth. "That is what the records in the crate tell us."

She still didn't understand what he was referring to.

Baris let out a huge yawn. "I'll sleep the first shift; you sleep the second shift. There's only one bed. If anyone knocks or tries to get in, wake me up. Otherwise, wake me up in three hours."

Leyla watched him pick up the crate and leave the room, carrying it with him. She turned back to the wall, her hands growing clammy. As she listened for Baris's movements to grow quiet, she used the location feature on her phone and dropped a pin, then sent it to Naim. Next, she sent a text.

He trusts me enough to go to sleep. Should I leave? I can meet you somewhere. Or maybe I can find a taxi.

She crossed to the single couch and sat down, waiting for Naim's reply. Several moments passed, but nothing came. She stood and walked over to the door. She was locked in. Next, she silently walked to the window in the front room. No balcony and four stories up. The window in the kitchen was even more precarious. She checked the bathroom, wincing as the door creaked as she opened it. No window.

That left the bedroom. She moved quietly to the door that was ajar. She couldn't hear snoring, and wasn't even sure Baris was asleep yet. She crept back down the hall.

Even if Baris told her it was her turn to sleep, she wouldn't have been able to. She crossed to the wall again. The lineage was fascinating, really, but she was startled that her name was on this man's wall.

She looked at the final names at the end of each lineage and her curiosity grew about the red marks and blue marks. She then saw that some of them had dates of death entered that were recent. As in a few weeks ago. One was last week.

An odd jolt passed through her, and she pulled out her phone and did a search on one of the names. An obituary came up, and Leyla read the details. The death was called "tragic" and "unexpected" but no explanation of the how the person died. Leyla peered at the birthdate. The man was twenty-two years old.

With unexplained dread, she typed in another red-marked name. The obituary that came up was of a thirty-eight-year-old man who had fallen asleep while driving. Perhaps Leyla was just being paranoid, but all of the names with red marks by them were males. And all of them were the descendants of Roxelane, wife of the sultan.

She Googled a third name. Another young man who'd died unexpectedly.

Guilty rang through her head. Baris had told her the red-marked names were guilty of something.

Her name was listed on the far side, and she realized she had one thing going for her. She was female. And possibly a second thing. She wasn't descended from Roxelane. But what did it all mean?

She pulled a chair over and sat a few paces from the wall, close enough that she could read the lettering of the names. Her mind tumbled as she followed the lineage of the red-marked names. Sure enough, they all led to one person: Roxelane.

What would they be guilty of?

She thought of the records that Baris was so obsessive over, obsessive enough to gun down a man who appeared to be a threat. Was that man looking for Baris? Or the records?

She leaned forward, her eyes scanning all the male names with red marks. She was missing a connection, she had to be. Pulling out her phone again, she took pictures of the red-marked names, starting with the ones with death dates written below, and moving onto names with only birthdates. Hovering over one of the names, she frowned. This one had a death date written below it that was still a week away. Had Baris written it down wrong?

Omar Zagouri.

He was descended from Roxelane through his mother.

Leyla wondered why this name had been singled out from the rest. She typed in Omar Zagouri into her phone and came up with three hits. After browsing each of them, she decided none of them appeared to be in his thirties. None of them was the Omar on the wall.

Every part of her body prickled. How would Baris know when Omar Zagouri was going to die? Unless . . .

A soft rattle from the direction of the front door stole her breath away. She turned just in time to see the knob turn and the door slowly swing open.

❖ CHAPTER TWELVE ❖

KINGDOM OF POLAND

AD 1521

Aleksandra rose from her filthy bedroll on the fifth day of living in a military camp. She didn't think anything could be worse than the first three days, but she'd been wrong. Yesterday, she'd been assigned to collect the human waste of the soldiers. It was an all-day process, and the only thing that stopped her from running to the hills and getting stabbed by a soldier for rebellion was that Roma worked by her side.

Together the two women went grimly about their task, ignoring the disparaging calls from the soldiers and enduring more than one incident of groping.

"Don't look them in the eye," Roma had whispered in a fierce voice. "Our filth is a gift. It will repel them if they get too close."

This morning, Aleksandra prayed that she'd be assigned any duty except collecting human waste. She moved quickly to join the other women leaving the tent. She was familiar with the routine now and knew not to speak around any guards or soldiers. It only drew unwanted attention, and in a camp full of thousands of men, female slaves had to be extremely careful.

For the first time, Aleksandra gingerly washed in the foul water at the trough. Five days without bathing had made her desperate, and although she knew she didn't smell any better, at least the water had a cleansing effect. She'd learned to eat their single meal almost without tasting a drop. She tipped the bowl back, swallowed a few times, and then trudged on. She felt just as hungry as she did before she drank the soup.

Roma stayed by her side, which usually meant they were assigned to the same duties. The guards would pick women in twos or threes or fours and send them off to a task. The shackles on their ankles made the going slow, but they were still expected to complete all tasks.

The guard who approached them now was one of the nicer ones. He hadn't made any slurs or advances toward them. Aleksandra stayed close to Roma, hoping they'd be chosen together whatever the task might be.

The guard spoke in Turkish, knowing that Aleksandra could understand.

"You'll be helping to clean out the harem tent today," the guard said. "Everything must be scrubbed down, then start packing their bedrolls and clothing."

Aleksandra nodded. "Where is the harem tent?"

"I'll take you there. Choose three women to bring with you."

Aleksandra turned to Roma and explained what the guard had said. Roma wrinkled her nose slightly. "I know where the tent is. We'll bring Urszula and Zofia. They'll work fast and stay out of the harlots' way."

Roma motioned for the other women to join them, and they set off, following the guard. As they walked, Aleksandra tried to find out more information about the women in the harem. She knew that Roma was insulting them by calling them harlots. The women in the harem enjoyed an elevated status compared to a harlot. The harem women were servants to the sultan, and only the most privileged ones ever shared his bed. Some went on to marry or retire. The harlots were the women used for entertaining the men in the camp. Roma had told her the harem women had a nicer tent, fine clothing, plenty to eat, and their own set of female slaves.

"I'd rather die than be a harem woman's slave," Roma had confided. Nothing in this military camp was appealing to Aleksandra. Every slave was just trying to survive as best she could.

They skirted the camp and slowed when they reached the eastern end. Aleksandra nearly stopped when she saw what must be the harem tent. From first glance, it looked quite ordinary, but there were small, luxurious touches. A rug covered the ground in front of the entrance so that dirt and leaves wouldn't be tracked inside. A smaller tent was set up nearby and the most delicious aromas came from it. Apparently, the harem had their own cook as well.

And the faint strains of music came from inside the tent. Someone was playing the lute. Aleksandra hadn't heard anything so beautiful since being forced from her home. But she didn't want to enjoy it or find pleasure here in any way.

The two guards lounging outside the tent entrance straightened when they saw the approaching guard and slaves. The soldiers' eyes raked over Aleksandra, and apparently not finding anything interesting, moved to Roma, then Urszula and Zofia.

Aleksandra knew that all the female slaves were beautiful women, but with the measures they'd taken to stay dirty and foul smelling, it was difficult for even the most discerning eye to see through the layers of grime.

Even so, Aleksandra kept her gaze lowered and tried to emphasize her pitiful, shackled shuffle.

"Are the women within?" the guard asked who had brought Aleksandra.

One of the soldiers spat. "Do you have a statement from the sultan? No one visits without a signed statement."

"I'm not here to ogle. I'm bringing the slaves in to clean and prepare for moving the harem tent," the guard retorted.

"We're leaving?" the soldier said. "Has there been a defeat?"

"I don't know," the guard said. "I'm just following orders." He turned to Aleksandra. "Go inside the tent and begin your duties."

The other women followed her as she moved past the soldiers. Walking into the harem tent was like stepping into another existence. The interior was spacious and oil lamps burned brightly.

Young women wearing fine linen tunics and silk shawls sat together in groups. A young man, his torso bare, was the one playing the lute. Several of the women had platters of food near them as they reclined on cushions. A few pairs of dark eyes turned in the slaves' direction when they entered, but most of the other women ignored the intrusion.

"Where do we begin?" Aleksandra murmured to Roma.

"We announce our task and ask them to cooperate."

"In Turkish?"

Roma studied the lounging women for a moment. "Yes, I don't think any of these women are former slaves of our land."

Aleksandra turned to the few women who were gazing at her with curiosity. "We've been commanded to begin packing your bedrolls and preparing the tent to leave camp."

One of the women shot to her feet. She wore yellow silk wrapped around her bust and hips, leaving her stomach bare. Dozens of gold bracelets clanged at her wrists and ankles as she moved. "Where are we going?"

Aleksandra didn't have the answer, and she knew that the other slaves didn't either. When she paused too long, the woman crossed to her and narrowed her painted eyes as she stared Aleksandra down. "How is it that a slave knows our language? Where are you from?"

The tent grew absolutely quiet. It seemed everyone was interested in the harem woman's questions.

"I am from a village not far from here," Aleksandra said, wishing that not everyone was looking at her. One of the first things Roma had taught her was not to draw attention to herself. It was too late now. "I learned Turkish from a tutor."

"You are learned, then?" the woman asked. Her tone had grown calculated, cold. "Why are you a slave?"

"I . . ." Aleksandra swallowed against the dryness of her throat. "The sultan demanded that I be captured."

If the tent could have grown any quieter, the women would have all been dead.

"The *sultan*?" the woman asked, her tone rising in pitch. "*He* captured you?"

Every single woman in the tent was staring at Aleksandra. The lute player had stopped and was watching with intense interest. She realized that even Roma and the other slave women were staring at her. Aleksandra hadn't told anyone, and she was baffled why she'd said anything now, especially in front of a tent full of strange women.

"Well, well," the woman continued, her gaze scanning along Aleksandra as if she were making a careful study. She gave a half smile. "It seems you've been favored."

All the words that Aleksandra had kept to herself for the past several days tumbled out. Even if she'd tried to stop them, she wouldn't have been able to. "Is being a slave considered favorable? I don't know about Turkish women, but I was about to be betrothed in a beautiful village and enjoy a life with a husband and children."

Now more of the women were standing, some watching with apprehension, some looking at her with defiance. Surely, she'd insulted them. She hadn't meant to, but how could they think a slave chosen by the sultan was somehow desirable? Was cleaning up the soldiers' waste and eating one scant meal a day any way to live life?

No one spoke for a moment then the woman smiled. A genuine smile. Aleksandra didn't know what to make of it.

"We do what we need to do to survive," the woman said. "Do you not think life is better than death?"

Aleksandra had to think about her answer for a moment, especially if she were to answer truthfully. More than once, she'd been willing to plunge a knife into her own heart. Perhaps only the hope of one day escaping and returning to her village kept her from doing so, that and the fact that she hadn't been able to gain possession of a knife.

Tears burned in her eyes, and Aleksandra blinked them back. She didn't realize she had any left. "I do," she said at last. "I do think life is better than death."

The woman smiled again, and it warmed its way to Aleksandra, surprising her. It was the first time since being abducted that she'd any sort of encouragement. "Welcome to the harem tent," the woman declared. "I am Verda, and these women are like sisters. We are all in this life together, and we help take care of each other. We'd be pleased to have you help us prepare for departure. But, why don't you and your women eat something first. At the first breeze, you'll blow over."

It was a dream unlike Aleksandra had ever experienced. Real food after days of watery soup. She and the other slaves sat on the ground, refusing to soil the silk cushions, and found more food handed to them than they could eat in a day. Aleksandra took small bites of a sweet bread she wasn't familiar with. The taste was divine, and she wished she had two stomachs to eat more. But she was afraid of eating too much, then becoming sick. Long before she was full, she set aside the platter of delectable food.

Then Aleksandra and the other slaves set to work, rolling the silk hangings decorating the tent walls and fastening the fine fabric with ropes. The harem women chatted more than they helped, but Aleksandra enjoyed listening to them talk. They folded tunics and veils into bundles. Even at home, Aleksandra hadn't seen such finery among the wealthier women of the village. She began to understand the appeal of living in the harem.

She studied the harem women as she worked, wondering what each of their stories were and how they'd come to be a part of the harem. They'd given up the chance of marriage and a family in order to serve in such a life. They were all beautiful in their own way, and the way they talked and laughed together struck a chord of envy in Aleksandra's soul. She'd never had sisters, and her mother had been a distant figure to her as someone who did what she could to feed her children, but didn't cultivate any sort of relationship.

Inside the harem tent, it was almost like watching mothers and daughters or sisters interacting. The women were comfortable with each other, even kind to each other, something that Aleksandra wouldn't have considered. Not that she knew a lot about harems. As she worked, Aleksandra became more and more aware of the stench of her own body. What must the harem women think of her? Their skin smelled of the sweetest perfume. If Aleksandra could close her eyes, she might believe she was standing in a garden of wild roses.

The tent was nearly packed with the exception of the clothing the women would be wearing the following day and their bedrolls, when silence again fell on the women. They all stopped what they were doing, turned toward the tent entrance, and sank to their knees in a bow.

Aleksandra looked over her shoulder to see who'd entered the tent and caused such obeisance.

A tall man stood just inside the entrance. Even if Aleksandra hadn't recognized his brown-green eyes and his sculpted jaw, she would have known he was royal. Süleyman the sultan was staring past all the women bowing before him, his gaze burning into Aleksandra's.

❖ CHAPTER THIRTEEN ❖

IZMIR

Leyla couldn't explain how she did it, but somehow she flew across the room and hid behind the couch in a single motion before the door opened more than a few centimeters. She didn't dare breathe, although she was sure that whoever the intruder was could hear her heart beating like a megaphone.

The first thing Leyla saw was a man holding a gun. And it was pointed right at her head.

"Stand up," the man said.

The voice restored her breathing.

"Naim?" She stood, although she felt like she might collapse. Holding onto the arm of the couch, she stared at Naim as he lowered the gun, then closed the door.

"I thought . . . I thought you were still hours away," she said in a shaky whisper.

His gaze shifted from her to the wall with all the names scaling down it. "Where's Baris?"

"Sleeping. I sent you a text." She moved toward him, still unsure about how he'd get her out of here, but wondering at the same time why he had a gun. It both relieved her and worried her.

"He's still sleeping, then?" Naim said, not looking at her anymore, but scanning the wall.

She couldn't quite comprehend what he was doing. Didn't he want to leave right away and take her with him?

But he seemed fascinated with the charts on the wall. He moved closer and started tracking lineage lines with his eyes. He still held his gun, though it was now pointed at the floor.

"Naim?" she whispered.

He held his hand up as if to tell her to wait. Then she heard a shuffle coming from the next room. In an instant, Naim grabbed her arm and pushed her behind him, while he faced the hallway, gun raised again.

"Forget about those names," Baris's voice boomed as he walked casually into the room, his own gun in his hand and pointing at Naim. "You won't need them."

"Where are the records?" Naim asked, his voice a growl.

Leyla wished she could see Naim's face. How did he know about the records? How had he gotten to Baris's apartment so quickly?

Baris scoffed. "Those records are mine. I paid for them, and that means they belong to me."

"You killed our courier, which means all bets are off. We aren't playing nice anymore." Naim released his grip on Leyla's arm, then said over his shoulder, "Get behind the couch, Leyla."

"Ah. You know her," Baris said. "Why am I not surprised?"

Leyla had no idea what was going on between the two, but she scrambled behind the couch for the second time that night.

Naim's laugh was harsh. "Your surprise will be your downfall. Hand over the records, and we'll part ways with both of our hearts still beating."

It was Baris's turn to laugh. "You make idle threats. If you knew who you were dealing with, you wouldn't be in this apartment."

"I never make idle threats," Naim said, taking a step forward.

Baris shook his head. "I'd believe that of your father, but you . . . Naim, is it? You're too much in the world. You have a girlfriend hiding behind you. And you're an educated man. Why would you want to be a thug like your father? Family loyalty?"

Naim kept his gun steady and took another step toward Baris.

Leyla wanted to scream at him to stop. At both men to stop. Then she wanted answers. Who was Naim's father?

Naim began to speak in a low voice. "You're on my father's hit list. If you don't give me the records, I'll shoot you. I have no choice. You know my father . . . it's my life or yours. There is no compromise."

The front door banged open, and two men stepped in, both with guns trained on Baris.

The color drained from Baris's face.

"The records, sir," Naim repeated.

Baris dropped his gun, and it spiraled away from him. He raised his hands, and said in a choked voice, "They're in the bedroom."

Naim nodded at one of the new men, and he quickly moved past Baris. He returned with the crate a moment later.

"If you have switched the records out, we'll find you," Naim said. Then he strode right up to Baris. "The only reason you live is because I don't want Leyla to witness two killings tonight. But don't think you're free."

Baris's face reddened, but he said nothing, his eyes dark with fury.

Naim turned toward Leyla. "Let's get out of here."

For a moment, Leyla froze. She had no idea who Naim really was. Who was to say he was the safer of the men in the room?

Naim just waited, his gaze steady on hers, and finally, she rose to her feet.

He nodded and she passed him, not daring to look at Baris. She'd been employed by him less than a day, and now it was over. Her mind couldn't quite catch up. But she did know she couldn't remain in this apartment any longer. Not with the names of dead people on the wall, and not with Baris.

She followed one of the men into the corridor, and then Naim was behind her, shutting the apartment door. He grabbed her computer bag. His hand touched her back as he guided her ahead of him, down the stairs she'd come up, and out into the street. They exited the back of the building and walked toward a small sedan parked next to Baris's truck.

It was all surreal, and the night enveloping them made it seem like a dream.

But Leyla knew she was far from dreaming.

Naim guided Leyla into the front passenger seat where she sat down, and the other two men loaded the crate in the trunk of the car, then climbed into the back seat. Leyla didn't speak, didn't move, just stared through the windshield. A light rain started up as they drove along a deserted street, then suddenly Naim pulled over and stopped. The two men in the back climbed out of the car without a word.

When they shut their doors, Naim pulled back onto the street. "I'm sure you have a lot of questions," he said. "Unfortunately, I won't be able to answer most of them."

"Who are you?" Leyla said, finally looking at his profile.

"I'm everything I said I am," he answered. "But there are other parts that I keep quiet about."

Leyla clasped her trembling hands together and let out a long breath. "Are you the good guy or the bad guy?"

It was Naim's turn to release his breath. "It depends on who you ask."

She squeezed her eyes shut. How had she gotten into this situation? "Who's your father?"

"Ah. That I can answer." He glanced over at her. "But then you'd have to go undercover for many years," he said. "So it's best not to know."

"Naim," Leyla said. "Take me to a hotel and drop me off. I'll find my own way back to Istanbul."

He fell quiet. "We'll go to a hotel, but I'm not leaving you."

They rode for another ten minutes in silence until Naim pulled up to a hotel. Leyla walked in with him, and although he booked only one room, she said nothing.

She was exhausted and only wanted to sleep. Maybe her mind would be clear when she woke up. But for now, she didn't believe Naim meant her harm, although she would be more than happy when she saw the last of him.

Naim pocketed the hotel key and led her back to the sedan where he lifted the crate out of the trunk. As they walked to the side entrance, another vehicle pulled into the hotel parking lot. "Don't move," Naim whispered to Leyla. They stopped beneath the awning that spread over the side entrance. In the dark, they weren't visible beneath the added covering.

Leyla watched as a lone man climbed out of a car and made for the hotel entrance.

"We're going back to our car," Naim said. "Hurry."

"What?" Leyla said.

"That man followed us, and I can't bring you into this any more than you already are. I can't risk him seeing you."

She hurried with Naim back to the car. He loaded the crate in the back seat this time, then started the engine. Leyla clicked on her seatbelt just as Naim accelerated out of the parking lot.

"Who was that man?" Leyla asked. Her head was pounding and her throat dry.

"My supervisor," Naim said. "He doesn't know how I tracked down Baris. We're not supposed to involve . . . innocent civilians."

"And I'm the innocent civilian?"

He nodded.

Leyla let her head fall against the seat's headrest. "You're not back at school to get a graduate degree, are you? And you didn't just happen to get a job as a taxi driver?"

"I am going to get a graduate degree, but you're right about the taxi part." His hands tightened on the wheel as a car pulled out in front of them. They were nearing the highway again, and traffic was getting heavier.

"Look," he said, in a calmer tone than he'd used all night. "The more you know, the more dangerous it is."

"*What* is dangerous?" she shot back. "I watched my new boss kill a man tonight, then I was shuttled across the country, and suddenly, you're some sort of criminal. What is going on?"

"You'll just need to trust me."

Leyla laughed, but it wasn't a cordial laugh. "You have your own gun and you somehow appeared in Izmir only thirty minutes after I told you where I was. Either you were randomly flying a jet around the country, or you were already following me."

Naim started drumming a finger on the steering wheel as he merged onto the highway.

She didn't expect him to answer; after all, it would just make things more dangerous. She reviewed the events and all that Naim had said from the moment she climbed into his taxi. "You did something on my phone when you put in your number, didn't you? And that was before the interview. How did you know Baris would hire me?"

"I didn't know, but I wasn't going to let the opportunity pass," Naim said, surprising Leyla with his response—that he'd responded at all. "Baris is not the typical antiques buyer."

His phone buzzed, and he picked it up from the console and glanced at the message glowing on the screen. "Dammit."

"What now?" Leyla said, knowing Naim would probably stay silent about whatever the message was.

"We're not going back to Istanbul," he said, then slammed his hand on the steering wheel, making Leyla jump. "My dad knows about you, and he wants you out of the picture."

A wave of nausea clenched her stomach. "He wants you to kill me?"

"No," Naim rushed to say, but she wasn't entirely convinced. "At least I don't think so." He grabbed her hand which was now shaking again. "I won't let anything happen to you."

Another text buzzed his phone. This time Leyla was able to read it before Naim snatched it up.

Drop the woman off at the next gas station. Raam will take care of her from there.

"Who's Raam?"

"The man at the hotel."

"Is he following us now?" she asked.

"Probably," Naim said. He handed her the cell phone. "Reply for me. Write, 'The woman can be trusted. Call off Raam or I'll do it myself.'"

With trembling fingers, she typed in the words, then pressed "Send. "Done."

"Now take out the battery from the phone and remove the sim card," he said, glancing at her. "Throw it out the window."

She did as instructed, and it was at that moment she decided she would have to trust Naim. She really had no choice, but it seemed he was intent on protecting her.

"Is that enough to throw off Raam?" she asked.

"We'll be changing course soon. It won't take him long to figure out what we've done."

"So the text to your father won't be enough to stop him from coming after me?" Leyla asked.

"If it was one of my father's other employees, then yes. But I don't trust Raam."

Leyla fell quiet, watching the dark countryside speed past.

"All right, so you followed me—to get that crate back from Baris," Leyla said. "You have the crate now, but there is another problem." She saw his jaw clench. "I looked up some of the names on Baris's wall with very recent death dates. Men who have died in the last few weeks. All suspiciously. He's killing them, Naim. He's killing the male descendants of the sultan's chief wife."

"*Killing* them?"

"He told me that names with the red marks are 'guilty.' Of what, he didn't say, but it's pretty clear to me." She could tell Naim was listening carefully. "They are all descendants of Roxelane, the sultan's favorite wife."

"What would they be guilty of?" Naim asked, sounding like he was talking more to himself than her.

"I think the answer is in the records in that crate," she said, pulling out her phone. "I took pictures of several names on the wall, and one in particular stood out since he has a death date listed that's not until next week." She scrolled through her pictures then said, "Omar Zagouri is in his thirties and is expected to die next week."

"What did you say?" Naim asked in a rushed voice.

"The death date is—"

"No, the name."

"Omar Zagouri."

Naim blew out a breath. "It can't be," he said.

"What can't be?"

"Omar Zagouri is my father's worst nightmare," Naim said. "He works for the Israeli government and his sole purpose in life is to take down people like my father."

"Who exactly is your father?" she asked. "And what does an Israeli government job have to do with him?"

Naim exited the highway and turned west onto a long straight road. "Everything I'm about to say to you can't leave this car." He glanced at her. "It could be a matter of life and death."

"All right," Leyla said.

"My father deals in antiques on the black market. He connects collectors with sellers. As with any business where transactions of millions of dollars are made, some things go awry. And people have to be threatened."

Leyla decided he was understating the word *threatened*. But she didn't comment. At least he was talking now.

"Omar had stopped some of the deals from going through. Claimed that the artifacts were wrongfully procured in the first place, but my father is always careful with his sources. Yet Omar continues to pursue some of his best clients. A couple of them have been imprisoned because of Omar."

Leyla didn't know what to say to that. She was still trying to figure out who the good guys and bad guys were. "I always understood black market meant illegal," she finally said.

"Black market might be technically illegal, depending on the country in which the transaction takes place, but really it's just a government's way of complaining about not getting paid taxes on a transaction between two private citizens." Naim slowed the car and turned onto a narrow road. "Antiques change hands more frequently than you might imagine. If the buyers and sellers were to pay taxes on every transaction, the antiques would eventually be worthless."

Leyla wasn't sure she entirely bought his story, but she could perhaps sympathize a bit. "Your father certainly gets a cut. I suppose that's sort of like charging a tax?"

"Every dealer takes a commission—they do all the work of procuring the antique, then authenticating it and putting out the word that it's for sale," Naim said. He pulled into a driveway, and Leyla was surprised to see they'd stopped at a small apartment building.

"Where are we?"

"My cousin's place," Naim said.

Leyla raised her brows. "You have a lot of cousins."

"It will be safe for tonight." Naim popped open his door. "We'll need to keep all the lights off, though."

"Wouldn't your father and Raam know about this place?"

"My father certainly does, but not Raam, and he's the one I'm worried about," Naim said.

Leyla climbed out of the car, her legs feeling the stiffness of so much traveling. Naim once again removed the crate from the car, then walked to the building.

He typed in a combination on the keypad of the metal gate then they walked into the flower-filled courtyard. Naim unlocked the door to the first-level apartment. The place itself smelled musty but clean, as if it hadn't been occupied in a while. The owner had been tidy.

"Where's your cousin?" she asked as they entered the dark kitchen. Moonlight came through the window, giving everything a pale glow.

"Not sure," Naim said. "Come on, you can sleep in the bedroom. I'll stay out here."

Leyla was too tired to protest. She followed him along a hallway, then into a dark room. Naim twisted open the blinds on the window, and Leyla was able to make out a narrow bed and a desk and chair.

"The bathroom's the next door along the hall. In the morning, we'll put together some food."

As if in answer, Leyla's stomach grumbled. When Naim left the room, she turned toward the window. The moon had been the constant all night, and even though she had no idea what might happen when the sun rose, she'd try to shut off her mind.

She curled up on the bed and drew the top blanket across her legs, then somehow fell asleep.

❖ CHAPTER FOURTEEN ❖

KINGDOM OF POLAND

AD 1521

Aleksandra dropped to her knees, clutching the silk robe she'd been folding. As she bowed her head, she felt the sultan's gaze bore through her as if he could see every bit of dirt on her skin and every scratch on her arms and legs.

The harem women kept their heads bowed respectfully, but a few of them tittered. Aleksandra realized then that some of these women probably knew the sultan quite intimately. And his imposing presence might not have the same effect on them as it did on the soldiers beneath him.

"Stand, please, and continue your activities," the sultan said.

Hearing his deep, rich voice brought unwanted awareness to Aleksandra. She was sure that most women felt in awe of such a powerful man when they were in his presence. She was no different. But he was her enemy, and he'd torn her from her home. It hadn't been quite yet a week since her abduction, but it felt as fresh as if her wrists had been untied moments ago. She didn't need to look at her arms to feel the raw skin that remained from being tied to a horse.

She half turned from him and finished folding the silk robe with careful movements. She didn't want to snag the fibers against her chafed fingers. Even though she was sure she'd never wear anything as fine as silk, she took pleasure in being able to touch the cloth.

The women slowly resumed their chatter as the sultan looked on. What was he doing here? Looking for a woman to take back to his tent for the afternoon? A shudder of warmth passed through her at the thought of being with a man such as the sultan. Aleksandra chided herself firmly for allowing any such thoughts to stray through her mind.

Conversation rose around her, and it was easy to distinguish the sultan's voice from that of the women as he spoke to a few of them. Aleksandra tried not to listen to his questions after their well-being, for if she let the words wash over her, her face would heat.

The other slaves began to carry the prepared bundles outside of the tent, and Aleksandra took her place with them, carrying a couple of bundles at a time. She passed by the sultan with no comment, and she didn't think he noticed her exit, until suddenly, he was outside too, standing in front of her so that she had no place to turn.

"Come to my tent tonight," he said, his eyes on her. "I must speak with you."

She kept her gaze on the bundle she held, not sure if she had heard him right.

He spoke again, this time in her language. With that, she snapped her head up and looked at him. "You've spoken my language all this while?"

His mouth lifted into a smile, and she didn't let herself read into the fact that a sultan was smiling at her.

"Do your soldiers speak my language as well?" she asked, thinking of the conversations they might have overheard when Aleksandra and the other slaves didn't think they were listening.

"Some of my men speak many languages," the sultan said, his green-brown eyes lighter out in the afternoon sun. He tilted his head. "It's unusual to meet a woman from the Kingdom of Poland who is well versed in Turkish."

"I'm not that fluent," she said, lowering her gaze again. "I couldn't read it if I was held at knifepoint."

The other slave women returned from where they were stacking the bundles and passed by Aleksandra on their way back inside the tent. She felt their curiosity but refused to look at them. Heat crept up her neck.

"No one said anything about holding you at knifepoint," the sultan said, as if they weren't drawing curious stares from everyone within sight of the harem tent. "As I recall, you were doing that with your own knife."

The emotions of that fateful night came rushing back through Aleksandra, and the familiar anger pulsed hot. "I would do it again if I could but find a knife." She knew her words were harsh, and she fully expected a reprimand.

Instead, the sultan threw his head back and laughed. She raised her eyes again to look at this man whose very presence made her heart skip ahead. When he stopped laughing, he looked at her again and grasped her arm, looking straight into her eyes. "Tonight." Then he turned and strode away.

Aleksandra couldn't stop herself from watching him walk away. Soldiers fell into place, surrounding him as he walked, acting as bodyguards.

She turned and looked toward the tent again. Curious faces peeked out of the entrance. Then Roma was there, motioning her inside.

As soon as she entered the tent, the harem women crowded around her, asking question after question. What did the sultan say to her? Why did he laugh? When was she supposed to visit him? What would happen inside his tent?

It seemed everyone had overhead their conversation, yet she didn't have any more answers than they did.

Hours later, when most of the tent's contents were packed up, Verda approached Aleksandra. "Take this tunic, I no longer have use for it."

Aleksandra looked down at the clothing Verda held out. It was a soft blue, made of delicate linen. Aleksandra knew it was finer than any slave was ever allowed to wear, which was why she could not wear it.

"Thank you, but I cannot take that," Aleksandra said. "I don't want to give the sultan any reason to find me acceptable. The more he hates me, the more he'll be willing to send me away."

Verda shook her head with a sad smile. "You will learn soon that this is your new life. Your old life can never be recaptured. Take the tunic, wear it tonight, and try to improve your station. You are under Turkish rule now. Do you want to remain a slave forever?"

Aleksandra still refused to take the tunic. "This is what the Turks made me into. This is what the sultan will see."

"You are a stubborn woman," Verda said, but her voice had a touch of fondness in it. "I suppose that is what intrigues the sultan. Speaking your mind is your second nature." She looked over at the other harem women. "None of them would dare what you've done. None of them would ever refuse a sultan. Remember that. Look at these women. Are their lives so bad?"

Compared to the slaves' tent, the harem tent was paradise. Aleksandra swallowed against the perpetual dryness of her throat. "Thank you for your kindness," she said, then turned toward the entrance. By the time she stepped outside of the tent, the other slaves had joined her.

They walked their slow shuffle back toward the slaves' quarters, following their guard, as the chains linking their ankles kicked up the dirt. All around them preparations for departure were being made. Part of the camp was moving on, and Aleksandra had no idea if she'd be sent with the caravan or stay in the camp.

Hot tears burned her eyes, and she blinked them away, lest Roma or one of the other women see them. Or even worse, one of the leering soldiers passing by them.

Once back at the slave tent, she fell into an exhausted heap on her bedroll. With the sun setting, the various parts of the camps prepared their evening meals, but the slaves had no such hopes to eat until morning. Sleep seemed to be the best way to pass the time. This night, though, Aleksandra was not hungry.

She was just drifting off to sleep as the darkness stole around her, when someone shook her shoulder. Aleksandra woke with a start and stared bleary-eyed at the man above her. He was a soldier, that was for certain, but she had never seen him before.

"Are you the woman from the Rohatyn village?" he asked in her language.

Aleksandra licked her dry lips and nodded.

"The sultan is expecting you." His thick brows furrowed as he studied her. "He has been waiting. Why did you not report to his majesty's tent?"

"I didn't think he was serious about his request."

The soldier's eyebrows straightened. "He is always serious. You'd better come with me."

Aleksandra shuffled after him, and the soldier glanced down at her shackled feet. Something like disapproval crossed his face. She was certain he was as confused as she as to what the sultan wanted with her.

"My name is Ibrahim," the soldier said. "I'm one of the sultan's personal guards."

Aleksandra nodded, but didn't offer up her name. She was impressed he spoke her language and treated her with more deference than any of the other soldiers had. "Are you Turkish?" She had noted his stockier build and shorter legs.

The man glanced over at her, his mouth turned up in amusement. "You are observant. I am Greek, or at least I was. As a young boy, I was abducted by pirates and became a slave."

Aleksandra slowed her step, stunned at the news. "*You* were a slave?"

Ibrahim chuckled. "It is a story to be told another time. But I was brought to work in the Manisa Palace where the crown princes of the Ottoman were being educated. Süleyman was among them, and we became fast friends."

Aleksandra didn't know what to think. This sultan was not what she expected.

"The most shocking thing of all is that I used to be Christian," he said in a lowered voice.

"Are you Muslim now?"

He nodded and continued to lead her along the path through the rows of tents. She wondered if his religion change had something to do with the sultan as well.

"Süleyman has worked hard to be a respected leader," Ibrahim said. "Even though he was trained up his whole life to take over as sultan, it wasn't a smooth transition. His father's viziers and generals saw him as young and inexperienced when he took over, even though he was twenty-six. He used battle to prove his value. It was only after he conquered Rhodes that he became a sultan to be respected and taken seriously."

Aleksandra had never considered that a new sultan might have these types of challenges within his own kingdom. She continued to walk with Ibrahim as he told her about other battles won by the sultan. With darkness fully enveloping the camp, the only light came from a few of the supper fires, and the moon and stars above. They wove their way through rows of tents to the very center of the sprawling camp. Aleksandra was expecting a massive tent, as elegant in nature as the harem tent, but when the Ibrahim stopped, they were standing in front of a tent that looked like any other. It was the same size as the slave tent, though everything about it seemed much cleaner, even in the dimness.

Ibrahim brought up a hand to stop her from walking. Then he moved away from her to talk to one of the guards posted at the entrance. The guard bowed to Ibrahim, indicating that the man who'd led her through the camp was of greater status than she'd first thought. Ibrahim motioned for Aleksandra to step forward. The guard moved toward her and checked her body for weapons.

She wanted to strike him for touching her, but she clamped her teeth shut and didn't move. When the guard was finished, he waved her inside. She followed Ibrahim into the tent. The first thing she noticed was the spicy scent of incense filling the first section they walked into. A metal basin of water stood on a pedestal and a woman sat on a low stool by the basin.

The woman looked similar to the women from the harem, wearing a fine linen tunic, her dark hair swept back, partially covered with a silk scarf. The woman didn't look too pleased to see Aleksandra. She tsked and shook her head. Then she said in Turkish, "You filthy dog. You can't see the sultan like that."

Aleksandra knew the woman didn't realize she understood every word. So she kept her expression bland.

Next to her, Ibrahim scoffed. He very well knew that Aleksandra had understood. "You wouldn't look much better if you lived in the slave tent. She will wash, then be presented to his highness." He cast a sideways glance at Aleksandra, and for the first time she felt as if she had an ally among the Turks.

The woman rose to her feet and collected a cloth, then handed it to Aleksandra. "Tell her to wash, although I doubt it will do any good. I can't help her now." The woman departed through a curtained doorway, moving into another part of the tent.

Aleksandra handed the cloth over to Ibrahim. "The sultan forced me into slavery, so there is no reason for me to appear as something I am not. He will see me as I have become under his rule."

The corners of Ibrahim's mouth twitched, and Aleksandra didn't know if he was amused by her or annoyed. He motioned for her to follow after the Turkish woman and step through the curtained doorway.

Aleksandra crossed the small section, then parted the curtain and entered. Dozens of oil lamps burned brightly in the next room, nearly as bright as daylight. The first person Aleksandra saw was the sultan, sitting on the other side of the space, behind a low table. Squares of parchment spread across the table along with several inkpots.

The sultan didn't look up as she entered, but continued to write. Several people were in the room. A thick-shouldered man sat at another table, studying some scrolls. His dark-skinned face was drawn into a frown. He looked up as Aleksandra entered the room and immediately rose to his feet. Not to welcome her or offer deference, it was more of a protective move, she realized.

"This is Hadim Suleiman Pasha," Ibrahim said. "He is an Ottoman admiral."

Hadim simply stared at Aleksandra, offering no greeting.

The Turkish woman who'd been in the first room was sitting with another man in a cozy fashion. It confused Aleksandra for a moment, who had assumed the woman was the sultan's consort. Perhaps she wasn't particular in her men. The woman pulled a piece of fruit from a basket and peeled the skin, making Aleksandra's mouth involuntarily water. Today she'd eaten much more than most days, but her stomach was a tough mistress.

"You need to kneel," Ibrahim whispered. "When the sultan asks you to rise, you may then stand in his presence."

The last time she'd seen him in the harem tent, all of the women had knelt immediately, all except for Aleksandra. Somehow she hadn't been punished for it, but the way the dark-skinned man and the Turkish woman were staring at her, Aleksandra knew she wouldn't get away with it for a second time. After all, she was a slave to the sultan of the Ottoman Empire. Even if she'd been abducted against her will, he was now her master and held her fate in his hands.

She sank to her knees, feeling the exhaustion of her weary and underfed body anew. The sultan continued to write, apparently lost in his own thoughts. The Turkish woman turned back to her companion and resumed a murmured conversation, though every once in a while she cast a disdainful glance in Aleksandra's direction.

So much time passed that Aleksandra's knees and ankles began to ache. But she was determined to hold still, her gaze fixed on her folded hands that rested in her lap. She'd remain in that position as long as was necessary. She wouldn't give the Turkish woman anything to gloat over.

At some point, her body would give out and she'd collapse, but Aleksandra still had hours left until that had happened.

It turned out that she didn't have much longer to wait.

"You've finally arrived," the sultan said.

Aleksandra didn't look up. "Yes, I had forgotten our appointment. Forgive me."

There was a pause where even the Turkish woman went silent. Now everyone in the room knew that Aleksandra spoke and understood their language.

"Do you often forget appointments?" the sultan asked.

Without looking at him, Aleksandra couldn't read the tone in his voice. "I have rarely forgotten an appointment. But I have also rarely spent day after day starved and worked to exhaustion."

The sultan chuckled, and at that, she looked up. He stepped around his table, still holding one of the parchment pieces. He didn't seem at all bothered that she'd complained about her circumstances. Yet she wondered if he was going to leave her kneeling on the ground all night.

"Do you enjoy poetry?" the sultan asked.

Aleksandra felt, rather than saw, the surprise coming from those in the room. Perhaps this was a strange question from a sultan to a slave. "I've read little poetry," Aleksandra said. "And nothing in Turkish."

The sultan continued walking toward Aleksandra until he stopped right in front of her. "You may rise," he said, his voice deep and soft, as he extended his hand.

For a moment, she didn't know what she should do. Did he expect her to take his hand? She glanced at Ibrahim, who gave her a slight nod. She reached up and placed her hand into the sultan's, and he effortlessly drew her to her feet.

The movement made Aleksandra breathless, when all she had done was stand up with the help of a man. He released her hand, but the damage had been done. The touch of his elegant fingers had imprinted itself on her memory. It had been too long since she'd been extended any courtesies. The interactions with the men in her village seemed to be a lifetime ago.

Standing so close to the sultan, she realized how tall he was. The man was slender, but the breadth of his shoulders indicated that he had plenty of strength. She had no doubt that he would match up with any trained soldier. And as royalty, he was probably an expert in swordsmanship himself.

The steadiness of his gaze on her face, her dirty and scratched face, brought heat to her skin. She had to look someplace else so she lowered her gaze to the parchment he held in one hand. "Are you speaking of what you were writing? Is this the Turkish poetry you referred to?"

"Ah," he said. "You are observant. I knew there was a reason I invited you here tonight."

Aleksandra's eyes darted to his face, then away again. She'd imagined many other reasons, but the least of them would have been to read poetry. "You did not give me a reason for the invitation."

"I didn't?" the sultan said, almost as if questioning himself. "I don't suppose I was entirely clear myself."

Aleksandra commanded herself to breathe. In and out. Another glance up at him. "Will you read it to me?"

His face changed then. From the wry amusement, and did she dare observe—interest? To a wonder, as if he had been waiting for this question from her. "You would truly want to listen?"

Another breath. "I would." Although the tent room contained several people, at the moment, Aleksandra didn't notice any one of them. It seemed the tent possessed a single being. The sultan.

He looked down at the parchment in his hand, and a faint pink stole across his cheeks. She didn't allow herself to identify how he made her feel in that moment. Later she'd remind herself that this man was her prison keeper. That he was all powerful and had used that dominion to rip her away from her mother and brothers, from the men she was choosing between to marry, from the fields and flowers of her village.

But as the sultan began to read the poetry's words written by his own hand, in his rich and mellow voice, Aleksandra knew her life had changed forever.

◆ CHAPTER FIFTEEN ◆

AHMETBEYLI, TURKEY

Dawn was just beginning when Leyla opened her eyes. She was both surprised she'd slept so long and surprised she woke before the sun rose; the moon was long gone now. Leyla dragged herself into an upright position. Her body felt hollowed out from all the adrenaline of the night before, and she wondered if her pounding headache would ever subside.

She climbed off the bed, straightened the blanket, and made her way to the bathroom. The house was completely silent, except for the distant call of a few birds outside. Barefoot, she walked into the kitchen to see Naim sitting at the table. He'd drawn the curtains and was reading what looked like old parchment scrolls.

On the floor sat the crate, its lid opened and old pottery sitting next to it.

"Look at this," Naim said to Leyla, with no preamble. His hazel eyes were dark, and the skin around them appeared bruised. He hadn't shaved, and dark stubble had grown along his chin and cheeks.

"You didn't sleep."

"No," Naim said, rubbing his face. In his other hand, the flashlight wavered. "We need to leave soon, and I wanted to understand what we are carrying."

She pulled a chair around to sit next to him and leaned over the table.

The flashlight shone on beautiful lettering—ancient, carefully written Turkish lettering that preserved the Arabic script. It was a salutation that read *My Love*, followed by flowery text, which might have been written between two lovers. But they were married lovers, Leyla realized, as she read the signature at the bottom of the parchment.

"What do you think?" Naim's voice cut through her thoughts.

She didn't answer him, but continued to read, skimming mostly, then started over and read more slowly. Roxelane spoke of her son, Selim, as well as her stepson, Mustafa—who would be in attendance at the birthday celebration for Selim.

She thought about the PDF she'd read on Baris's laptop and the claim that letters existed between the sultan and his wife detailing a plot against her stepson. Could these letters be what Baris had discovered?

Leyla looked up at Naim, her voice trembling as she told him about the PDF she'd read and Baris's claim. Then she said, "These must be those letters." She looked at the others on the table. "Have you read them all?"

"Yes, but none of them outline a nefarious plot against Mustafa."

She scanned the letter that began: *To my most noble husband, the sultan.*

Leyla read through a description of an outing Roxelane had taken through the city, then she paused when she saw Mustafa's name.

Mustafa met with the military council this past week to discuss the Persian campaign.

"This feels tacked in," Leyla said. "Like it's a deliberate reference to Mustafa. Clues or hints. Are these all written by Roxelane?"

"Yes, and every one of them mentions Mustafa in some way."

"Some historians believe that Mustafa was set up by the sultan's grand vizier Rustem Pasha, during the sultan's Persian campaign," Leyla said. "Rustem told Mustafa that his father needed their armies to join together, and then when Mustafa took his army to meet his father, Rustem told the sultan that his son was coming to kill him."

Naim nodded. "So when the sultan saw Mustafa approaching with his army, he saw it as a threat."

Leyla looked from one letter to the other. She stopped when she reached the third one. "Here's a mention of Rustem Pasha." Naim leaned close to her, and Leyla translated, "Last night Rustem Pasha dined with us. He sends you his fondest wishes."

"Do you think Roxelane and Rustem plotted together?" Naim asked.

"Possibly," Leyla said in a quiet voice. "It would have to have been extremely convincing, for when Mustafa arrived in his father's tent, the sultan was so entirely persuaded that his son was a traitor that the sultan's guards set upon him and killed Mustafa without so much as an explanation."

"Of course not all agree there was a conspiracy against Mustafa," Naim said.

"There was always a conspiracy, we just don't know the right one." Leyla picked up one of the letters. "Although these letters might lead us closer to the truth."

"My father has the rest of the collection stored in one of his warehouses. These pieces were missed at the excavation since they were hidden in pottery." Naim tapped the table. "If these letters are what you say they are, as a set they're worth more than ten million."

"That's enough money to kill for," Leyla said in a quiet voice. Baris had killed for it already.

"Now you understand the stakes," Naim said. "If Baris could prove that his ancestor was wrongfully executed, then it means that he is a descendent of the true line of sultans."

He pulled one of the other parchment pieces closer. "Here. Take a look at the other ones." Naim aimed the light at the end of the writing. Like the other pieces, there was a small drawing of a curved knife.

"I wonder why there's a yataghan on each piece."

"I noticed that too."

Leyla continued to read Roxelane's writing about a banquet that Mustafa would be attending. The text's change of subject stood out from the surrounding sentences. And there were more references about her interactions with Rustem Pasha and plenty of praises included about his political views.

"What did Baris want with these letters?" Naim asked.

"Baris was seeking revenge in some twisted way," she said. "As a descendant of Mustafa, he's targeting the descendants of Roxelane. Nearly four hundred years later."

"Madness. Not that I understand it," Naim said. "On the other hand, family is important to all Turks. There's a reason you haven't told your parents about your new job. You don't want to disappoint them."

Leyla looked back down at the parchment. If she'd listened to her parents, she'd be home in her own house right now. "So, now what?"

"I'm going to do something I never imagined I would," he said.

She snapped her gaze back to him.

"I'm going to warn Omar Zagouri that there's a madman looking for him." He grasped Leyla's hand. "And I'm going to need your help."

"In what way?" she asked. How could she possibly help Naim with a man she'd never met?

"There's no way I can access him because of the past between him and my father," Naim said. "Our one and only meeting wasn't pleasant. He'd know who I am on the spot. I'll either be shot or arrested, so the warning has to come through you. It will be difficult for him to believe you, especially if he discovers that I'm behind this. He'll think it's a trap. But even though he's at odds with my father, whatever happened four hundred years ago between the sultan and his family needs to end now."

Naim rose to his feet, still grasping Leyla's hand. She stood up with him, surprised when he touched her cheek with his other hand. "Leyla, I need you to understand that if you agree to help me, it will be dangerous for you."

She looked into his hazel eyes, which were growing lighter with the rising of the sun beyond the kitchen window. "What about you?"

"When I agreed to work for my father, I agreed to embrace this life." He released a warm breath of air. "He did give me a choice, you know. Like you, family has always been a priority for me. I am my father's only child."

"Except I turned away from mine," Leyla said.

"Only for a short time." Naim paused and lowered his hand, letting it rest on her shoulder. At any other time, Leyla might see his actions as romantic. But even though a small part of her might still have a crush on him, she knew he was deadly serious. "Your devotion to your family makes it all that much harder for me to make such a request."

"What is it?"

"You need to call and tell them you've accepted the university position. You need to let them know you're working in Istanbul for the summer—like you originally planned. They don't need to know you'll be traveling with me, but they need to hear from you. They can't be kept wondering and waiting."

Leyla looked down, away from Naim's intense gaze. He was right, she knew it, but she didn't want to call her parents. Not yet. She'd barely caught her breath from the events of last night, and she knew once she heard their voices, her emotions would surface. "It won't be news they want to hear. I don't want to break their hearts."

"Would it break their hearts so very much?"

She looked up then and nodded. Tears burned at the back of her eyes, but she kept her gaze steady. "I told myself that the next time I called them I'd tell them the whole truth. I'll have to break the news that I have no intention of marrying Ruslan. And I would make it clear that there is nothing they can do to change my mind. Whether or not I return home to live and work is a different story, but I will not accept an arranged marriage."

"You're a courageous woman. I know your parents will be hurt at first, but then they'll be proud of you too." He released her shoulder and leaned in slightly, his next words just above a whisper. "And I'm glad you aren't marrying Ruslan."

He drew away before she could process what he might have meant. But the questions plagued her anyway. How well did she really know Naim, and could she rely solely on her attraction toward him to trust him? He turned back to the table, and using an old T-shirt he must have found among his cousin's belongings, he wrapped up the rolled-up parchment. "Let's put this in your computer bag."

She saw that he'd brought it in from the car. Grabbing it, she unzipped the bag and took out the laptop. "The PDF's from Baris are on this laptop," she told him. She knew she had to trust him, or else she would not be able to completely free herself from Baris. "I didn't explore the other files on the computer yet. Perhaps they will give us more information."

"Let's hope so," Naim said, loading the wrapped parchment against the stiff part of the bag, then carefully replacing the laptop. "Sorry we can't stay and rest longer, but we have a boat to catch."

She stared at him.

"We're going to Crete, then we'll track down Omar Zagouri."

Thirty minutes later, they were on a rented high speed motor-boat, and Naim was driving them across the Aegean Sea. At least Leyla thought the boat was rented; Naim seemed awfully familiar with the mechanics of the thing.

She sat near the captain's chair, the brisk cool air blowing against her face as Naim glided them across the low swells. The sun made its daily debut over the eastern horizon, lighting up the shores of Turkey as they moved farther and farther away. Watching the disappearing shore brought an ache to her stomach. She was traveling into the unknown, in so many ways, not only with what had happened with Baris and the fact that she was apparently on the run like a fugitive, but she was with a man she didn't know nearly well enough to be in such intimate circumstances with.

"Are you warm enough?" Naim called over the wind.

"Yes," she shouted back. He'd found a couple of wool blankets and draped them over her bulky life jacket. He wore no life jacket, which she wasn't happy about, but there had only been one on the boat.

She hadn't called her parents yet; and what would she now tell them? Their reaction to her decision to remain in Istanbul would be nothing compared to what they'd think of what she was doing now. One of the only things that was keeping her grounded and able to put trust in Naim was that he seemed adamant that she contact her parents. And she'd promised that she'd do so. She didn't look forward to the conversation, and she could only imagine what they'd think if they knew she was on a speed boat cruising across the Aegean Sea with a man who wasn't her relative. Leyla could hardly believe it herself.

She looked up to see Naim watching her. He turned away his gaze when Leyla made eye contact. Her breath was already unsteady. What had she gotten herself into?

❖ CHAPTER SIXTEEN ❖

MOROCCO

Omar gripped Mia's hand, more to keep himself in the present than to guide her across the congested street. He'd opted to walk from the hospital back to his parents' apartment. He was hoping that the cool night air would clear his mind as he was trying to make sense out of what Deniz had confessed.

"Deniz said that Baris had bought artifacts from Bata Enterprises," Omar said.

Mia drew in a sharp breath. "If that's true, then this is bigger than just us, Omar."

They stepped up on a curb where a row of cafés had started. Music, lights, and the sound of conversation and laughter reached them, but it all seemed a world apart from Omar's inner turmoil. "You're right," he told Mia. "If Bata's involved, then we need help."

Mia squeezed his hand in agreement, then released his hand to turn on her phone. "I'm texting Simon Greif. He needs to know about this."

Omar released a sigh. He hadn't wanted to bring the big boss into what had turned into a personal vendetta, but Bata's reach was international and the man was filthy rich, his holdings spanning the globe. There was no other choice but to reach out to Simon Greif. Suddenly, Baris's tracking of Omar started to make a strange sense. Omar and Mr. Bata had been at odds . . . was Bata behind Baris's quest? Had Bata been paying Baris a price he couldn't turn down?

"Sent," Mia reported. "I asked Simon to put out his feelers, to find out if there's unusual activity going on with Bata Enterprises. Large sums of money being transferred to unnamed accounts, or archaeological digs suddenly closing down, or private collectors suddenly going quiet."

"That's my girl," Omar said, gratitude rushing through him. He captured Mia's hand again, pulling her to a stop in the middle of the sidewalk. He leaned down and kissed her.

He expected Mia to pull away quickly. Instead, she snaked her arms around his neck and pulled him in for another, lingering kiss.

Those walking past on the sidewalk skirted around them. One man even let out a low whistle. Omar didn't care. Mia was with him, here and now. Despite the frustrations he had about his mother's situation and the task of tracking down Baris, Mia was helping him, and he couldn't think of anything better.

The world gradually came into focus, and the sounds of night life reached Omar as Mia finally drew away from him, a smile on her face. She was watching him, as if she could read his mind.

"Should we check out the club?" she asked.

Omar laughed. "Yes, how did you guess I needed a drink?"

Mia slipped her hand into his, but he didn't need any prodding to walk with her into the club that was throbbing with music just beyond the last café. Omar entered the club and was immediately surrounded by colored strobe lights and an all absorbing beat. He ordered a couple of beers from the bar while Mia found a small corner table.

After he downed the first beer, Mia tugged him toward the dance floor. He was about to protest that he was too tired to dance, but Mia's hands on him and her sultry moves against his body convinced him otherwise. He drew her close, and buried his face against her neck and hair, and let himself breathe her in as the music drowned out all other thought.

All too soon, Mia was breaking away, pulling her phone out of her pocket and holding up the screen so Omar could see the text. It was from Simon Greif.

Bata Enterprises has transferred several payments to a small business in Izmir over the past six months. What's unusual about it is the shop is registered as a jewelry and antiques business. Typically, those types of businesses are paying Bata Enterprises, not the other way around.

Omar took the phone and typed back a reply to Simon: *What's the name of the registered owner?*

The reply took a couple of moments to come in: *Baris Uzuner.*

Omar and Mia both stared at the screen.

Send me everything you can find, Omar typed. *I'll be at a computer in a few minutes.*

Another text came in: *What's going on? Where are you guys?*

Where we are doesn't matter, because our next stop is Izmir. Omar handed the phone back to Mia, regretting his night had only included one drink and one dance, but he'd have to make up for it later.

"Let's go," he said.

Mia nodded and they left the club together. Out in the night air again, Omar hailed a taxi after all, and they made short time returning to his parents' apartment. His father was still awake when they entered, so Omar filled him in on the latest news.

Then he turned to the laptop on the kitchen table, and the three of them pored over the information that Simon had started sending over.

One of the scans was of payments made to the antiques business. Each transaction paid to Baris Uzuner was equivalent to about twenty thousand dollars.

"Where is all the money going?" Omar's father asked.

Mia opened a new e-mail from Simon. "Here are Baris's recent bank statements."

Omar started to read through the transactions, taking note of the transfers of large amounts to other banking accounts. "Wait," he said, before Mia could click on the next page in the document. "Deniz," he read. "This transfer is to Deniz."

Mia sat back in her chair. "So Bata Enterprises is funding Baris—whether directly or indirectly, I'm not sure."

Omar scrubbed a hand through his hair. The last time he'd dealt with Mr. Bata had been through his only son, Naim. Omar had Naim arrested for a blackmarket deal that he swore hadn't gone through Bata Enterprises, but Omar had enough proof for the police. What Omar was surprised at was how vehemently Naim had protested his involvement.

In the end, Omar had told Naim that he was guilty by association—whether a transaction was made by Mr. Bata, or Naim Bata, it was one and the same to Omar . . . and the police agreed. Although, three days later, Naim was released from prison. It seemed that Mr. Bata had friends in every organization.

"They're connected, that's all I need to know," Omar said, looking over at his father.

"What can I do to help?" his father asked. "Anything."

"Just take care of mother," Omar said. "I don't know when I can be in touch again."

His father's thick brows lifted. "When are you leaving?"

"Tonight," Omar said, glancing at Mia.

"Are you sure?" Mia asked. When he nodded, she said, "We need to hire a security guard for your parents."

"Why?" Omar's father asked. "We aren't going anywhere for a while."

"Mia has a good point." Omar powered off the laptop. "Bata Enterprises brings a new dimension to this whole operation. When

Baris and Mr. Bata discover that Deniz failed, they're going to follow Deniz's trail and find out why he botched locating me." He turned to look at his father in the eye. "You need to relocate until this is all over."

His father looked down at his hands, clenched together on the table. "Will hiring a security guard help? I'd hate to move your mother in her condition."

"Hire two guards, twenty-four seven, and I'll be happy," Omar said. He embraced his father. "I'm sorry that my history has affected the family."

His father patted him on the back. "We're survivors, Omar. You know that. Now go do what you have to do. I'll watch your mother."

Omar and Mia made short work of packing, and within the hour they were at the airport, booking the first plane to Turkey.

The Casablanca airport was quiet, and Omar found a row of empty seats, which wasn't too hard in the middle of the night. Mia leaned her head against his shoulder and closed her eyes as he powered on his laptop and connected to the Internet.

"What did you bust Naim for?" Mia asked, stifling a yawn.

"A few years ago, there was a dispute between Turkey and Germany over artifacts that Turkey claimed Berlin had stolen from them," Omar said as he started to scroll through Simon Greif's e-mails for a second time. "Berlin accused Ankara of not preserving the artifacts in the first place, and Ankara insisted that German archaeologists in the early nineteenth century had stolen artifacts they'd excavated on Turkish soil."

"What does Berlin have?"

"The most notable treasures include the sarcophagus from the tomb of Haci Ibrahim Veli, the prayer niche from the Beyhekim Mosque, and a fisherman statue from Aphrodisias."

"So how do Naim and Bata Enterprises fit into this?" Mia asked, lifting her head to look at him.

Omar gave a laugh. "You'll find it hard to believe. Mr. Bata thought he could act as the courier, and then when a few of the smaller items went missing, he claimed theft and filed an insurance claim. *If* the items had been stolen, the insurance should have gone to the country of Turkey, not Bata Enterprises."

"Let me guess," Mia said. "The items were later discovered in a private collection."

"Three of them were, including dozens of Iznik tiles from the Piyale Pasha Mosque. I traced the transaction directly to Bata, and when I arranged a private meeting with him to negotiate, his son Naim showed up."

"How long ago was this?"

"It's been two years now."

Mia went silent and laid her head on his shoulder again.

Another e-mail came in from Simon, and Omar clicked it open. He'd asked his boss to find the most recent known location of Naim Bata. "Well, well."

Mia lifted her head to look at the screen.

"It looks like we're closer to Naim than we thought. He rented a boat off the coast of Izmir, chartered for the island of Crete." Omar checked the time on his watch. It was 2:00 a.m. "It looks like I'm changing our flight reservations."

❖ CHAPTER SEVENTEEN ❖

KINGDOM OF POLAND

AD 1521

The sultan's poetry was like music infusing into Aleksandra's soul. She'd never heard such use of words or turns of phrase and attributed it to the Turkish language. But it was more than that, she knew, it was the poet behind the phrases. The sultan of the Ottoman Empire. A man who ruled countries and continued to conquer more, just as he'd conquered her village.

Throne of my lonely niche, my wealth, my love, my moonlight.
My most sincere friend, my confidant, my very existence, my Sultan
The most beautiful among the beautiful . . .
My springtime, my merry-faced love, my daytime, my sweetheart, laughing leaf . . .
My plants, my sweet, my rose, the only one who does not distress me in this world . . .

Everything else in that secluded tent room faded. The watching admiral, the glowering Turkish woman and her male companion, even

Ibrahim seemed relegated to the background now. The world grew small, or was the sultan's presence growing larger until only he occupied it?

When he finished reading his freshly written poem, it took Aleksandra a moment to realize it. The words continued to echo, living well past their spoken presentation. She had been staring at his tanned, elegant fingers as they grasped the piece of parchment, and now, as he lowered the parchment, Aleksandra finally met his eyes.

To find them on her. Waiting.

She knew something inside of her had been transformed, and she wondered if she could still speak. Perhaps she'd have to relearn words and phrases like a young child. The sultan continued to watch her, not demanding a critique, as if he knew it was best to wait.

And as of now, Aleksandra didn't have the words, at least not in Turkish. So she replied in her native language. "I have never heard a more beautiful poem. It has filled my heart where I didn't think it would be possible to fill." She gestured about the tent room. "It's more beautiful than the finest silk, the most graceful woman, and the sweetest child."

The sultan bowed before her, then grasped her hand and bent over it to kiss her fingers. Aleksandra's breath caught at the gesture. This was beyond what a slave would ever expect from a ruler. When he released her hand, his eyes told her that he'd basked in her compliments, and that he appreciated them.

"You are the first to hear that poem," he said.

And although Aleksandra knew other people in the room had heard it the same time as she, she realized he'd been reading it to her alone. She was beyond flattered, even though she didn't want to be. She wanted to still be angry with him and bitter about her situation. But she knew if she'd remained in her village, she would never in her entire lifetime have heard such eloquent words spoken with such feeling. Until just moments ago, such poems had been beyond her comprehension.

"I am honored," she said, and she meant it from the deepest part of herself. His green-brown eyes held hers, and she allowed herself to fully gaze at him. If she hadn't known him as the sultan, she would have felt his magnetism anyway. A man like this, no matter what station he was born to, would have excelled, and excelled greatly. His gaze was clear and intelligent, his manner careful and observant, he was quick to laugh, yet firm as steel in his resolve.

"Thank you," the sultan said.

She saw true gratitude in his expression and marveled how a man such as he would seek out a lowly slave and read his poetry to her, then be grateful when she complimented his writings. Was it because she spoke his language? She didn't allow herself to consider further, or to allow herself to hope more than the smallest latitude she'd already given herself.

And then she waited for the sultan to tell her why he'd requested her presence.

"I am moving a small part of my army north tomorrow," the sultan said. "You are to join the harem and travel with us."

Aleksandra opened her mouth to reply, but nothing came out. What did he mean by *joining* the harem? Did he want her to be a harem woman or a slave to them? She took a step back, feeling her hands start to grow cold. "Where are you going?" she said, her voice just above a whisper.

"That is not your business," the admiral barked. He strode swiftly to the sultan's side. "Why you entertain this varmint is beyond me, your highness."

The sultan's face stilled, and he raised his hand to silence the admiral. "This is not the time for rash judgment."

"Rash?" the man continued. It seemed he was not cowed by the sultan's status or power. The sultan seemed to allow freer speech than Aleksandra would ever expect.

"You are elevating a slave, a new slave at that, to your personal harem?"

The sultan merely stared at the admiral, a warning look in his eyes.

Aleksandra found herself growing hot with anger toward the admiral. Who was he to question the sultan in this way? She wanted to stand between the two men in the sultan's defense. An unexpected reaction for her as she realized he was still her enemy.

The admiral stalked away and turned his attention back to the table of scrolls. But it was clear he wasn't truly paying attention to whatever work he was pretending to do.

"I don't think the admiral likes me," Aleksandra said in a hushed tone.

The sultan smiled, and once again she was breathless. "Hadim is never easy around strangers," he said.

From his corner, Hadim scoffed.

"I'm sorry, I didn't mean to interfere—" she started.

"Hadim is the admiral of my fleet," the sultan said. "He's with us temporarily." He cast a meaningful glance back at the admiral, who met the sultan's gaze with a glare.

"You promote someone, and then all they do is talk back to you," the sultan said, still smiling.

Aleksandra let a smile creep to her face, then quickly sobered, hardly daring to believe she was in such a conversation with the sultan. She'd have to withdraw her emotions around this man. She didn't want to allow any vulnerability.

He continued to watch her closely, as if he were waiting for her to say something else. She had dozens of questions about her assignment to the harem, but she didn't want to ask them in front of the others. So she kept her questions silent.

"The night grows late," Aleksandra finally said.

The sultan seemed to snap out of wherever his thoughts had been. "Take her back to her tent and make sure she has everything she needs for departure tomorrow."

Aleksandra had no idea what things he thought she needed. She had nothing but the clothing she wore. But then she remembered. "Will the journey be perilous?"

The sultan turned his eyes back to her. "We are making our way to the Black Sea and then returning to Constantinople."

"Your home," she said before she could stop herself. She was going to the sultan's home.

"I don't expect peril, but we will be prepared if we meet it."

"Are your battles over then?" she pressed, unsure of where her courageous questions came from. "Have you conquered what you came to conquer?"

"Süleyman," the admiral said in a warning tone.

"Always the commander," the sultan said, a half-smile on his face. He stepped forward and touched Aleksandra's arm, guiding her to the curtained doorway and lifting the cloth that hung there.

She stepped through, her breath growing faint at his closeness. She could very well imagine the disdain in the Turkish woman's eyes as she watched them leave together, not to mention the tension radiating from the admiral.

Ibrahim walked with them, escorting them into the smaller room at the front of the tent. With a single look from the sultan, suddenly Ibrahim exited out the front entrance and for the first time ever, Aleksandra stood alone with the sultan. No one was watching them. No one was listening.

Aleksandra feared that if the sultan spoke, she wouldn't be able to hear a word he said over the thundering of her heart.

"Sleep well," the sultan said, his gaze lingering on her face.

The words were plain, but his voice was like a caress, and her skin warmed as if he had touched her face.

She wanted to tell him she didn't know what a peaceful sleep was, not since being abducted. Her nights consisted of a hard bed on the ground, dirt in her face, and the occasional moans from women who were hungry and in pain.

Did the sultan know how much he was confusing her?

"I will try to sleep."

He didn't question her answer. He only gave her a small nod. Something in his eyes told her that he wanted to say something else, but that now was not the time. Perhaps there would never be a time, but in this space, it seemed that nothing stood between them. She stepped toward him, involuntarily, and closed the already small space. She didn't need to touch him to feel his presence from head to toe.

She thought she heard his breath shorten, but she couldn't be sure. And even if she had, she would have doubted it. Her perception of this man was changing. And it would not save her. It would not return her to her village. It would not rescue her family from whatever fate they were suffering now. It could only bring her more pain.

Her questions rose to her lips. "What will I do in the harem?" she asked in a soft voice. "Will I serve the women? Clean and prepare for them?"

The sultan's brows lifted as if he were surprised by her question. Perhaps she was naïve, but she wanted to know what to expect.

"You will recover your strength. I need a female advisor who is well versed in the languages and customs of the villages we'll be passing through on our way to the coast."

Aleksandra was the one who was surprised now. "You wish me to be an advisor? Not . . . a harem woman or a slave?"

He took a moment to answer. "Your duties may seem blurred at times."

She didn't know how to reconcile that. "What do you mean?"

"You are an intelligent woman," he said. "I won't let that go to waste." He leaned down, so close that Aleksandra wondered if the impossible was about to happen. Would the sultan kiss a slave woman?

"May I make one request?" she whispered.

He didn't move, but said, "What is your request?"

"I'd like to bring the slave woman Roma with us on the journey. She is a hard worker and can serve the harem women."

"This Roma is your friend?"

She lowered her eyes, not sure where his sentiments lay. "Yes. But that will not get in the way of my service."

"I will decide in the morning," he said, and Aleksandra knew the matter was closed.

"Will you tell me your name?" The way he said it told Aleksandra that he knew there was a reason she hadn't given it to him before.

She battled against her common sense and her desires.

After a moment, he straightened. "If you will not give me your name, I'll give you one." Staring at her so that she felt he could surely see every thought moving through her mind, he said, "Roxelane."

She met his gaze, feeling herself getting lost. "Roxelane," she repeated.

"Very good," the sultan said. "I'm glad we agree."

She didn't know how to answer. He stepped around her and lifted the flap that opened the tent to the outside. Then he looked over at her. "Until tomorrow, Roxelane."

⬥ CHAPTER EIGHTEEN ⬥

CRETE

"There are a couple of ways we can get Omar Zagouri's attention," Naim told Leyla as they stood on the balcony of a Crete bed and breakfast hotel. The blue of the Mediterranean seemed to surround them on all sides.

Leyla glanced over at Naim, who had propped his hands on the balcony rail. He'd crashed for about two hours when they checked in, while she had sat on the balcony, staring across the moving water. Still, she hadn't called her parents.

"Can't you just email him or call him?" Leyla asked.

Naim laughed. "He probably doesn't keep the same phone number for longer than a week. I know my father is always changing his number. I have to call a secure line to get it."

Leyla raised her brows. "Is that something else I'm not supposed to know?"

A sigh escaped Naim, and he looked over at her, studying her openly.

Leyla should have squirmed under his close observation. She was sure her long dark hair was tangled, her makeup a thing of the distant past, and she'd been in the same clothes for forty-eight hours.

"Look, Leyla," he said. "I think you need to understand that I like you."

She felt her breath catch. Apparently Naim didn't mince words much.

"Right now, that might not be a good thing. My family life is beyond complicated."

Leyla exhaled. "My family life has its own complications."

But he was smiling at her, as if he hadn't just told her he liked her and dismissed her all in the same breath.

"And . . ." She couldn't believe she was about to say it, but apparently, this morning looking out over the Mediterranean was one for confessions. "I like you too."

Naim just nodded, then turned back toward the sea. "I have Omar's father's contact information. It's something that not even my own father knows about. I'm not sure why I kept it when I came across it a few years ago."

"So, call Omar's father and explain that we need to reach Omar right away?"

"I wish it were that simple," Naim said. "Omar is very private about his family."

"Sounds like someone I know," Leyla said, lifting one of her brows. "We've been in classes together for what, three years? And I learn about your family only because you put a tracer on my phone and I was kidnapped."

Naim straightened and turned, leaning against the rail, and faced Leyla. "That's what makes this so complicated."

Leyla watched him, waiting for his explanation.

"You and me. I can't bring a woman into my life. At least not one who wants to live a normal life. My mother lived in seclusion her entire marriage."

Leyla combed her fingers through her hair and glanced from Naim to the sea, then back again. "Where did she live?"

"Oh, it's a beautiful island, and she was surrounded by her child and my father's relatives. My father flew in her every request. But she never left, never saw the world, and never interacted with people she wasn't related to or who didn't work for her."

Leyla asked the question she had to. "Was she happy?"

Naim was silent for a moment. "I believe so. She loved my father."

"What happened to her?"

"Cancer," Naim said. "My father flew in the best doctors, but in the end she didn't want to leave the island to undergo extensive chemotherapy."

"I'm sorry, Naim."

He nodded and closed his eyes.

Leyla wanted to give him a hug, but didn't want him to misinterpret it after their joint confessions.

When he opened his eyes again, his expression was less troubled, and the hazel of his eyes more green than brown. "Tell me about your family."

So Leyla did. Her mother's tendency toward hysterics any time Leyla wanted to do something other than stay home, marry, and have babies. Her father's strange pride in what Leyla did, and her brothers who were married and producing children at a rapid rate.

"You must be the darling of your parents' eyes, as the only daughter."

She shrugged. "Pretty much. It was wonderful until I became a teenager and developed a mind of my own."

Naim moved closer to her, and she became increasingly aware of his open-collared shirt and the warm brown exposed skin of his neck and chest. "I like your mind."

Leyla laughed. "At least someone appreciates it. My mother will never understand me."

Naim reached for her hand and threaded his fingers through hers.

Leyla was surprised at this move after what he had said, yet she couldn't have been happier. Warmth tingled through her as he brought her hand to his mouth and pressed a kiss on her palm, still holding her gaze.

"Are you ready to make that phone call?" he asked.

Her heart stuttered. "To my parents?"

"I was referring to Zagouri's father, but we can wait until you call your parents."

His fingers were still wrapped around hers, and it made her feel more courageous, like she could have the conversation with her parents and deal with whatever outcome it brought.

"I should speak to my parents," she said. "You're right." But she was reluctant to release Naim's hand. Was there any hope of their relationship moving beyond helping him track down an Israeli government agent?

She looked down at their intertwined hands. "All right. I might as well get it over with—since you're pretty much forcing me."

Naim chuckled, and squeezed her hand, then released it.

The warmth fled from her fingers, but it was still pulsing through the rest of her.

She left Naim on the balcony and unplugged the phone from the charger Naim had given her. She checked the time. Her parents would be going about their day, unaware she was about to make them extremely distraught. Then again, she realized that if they knew what she'd been through since meeting Baris, they'd hire a car and fetch her from Istanbul right away.

Except she was no longer in Istanbul.

She sat at the edge of the single bed in the room that was still rumpled from Naim's nap. Taking a deep breath, she glanced toward the balcony, where Naim was once again leaning against the rail, looking over the sea. She pulled up her parents' number and pressed "Send."

The phone rang five times then her mother's voice answered. "Leyla?" a hint of panic laced her tone.

"Yes, it's me, Mother. Sorry I haven't called earlier."

Her mother began to cry, and guilt pounded through Leyla. Her mother could be so dramatic sometimes, but Leyla knew for her mother the emotions were real.

"Mother, I'm sorry. I've been very busy, and only had time to call just now," Leyla tried to explain. "I have something to tell both you and Father. Can you get him on the phone too?"

"I'm here, Leyla," her father said, seeming to take the receiver from her mother since the crying quieted significantly. "Where are you?" His voice was unusually gruff and demanding.

Something in Leyla's heart twisted. A warning.

"I've news to tell you and Mother, but she's so emotional right now," Leyla said. "Should I call back later?"

"A man came to the house looking for you," her father said. "He said you stole something from the university, and he has questions. He thought you came home because you left Istanbul two days ago. Where are you, and what's going on?"

Leyla stood. She couldn't think. Which man had come to her home . . . To question her parents? Fear and anxiety collided in her breast. "Who was it?"

"I don't know who he was. What's going on?" Her father's voice grew sharper and louder. "If you're in some kind of trouble, it's foolish to run from the police. You'll just have more charges brought against you. This is what Mother and I have been telling you for years. The world is not a kind place. And now you've *stolen*, Leyla. You've broken the law and the commandments of Allah."

Leyla opened her mouth, then closed it again, her eyes stinging. "I didn't steal anything." Her mind turned to Baris. She had his laptop. Had he gone to her village? "Can you describe the man? Please, Father. It's important. I need you to believe I'm not a criminal."

Naim had straightened from the rail, obviously hearing the stress in her voice.

He walked into the room, stopped in front of her, and mouthed, "What's going on?"

She met his gaze and knew hers was full of panic. She didn't want to tell her father that she was traveling with Naim, a man who worked for a black market antiques dealer, and that she was on a quest to stop a dangerous man from killing more people?

"Where are you?" her father demanded. His voice was loud enough to echo through the phone so that Naim clearly heard it.

She took a shaky breath, forcing herself to keep her emotions steady so that she could make her father listen to her. "I can't tell you where I am right now," she said. "Or my safety will be compromised. Please describe the man to me. Did he give you a name?"

"He said he was from the university, that was all." Her father was quiet for a moment, and in the background, she heard her mother speaking rapidly.

Then suddenly her mother's voice came onto the phone. "His eyes were black, Leyla. Black!" Her voice broke. "He was not a nice man, and I told your father that I didn't believe he was from any university. How did this happen? How did you get involved with this man? Are you pregnant? I never supported you leaving. Istanbul is not a—"

"No, Mother," she shot back. It was too late keep emotion out of her voice. "I'm not pregnant, and I'm not a criminal. What else can you tell me about that man? I need to know."

Her mother paused. "He was taller than your father, but his shoulders were hunched like he grew too fast as a child, or spends too much time slouching over one of those computer machines."

Leyla had turned the phone out so that Naim could hear his mother's voice. She met his eyes and knew he was thinking the same thing she was. *Baris.*

"Anything else? Please, it's important."

Her mother's voice was clearer when she said, "He wore a turban, which I thought unusual. I didn't know university men wore turbans."

"He's not a university man," Leyla said.

Her father spoke next. He must have picked up one of the other receivers in the home. "Who is he? Is what he said true?"

"I can explain everything when I see you again," Leyla said, a catch in her throat. She met Naim's eyes again, and wondered if she now had to worry about her family's safety. "I'll call soon, but for now, please call me if you remember anything else about the man."

"Leyla—" her father started, but she cut him off.

"You need to believe me, Father. Please trust me. It's safer that I don't give you any more information right now."

She hung up before he could say anything else and tossed the phone onto the bed. The emotions rushed through her, almost overwhelming, and she found herself in Naim's arms.

He held her tightly and stroked her hair. She couldn't cry, but she wanted to.

"Are my parents safe?" she whispered against his chest.

"I'll make sure they are," Naim said, his deep voice vibrating her cheek.

She looked up at him. "How? How will you make sure they're safe?" He brushed the hair away from her face.

"Or is this something you can't tell me?" she was speaking loudly now, but she couldn't stop the anger and fear pulsing through her. How dare Baris go to her village, to her home?

"Leyla, take a deep breath." Naim placed his hands on each side of her head, cradling her face. "We'll contact Zagouri's father, and then we'll contact my father. Your parents will be protected, and Baris will be stopped."

She inhaled then exhaled, focusing on Naim's multicolored eyes. "All right. Tell me what to say to Mr. Zagouri."

Naim leaned down and kissed her forehead. It wasn't a romantic gesture, so much as a comforting one. He released her and grabbed his phone, then pulled up a number.

"This line should be clear," he said. "But we can never be too careful. Speak in English. He should know enough to communicate with you." Naim instructed her what to say, then dialed the number and handed it over to Leyla.

Her heart thumped with each ring, and she was about to give up after the fifth ring when an older man answered the call. "Hello, Mr. Zagouri," Leyla said. "I'm calling for your son, Omar. I know he's not at your residence, but I would like to pass on a message—"

The phone line went dead, and Leyla looked over at Naim. "He hung up."

Naim took the phone from her and dialed again, then handed it back. "If he doesn't answer, then you know he's going to pass on the number to Omar. If he does, then proceed with giving him the message from me."

The phone rang seven times before it stopped. "Nothing," Leyla said, not sure if she should be surprised. "How do you know that this will lead us to Omar if his father won't even listen to a message?"

Naim lifted the side of his mouth. "Omar keeps his family life very private, but we can be assured that he's in contact with his parents. The fact that his father hung up tells me that his father has received specific instructions from his son."

"So now what do we do?" Leyla said.

"We order some room service and wait." Naim set the phone on the desk and plugged it into the charger. "If he doesn't call back by the end of the day, we'll have to relocate, and I don't know how long it will be before we can charge the phone again."

"So we just wait," Leyla said under her breath. She crossed to the balcony doors and leaned against the doorframe. Beyond, the sea was deceptively calm, unlike the impatience pulsing through her.

Naim came up behind her, and although he didn't touch her, Leyla felt as if he were. The warmth from his body arced between them, and she realized she was becoming much too attracted to him. She'd always liked him, had been interested in him, but sharing a hotel room probably wasn't the wisest decision. If they didn't stay another night, was it worth making a statement over it?

"What will your father do?" she asked, just to put space between them. She was starting to lose her sense of reality. It was becoming perfectly acceptable in her mind to turn around and kiss Naim.

It worked. Naim blew out a breath and stepped around her, moving out again onto the balcony. "He won't be happy that I'm keeping you involved and it's affecting your family now, but I won't give him a choice. He'll have to open the way for us to help Omar." He scrubbed his hands through his hair, which only made Leyla want to offer him comfort.

Leyla was about to respond when the cell phone on the desk rang. She crossed to it with Naim. The caller ID screen said, "Private."

"Is it Omar?"

Naim pressed his lips together with a shrug, then handed her the phone.

She answered, and there was a brief pause, then the phone clicked off. She looked at Naim. "Omar?"

"I assume so." He walked back to the balcony and leaned against the rail, hands gripping the top bar.

"Why wouldn't he say something? Ask who I was at least?" Leyla asked, walking out.

"That would make too much sense, and would also be a stupid move on his part." Naim glanced over at her. "He's too careful to give himself away, although he essentially already did."

"So what's going on, then?" she prompted. She was finding that a lot of stuff that went through Naim's mind didn't necessarily make it into a conversation.

"I'm guessing that he's now tracking us."

Leyla froze at the comment. "How?"

"Omar just confirmed that the cell number was a live connection, and now he'll track that number . . . which means that he's coming our way."

"So, we just wait here for him to show up?"

He gave a brief nod. "I hate to keep you involved, but if Omar shows up here and sees me, he won't hesitate to shoot me. If you're here, he'll hesitate and it might give me enough time to convince him we're now on the same side."

"Whoa," Leyla said, holding up her hands. "He's going to shoot you without asking why you're trying to contact him?"

Again, Naim scrubbed a hand through his hair. "Our history isn't exactly . . . squeaky clean. A couple of years ago, he might have used me to get to my father, but now, with some events this past summer, I'm just as much of a target as my father. He'd be happy taking either of us down."

Leyla folded her arms and stared out across the pulsing waves. "Do you belong in prison, Naim?" She figured the question needed to be direct. And then depending on his answer, she needed to get out of this place. She'd get the police involved, tell them everything, and find a way to protect her family.

Naim moved closer to her and ran his fingers along her arm until he reached her hand. Then he turned her hand upward and linked his fingers through hers. "I'm employed in a volatile industry. Whenever there are millions at stake, you always have to watch your back. You can trust very few people. My father's company provides a service that's in demand. No one ever needs to get hurt, but money can change people. Priorities and morals aren't always so black and white."

She looked down at their intertwined hands. How was it that this man was finally paying attention to her, when she wasn't sure she wanted that attention?

"Selling ancient artifacts to collectors has always been a business, even when the first mummies were discovered. But the modern governments put so much red tape in place, and their primary interest is collecting fees and taxes, so that it's impossible to make a proper bid for a piece you're interested in. Until there is world peace, I don't see the black market dying anytime soon." He held her gaze for a moment. "Perspective can lead you down different paths."

Leyla pulled her hand away, and his dropped by his side. "Just tell me, Naim, can I trust you?"

His dark eyes seemed to be pleading with her, as he brushed her hair from her shoulder. "You can trust me," he whispered.

◆ CHAPTER NINETEEN ◆

KINGDOM OF POLAND

AD 1521

When Ibrahim appeared at the slave tent in the morning and requested that both Aleksandra and Roma follow him, Aleksandra was pleased, if only for a moment. Ibrahim stopped them outside the tent and said, "Your request has been denied."

Aleksandra knew immediately what he meant. Roma would not be coming. She turned to her friend, her only friend, and embraced her fiercely.

"I will pray for you," Roma whispered, then released Aleksandra. She went back into the tent without even another glance.

Aleksandra immediately missed her. The night before, she'd whispered the details of her meeting with the sultan, and Roma had declared that the move was a good one. Traveling with the sultan was better than the slave tent in the military camp.

Roma had also marveled that the sultan had given Aleksandra a name. She had marveled as well, repeating the name of Roxelane over and over in her mind as she drifted into sleep.

She'd been surprised that sleep had come, but exhaustion usually won all of its battles. Now, walking away from the slave tent, Aleksandra thought of Roma. Would she ever see her again?

Aleksandra thought of the other slave women she'd been working side by side with. She'd keep their names secret, just as they'd keep hers. It was the only way to survive the injustices and griefs when forced to leave their homes.

The morning was still early as Aleksandra followed Ibrahim. Scents of food being cooked over fires reached Aleksandra, and she hoped they'd be fed at least before setting out. There was none of the friendliness Ibrahim had shown her the night before when walking to the sultan's tent. She didn't know what to make of it, so she stayed equally quiet. Did Ibrahim disapprove that the sultan had given her a name? And that he'd asked her to act as an advisor?

The sun topped the eastern hill as they reached the edge of camp, the brilliant light washing out the shadows of the night. Dozens of horses were being prepared and mounted by soldiers, who wore dark cloaks over their armor. Another dozen camels were loaded with baggage. Aleksandra had not seen the camels at the camp before and wondered if they'd been confiscated from one of the outer villages. The beasts didn't sound too pleased and bellowed their irritation as they were prodded to stand.

Goats had been tethered together, and a couple of young shepherds stayed busy swatting them with sticks when they strained against their ropes. This caravan was going to be far from the legion of soldiers that had invaded her village. It looked more like a traveling merchant group.

Aleksandra realized that this was the disguise the sultan was using. It was quite brilliant, now that she thought about it. Then she spotted the harem women. They were veiled and demure, hardly speaking this morning.

"Sit here," Ibrahim said to Aleksandra.

She looked behind her to see a low rock. She sat, and Ibrahim knelt and removed her shackles. The removal of the metal weight from her ankles nearly made Aleksandra cry with relief. She blinked back the burning tears that threatened and lifted her chin to look at Ibrahim, gratitude flooding through her.

He gave her the barest of eye contact, but Aleksandra saw understanding there. He'd been a slave once. Her battered spirits lifted, with promise of change and a new day. One free of heavy shackles. It felt strange to walk unencumbered as she was led over to the harem women.

"This woman will be joining the harem," Ibrahim said to the women. "Clean her up."

When Ibrahim left, Verda was the first to grasp Aleksandra's arm. "You have been reassigned?" She lowered her voice. "This is what the sultan wanted last night?"

"Yes," Aleksandra whispered, wishing that Roma was with her. "I asked that my friend come with me, but the request was denied."

Verda's eyes widened a fraction. She drew Aleksandra away from the other curious women. "The first thing you must learn about the harem is that there are no friends."

Aleksandra stared at the woman. Yesterday, she'd seen nothing but kindness and caring. Verda had been kind to her, and Aleksandra had felt a friendship forming. But the ruthlessness in Verda's eyes now told her that she'd been mistaken.

She swallowed back her questions, sure that they'd all be foolish. If she could sorely misread the women in the harem, what else had she been wrong about? The sultan's kindness?

"Come with me," Verda said. "You need to wash and dress. You won't begin your training until we return to the palace in Constantinople and the Master of the Girls can place you. But until then, you at least need to be cleanly attired." She looked over at one of the other harem women. "Hatice, bring clothing to the bathing tent."

Aleksandra did not know what type of training she was expected to go through. But she followed Verda away from the assembling travelers, impatient horses, and bellowing camels to a bathing tent. Verda stepped up to the guard at the entrance and said, "We have a new harem woman."

The guard nodded and pulled open the curtained entrance. Aleksandra stepped inside to the steamy interior. The darkness was broken up by oil lamps set on wooden crates along the perimeter of a small natural spring. Aleksandra thought it clever that the Turks had erected a tent over the natural spring. The steam rising from the water had nowhere to go and remained inside the tent.

At first it was difficult to take a regular breath, but by the time she began to undress, Aleksandra was getting used to the heavy, moist air.

"Quickly," Verda said. "There's no modesty here. Remove your clothing and get in the water. We only have a short time."

Aleksandra kept her gaze lowered as she slipped out of her filthy tunic and walked into the warm water. She sank into the steaming warmth and released a sigh of contentment. The warm water was like a caress, a healing caress.

Then Verda was handing over a small casket of oil and commanding that she wash her hair. First Aleksandra used the oil on her hair, threading her fingers through her long strands. The scent of lavender surrounded her, and Aleksandra wished she could close her eyes and float in this spring, forgetting the outside world.

Another woman came into the tent, carrying fine linen tunics. Once Aleksandra was clean, her hair scented, and wearing luxurious clothing, she knew the men would finally see her. And she'd be the subject of leering.

Cold dread replaced the warmth of the spring, and she started to shiver.

"Come out of the water, we must get you dried and dressed," Verda said.

Why had she let her guard down? She'd given herself over to a few moments of pleasure, and it felt like a betrayal now. To herself, to her village, to those who'd died fighting against the Turks. Here she was, bathing in a warm spring and dressing in fine clothing.

Verda surveyed Aleksandra as she finished dressing. "As the new woman, you will attract a lot of interest once we reach Constantinople. And if you're ever to have a chance to rise up in the hierarchy of the harem, you'll need some curves. We need to fatten you up."

Aleksandra wanted to look anywhere but Verda, and a hard knot was tightening in her stomach at the thought of everyone assessing her physical appearance.

"How does the hierarchy work?" Aleksandra asked in a whisper.

Verda arched a brow. "The women can be quite competitive, ruthless, in fact. The women chosen to travel with the sultan on this conquest are little more than servants back home. The sultan left his favorite consorts in his palace, where they face no danger." She offered a slight smile. "Time will tell whether or not you'll rise to status of favorite. If you do, know that you'll have hundreds of women hating you."

"Hundreds?"

Verda's smile widened. "The harem court is quite extensive. And if you want to continue in the sultan's attention, you'll have to please more than just him. Not only do we need to work on your physical upkeep, but you will learn the art of how to please people."

Verda turned to Hatice. "Burn the old clothing. Then meet us at the caravan. We don't want to be the cause of any delay."

Aleksandra watched as Hatice left, feeling as if the woman was taking a part of her with her. The clothing might be filthy, but it had been her last link to her village and former life. Now she would either be a servant for life, or have to compete with other women for favor from the sultan.

This. This was infinitely worse than her mother's life.

Perhaps there was a way not to pass the harem training? What happened to expelled harem women?

"Put these on," Verda said, holding out a silk veil.

Aleksandra had never worn a veil, but she had never been so grateful for a piece of clothing. Verda helped her put it on right, and then she gave her a pair of sandals. The sandals felt foreign to Aleksandra's feet, since she'd been barefoot and shackled for so many days. Verda then pronounced that she was clean enough now to travel with the harem.

Stepping outside the tent, the warm morning air was almost cold compared to the steamy interior of the bathing tent. The cold brought all of her senses to alert, and she became aware of the soldiers' attention as she took her place with the rest of the harem. Their gazes were not subtle, and Aleksandra began to feel light headed. She hadn't eaten since the night before and the time in the steamy bathing tent had depleted any of her reserves.

"Drink this," Verda commanded, holding out a goatskin. "The sweet tea will revive you." It seemed Verda missed nothing.

Aleksandra took several long swallows, then climbed up in the litter perched on top of a camel. A white canopy covered the litter, and Aleksandra knew it would be much needed in the heat of the day. Soon Verda joined her, settling on one end of the litter. It was remarkable that two women fit.

"From up here, I feel quite royal," Verda said, her smile flashing, her eyes bright.

It was the first time Aleksandra had seen behind the formal shell Verda seemed to hide behind.

"How long is the journey to the coast?" Aleksandra asked.

"Three days with this caravan," Verda said, turning her eyes to look to the east. "The sultan has arrived."

Aleksandra peered down from the litter. She did, indeed, feel tall and important perched on top of the camel, even though it hadn't risen to its feet. She didn't think the sultan would notice her, but he strode toward the harem women, sending Aleksandra's pulse soaring.

He seemed to be looking for someone. He stopped when Verda lifted her hand. Then he moved more slowly toward their litter.

"I almost didn't recognize you," he told Aleksandra, his voice deep with the early morning.

Aleksandra let her lashes fall and her gaze settle on her lap. She realized that even though she was wearing a veil, up close, it did little to conceal her from the intensity of the sultan's gaze. "I was ordered to wash and given a veil to wear," she said.

"I can see that," the sultan said with a soft chuckle. "I hope the journey is smooth for you."

Aleksandra wanted to tell him to stop talking, to stop saying nice things to her. Verda was listening, and standing not far from the Sultan was Ibrahim, surely hearing every word as well. What were the sultan's intentions with her? Could he really use a woman from the harem to translate for him?

"Moments ago, I was sleeping on the dirt ground of the slave tent. This litter is infinitely better than any stretch of dirt, and shackles about my ankles." Aleksandra didn't know why she dared to speak so boldly around him. She should not be speaking at all. She could very well feel Verda's sharp eyes on her.

It was as if they were both holding their breath, waiting to see how the sultan would respond.

"Indeed you were," the sultan said, no hesitation in his voice. "Then everything you are about to experience will be comfortable compared to your previous circumstances. Perhaps all of my leaders should serve as a slave before they are promoted. They would have more gratitude. And there's nothing a sultan cares for more than a grateful people."

Aleksandra raised her gaze then and looked into his brown-green eyes. In the morning, their color was clearer, as if the freshness of the day was still upon him, and the duties of a sultan hadn't happened to turn them murky. Had he planned for her to join the harem all along? Had he known she'd resist if he assigned her here first thing? Is that why he sent her to the slave tent to be shackled and to clean up the waste of the soldiers?

His mouth lifted up on one corner as their gazes held. Verda's widened eyes faded from view, and even Ibrahim's sharp attention seemed to be leagues away. The space between Aleksandra and the sultan was warm and close.

"I only wish you well, Roxelane," he said, and she realized he'd spoken her new name. The name he'd given her. He tilted his head, as if expecting her to say something like *I only wish to serve you*.

But the words refused to come, and she didn't know if they'd ever come. She'd noticed that Verda carried a very small dagger. Did all the harem women possess them? It would be one of her first questions when she was left alone again with Verda. Would Aleksandra be able to resist taking it if Verda fell asleep in the litter on their journey? Without shackles, she could make it a good distance, quickly.

Aleksandra had not spoken any of her thoughts, but the sultan had watched her closely. And something in his eyes told her that he knew she was not wholly present. Not even in the sultan's company.

"Verda will train you well," he said, his tone more formal now. "We do not let our harem women get neglected."

With that, he turned from them and joined up with Ibrahim, speaking with him quietly. Aleksandra watched the two men weave their way through the assembling caravan.

"You foolish girl," Verda spat out.

Aleksandra felt as if she'd been slapped. "What?"

"He likes you." Verda shook her head. "Why in heaven's name. I do not know why the sultan would like a simple village girl like you. You're probably Christian as well."

Aleksandra could only nod. "I am not here by choice."

"Oh, be quiet," Verda said. Aleksandra had suspected Verda could be forceful, but she hadn't expected to see it aimed at her so soon. "You have attracted the attention of the sultan of the Ottoman Empire. One of the most powerful men in all the world. He commands armies and leads millions and millions. And yet . . . all you can do is complain that you wore shackles for a few days."

Verda pursed her lips and turned her head as a young man approached their litter. He was clearly a slave but wore a relatively clean tunic. He threw appreciative glances at both women before grasping the camel's reins and urging it to get up.

The camel bellowed its displeasure, then rocked forward and back, staggering to its feet.

Aleksandra grasped the edges of the litter, holding on as it rocked precariously to and fro. Verda was still looking away, her face red with anger.

The caravan started out slowly, as the camels and horses fell into place, moving forward as one great mass. Soon they'd drifted into a steady rhythm. The young slave held the reins as he led their camel. Aleksandra studied his bronze skin and bare feet. He walked with an easy gait, as if he might even enjoy his task. She estimated his age as thirteen or fourteen, and she wondered if he was Turkish or had been abducted from a village. Aleksandra kept her gaze away from the furious Verda and watched the terrain as they traveled. She'd never been this far from her home village and with every league they traveled, she felt more and more hopeless that she'd never see her home again.

Verda opened a basket that was next to her and pulled out small seed cakes. She handed one to Aleksandra, who took it gratefully. But still Verda didn't speak to her.

Aleksandra ate the corn cake, feeling stronger than she had in a long time. She was lounging in a litter and eating. Her life had definitely changed. After some time, she was lulled to sleep with the rocking motion and the increasing heat of the day.

She didn't know how long she'd slept, but when Verda slapped her arm, she felt as if she were coming out of a cloud of mist "Cover your face and as much skin as possible," Verda said in a sharp tone.

Aleksandra scrambled to fix her veil and adjust her tunic.

"Here, put this on." Verda shoved a rough-sewn robe of heavy cloth in her direction. It looked like something a servant would wear.

"What's this for?"

"There are marauders up ahead. The page boy just came through and announced an impending ambush. Several dozen soldiers are waiting, and there's no place for us to turn back to take protection. It looks like a battle is about to happen. And the last thing you want the marauders to see is a group of beautiful women."

Aleksandra's pulse throbbed wildly as she dared to turn around and see what lay ahead of the caravan. Surely the sultan would find a way to protect himself, but to her surprise, he was riding in front of the caravan, straight and tall in his horse's saddle. His sword was gripped in his left hand as he held the reins with his right. It was as if he were looking forward to a fight.

❖ CHAPTER TWENTY ❖

CRETE

"He's not alone," Mia whispered to Omar.

"One of his thugs must be with him," Omar grumbled next to Mia as he kept low behind the balcony of a hotel adjacent to the one where they'd tracked Naim Bata. "Maybe it's Deniz's twin."

"Not unless his twin shaves his legs and wears rather short skirts."

Omar reached for the binoculars that Mia peered through. She released her hold and sighed as he scoped out the hotel room. The sun had set, and Naim had left a lamp on inside, making his room like a lighthouse in the middle of a wild storm. Naim was either very stupid and not at all like his father, or he was deliberately baiting Omar. The second happenstance, Omar could actually respect.

A woman sat perched on the end of a bed. She indeed did have long legs. And she was definitely a woman. A girlfriend? A one-nighter? It seemed that Naim had grown overly confident.

"She must be the woman who called my father," Omar said. "This complicates things. We have to get Naim alone." Then a man came into view, his back to Omar. But it was definitely Naim. Omar never forgot his enemies. Since tracing the phone number to Bata Enterprises, Omar knew their organization was somehow connected to whoever was trying to track him down. Omar had infiltrated Bata Enterprises more than once, confiscating stolen treasures. And from Mia's research, there had been quite a bit of activity lately regarding Ottoman artifacts. The coincidence was too great. If Naim was somehow in the middle of Baris's agenda, this was getting personal.

Was Naim the middle man between his father and Baris? "I wonder how long Naim and his father have been supplying the Turkish Royalists with artifacts and money, fueling their fire?"

Mia grasped his arm. "Do you think he'll answer our questions?"

"If not, we can always shoot him."

"Which will get us back to exactly where we are," she countered. "With more questions than answers. Naim could be our key to breaking into the Bata empire. There's only so much Simon Greif can find for us."

Something clicked in Omar's mind. "That's because they don't use electronic paperwork for everything."

Mia looked at Omar in the darkness. "What do you mean?"

"I just remembered . . . when I interfered with an illegal purchase a couple of years ago between Bata and one of his clients, I found a pager on the client."

Mia scoffed.

"Yeah, I thought it was archaic too, but then I realized it was brilliant." Omar handed the binoculars back to Mia. "I confiscated the pager, and found it didn't hold any data. All communication disappeared after it was read."

"We found the outside transfers Bata made to Baris, but how does Bata track his purchases and sales?" Mia asked. "Even a black market tycoon needs some sort of accounting."

Omar thought for a moment. It made sense that Mr. Bata would do anything to prevent a paper trail, but Mia was right. He was still running a business.

Mia was looking through the binoculars again and she tapped Omar's arm. "Look. Like father, like son?"

Omar peered toward the hotel room. He didn't need binoculars to see that Naim Bata was writing in a small notebook.

"Handwritten ledgers?" Omar wondered.

"That and a bank account in Switzerland." Mia lowered the binoculars. "It's archaic, but might explain some things."

Omar nodded. It made a sort of strange sense. "We need to separate Naim from the woman," he said. "Do you feel like dressing up?"

"Neither of them know me anyway," Mia said. "A scarf should do it." She rose to her feet, and Omar followed after her, grasping her hand before she could reenter their hotel room.

"Thank you," he said, pulling her close and kissing her forehead.

Her hand slid around his neck, and she pressed against him and gave him a real kiss. Omar wasn't about to protest.

"Too bad we aren't on vacation here," she murmured against his ear. "Crete is a pretty place."

He wanted to ask her what she thought about his proposal, if she'd changed her mind. But for now, he'd stay silent, grateful that she wasn't running from him anymore, that she was speaking to him, and that, as usual, she was helping him. He, too, wished they were on vacation and not tracking down criminals. "When we get Baris arrested, we'll come back. Relax on the beach."

Mia lowered her hands, trailing them along his chest. "We'll bring your parents too."

Something in Omar's heart hitched. Having Mia speak like that about his family gave him more hope than ever. He smiled down at her. "Anything to please you."

She laughed, then pulled away from him. "I have a scarf to tie and a woman to distract."

Omar didn't have to think twice about having Mia distract the guest in Naim's room. He trusted her with his life and with everything else.

Mia entered their hotel room, closed the drapes and dug out a blue paisley scarf from the recesses of her bag, then tied it about her head, covering her hair. Her final touch, a pair of blue-rimmed glasses. The scarf was a good look on her, framing her face and bringing more attention to her eyes.

"Where will you be?" Mia asked him, turning from the bathroom mirror to look at Omar.

"Naim's balcony."

She eyed him, scanning him from head to toe. "You've still got it, babe."

Omar laughed. "Only for you."

She smiled. A real smile that lit up her face, and Omar wished he could capture it on film and keep it forever. "I assume we won't be coming back to this room after."

He reached for her bag and his. "Not planning on it, even if things with Naim go 'well.' I'll drop these bags into the car before I meet with Naim. He'll figure out pretty quick how we spied on him."

"Be careful," Mia said, grasping his hand for a moment, then quickly releasing him. She walked to the door, adjusting her scarf, then she was gone.

Omar did a quick scan of the room. It was free of any evidence that he and Mia had been watching Naim's room for the past hour. He loaded his pistol, then secured it in the strap about his waist and pulled his shirt down over it. Finally, he grabbed the two bags and headed out of the room.

He avoided the elevator and took the stairs down to the main level. Then exiting out the back door so he wouldn't have to pass the check-in desk and the employee he'd had to argue with to get a specific room, he crossed the parking lot to his rented car. Dumping both bags in the trunk, he locked everything up, then turned in the direction of Naim's hotel. It was nearly midnight, but a few people were in the lobby.

Omar walked around the white building until he reached the beach-access gate. Soft music sailed across the sand from a nearby café, creating a calming atmosphere. Omar hoped things were going well with Mia's distraction as he strode toward the balcony where Naim's room was. Omar had three floors to scale. He supposed it could have been worse; it could have been four floors.

He paused below the balcony, reviewing his options. The thick plaster looked a bit ominous, but there was no help for that. At least the moon was plenty bright and bounced off the white building. His eyes tracked a possible route, and then without second-guessing himself, knowing that Mia was probably knocking on the door right at that moment, he started to climb. If he'd had gloves, it would definitely be less painful. As it was, the thick plaster on the outside had enough grooves that would make climbing the wall possible, but the skin on his palms chafed immediately as he gripped his first few handholds.

He swung up onto the second-floor balcony with only a few scrapes and likely bruises on his shins. The light was on inside the room, and Omar heard the sound of a TV. He took a couple of deep breaths, then climbed up on the rail and balanced there, looking for his next handhold.

The wind had picked up, cooling Omar, but he still had a way to go. The third-floor balcony was about two meters above him, off to the right, not in a direct line. Light filtered from the balcony above, and Omar wondered if Mia was there yet. Had she been able to lead the woman away?

Omar strategized the first set of hand and footholds, hoping that as he climbed, he'd be able to figure out a good path. He pulled himself up along the wall, fingers clenching at the rivulets in the stone, his feet finding purchase below. He reached again, and moved up another half meter. The wind tugged at his clothing unexpectedly, throwing off his concentration for a moment. When he regained his focus, he searched for his next hand hold. He found a decent indentation about a foot above him.

He reached for it and grasped the white stone. As he pulled his weight with him, his hand slipped, and the plaster scraped Omar's arm. His arm was bleeding, but there was nothing he could do about it.

Slowly, tightening his stomach muscles, he lifted his left foot and perched on an indentation that was only a couple of centimeters deep. He could only hope it would hold his weight. He moved quickly now, reaching for the lower part of the balcony. The stone beneath his left foot chipped, and Omar barely latched onto the balcony before his foot struck nothingness.

He gritted his teeth and used every bit of strength to pull himself up until he found purchase. Then he silently hauled himself over the rail. His breathing became rapid, but he kept absolutely still. Light spilled from the hotel room out onto the balcony, but he could see no one from this angle.

Was Naim still inside? Omar drew his pistol from the strap around his waist and waited for the pounding of his pulse to mellow. But by the time his breathing had calmed, his heart was still racing.

Then, the light inside the hotel room clicked off. Omar let his eyes adjust to the new darkness, not taking anything as a coincidence, he left his position at the rail and grasped the handle of the sliding glass door. One pull told him it was unlocked, and he slid it open and stepped inside, pistol ready.

"Hello, Omar," the voice came from his right, and Omar turned, clicking on the laser sight of the gun. The red dot easily found the head of Naim.

The man raised his hands. "You arrived much faster than I expected."

"Who is the woman?" Omar asked.

"No one you know," Naim said. "But she might quite possibly have saved your life."

This turn of conversation was not expected. "How so?" Omar took a step more fully into the room and faced Naim's dark form sitting in a chair by the bed.

"Leyla Kaplan is a graduate student of the Istanbul University," Naim said. "She was hand-selected by Baris Uzuner to work on tracking down and authenticating documents from the sixteenth-century Ottoman Empire."

"Baris?" Omar asked. He reached toward the wall and flipped on the light switch. Yellow flooded the room, and Omar got his first look at Naim. The man was much as he remembered him, although his dark hair was longer. "Tell me about your connection to Baris and why you called *my* father."

Naim nodded, eyeing the gun that was still pointed at him. From his vantage point, Omar couldn't see any weapon on Naim—interesting.

"Baris is a zealot, who also happens to be the director of the Turkish Royalists," Naim said, leaning slightly forward, his gaze staying on Omar. "On my phone there," he tilted his head toward the cell phone on the bed, "are pictures of the wall in Baris's apartment. Baris has created a massive genealogical chart of people descended from the Sultan Süleyman and his chief wife Roxelane. Baris has records, letters . . . that were mistakenly sent to him by my father . . . they are letters written between Roxelane and the sultan. Each letter reveals information about the sultan's oldest son Mustafa by his other wife. The son and heir who was executed and resulted in Roxelane's son becoming sultan."

"What does that have to do with me?"

"Through your mother's line, you're descended from Roxelane," Naim said. "Baris is systematically tracking down all descendants and killing them."

"Killing them? Why?"

Naim waited a few breaths, and in those moments, the larger picture began to merge in Omar's mind. He knew that the Turkish Royalists' biggest enticement to potential recruits was the promise of putting a royal descendant on the throne. As was common in the sixteenth century, numerous siblings and other relatives were frequently executed to make room for one of the heirs.

"Baris is descended from Mustafa," he surmised.

"Correct."

"And if the descendants of the other wives, more specifically Roxelane—who it appears plotted Mustafa's demise—were dead, the only claim to the throne of Turkey would be Mustafa's line."

"Yes," Naim said. He spread his hands. "Leyla took a picture of your name that was written on Baris's wall. Something about it caught her eye." He took a breath. "Your death date was already written in."

Omar let that information settle over him. "May I?" he asked, although he really didn't need permission to take the phone from the bed. He was the one with the gun.

"Of course," Naim said, being equally cordial.

With one hand, Omar powered on the phone, and clicked on the photo app. He scrolled through the most recent pictures then he backed up and counted the ones with recent death dates written next to them. *Six.* There had been six transfers of $20,000 each into Baris's bank account. Coincidence? Omar didn't think so. He wondered what Naim's reaction would be. Then Omar stopped on the final name with a death date listed. His own name. "Sunday. I'm to die on Sunday it seems."

"It's as good a day as any other, I suppose," Naim said.

"I always thought a Monday would be better. Then the funeral could be Friday before Sabbath begins and give everyone time to book their flights. They could be back to their normal lives by the following Monday."

"Perhaps we could get word to Baris about your preference."

Omar tossed the phone onto the bed. It was a bit disturbing to see his death date listed. "Why would you warn me? Wanting me to overlook one of your black market deals?"

"My job wouldn't be nearly as exciting if I didn't have you on my heels trying to ruin a good business transaction."

Omar waited.

Naim blew out a breath. "Although we've been on opposite sides of . . . business strategy . . . up until now, I could use your help. And it makes more sense if you're alive to help me. I want Baris. He's killed two of my father's couriers. He kidnapped Leyla. He's even gone to her hometown looking for her. He won't stay quiet and is pushing every door he can to get the rest of the sultan's records. And now I'm on his short list."

"Just have your father take him down," Omar suggested, watching for Naim's reaction, and wondering how much he really knew.

Naim shook his head. "It's not that simple. The entire organization needs to be stopped once and for all. My father doesn't have the manpower for it."

Omar scoffed. "And I do?"

It was Naim's turn to be silent, waiting.

The man must not suspect that his father was the one funding Baris's assassination spree. Either that, or Naim was aware but very good at playing the innocent. "How deep does this organization of the Turkish Royalists go?" Omar asked.

Naim eyed him. "Whose side was Turkey on in World War II?"

"They were neutral until the very end."

"And who did they help?" Naim pressed.

"They sided with the Allies against Germany and Japan," Omar said. "But that was only a few months before the war ended."

"Yes," Naim agreed. "But more specifically, President Ismet Inonu met privately with Winston Churchill during the war years, and only when Churchill deemed it to be to England's advantage for Turkey to finally take a stance, did Turkey join."

"Churchill must have offered a sweeter pie than the Axis." Omar thought of something else. "Do you think Churchill wanted Turkey to restore a monarchy?"

"I don't think Churchill did, but those connected with him were charmed by the life of a sultan and the many luxuries a monarch enjoys. Private English benefactors to the Turkish Royalists guarantee a piece of the life. Money, power, greed. It all combines into one fierce desire."

"A desire to support a monarchy and expect perks in return." Omar looked toward the door, wondering what was going on with Mia. "England has supporters, who else?"

"Your imagination is as good as mine," Naim said.

Omar considered this, but he couldn't make any valid conclusions until he dug deeper. Mia could help him with that.

"Tell me about Leyla. Why is she still with you?"

"To piss off my father?" Naim gave a dry laugh. "She knows more about the Ottoman dynasty than most tenured professors." He propped his elbows on his knees and clasped his hands together. "I have the letters—we took them back from Baris, and he's livid."

"Ah," Omar said. "His proof has been stolen. I'm sure that will affect his ability to get his funding." Omar waited to see if Naim would take the bait when funding was mentioned. But Naim just ignored it.

"You're right," Naim said, lifting a brow. "I hadn't thought of that."

Omar studied Naim, deciding that the man didn't know the full extent of his father's involvement. Right now, Naim was playing noble and trying to thwart Baris. At least that told Omar that Naim had a conscience, whereas his father did not. It was time to find out for sure. "This is beyond just Baris's personal vendetta now, as twisted as it is," Omar said. "If he's bragged to anyone about the letters and the proof they carry, he'll have to deliver on his word." Omar eyed Naim. "I don't know if you're aware of who's funding Baris, but once you find out, we'll see if we're going to join forces."

"What do you mean?" Naim asked. His eyes widened. "Do you know who's funding Baris's assassinations?"

Omar lifted his gun slightly, still holding it casually in his hand. Naim followed his movement, not missing a detail.

"We have bank statements that show six transfers of $20,000 apiece. Six men have been assassinated. The connection is too obvious, so it seems the investor is paying twenty thousand per hit."

"Really?" Naim blew out a breath. "How did you get bank statements from the investor?" Then his face paled. "Is this why you haven't shot me yet? You think I know who it is?"

"Do you?" Omar waited almost a full minute for Naim's answer. When it didn't come, Omar said, "Bata Enterprises has been making large transfers of money into Baris's business account for the past six months, each in the amount of twenty thousand. Is there any other explanation you can come up with?"

Naim's face drained of all color. Then he said in a strangled voice, "Prove it."

Omar shook his head slowly. "I'd be happy to, but I think you already know I'm right. Think about it. Baris is a descendent of Mustafa. I'm willing to bet that your father is a descendant as well."

Naim sucked in his breath, and for a moment, Omar wondered if he were holding it. Then Naim turned from Omar and sank onto the bed, burying his face in his hands, and taking several deep breaths. When he finally lifted his head, his eyes were red, his voice hoarse. "Damn my father."

❖ CHAPTER TWENTY-ONE ❖

KINGDOM OF POLAND

AD 1521

Aleksandra's breath stuck in her throat. Over the crest of the hill in front of the caravan, a group of wild-looking men with bare torsos and red-stained leather bands tied about their arms rode their horses straight toward the caravan. The Turks had plenty of armored soldiers, but they were also encumbered with supplies, women, and child slaves.

One of the harem women in a nearby litter screamed, and this seemed to release the fear that everyone else was holding back. Verda grabbed Aleksandra's arm, tightly. "Stay with me, whatever you do. Don't scream. Don't even speak." From beneath her tunic, she unstrapped a knife from her leg. "Take this and don't be afraid to use it."

Aleksandra stared at the knife. "They are my people."

"Not anymore," Verda hissed. "You're Turkish property now, and you will be seen as a traitor if you turn on the sultan."

Aleksandra's body started to tremble as she took the knife. The blade was of fine steel, the hilt jeweled. There was so much she could do with it. She could plunge it into Verda's throat, then escape the litter and run for the trees. She'd find a way back to her village. She could fight off the slave boy who was leading their camel. Her desperate adrenaline would overpower him. She could turn the knife on herself. End everything now.

She could . . . she could fight for the sultan. The man who'd abducted her, then put her in shackles and starved her, then because he was amused, had sent her to the harem where she'd be trained to serve him.

Hot tears burned in her eyes as the caravan slowed to a dead stop, and soldiers ran past the camels, strapping on armor, drawing out their swords, and readying themselves for battle. Women were crying, one was screaming, men were shouting, and the thundering of horses' hooves grew ever closer.

Someone tugged their camel to a sitting position. It was the slave boy. "Run!" he shouted, pointing toward the line of trees. "All women will hide in there!"

Aleksandra was never so grateful she understood Turkish in her life. She was off the litter before the camel was properly kneeling. Verda landed on the ground next to her, and the two women started to run, not needing to be told twice. They reached the line of trees, the other harem women following close behind, several of them in hysterics.

"You must be quiet!" Verda told the crying women. She grabbed one and slapped her. The woman stared at Verda, dazed, but her hysterics quieted.

Verda turned to Aleksandra. "Take us to a safe place in the trees. You are most familiar with this country and can protect us."

Aleksandra felt no such sentiments, but the first sounds of metal upon metal between opposing soldiers a hundred paces away convinced her that now wasn't the time to point out that she was not familiar with *this* terrain. Her home was far away.

"Come with me," she said, hurrying into the trees, heading straight up a hill. She only stopped when she came to an outcropping of rocks near the top of the incline. Here they could hide and watch at the same time. It wasn't nearly far enough to have a good start if the soldiers tried to catch them. But if they weren't seen, it might be good enough.

Crouched behind the rocks, Aleksandra kept her sight on the battle below. She'd seen men sparring plenty of times in her village and had been horrified when the Turks had invaded her village. Yet this battle wasn't fought in the darkness, but in the brightness of the afternoon. She estimated about three dozen Polish men fighting fifty-plus Turkish soldiers.

By just counting the numbers, she expected the Turks to overpower the Polish soldiers, but the natives were fighting with a fierceness that made Aleksandra both proud yet ill to her stomach. She couldn't turn away from the blood, and she couldn't block out the moans of pain as the men fought. Around her, the harem women were covering their ears, closing their eyes, giving off their own moans.

Only Verda had settled close to Aleksandra and was watching the battle below with open eyes.

"Why?" she whispered, mostly to herself. "Why must anyone fight? Does not the earth have room for all of us?" Frustration pulsed through Aleksandra. She'd seen brawls in her village over simple misunderstandings about a property line. It seemed no one could be satisfied with what he had, and only wanted more. And even in times of peace with other countries, there was strife within villages and governments.

"Countries will never stop fighting," Verda said. "Not until every civilization is destroyed. Power and greed are the greatest of the human failings."

Aleksandra gripped the rock in front of her, wishing she could somehow put a stop to the acts of death taking place below. "Can we not just want every human to live a peaceful life?"

Verda scoffed. "Human nature is too raw for that. Think of any time you've been filled with love toward someone, and then in a matter of moments, you are bothered or angry by something they did."

It was true. She'd imagined herself marrying three different men, then immediately found things to dislike about them. She thought of her mother and how she should feel only love for her, yet she despised many things about her. And she'd had no intention of sharing a home with her mother one more moment than she had to.

Aleksandra caught site of the sultan, who was engaged in a fierce sword fight with a Polish soldier. She straightened as she watched the deadly dance between the two men. "Why does the sultan not seek protection?" she asked Verda. "Surely his life is more valuable than every man below."

Verda was also focused on the fight. "He's a young sultan and has too much confidence."

They watched as the sultan defeated the Polish soldier, only to immediately begin fighting another man. "He is certainly skilled," Aleksandra said, although her stomach was turning over at the particular skills the sultan was demonstrating. It seemed that killing a man in battle was an art form, an art form that the sultan was well versed in.

"Look," Verda said, grasping Aleksandra's arm. She looked to where the woman pointed and saw four Polish soldiers running toward the line of trees below them. Had they seen the women escape?

Aleksandra watched as the men started up the hill. "Have they seen us or are they deserting?" she whispered.

"It doesn't matter. What do you think they'll do when they come across us?"

Even though they were her own countrymen, Aleksandra was dressed as a Turkish harem woman. She'd heard of the terrible things done to women by soldiers in war. No line was too thick to be crossed. "There will be no mercy," Aleksandra said.

Verda withdrew the dagger from her tunic, and Aleksandra did the same.

Some of the other women had seen the approaching soldiers and withdrew their own daggers. Hatice collapsed, silently crying, already giving up. Aleksandra wanted to shake some sense into her. One woman could ruin it all for them.

The men were growing closer, and Aleksandra knew it would be all over if they didn't do something drastic.

"We must make noise," she told Verda. "We'll scream for help, and the Turks will hear us."

But Verda shook her head. "Our soldiers will never get here in time. We must run."

"Where are we going to run?" Above them the rocky hill continued nowhere, below them men were slaughtering each other.

"You're right," Verda said. "We must fight. Some of us will survive."

Aleksandra wasn't so sure. Even though there were nearly a dozen women, and only four soldiers, no outcome would allow them to live. If they were to have a chance at all, it would be getting closer to the Turkish soldiers. But Aleksandra knew that survival still wasn't guaranteed with the Turkish men already in a battle for their lives. The women were on their own.

"Everyone have your dagger ready and be prepared to fight," Aleksandra said in a commanding tone. She ignored the woman who had collapsed. "We'll run back toward the caravan, but the soldiers will try to stop us. Some of us will make it through, some of us might have to sacrifice to free another woman."

The eyes that were upon her were wide with fear, but most of the women looked determined. Even if they did make it back to the caravan, death could very well await them there.

The moment the first soldier saw them, Aleksandra said, "Let's go," at the same time the soldier alerted his companions. Their drawn swords and fierce expressions sent Aleksandra's heart into a dangerous race.

These men might be her countrymen, but they'd only see the women as an extension of the Turkish army.

The women rose together and scrambled over the rocks. Aleksandra led them down the hill, veering away from the Polish soldiers. The men changed their direction and started running straight toward them.

"Go!" Aleksandra yelled at the women. "Don't slow down for anything." Her breathing already came in gasps, and as the men reached Hatice first, her curdling scream seemed to fill the entire valley.

Aleksandra urged Verda and the others forward. She couldn't leave Hatice behind. With her dagger gripped in her hand, she turned to see one of the soldiers dragging the woman by the hair as she sobbed. "Where's your sultan now?" the man shouted at her, although Hatice couldn't understand his words. He hit her hard, and she stopped screaming.

Anger boiled through Aleksandra, propelling her legs faster as she ran toward the Polish soldiers. Then she realized that Verda was beside her. "Take the women down the hill," Aleksandra gasped. "I'll be the distraction to slow them down. There's no reason for both of us to die."

The Polish soldiers had demonstrated to Aleksandra that men on both sides of the battle were ruthless killers. She might be able to save Hatice if she only sacrificed one person—herself.

But Verda accompanied her as she ran straight toward the Polish soldiers. Aleksandra started screaming at the men in their language, momentarily startling them. "Leave her alone!" she yelled at the man who was dragging Hatice.

He looked over his shoulder and released Hatice just as Aleksandra threw herself at him. The other three soldiers were there in a minute, pulling Aleksandra from the soldier she was trying to attack. Somewhere in the melee Verda was fighting as well.

With her surprise attack, Aleksandra had the advantage and plunged her dagger into the soldier's thigh. He screamed and fell to the ground just as Verda was pounced upon by three men. Aleksandra grabbed the yataghan from the Polish soldier's hand, knowing she'd have a better chance at defending herself with the larger knife than with a small dagger.

Aleksandra also knew Verda had little chance of survival, so there was nothing to lose. She turned on the three men, her yataghan ready. She lunged toward the one who was closest. He laughed at her as he caught her wrist before she could do him any harm. That only made her more furious. As the soldier twisted her arm painfully behind her, she kicked at him as hard as she could.

He jerked back, but to his credit, he didn't release his hold. Before she knew it, she'd been shoved to the ground and the soldier's heavier body was pinning her quite securely. He smelled worse than Aleksandra ever had. By the wildness she saw in his brown eyes, she knew he was beyond reason.

She wondered if this perspiring soldier would be the last thing she'd see before dying. She closed her eyes, trying to conjure up another, more pleasant image, but her thoughts were in chaos. She felt along the ground, hoping to reach the yataghan. Suddenly, the man collapsed on top of her, unmoving.

Aleksandra wriggled out from beneath him, using all of her strength to get herself free. A carved arrow protruded between his shoulder blades, and blood was spreading across his bare back.

Aleksandra picked up the yataghan on the ground and scrambled out of his reach in case he wasn't quite dead. On the other side of the fallen soldier, Hatice lay unmoving. Aleksandra didn't know if the woman were dead or just injured. She looked up just as another arrow sailed through the sky and sliced into the neck of one of the soldiers. He toppled to the ground. The third soldier started running, but didn't get very far before he was struck with an arrow. The fourth soldier grabbed desperately for Verda, wrenching her against him, using her as a shield against any flying arrows.

Verda screamed, and Aleksandra could think of nothing else except that Verda was being hurt by a soldier. She flew at the soldier, grabbing at his arm and trying to set Verda free. The soldier threw Verda to the ground like she was little more than a sack of grain, and then he turned on Aleksandra. She saw immediately that she'd underestimated his size. He towered over her, and the brute strength in one of his arms was greater than what she had in her entire body.

She took a step back, hoping to lead him from Verda's collapsed form. Even if these next breaths were her last, she'd die knowing that Verda still had a chance. Hatice hadn't moved at all, and Aleksandra had to assume she was dead. But Verda was still moving, still breathing. That was enough for Aleksandra.

"You deserve whatever the Turks do to you," Aleksandra spat out.

"And you're a traitor," the soldier said, advancing on Aleksandra, his sword held out in front of him.

"I was abducted, but now that I watched you and your men kill innocent women, I'm appalled." Her voice cracked. Hatice was dead. Verda nearly so. She gripped her yataghan with both hands.

"You think the Turks don't kill women?" he scoffed. "Have you lived in a hovel your whole life?"

How long could she distract him? Were there still archers watching this soldier?

"Come with me," he said, his voice softer now, but Aleksandra didn't miss the leer in his gaze. "I can protect you and get you back to your village."

His words alone might have convinced Aleksandra had she been desperate. But she wasn't desperate; she was angry. Verda lay a few paces away, and she couldn't leave the woman behind, even if Verda claimed there was no such thing as friendship in the harem. The woman had watched over her, scolded her, and protected her.

"I can't return to my past," Aleksandra said, knowing the words were true. The moment she was abducted, she'd begun to change from

Aleksandra to Roxelane. And now, she'd probably killed one of her own people, making her now more Turkish than Polish. Guilt should have burned through her, but instead, she knew she'd do whatever it took to lead this man away from Verda.

The soldier smiled, his eyes soaking in her every feature. "Tell me your name, and I'll tell you mine. We don't have to die today. We can escape into the hills, and I'll return you to your family. You must miss them."

She did miss them, but she didn't even know if they were alive.

Her gaze involuntarily went to Verda, and the soldier stopped, looking back. "Ah. You're trying to distract me. Clever minx."

Before she could respond, he'd charged her, faster than she thought possible. She screamed as she fell backward with a thud, then all the light darkened around her.

When the world lightened again, Aleksandra realized two things. Her skull felt as if it had been shattered. And the man speaking soothing words to her was the sultan.

"There you are," the sultan said, his honeyed words a cocoon.

"I'm Roxelane."

"Yes."

Then she remembered the fighting, the arrows, Verda's screaming. She tried to sit up but the pain in her head intensified.

"Don't move," the sultan said. "The healer will be here soon. He's attending to a few of the men first."

Aleksandra exhaled, wishing she could think more clearly. "Where's Verda? Is she alive?"

"Thanks to you, she's alive."

"Hatice?"

"She didn't make it."

Aleksandra felt the rest of her breath rush out. She'd known Hatice had to be dead, yet hearing it confirmed was something else altogether.

Tears burned in her eyes, and she couldn't stop them from sliding down her face. "I'm sorry. I tried to save her. I should have been faster."

The sultan shook his head. "You saved Verda, and you saved the rest of the women. You defeated four warriors, Roxelane."

She lifted her head, intent to argue with him, but the pain cut off her words. She had to lie back down, close her eyes, breathe in and out.

She thought of Hatice's life cut tragically short, and her heart broke all over again. She'd barely known the woman, but the life of one of the harem women had been lost today. "Did we win the battle?" She assumed so since she and the sultan were here.

He gave her a sad smile and a nod. "We did. The price was high. But I am grateful for what you did for the women. They are fortunate to have you."

Aleksandra wanted to protest, but all this conversation was making her very tired.

She just had to know one more thing. "Where is Verda?"

"She's resting in the litter," the sultan said. "In a few days, you and Verda will be completely healed."

◆ CHAPTER TWENTY-TWO ◆

CRETE

Leyla twisted away from the dark-haired woman who grasped her arm. The woman had come to the hotel room and said there was an urgent call for her at the front desk. Thinking it had to be her parents, she'd turned to Naim with a questioning look. He'd nodded for her to go and take the call.

But when the woman insisted on taking the stairs to the lobby, Leyla knew something was wrong. She'd stepped away to head back down the hallway, when the woman grabbed her. Leyla didn't think she could outrun the stranger, if the strength of her grip was any indication of the woman's speed.

Panic shot through Leyla and as the woman's scarf slipped from her hair, she suddenly had a thought. "Are you with Omar Zagouri?" Leyla asked, backing away, although the look in the woman's eyes told her she wouldn't get very far.

The woman's eyes flashed, in surprise or annoyance, Leyla wasn't sure.

"What do you know of Omar Zagouri?" the woman asked, stepping closer to Leyla, although she no longer gripped her arm.

"I know that Baris Uzuner is looking for him," Leyla said. "That's why I called Omar . . . to warn him."

"Warn him of what?" The woman's stance had changed. It was less aggressive now, and her gaze seemed to be genuinely curious.

"Naim needs to speak with Omar," Leyla said, narrowing her eyes. "Did you come with Omar? Is he in the room with Naim now?"

The woman tugged the scarf and pulled it completely from her hair. Short dark curls tumbled about her face. She took off her glasses too, then folded her arms across her chest, which didn't make Leyla feel any more relaxed, but at least she wasn't being pulled in a death grip into a stairwell.

"My connection to Omar Zagouri is none of your business." The woman tilted her head. "Why are you making phone calls for Naim Bata?"

Leyla exhaled and looked back in the direction they'd come. She couldn't see the door of the hotel room because they'd turned more than one corner. She turned back and faced the dark eyes of the strange woman. "We shared a few classes together at Istanbul University."

The woman blinked as if she were surprised. "Does this have anything to do with my question?"

Leyla tried again and told her about getting hired by Baris Uzuner and how he'd shot a man, then driven Leyla across the country. "Baris has an entire wall in his apartment of madman scribbles depicting a genealogy chart of people connected to the Sultan Süleyman. He put the death dates next to people he was either killing or having killed." Another breath. "Omar Zagouri's name was listed."

"So you think he's being targeted?" the woman asked.

"I know he is," Leyla said. "I researched the names of the other men and read their death notices."

The woman was silent for a moment, then held out her hand. "I'm Mia Golding."

"Leyla Kaplan," she said, shaking then releasing Mia's hand.

"Tell me what you know of Naim," Mia said, her steely gaze less friendly now.

"I . . . don't know much." Leyla knew she had to choose her words carefully. "From the few things Naim's told me about his father and their antiques business, I think I only know half of what he wants me to know anyway."

"The good half, I'm sure," Mia said. "He must trust you a lot."

Leyla's face warmed. "What do you mean?"

"He wouldn't have told you anything about his job if he didn't trust you." Mia leaned against the wall, finally looking like she was easing off.

"Omar already knows about Baris." Mia lowered her voice. "In fact, we're on our way to find him. We just had this small detour to make."

Leyla exhaled. "So he'll work with Naim?"

"*Work* with him?" Mia laughed. "You don't know much about Naim, do you? Or Omar? They'd never work together in a thousand years. They have nothing in common."

Leyla narrowed her eyes. "It sounds like they have plenty in common, except for disagreeing about which side of the antiques tax law they're on."

Another laugh shot out from Mia. "Tax laws? Is that how Naim explained it to you? No wonder you're sharing his hotel room."

"It's not like that," Leyla said, her face growing even hotter now. "*We're* not like that."

"Not yet," Mia said, patting her arm. She straightened from the wall. "Come on," she said. "If you're really an innocent in all this, then it's too late to shield you from the truth. I've got a few questions myself to ask Naim." She set off down the hall, back toward the hotel room, without even a backward glance at Leyla to see if she was coming.

The woman had wanted her out of the room so urgently that Leyla suspected Omar was in there with Naim now. She wouldn't be left in the empty hallway to wonder. She hurried after Mia, catching up to her just as Mia reached the room.

She opened the door with a hotel card that left Leyla wondering how she obtained it.

Leyla walked into the room, following Mia, to see the two men standing out on the balcony, the sliding glass door open. One of the lamps in the room was on, but the rest of the room was in shadow.

"Mia Golding," Naim said in a stiff voice, looking over at the women. "Thanks for bringing Leyla back. The scarf and the glasses worked well for you."

"Still a charmer, I see," Mia said in a flat voice, crossing the room to the balcony.

Naim folded his arms, and his jaw twitched. What had Omar said to him? The tension in the room was almost palpable.

Leyla shut the hotel door behind her and followed after Mia, curious to see how everyone would interact. It seemed that not only did Naim know Omar, but he knew Mia too. Leyla paused when she saw a pistol on the desk. It hadn't been there earlier, and she couldn't help but wonder if it was Naim's or Omar's. She dragged her gaze from the gun to the three people now on the balcony. For a moment, a wash of emotions filtered through her. What had she gotten herself involved in? If she left now, would they come after her? Tell her she knew too much? One part of her wanted to flee, but the other part, the part that she listened to, wanted to stay and help put Baris away.

Mia sidled up to Omar and slipped her hand in his.

Leyla shouldn't have been surprised. So Mia was partner to Omar in more ways than one. But the way that Naim's gaze had roamed over her also made Leyla think there had been something between Naim and Mia. Thankfully, Naim's gaze didn't linger, although he had definitely looked at her.

Now he was looking at Leyla. "Are you all right?" he asked.

She nodded, unsure of the quality of her voice at that moment. She wanted to ask him the same. His face seemed pale and his voice rough.

"Omar Zagouri," Omar said, stepping forward, extending the hand that wasn't holding Mia's.

Omar wasn't as tall as Naim, but Leyla was sure that his physical strength made up for his average height and wiry build. His dark curly hair was cropped short, and there was a hint of a mustache on his upper lip. His eyes were surprisingly a warm brown, and they seemed not to miss a thing about her.

She shook his hand, feeling strange that she was in the presence of a man who was a name on Baris's wall.

"I understand I owe you a thank you," he said. He glanced over at Naim, then added, "Thank you for finding my name on that wall and deciphering Baris's plans to target me and some of the others."

"I . . . I told Naim, and fortunately he knew how to get in touch with you," she said.

One side of his mouth lifted, and she didn't miss the amusement in his gaze. "That he did." Another glance at Naim, then Omar said in a sober tone, "Baris has already made moves toward tracking me. He sent a thug to question my mother. She's currently in bed, on oxygen and living on pain medication."

Shock ran through Leyla. "I'm sorry," she said. "Will she be all right?"

"She will eventually," Omar said. He glanced at Mia. "The thug's in prison, and he gave us Baris's name after a little coercion." His gaze went to Naim's, a hidden meaning in them that Leyla couldn't decipher. "Do you think it's smart to include Leyla in our plans? Now would be a good time to send her back home."

Leyla stiffened. If she returned home, she'd be even more unsettled about her safety. What would stop Baris from coming to her village again? And what would he do when he found her? What if he sent a thug after her like he had to Omar's mother? He didn't seem to be afraid of hurting a woman to get information.

"She knows too much," Naim said vehemently. "Baris knows we took the letters, and he's already looking for her. I need to be able to guarantee her safety."

Leyla was surprised at Naim's tone of voice.

Omar was quiet for a moment, and Leyla realized everyone was waiting for him to speak.

"I don't want this to be messy," he said finally, looking directly at Leyla. Did he think she would mess something up? Put them all in even more danger?

"Tell me how I can help," Leyla said. "I don't want to get in the way of finding Baris."

Omar's dark eyes stayed on her as he tilted his head. "What do you think about the letters? Is there enough evidence to prove that Mustafa was set up and wrongfully executed?"

Leyla inhaled sharply, her eyes flitting to Naim, then back to Omar. "Truthfully, there is evidence, though it feels thin to me. But I can see where Baris is clinging to it so that he can advance his cause." She let out her breath, very aware that three pairs of interested eyes were on her. "He wanted me to analyze the letters and help him track down the rest of them. Altogether the collection might be very damning."

"Which will give Baris all the more fuel," Omar concluded.

"Correct," Leyla said.

Mia stepped away from Omar, moving closer to Naim and pinning him with her gaze. "Naim," she said. "How hard will it be to get those records . . . before Baris finds a way?"

A small smile touched his face. "I already have a request in to my father. I expect to hear from him soon where I can pick them up. But of course, I can't guarantee anything fully."

Omar scoffed, and everyone turned to look at him.

"Is there a problem?" Naim prompted.

"You're running around with this woman, putting her in danger, and you've already broken your father's policy of not using noncontracted sources by involving me, and you think he'll just hand over the sultan's letters to *you*?"

Naim opened his mouth to answer, then shut it.

"Surely Naim's own father trusts him," Leyla couldn't help but say.

Omar just lifted a brow at her then looked back at Naim.

A moment of tense silence passed, and then Naim said, "We'll have to get them ourselves if he isn't willing. It's the only way to guarantee . . . to put a stop to the killings. Whoever possesses the letters has the power."

Nodding, Omar said, "That's what I thought. He knows who I am, and who Mia is." His gaze found Leyla's. "That leaves only one person who can infiltrate his defenses."

Again all eyes were on Leyla, and she felt a shiver trail her skin. "What would I have to do?" she asked.

Naim was watching her closely, as if he would jump in and interfere if he needed to, but for the moment, he was seeing how she'd handle this.

"I'm assuming you'd have to do it as a dealer, maybe a new contact from an established dealer. Has Naim's father heard your voice or seen your face?"

"No," Naim said, although he didn't sound entirely convinced. "At least I don't think Baris would have sent anything to my father, although I know Baris was planning on using her to help him retrieve the letters."

"So she'll still be doing the job she was hired for, just for someone else," Omar said. "For us."

Leyla's mind spun as she looked between the men and then over at Mia. They all seemed unaffected that she was about to go undercover. She wasn't even sure she knew what it would all mean. But what other options were there? Even if they stopped Baris, another man could take up the gauntlet. No one spoke as they waited for her response. "I'll do it."

"I need to speak with Leyla alone for a moment," Naim said.

Omar and Mia didn't seem bothered by the request, and they walked into the hotel room, sliding the glass door shut between them.

Naim turned from Leyla and rested his hands on the rail, looking over the dark ocean. She walked toward him and leaned against the rail too. "If you don't think your father will let you see the letters, then I'll go in as an antiques dealer and request a purchase. Just tell me how to do it."

Naim shook his head. "Omar's right. My father isn't going to turn those letters over to me, or to anyone. He's already trying to get back the letters we currently have. My father already knows a woman was involved in getting the records in the first place. He'd see right through us if you suddenly showed up."

"Does your father not trust you?"

He met her gaze then, and Leyla realized there was a lot he wasn't telling her, and probably would never tell her.

"I don't know," Naim finally said. "I really don't know."

Leyla's stomach twisted. She understood what he meant. Her own father had put a lot of trust *in* her, but she didn't think he completely trusted her.

"The problem is that I won't know unless I ask him, and if the answer is no, then he'll make it even more impossible to get them. I'll be stealing from my own father, and he won't take that lightly when he finds out." He turned to Leyla and slipped his hand in hers. "But I don't see any other option. My father would never agree to work with Omar. He'd rather see Omar die instead of teaming up with him for anything. It would compromise his security too much."

"So your father is going to see you as a traitor?"

"Yes," Naim's voice was a whisper.

"Maybe you should drop all of this, then," Leyla said. She moved closer to Naim. "Omar's been warned, you did at least that. I can find a place to stay low for the rest of the summer, and hopefully Baris will lose interest. We send the letters back to your father, and he will be responsible for them instead of you—"

"Leyla." Naim stopped her from speaking by placing a finger on her lips. A warm shiver traveled through her. "I'm not going to let you fend for yourself. And it feels . . . right . . . to work with Omar. I can't explain it now. There's a lot more involved than I realized at first. But if I remove myself from this, I lose the ability to protect you, and my father might be able to intimidate Baris, but he needs to be stopped. I'm leaving the letters we got from Baris with Mia. Both Baris . . . and my father need to be completely stopped. You saw all those names on the wall."

"Once your father knows about those names, he'll want Baris stopped as well, won't he?"

Naim looked away for a moment. More secrets. Then he leaned forward, his forehead touching hers. "Can I trust you, Leyla?" he whispered.

"Of course," she whispered back.

"Omar has done some investigating . . . my father might be an anonymous member of the Turkish Royalists. Omar thinks he's funding Baris."

Leyla's breath stilled. "So he and Baris are on the same team?"

"Not exactly," Naim said in a quiet voice. "At least not that Baris knows. They are direct competitors in a sense. But if Omar is right, my father is actually pulling the puppet strings—Baris just doesn't know it. Both men are descended from Mustafa through different brothers. I don't know if Baris knows my father by his real name."

She could only stare at him. "Was your father's name on Baris's wall?"

"Yes."

"And yours?"

He shook his head, and relief shot through Leyla, but she didn't understand how Naim's name wouldn't be listed below his father's.

"When my father changed his name to work in the black market, he also had his own death staged—for his birth name." Naim released a sigh and straightened. "Baris doesn't know that my father is a descendant, and he also doesn't know my true identity."

Leyla tried to wrap her mind around all that Naim had told her. If his father was funding Baris, even anonymously, it meant that his father was no better than Baris—no better than an assassin. She pulled out her phone and opened up the picture app. "Show me where your father is."

"Eren Murat," Naim said, pointing to one of the lower names that had both the birth and the death date written below.

"So you would be right under him," Leyla said, then scrolled horizontally.

"If Baris thinks my father's line is a dead end, then he won't be happy to discover otherwise," Naim said. "My father is descended from the oldest son of Mustafa, and Baris from the second son. So my father has a stronger claim to the throne than Baris."

"And this is why your father wanted the letters back from Baris?"

"Yes," Naim said. "I suspect so. He's using Baris to get rid of any other claimants to the throne. And once my father has all the letters in his possession, there's no telling what type of move he'll make next."

Leyla put her cell phone away and looked into the hotel room, where Omar and Mia were standing near the desk, talking. Leyla was grateful she'd had this chance to speak privately with Naim. It made her decision easier.

She rose up on her toes and pressed a kiss against his warm, scruffy cheek. "I'll help you get those other letters, Naim. I'm on your side."

Naim exhaled and his hands wrapped lightly around her waist. "Thank you," he whispered.

❖ CHAPTER TWENTY-THREE ❖

KINGDOM OF POLAND

AD 1521

From the moment Aleksandra had awakened to see the sultan leaning over her, concerned for her health and safety after the battle, her heart had started to shift. It was as if fighting alongside the harem women against the Polish soldiers had bonded her with them.

Verda had quite recovered from the attack, although she walked with a slight limp. And Aleksandra felt infinitely tied to the woman, though Verda continued to be her stern self. The sultan had come to check on both women's health more than once, each time endearing himself more firmly to Aleksandra. How was it that a man with so many demands on his time had a thought for her?

"He's coming," Verda said, lifting her brows just slightly as she sat across from Aleksandra under a group of trees where the caravan had stopped to prepare supper.

"Who?" Aleksandra said, although she very well knew. There was only one *he* that she and Verda ever talked about. Aleksandra ignored the skip in her heart as the sultan approached the group of women, who all fell quiet as he drew near.

"How is your leg?" he asked Verda, although his gaze shifted to Aleksandra. Sitting as she was, the sultan seemed even taller, and the glow from the setting sun burnished his dark hair to a bronze.

"Doing well, thank you," Verda said. "I'm able to walk a fair distance now."

The sultan gave her the proper condolences and encouragement, then he turned to Aleksandra, as she knew he would. It was probably not a good thing to expect his attention, but she did.

"Your services are needed, Roxelane," the sultan said.

She rose to her feet now, her legs trembling.

"You will travel with Hadim to the next village and translate for the admiral."

She was thoroughly intimidated, but she followed the sultan to where his commander and several soldiers stood, planning out their strategy.

"Roxelane is here to help you," the sultan announced.

Hadim turned to look at Aleksandra. His massive build seemed twice as large at such close proximity. Aleksandra fell back a step and thought she saw triumph in the admiral's gaze. Let him have the triumph. She wasn't sure if he still considered her a Polish slave, but she hoped he wouldn't turn on her once they were away from the sultan.

"Do you think she's up for the task?" Hadim looked at Aleksandra, but directed his question to the sultan. "Or will she turn on us and stir up a rebellion, resulting in more deaths of our small caravan?"

Aleksandra had heard the whisperings among the women of how Hadim hadn't liked the sultan's plan to travel back to Constantinople without the whole of his army. The added responsibility of protecting the sultan had increased the admiral's burden.

"She will not defect, if that is what you're asking," the sultan said.

Ibrahim stepped forward from the group of men. "I agree with the sultan," he said, folding his arms across his chest.

Aleksandra was grateful for this. Hadim looked from Ibrahim to the sultan, then finally to Aleksandra. "Very well. I have not seen so much trust put into a woman, especially a Polish—"

The sultan raised his hand, and Hadim pressed his lips together. The sultan addressed Aleksandra. "I trust that you will serve us well."

His brown-green eyes were more green this evening, and she couldn't have looked away if she'd tried.

"Let's ride before nightfall," Ibrahim said.

Aleksandra followed the men to their waiting horses, and she was thankful when Ibrahim helped her up onto his horse, then climbed up behind her. She'd ridden a few horses, but not very far, and not any such horse as the Turkish men rode.

She sat stiffly in the saddle as Ibrahim urged the horse forward. "Lean against me and relax into the movement," he said. "Or you will have a sore back and joints by trying to fight the motion."

Aleksandra let herself lean against Ibrahim, and his hand settled at her waist, holding her securely. She was grateful for his firm hold. She exhaled slowly and tried not to think of what her harem training might prepare her for. She knew she was naïve, yet not as naïve as some other village women might be. Her mother's occupation had made Aleksandra more aware than most of the relationship between men and women.

The night air quickly closed around them as they rode along the hillside. As they rode, Ibrahim explained that this village was a gateway city which the sultan had defeated earlier that year. He wanted to pass through peacefully even if it meant they paid their passage through. "Your task is to make sure they understand our intentions and that they are satisfied enough not to retaliate when we're taking our caravan along their roads. If we fail, another battle will ensue, and our alternative route will add days to our journey."

"How can I be persuasive?" she asked. "Perhaps Hadim is right—it's foolish to send a woman. What will the village leaders think?"

"They will understand us through you," Ibrahim said. "That's all you need to know."

As the cool wind pushed against her face, and her back was warmed by the man holding her, she marveled at all that had happened since her abduction. Her pulse picked up as she felt the weight of responsibility descend.

When the village came into view, a stab of nostalgia pierced Aleksandra at the sight of the quaint village and the occasional trail of smoke indicating a fire in the hearth of one of the homes.

She felt like she was looking in on a life that was far distant for her, another lifetime in the past, one that was getting harder to remember. But seeing the village now felt like a slew of memories was being slammed into her. She stiffened as they grew closer to the village and men started to assemble in the market square.

She remembered the chaos in her own village's market square when the Turks had arrived. Breathing slowly, she tried not to let the images overwhelm her. She had to let the past stay in the past.

At the front of their group, Hadim slid off his horse and held up his hand in the sign of peace. The village men didn't relax their stances or lower their weapons.

Hadim looked over at Aleksandra. "Tell them we are here in peace. Do not tell them we are with the sultan, just that we are Turkish dignitaries."

Ibrahim urged her to take a step forward and she made the same hand gesture that Hadim had made. She took a deep breath, then said in a loud, clear voice, "We mean you no harm. We are a caravan just traveling through."

The men looked surprised to hear her speak their native tongue.

"We are only a small group and ask that we be given safe passage," Aleksandra said, her courage gaining by the moment. "Do you have a tribute we need to pay for your goodwill?"

One of them men stepped forward, away from the villagers. He was older, his shoulders stooped, but he still had the strength to carry a sword. "It would not be goodwill if we required you to pay a tribute."

"What did he say?" Hadim asked Aleksandra. When she repeated the words, he said, "Ask him if he's the village chief."

She did, and the man took another step. "Our chief is not in our village, but I am acting as his spokesperson."

When Aleksandra relayed the message back to Hadim, he frowned, and it was plain he didn't believe the old man. "They might be giving us a false sense of security."

"Do we have any other choice?" Ibrahim cut in.

"Offer to pay them anyway—a gift for their generosity," Hadim said, turning his attention back to the villagers.

Aleksandra called out to the men again. "We would like to present you a gift for your generosity in allowing our caravan to pass by your village unencumbered."

Ibrahim handed her a wooden box with metal hinges. It was quite heavy, but Aleksandra carried it several steps before setting it down on the ground and lifting the lid. In the moonlight, and the torchlight beyond, gold and silver gleamed. Aleksandra estimated at least a dozen beautiful necklaces were nestled inside.

The older village man stepped forward and bent forward with hesitation to inspect the box. After a moment of looking at the necklaces, he gingerly picked one and held it up, inspecting it from all angles. His gaze met Aleksandra's, who hoped she was concealing the fact that her heart was racing.

"This is a generous gift," the old man said.

"The safety of the caravan is important to us," she said. "We are traveling with women. We are hoping that we can rely on your generosity."

The old man picked up the chest and walked back to the other village men. Beyond the initial group, other villagers had come out of their homes and were silently gathering in the market square.

Aleksandra ached to see the men, women, and children, huddled together in family groups. She did not want this to turn sour, for all of their sakes.

When the old man walked back toward the Turkish caravan, he said, "We are willing to let you pass through unharmed. We will be watching, though, and will not be bullied."

"Thank you," Aleksandra said. She passed the message to the other men. They in turn bowed toward the men of the village.

"Quickly," Ibrahim said, urging her onto his horse. "We must signal the caravan before the villagers change their mind."

They rode hard back to where the caravan waited on the other side of the hill. As soon as they neared, Ibrahim called out, "We've obtained permission. We must move quickly. Everyone keep your eyes forward, and your mouths shut."

Aleksandra was somewhat reluctant to join Verda in the litter, feeling much more vulnerable than she did in the strong arms of Ibrahim. But she knew that now wasn't the time to complain. As their camel lurched forward, Aleksandra told Verda all that had happened.

When she noticed a soldier was riding quite close to their camel, she turned to look at him, and wondered if he was trying to eavesdrop. The man had turned up the hood of his cloak so that his face was cast in darkness. But something about his bearing, and the way he commanded his horse, told Aleksandra that the soldier was the sultan, trying to conceal his identity.

When he saw her looking at him, he drew his horse even closer, and said in a near whisper, "Thank you for your help."

"I'll accept your gratitude when we get through the village without incident," she said. The front of the caravan was nearly to the place where Aleksandra had offered the valuables in exchange for safe passage.

The sultan came closer, and she could see his eyes gleaming from beneath the hood. "You've been loyal to us, Roxelane."

He said it softly, but there was a depth behind his words. For a moment, she didn't know how to reply. What if things did go wrong and the village men turned on them? The battle would be fierce, and anything could happen to her, or to the sultan.

"I hope it will be enough," she said. Verda reached across the litter and grasped Aleksandra's hand. She squeezed back.

"There is no reason for bloodshed tonight," the sultan said, seeing the gesture between the two women. "Allah willing, we will travel in peace." And then he pulled his horse away, and slowed his pace as the front of the caravan reached the market square.

Aleksandra hardly dared to watch, but she had to keep her eyes peering through her veil. The villagers had lined up along the market square, the men holding their swords and spears, and some of the women clutching daggers. They watched quietly, not speaking, equal to the Turkish who were not speaking at all.

Aleksandra's heart hammered in rhythm to the sound of horse hooves and camel strides along the rocky road. She almost dared not breathe. Her gaze kept flitting toward the sultan, and she had to force herself not to look at him. She didn't want the villagers to notice her angst. Did they realize who was really part of the caravan?

She saw the old village man who'd spoken to her and completed the negotiations. From her place high up in the litter, it was hard to read his expression in the torchlight. Was this man honest? Would he keep his word? Or were they about to be ambushed?

It seemed Verda hadn't been breathing either, for as they crossed over the last part of the market square, she let out a breath. *It's not over yet,* Aleksandra wanted to say, but she kept quiet, watching now as the last half of the caravan made its way through the gathered villagers.

As they left the village behind without incident, Aleksandra had never felt more relieved. She reveled in the small miracle, and when the sultan sought her out, riding alongside the litter, she smiled at him.

"Well done," he said.

"We were fortunate indeed," she replied, her voice breathless.

"Allah has watched over us," the sultan said.

He knew she was Christian, yet his voice was strong and sure, demonstrating his conviction in the God Allah.

The sultan's gaze moved to Verda for a moment, and then back to Aleksandra. "Your help will not be forgotten," he finally said, then he pulled his horse forward, leaving Aleksandra and Verda to stare after him.

Verda leaned toward Aleksandra and grasped her hand. "You have captured his interest like no other, Roxelane of Poland. When we arrive at his palace in Constantinople, you will need a bodyguard to protect you from all the jealous women." Her tone was light and amused, but something in Aleksandra's stomach twisted painfully. She'd finally found a man who saw her for who she was and praised her for it. But he could never belong to her.

◆ CHAPTER TWENTY-FOUR ◆

CRETE

When Leyla pressed against Naim and kissed his cheek, she tried not to inhale his freshly showered scent. She'd become increasingly aware of him with each passing hour. Not that she didn't acknowledge she'd had a bit of a crush on him at the university, but he'd always seemed unattainable. And now that she knew about Naim and his father, it was clear that her world and Naim's were too far apart.

When Naim had rescued her from Baris she couldn't have been more surprised. In fact, he continued to surprise her. The way he was so protective of her; the fierce determination to be different from his father even though he'd been reared by the man.

And the way he was starting to look at her. She could quite positively say he liked her too. And now they would be working together to retrieve the rest of the letters, to put a stop to Naim's father and Baris, and their greed.

Leyla moved away from Naim, her thoughts scattering, and opened the sliding glass door leading into the hotel room. Omar and Mia both turned to look at her, and Leyla imagined what they must think of her disheveled appearance. She knew she was on the thin side, and her thick dark hair tumbled wildly down her back since she didn't have anything to tie it back with

She glanced back at Naim, who was watching her with his dark eyes, and for a moment she wondered what might have happened if Omar and Mia hadn't been present. If she'd kissed Naim on the cheek, and they'd been alone.

But before she could speak to Omar and Mia, her attention was pulled toward the TV console in the room.

A news reporter was speaking in Greek, but the subtitles were in Turkish: "Muhammed Emir was found dead this afternoon. Apparently having jumped from the fourth-floor balcony of his apartment. The police have blocked off the street in downtown Istanbul . . ."

Omar, Mia, and Naim joined her, watching the report. Leyla listened in stunned silence. The name of Muhammed Emir had been on Baris's wall. She fumbled with her phone as Omar muted the sound of the TV. Within moments, Leyla had the name zoomed in on with her cell phone picture app. "Look," she said in a breathless voice. "It's Muhammed Emir, as written on Baris's genealogy chart."

Everyone went silent as they stared at the name.

"Naim," Omar said in the stillness. "We can't wait to train Leyla. We have to act now. Tonight."

Leyla looked to Naim, whose face had paled. He scrubbed his hands through his hair, avoiding her gaze.

"We need the rest of those letters," Omar said. "Before Baris gets to them."

"All right," Naim said, raising his gaze and looking at Omar, then at Leyla. His eyes seemed vulnerable, darker than usual. "Leyla, you're coming home with me to meet my father. I'm going to introduce you as my girlfriend."

It was strange hearing those words from a man and knowing he didn't mean them. She'd be *acting* as his girlfriend. But this was no game. She might be pretending, but Naim's father would be real.

"My father will be upset that I'm bringing home a woman, but at least he'll be polite to you," Naim continued. "It will give both of us a chance to explore the house. I can get into his office and look through his ledgers."

Omar and Mia exchanged a significant look, and Leyla wondered what it meant, and what she was truly getting herself into.

"I'll act obnoxiously in love with you," Naim continued, "and my father will be distracted by trying to convince me otherwise. You will be who you are, an inquisitive university student who marvels at all of his antique displays. The closer we stick to the truth, the better." Naim looked at Omar. "Unless you can think of a better plan?"

Omar folded his arms. "I actually like it."

"Me too," Mia said. "I think it could work. There's not much that can stir up a father more than bringing home a significant other."

Leyla met Naim's eyes across the semicircle of people. "All right," she said, trying to keep the nervousness out of her voice. "I'll be your fake girlfriend."

Omar let out a short laugh, breaking much of the tension between the four people. "I don't think you'll have to act too much."

"Omar," Mia said in a warning voice.

Leyla's face heated, and she knew Naim had noticed her blush. She hoped he wouldn't read anything into it.

"We appreciate your help," Omar told her. "You'll be the perfect distraction." His gaze shifted to Naim. "I'll arrange for a pickup of the letters as soon as you secure them."

"I'll have to get them off my father's island first," Naim said. "If he gets suspicious, that might be difficult, or even impossible. What happens if I don't get the letters?"

"Those are too many steps to happen, and I don't believe in perfect storms," Omar said. "We'll come to the island and pick them up."

Naim laughed and spread his hands. "That will completely defeat the purpose of warning you in the first place against Baris. Walk onto my father's island, and he'll kill you himself."

Omar merely shook his head. "Who said anything about walking?" He looked from Naim to Leyla. "Best of luck to both of you. Mia and I will track Baris and find out how far his reach extends."

"I'll keep you apprised," Naim said.

"No more phone calls to my father," Omar said, walking with Mia toward the door. He opened the door and turned back. "Text my number directly."

Naim nodded.

A final glance at Leyla, and then Omar and Mia stepped into the hallway and shut the door.

As soon as the door shut, Naim turned to Leyla. "I should explain some things to you first, so you'll understand what you are facing in my father. I'm not going to force you to come with me. You can back out any time."

Leyla was surprised at how nervous Naim's words made her, especially now that Omar and Mia were gone.

"I'm the only son of a man who's built up a major black market empire," Naim said, "and since I learned to talk, I've been trained in his footsteps."

He exhaled heavily. He was nervous too.

"My father always planned that I marry a daughter of one of his business associates," Naim continued. "There are a couple of women he's already mentioned to me. Of course it would be more of a business deal, mostly because being married to me would mean living a life under heavy security."

Leyla wasn't sure why he was telling her all of this, but she found it fascinating. "Your mother lived that way?"

Naim nodded. "She was happy for a time, when I was younger. But as I grew older and started my schooling, she became lonely. Even as a teenager I could see her struggle between her love for my father and her desire to live a normal life among other people. She often told me she wondered what it would be like to go to the park with a friend, or to have coffee at a café."

Leyla blinked back the sudden emotion that rose as she thought of Naim's mother living a lonely life.

"When my father finds out the truth about you," Naim said, his voice dropping to a whisper, "he'll know that I betrayed him. You'll have to hide, Leyla." His gaze bore into hers as he lifted a hand and brushed the side of her face with his fingers. "I don't know if I can ask you to do that."

"I want to help," Leyla said. "I want to stop Baris."

Naim held her gaze for a moment, then grasped her hand. Slowly he pulled her closer and then into his embrace. She wrapped her arms tightly about his waist and wished ,for a moment, that they wouldn't have to pretend when in Naim's father's presence.

"What do you want to do?" he whispered.

She exhaled. "When do we leave?"

"Now." Naim released her, and Leyla was reluctant to step out of his warm embrace. But she followed his lead and gathered what was left in the hotel room. Before they left the room, Naim made a phone call, notifying security on the island that he'd be arriving that night.

His eyes met Leyla's as he ended the call. "He'll be up and waiting by the time we fly in."

He crossed to Leyla. "Ready?"

She nodded. They walked together to the hotel lobby where they caught a taxi to the airport. "You'll have to bring bags, or my father will wonder why you have so little," Naim said as they settled into the back seat of a taxi. "Are you all right settling for what you can get at an airport shop?"

It made sense, it also made this all the more real. "I'll make it work," Leyla said, sounding more positive than she felt.

Once they reached the airport, Leyla bought a duffle bag and a few items of clothing. Thirty minutes later, she was climbing onto a chartered jet with Naim.

"Mr. Bata," the pilot greeted them as they stepped inside. He was a short, thin man, with a carefully trimmed mustache and dark eyes that looked like they didn't miss a detail. "Miss . . ."

"A friend of mine," Naim said in a brusque voice, surprising Leyla. Apparently he wasn't too friendly with this pilot.

They settled into their seats, and a stewardess dressed in a well-fitted navy pantsuit brought them drinks. She disappeared into a curtained-off section of the plane. Naim didn't give her much of a greeting either. Maybe it was his Bata persona that was coming out.

As the jet taxied down the runway, Leyla looked out the window into the black of night seeing the lights of the airport skim by. "I feel like I'm in a dream."

Naim's hand slipped over hers, both surprising Leyla and bringing her some comfort. They weren't in front of Naim's father yet, so he wasn't pretending right now. "The closer we stick to the truth, the easier it will be to fool my father," he said.

"So it's not like we are completely fooling him because we're being honest?"

"Right." Naim held her gaze. "We'll tell him about your degree, your internship with Baris, how I rescued you, but he'll not know we are after the rest of the records. I'll tell him the letters are in a secure place. I'm hoping our 'romance' will be enough of a distraction for him. He won't be happy that I'm bringing a woman he hasn't investigated to the island."

Leyla's face flushed, but she wasn't sure if it was because she was about to enter into the greatest deception of her life or if it was because

Naim was still casually holding her hand. "Tell me about your family," she said. "Your father will expect me to know more than I do."

She was right. "As you've probably guessed, I'm the only child much to my mother's dismay," Naim started in a quiet voice. "She had several miscarriages. It was tragic for her and difficult for me to be the one and only son. I guess that I felt the pressure growing up. There was never any question of me working for my father. I knew too much to do something else, and my father's empire is worth a lot of money. He didn't want to leave it all to someone not related to him."

"If you had a choice, would you work for your father?" Leyla asked, genuinely curious.

Naim was silent for a moment. "Even if my father were an honest business man, his dominating presence and tight control are difficult to live with. Besides, I've never been able to truly consider that choice. If I broke off from the business, I would be too much of a risk. I know too much. There's not a way out that would result in keeping my life."

Leyla lifted her brows. "Your father would have you killed?"

Naim looked away, but it was clear in the set of his jaw and the tightening of his grasp on her hand that the answer was yes.

Sinking back into her chair, Leyla said, "It must be hard to know who you truly are if you've lived your life in fear."

He flinched, but then in an equally quiet voice, said, "I know who I am."

She regretted saying what she had. The jet lifted from the runway, creating a vortex of motion in her stomach.

Naim closed his eyes, his hand still surrounding hers. "I don't know if there's a way out," he said after a moment. "Sometimes I think I can leave, and other times, I know that I'm entangled too deeply."

The plane leveled out, and Leyla's stomach relaxed. "If you take over for your father, can you make the business better?"

"You mean more legal?" Naim said with a short laugh. He released her hand and leaned forward, propping his elbows on his knees. "It's possible, I suppose. But my father would have to die, and I'd have to fire everyone."

The plane started to descend, and Leyla looked out the window. "We're here already?"

"My father's island is not too far from the mainland, but he keeps most of the lights off at night to keep it as private as possible." He reached across her and pointed out the window as the plane dipped. "That's the runway."

Leyla peered through the darkness. A line of lights was barely visible along the private runway. Not until they grew closer, could Leyla make out the roofs of a large compound.

The pressure inside the cabin shifted as the jet landed. Naim stood and waited as Leyla unbuckled and rose to her feet. He grabbed her bag with one hand, then took her hand in his. "Remember, we need to convince my father that we're in love," he said, leaning over and whispering so that the stewardess who was unlatching the jet door wouldn't overhear.

Leyla squeezed his hand and exhaled. She was ready. She had to be.

They walked past the stewardess and down the stairs that had been wheeled to the jet. Two men stood on the tarmac, waiting.

"Kerem is in the tan shirt," Naim said. "He's the runway controller. And the other man is my father. Mr. Adem Bata."

Leyla found herself staring. Naim's father stood with his arms folded over his powerful chest. In the light spilling out from the jet, she could see his father's white and black peppered hair was slicked back, and he wore a suit jacket.

The man's narrowed eyes told Leyla loud and clear that he wasn't happy with her unexpected arrival.

❖ CHAPTER TWENTY-FIVE ❖

CONSTANTINOPLE

AD 1521

"There," Verda said, sitting across from Aleksandra on the other side of the litter, as they neared Constantinople. "Those spires are of the sultan's mosque."

A shiver of anticipation traveled through Aleksandra at the first glimpses of the great city. She was far from her home now, and she doubted she'd ever see it again. And she'd reconciled herself to this fact. Whatever lay ahead would be her new life.

She glanced at Verda and noted the woman's high cheekbones and deep brown eyes. Her mouth had softened and there was something akin to contentment in her gaze. It was clear to Aleksandra that the woman had missed her home.

A soft rain had started to fall, but the camels in the caravan picked up their pace, as if they sensed the approach of their destination and were looking forward to rest and food.

Around them, the other women sitting in their litters started to point and exclaim. The soldiers on their horses both in front and behind the camel train were talking, laughing. It seemed that everyone had been infused with high spirits. Aleksandra could only imagine what might be going through the sultan's mind. He was approaching his home after months of absence and many battles fought and won.

In Constantinople, he was ruler and all powerful. On the road, he'd been at the mercy of a well-aimed arrow or sword-wielding enemy. Aleksandra was almost relieved for him. Although he hadn't spoken to her since he'd seen that she was cared for, she hadn't forgotten his tenderness and concern. Her head injury had healed thoroughly, and she hadn't had any head pain the past few days.

She had been impressed with the concern he had for all of the harem women, especially Verda, to whom he'd sent the healer to check on each day.

"Will there be a great celebration?" Aleksandra asked Verda.

"Oh yes," Verda said. "Constantinople will be proud to have its sultan back, but there will be sorrow also." She paused before saying, "While on his campaign, the sultan's young son, Şehzade Murad, died of small pox. Fortunately his heir, a healthy boy of seven, still lives."

The news shocked Aleksandra. She did not know that the sultan had a son, let alone more than one. Of course he did, she told herself. All those consorts, and two wives, children would certainly result.

"A terrible thing to lose a child," Aleksandra said, thinking more about the sultan's living heir. Surely the sultan was anxious to return home to his wives and heir.

Verda must have seen the surprise on Aleksandra's face, for Verda leaned forward and said in a conspiratorial tone, "This will, of course, mean that more women will vie to become one of the sultan's wives. He has two wives, but only one living heir. He might be grieving the death of his wife Gülfem's son, but some of the harem women will be rejoicing."

"Because these women think they can rise to the status of a wife?"

"It happened with Gülfem," Verda said with a knowing smile. "I can see this conversation interests you."

Aleksandra tried not to let her emotions show so plainly. She was starting to feel charmed by the sultan, and she was beginning to understand how women might compete for his favor. But she stopped asking questions as a massive palace came into view. She might have gasped out loud because Verda said, "That's home. The Topkapi Palace."

The camels and horses had picked up their pace, as the soldiers urged their mounts forward, but Aleksandra could only stare.

Verda continued to narrate as they neared the small peninsula that was dominated by the massive structure and its collection of buildings surrounding the palace. "To the south is the Sea of Marmara, and the Bosphorus Strait is on the northeast side. We call it the 'new palace' even though it was completed by the sultan Mehmet II some fifty years ago."

A tall gray stone tower dominated the palace, surrounded by elegant spires. A red flag edged in gold and sporting an embroidered Zulfiqar sword waved merrily above the ramparts, as if beckoning the new arrivals. The expansiveness of the palace was larger than Aleksandra's entire village.

"How many people live in the palace?" she asked Verda.

"Nearly one thousand, I should think," Verda said. "You have been fortunate to see so much of the sultan these past weeks. Once in the harem quarters, you may never see him again."

Aleksandra didn't know if she should gape at Verda or stare at the edifice rising above their winding caravan. "Does the sultan not visit the harem?" She thought of his visits to the harem tent where he'd conversed kindly with the women.

"No one gets past the black-skinned eunuchs. Not even the sultan. Some of the harem women haven't even seen the sultan up close."

It was hard to believe that plenty of harem women didn't interact with the sultan, but the massive edifice before her crowded out all other thoughts. "What does Topkapi mean?" she asked.

"The Gate of Cannons." Just as Verda spoke, the main entrance to the palace came into view. To the sides of the massive door was a set of cannons, guarding the doors. Aleksandra had to tilt her head back to take in the full view of the two towers as they passed through the main entrance.

Inside the courtyard, dozens of servants waited to take the horses and camels and unload the baggage.

A servant couched the camel that Aleksandra and Verda rode on, and the women climbed off the litter, stiff from the day's travel. Three dark-skinned men approached. After a quick greeting to Verda and a curious glance at Aleksandra, they were led away from the disassembling caravan. Aleksandra glanced back before entering a doorway to see if the sultan was anywhere in sight.

He must have been escorted away already, and Aleksandra felt a sense of deflation run through her. What if Verda was right, and she did not see him again? What would her life in the harem be like, surrounded by competing, jealous women?

The corridor they'd stepped into was magnificent. Aleksandra had never seen such high ceilings, beautiful stone arches, and polished marble floors. Aleksandra cringed to think that her dusty sandals were leaving marks.

But the dark-skinned men moved quickly, their white robes billowing behind them.

"Where are we going?" Aleksandra asked Verda in a soft voice.

"The eunuchs are leading us to the bath house, then we'll make our way to the harem court. There you will be introduced to the Kizlar Agha, Master of the Girls." Verda touched Aleksandra's arm. "When he learns of your language skills, he will be pleased. The harem court is much nicer to foreign women when they are intelligent." She lowered her voice. "And you are certainly beautiful enough to cause a stir of envy right from the beginning."

Aleksandra was both surprised and pleased at the compliments. She felt the change in the air before they reached the bath house. The three eunuchs motioned them through a curtained entrance of an elaborate building decorated with colored mosaic tiles.

Scented, moist air caressed Aleksandra's skin from the moment she stepped inside. A series of deep blue pools were arranged in a circle. There were no burning oil lamps or torches, but only natural daylight seeping in from the latticed window openings. Yet, there was complete privacy from any outside onlookers.

The other women from the caravan were already inside, wearing small white robes while they soaked in the water.

The eunuchs motioned for Aleksandra to undress, and her cheeks flamed at the thought. But then she looked over at Verda, who unabashedly changed out of her dusty tunic into the white robe. It was quick and no one paid her attention.

Aleksandra was not used to being waited upon, especially by men, even though they were eunuchs. Taking a deep breath, she moved quickly to shed her clothing, then accepted the white robe offered by one of the men. She pulled it gratefully around her, when one of the men pointed to her ankles and said, "You've been injured."

She looked down at her scarred ankles. It had been many days since the shackles had come off, yet the evidence still remained. The eunuch met her gaze, his thin brows drawn together.

"She was captured as a slave," Verda said in Aleksandra's defense. "Then she apparently impressed the sultan enough with her intelligence that he promoted her."

The eunuchs listened to Verda's explanation. Then all three of them grinned.

"What are you smiling about?" Aleksandra asked.

One of the men said, "There is more than intelligence to this woman."

The other men nodded, and Aleksandra's face flamed. They had all just seen her in an undressed state . . . and now this observation.

Verda smiled and said, "Come, the baths are waiting."

First they stepped into a pool of hot water.

"This pool will cleanse all the impurities from our journey." Verda handed Aleksandra a square of thick soap. "Rub it all over your body, then rinse, and we'll enter the next pool."

The hot water felt divine even though the room was warm and Aleksandra was far from cold. The hot water made her aching limbs feel rejuvenated. Once they'd washed, Aleksandra followed Verda into the second pool.

Two of the men approached them carrying vials of oil. Aleksandra leaned her head back as the eunuch massaged the oil into her hair. A deep floral scent mixed with a sharp spice surrounded her as the eunuch worked on her hair. Slowly her limbs started to relax, and she felt as if she could sleep for a very long time.

The bathing was all too short, and soon Aleksandra was dressing in a long silk robe the color of the morning sky. She glanced over at Verda who was dressed in a brilliant yellow, setting off her warm coloring and deep brown eyes.

One of the eunuchs turned his attention to watching the other women in their bathing. "Where is Hatice?" he asked, turning to Verda.

Verda let out a breath. "The caravan was attacked on the way, and there was a terrible battle."

Aleksandra was surprised to see the eunuch's eyes well with tears.

"She is gone," Verda finished in a quiet voice.

"She is buried in a foreign land," the eunuch stated in a flat voice.

Aleksandra moved to the man's side and placed a hand on his arm. He looked at her with surprise, but didn't flinch from her touch.

"The sultan had her buried next to a wild rose bush," she said. "The Kingdom of Poland has many beautiful hillsides, and Hatice was laid to rest in the most beautiful one of all."

He didn't speak for a moment but simply stared down at his twisting hands. It touched Aleksandra that this servant had cared so much for Hatice. "Thank you for telling me that," he said. Then he raised his gaze to meet Aleksandra's and extended his hand. She took it in hers and was surprised when he bent to kiss the back of her hand. "My name is Kaan. What is yours?"

She hesitated only for an instant. "Roxelane."

His lips twitched as if he knew that wasn't her real name. "Roxelane, tell me of your country."

She had not been asked this question by anyone, not the sultan, not Verda, not even Roma.

It was her turn to let out a breath. "I lived in a small village called Rohatyn. We raised crops and sheep. Most of the villagers lived a simple life, a peaceful life." She closed her eyes briefly, thinking of the night that everything changed. Her innocence about how her life was about to be turned upside down. And now here, in the opulent palace of the sultan of the Ottoman Empire, surrounded by servants and stone masterpieces.

"How did you learn our language?" Kaan asked.

"My father," Aleksandra said, her chest expanding with emotion—emotion she'd tried hard to keep suppressed.

"You will be a great asset to the harem's court." Kaan turned to the other eunuchs, who were busy folding white robes, but had heard every word Aleksandra had spoken.

"We will watch over Roxelane with care," he told the other two men.

They nodded, and she realized Kaan was a sort of leader among them.

Aleksandra caught Verda's pleased look. She cast her own look of gratitude Verda's way.

She couldn't know how fortunate she was until she entered the harem court and all eyes turned on her. At first, she was too overwhelmed by the grandeur of the main hall to pay attention to the whispers floating about.

A series of columns rising into gold-leaf arches divided the massive room into sections. From the floor to the ornate ceiling, Aleksandra felt she was looking into a painting. Windows set high on the walls let in the streaming sunshine, which lit the grand hall and reflected the gold thread in the tapestries and cushioned benches. In the center of the back half of the hall, a low fire burned, and several women stood around it, talking. Other women were grouped in clusters, some sipping tea, others lounging on cushions, a few carrying babies. Aleksandra wondered if these children were the sultan's as well. Daughters?

The eunuchs led her to a low table set with bowls of fruit, warm meat, and honey cakes topped with nuts. Aleksandra reached for one of the cakes first and heard a series of titters around her. She took a bite of the delicious food before turning. Verda had crossed to the other side of the room and was speaking to women Aleksandra didn't recognize.

Watching Aleksandra was a woman who looked like royalty herself. Her body was draped with silver-threaded, blue silk; and red jewels adorned her neck, earlobes, wrists, and ankles. Three women surrounded her, all of them well dressed, indicating that they were harem women as well.

Aleksandra stared back, curious, unwilling to be cowed during her first moments in the harem. Besides, Kaan and Verda had given her courage.

"We've heard about you already, Roxelane," the woman said in a slightly lazy tone.

Something told Aleksandra that this woman was anything but lazy. Her eyes missed nothing of Aleksandra's simple robe and appearance.

"It seems the sultan gave you a Turkish name," the woman continued. "Perhaps he couldn't stand to hear your foreign one."

"Your name burned his ears," one of the other woman said.

"My name *is* Roxelane," Aleksandra said. "I no longer remember any name before the one the sultan declared for me." Clearly, the fact that she was afforded so much attention by the sultan really bothered this woman. A quick glance of the other women revealed that most of them were paying close attention, and it wasn't kind curiosity. Verda had been right.

And then to Aleksandra's relief, Verda was walking toward them quickly, which only made her limp more pronounced.

"Gülfem," Verda purred, stopping in front of the woman and grasping her hand. "You've met the sultan's heroine, Roxelane. Isn't she lovely?"

Gülfem. She was the sultan's wife who'd lost a baby. It was hard to feel compassion for a woman with such a vicious tongue, yet Aleksandra did feel some pity.

"Sweet Verda," Gülfem said. "It's nice to see you survived your travels."

The endearment was far from endearing coming from Gülfem. Most of the women had gone back to conversing in their groups, but a general hush had settled over the hall.

Verda's smile widened. "Thank you for your concern. The harem women who were with me owe their life to Roxelane." Her words of praise caused Aleksandra's neck to heat. Verda was making too much of the battle. Many unfortunate things had happened, Hatice's death among the worst.

"Is that true, Roxelane?" Gülfem asked. She turned her wide, almond-shaped eyes upon Aleksandra, who could see why men would think her beautiful. Gülfem's cheeks were colored and her lips painted in a perfect arc. "Do you use your tongue, or have you suddenly become mute?" The women around Gülfem laughed.

Aleksandra waited for the laughter to stop before she turned to Kaan. "You said you'd show me my bedchamber?"

He suppressed a smile as he bowed before her. "This way."

Aleksandra felt, rather than heard, the shock from Gülfem at being ignored. It was Aleksandra's only defense at the moment. She didn't know what the consequences might be, but she also felt her emotions becoming raw. And she couldn't imagine anything worse than being reduced to tears in front of a powerful woman like Gülfem.

When Kaan set off toward one of the doors leading out of the hall, Gülfem said, "You're not to establish her down that corridor."

Kaan's step hesitated, then he turned and said, "Sultan's orders."

The woman's face went red and her lips parted. For a moment, it seemed she was about to say something, but couldn't find the words.

Kaan turned around and started walking again, passing beneath the arch of the door that Gülfem had questioned. Aleksandra wasted no time in following him into the cool corridor that branched from the main room.

The corridor was much quieter than the main hall, yet servants scurried along the passageway, most of them without so much as a glance in Aleksandra's direction. This she was grateful for, and she'd be even more grateful to be inside her own bedchamber.

"Here we are," Kaan said, opening a door painted green.

Aleksandra stepped inside. It was clear the room was occupied, although it was very orderly. Silk slippers lined one wall, and fine robes hung from metal hooks drilled into the stone wall. A green, blue, and red tapestry had been hung over the single bed that was shrouded with transparent gauze cloth.

"Someone is sleeping here already?" Aleksandra said, walking into the room. It was small, but beautiful. A window opened out into a courtyard. Peering through, she saw fountains, ponds, patches of gardens, and stone benches. It was like an indoor garden. Fascinating.

"The concubine who lived here has left recently," Kaan said.

Aleksandra turned to Kaan. "Left? Is she working someplace else in the palace then?"

He met her gaze, steady with his own. "She was banished from the palace. She was found breaking a rule and was dismissed immediately. I wouldn't be surprised if she is now begging in the streets. You will live here and are welcome to any of her things."

Aleksandra gave a small nod and bit her lip. "What are the rules?" she asked. While traveling with the caravan, she'd thought of what types of things she could do in order to get herself dismissed from the harem. But now, the thought of an actual dismissal only tied her heart into knots.

"That will be part of your training," Kaan said in a gentle voice. He must have noticed her anxiety and he was kind to address it.

"Is there anything I should know now . . . so that I don't meet any such fate as the woman in this room?"

Kaan crossed to the platform bed and straightened the already neat coverlet. "She was found in the bed of one of the sultan's guards." He shook his head. "Even a concubine can't be unfaithful to the sultan."

Aleksandra let the words settle. "Tell me about the hierarchy of the harem. Verda told me a little, but I'm not sure I understand."

"There are many layers, and things are always shifting as women go in and out of favor." He turned to face her. "The queen mother is second only to the sultan himself. She holds her own court and shares her ruling chambers with the sultan. Mahidevran Sultan is the chief wife, and her son, Şehzade Mustafa Muhlisi, is the crown prince."

"He's seven years old?"

"Yes, and he is already as ruthless as his mother."

This comment surprised Aleksandra—that Kaan would speak so freely to her.

"As much as some of the women despise Gülfem's cunning ways, most still prefer her to Mahidevran, who is colder than an eastern storm. But Gülfem's son died last year. She will be anxious to get herself with child again, and it must be a son to contend with the crown prince."

"There are only two wives then?" Aleksandra asked. "What of the concubines? Can they rise in status?"

"It is possible. The women of the harem enter as a servant, then they can be chosen by the Master of the Girls to be a concubine to the sultan," Kaan said. "That puts her into a circle of influence, but the sultan has only taken two wives, and he has not sought out any more. A concubine might have greater wealth, more servants, and her own set of chambers, but her children will have no inheritance."

Aleksandra could see the greater appeal of achieving legal status since children born to the wife would be an official part of the royal family.

"Thank you for your kindness," she told Kaan. After he left her alone in the room, she spent several moments looking outside to the beautiful courtyard. A short time ago, another woman had lived in this room. Aleksandra had never been more aware of how life could change in an instant.

❖ CHAPTER TWENTY-SIX ❖

ISTANBUL

The morning promised to be a hot one. Omar and Mia walked through the Istanbul Ataturk airport, which only added to Omar's frustration. Both he and Mia had been searched at customs, and even though they'd both produced their Israeli government IDs, the Turkish officials had confiscated their guns. Omar was just glad that they hadn't inspected the ancient letters Naim had passed to him. Omar had kept them in a regular manila folder, wedged between two newspapers.

While Omar worked on his cursing skills, Mia scrolled through her phone, searching for any information on the death of government official Muhammed Emir. "Do you think Baris is still in Turkey?" Mia asked him.

"I'm not sure what to think," Omar said. The fact that Emir was a government official made his death a higher profile compared to the other names on Baris's wall. Omar had had Naim forward him the pictures so that he and Mia could start looking into all of them.

Mia stopped ahead of him, her eyes riveted to her phone, watching a video news clip. Omar crossed to her and read the English subtitles detailing the report. Mia understood Turkish much better than him.

"New information is coming in that Muhammed Emir was possibly pushed from his balcony. A witness has reported seeing a man coming out of Emir's apartment minutes after Emir fell."

"Baris?" Mia whispered.

"If it was Baris, he's an idiot. He probably sent another thug to do the dirty work."

"Why do you think he's still in the city with all of this publicity?"

"We'll find out," Omar said, powering on his phone and pulling up the address that Naim had given him for Baris's antique shop. Mia looked at the screen with him. "What if he's there?"

"Then this will be over quickly."

"We can't just kill him you know," Mia said. "He's our link to the entire Turkish Royalist organization."

"I know," Omar said, although he didn't think he sounded convincing. It would be hard to play nice with a person who already had Omar's death date written on his wall.

They watched the rest of the news report on Mia's phone, not hearing anything significant that hadn't been said in the first thirty seconds. "Let's get out of here," Omar said.

It had been a couple of years since Omar had been in Turkey, and as they stepped outside, he remembered the chaos surrounding the airport. A tangle of taxis crowded the curb, and in the distance sat big tanks of gasoline and a small mosque. He knew that once they got into the city, mosques would dominate the landscape.

Omar grabbed one of the taxis waiting at the curb, and finding out the driver spoke a little English, Omar gave his directions. Mia clarified the directions in her broken Turkish. As the taxi driver nodded his understanding, Omar leaned back on the vinyl seat and looked over at Mia.

"Do you remember that first time you met Naim?" Mia asked in Hebrew so that the taxi driver couldn't listen in.

Omar nodded. About two years ago, he'd received word of a bronze statue of Mars that had been discovered missing from Zeugman Mosaic Museum. Omar had been assigned to track down the statue and when it led him to the Bata empire, he'd arranged to meet Mr. Bata at a hotel restaurant to speak about the "transaction" like gentlemen. Mr. Bata hadn't shown up, but Naim had. Omar told Mia this, then said, "It was plain that Naim was green; he was like a loose cannon. Given too much power too quickly."

"What happened?"

"I threatened, and he justified, then *he* threatened *me*."

Mia smiled. "That probably didn't go over too well."

"When I showed him the list of stolen antiques I had for his father, he backed down," Omar said.

"And I'm guessing you were armed and let him know it."

Omar laughed. "Yes, that too. But I think he was more impressed with my undercover work."

After what seemed an eternity, the taxi finally slowed, then stopped at the curb in front of a shop front with a wide glass window spelling out "Antiques & Gold Shoppe." "Looks like the place is closed," Omar mused. Then he paid the driver and climbed out with Mia.

They walked to the shop front, and Omar tried the knob of the shop's front door and found it locked.

"Let's go around back," Mia said. She walked to the corner of the building and turned down the narrow alley that ran alongside of it. Omar followed.

Omar stopped at the corner of the building. "Are you ready for this?" he asked, looking around the rear parking lot. The place was deserted.

"Yes," Mia said, crossing to the rear door. "Let's see what Baris's shop looks like." She twisted the knob. "Locked," Mia pronounced. She looked over at Omar. "How far do you want to take this?"

"All the way." He knelt by the door, pulled out the thin lock pick he kept in his cell phone case, and set to work on jimmying the lock. Within moments, the back door swung open.

Mia put her hand on his shoulder and squeezed. "Nice job." Then she stepped inside, turning on the flashlight of her cell phone.

Omar's first impression was that the place needed to be dusted. It looked like a high-end functioning shop, but the air tasted stale and abandoned. He switched on his own cell phone light and passed by the register, then a door that led to what was probably a storage room.

Mia lifted a heavy drape, and stepped into the main part of the shop first, and Omar hurried to catch up when he heard her gasp.

"What is it?" He stopped as he reached her, taking in the scene before him. But then the smell hit him full force. Something long dead and rotting. He covered his mouth with his hand, fully expecting to see a corpse lying on one of the rugs. Instead, he saw a form much too small to be human.

"It's a slaughtered pig," Mia said, her voice thick with repulsion.

❖ CHAPTER TWENTY-SEVEN ❖

CONSTANTINOPLE

AD 1521

Aleksandra woke in absolute darkness. Unusual, because due to her window's location, the moonlight shone in most of the night. Something was different now. It was too quiet. The harem court had a curfew, but it seemed a servant was always being called to one chamber or another, or Aleksandra could hear the distant cry of a child in one of the family sections.

Awake when it seemed everyone else was asleep or silent, Aleksandra went over the day's events. Looks from the harem women that felt as sharp as daggers, and words that might as well have been soaked in poison had all been aimed at Aleksandra. The women who hadn't been in the caravan blamed Aleksandra for Hatice's death. And some who were in the caravan, and witnessed the battle firsthand, blamed her as well for not being able to hold off her Polish countrymen.

Hatice had achieved sainthood status—or would have if the harem women were Christian. Gülfem had been the most vocal, of course.

She'd been whispering to other women in corners, creating a division among the women: those who welcomed Aleksandra and those who didn't.

Verda had been quiet for the most part. Aleksandra didn't blame the woman. It seemed that Gülfem had a lot of influence, and no one wanted to speak too boldly against her.

Some of the women who would speak to Aleksandra told her to keep clear of Gülfem. They told her stories of other women who had crossed Gülfem and then had been found guilty of breaking a rule. Soon after they were sent away. Aleksandra had no doubt Gülfem had orchestrated the women's dismissals.

That was why now, in the silent dark, Aleksandra felt the first traces of dread brush her skin. Something wasn't right. It was too dark and too silent.

Slowly, Aleksandra sat up on her bed, grasping the coverlet close to her chest. She blinked a few times, but couldn't make out any forms, not even the shape of the door across the room. That meant there was no light in the corridor either. What had happened to the torches that were kept burning throughout the night?

A shiver went through her. She hadn't been cold one night since her arrival. It seemed even the temperature had turned. Was the sky cloudy? Was that why no moonlight came from the window? She turned her head to look at the window, but saw only darkness. She blew out an unsteady breath. Perhaps she was dreaming. Perhaps this wasn't happening at all.

"Kaan?" she said into the darkness, although she knew the eunuch was not standing guard outside her chamber. There were guards about the harem court, but not stationed outside each woman's chamber.

"Verda?" she called out in a soft voice. She wanted to be heard, but then again, she didn't want to alert anyone needlessly. She had to reach the window, or the door, to see what happened to the light, to see what was real.

The window was closer, so she drew off her coverlet and moved her legs over the side of the platform bed. She didn't know why she was hesitating, but she held her breath as she let her feet slide to the floor. The familiar coolness of the wood floor should have brought her comfort, but it only made the room seem more empty.

She ran her fingers along the wall until she reached the window. A thick drape covered the window. Her hand stilled. She'd never had a drape on the window, which meant that someone had put it up while she was asleep. Someone had been in her bedchamber. She took a breath, trying to collect her thoughts, and then she tugged down the drape.

Immediately the chamber flooded with blessed moonlight. Aleksandra would have been relieved if she hadn't suspected that whoever came in had done so for a reason other than blocking out the moonlight. She didn't believe that Kaan or one of the other eunuchs would have done that without her permission or knowledge.

Her breath was stuttered when it came out next. And then she heard it. A whisper that wasn't human, and then a shifting, a light scraping.

Every hair on her body stood on end, and she slowly turned, keeping her back to the window. The snake moved near the door, as if it had been set just inside, and then the door pulled quickly shut before the snake could escape into the corridor. Aleksandra had the odd thought of wondering if the snake was as upset as she was.

She couldn't move, didn't dare move, as she watched the slithering creature slowly explore its surroundings. Aleksandra was not familiar with snakes in Constantinople, but she could have bet her life on the fact that this snake was poisonous, if not lethal.

Whoever had slipped it inside after casting the chamber into absolute blackness knew exactly what type of snake it was. There would be no other reason to exert so much effort in placing a harmless snake in her chamber.

Why, she might ask herself, but she already knew the answer. She was a threat to the other women in the harem. Even if she was only one woman, there were only so many women who could rise in status. Verda had warned her to keep to herself, and she had. Verda had told her that foreigners were often despised by the Turkish-born women.

But this was a deliberate act to either scare her or get rid of her. Did the person who had placed the snake think that Aleksandra would leave the harem at the first sign of a reptile in her room in the middle of the night?

Slowly, Aleksandra moved to her bed and reached beneath her head cushion where she kept the yataghan she'd taken from the Polish soldier. It had served her well during the battle, and it would serve her well now. Gone was the sentiment of turning the knife on herself and leaving this existence and all the challenges behind. Aleksandra was ready to fight.

She would not scream or call out for someone to rescue her. She would not panic and run from the snake, which would probably result in the creature attacking her anyhow and sinking its venomous fangs into her flesh. No, she would use her wits.

Aleksandra picked up the small cushion from the bed and clutched it with her left hand. It would act as a shield if things went wrong. In her right hand, she held the yataghan. Lifting her arm slowly, so as not to startle the snake with sound or movement, she brought her hand back, over her shoulder, keeping her eyes on the movements of the slithering snake.

Its black scales caught the moonlight as it coiled around the wood chair. She thought of Sabu and how he'd challenged her to a knife-throwing competition. She hadn't practiced then, yet had thrown straight and true. But that target hadn't been moving. She figured she had one chance now. One opportunity.

She let her heart rate settle, and then she aimed, and threw the knife straight at the head of the snake. She almost closed her eyes as she released the knife, but she knew she'd have to get out of the way if she missed.

In one motion, she leapt onto her bed, even before the knife hit its target.

She watched as the snake jerked, then slithered beneath the chair, its head pierced straight through with the knife. Twisting, the snake turned over once, then again. Aleksandra wasn't breathing, merely floating as if suspended above the ground. She'd struck the snake, but it was still moving, still living.

She waited a moment, and finally the snake went still.

Aleksandra continued to sit on her bed, huddled against the wall, arms wrapped around her trembling legs. It wasn't so much having thrown a knife at the snake that disturbed her, but the fact that someone had deliberately made her room dark and placed the snake there.

She stayed in her huddled position until the moon faded and the sun crested the horizon, chasing the cool shadows from her chamber. Still, she kept her eyes trained on the lifeless creature.

It wasn't until the first bells sounded for the morning meal that she rose from her bed, washed in the basin of tepid water, replaited her hair, and changed into the most elaborate tunic left by the banished concubine.

She crouched over the snake and pulled the yataghan from its head, then she speared the central part of its body and lifted the snake from the floor. The brown and gold scales shimmered with eerie beauty, and even in death the snake exuded peril.

Aleksandra opened the door and stepped out into the corridor. A servant girl was scurrying by, but stopped when she saw what Aleksandra was carrying on the tip of her dagger. The servant let out a gasp, but Aleksandra kept walking, ignoring her and any others who stopped and stared, or hurried to get out of her way.

Aleksandra entered the harem court, amid the smells of the morning meal set out on the tables. As usual, Gülfem sat at the head of the table, surrounded by her greatest female supporters. She appeared to be telling an entertaining story by the rapt attention of those around her.

One of the harem women shrieked as she noticed Aleksandra striding toward the table. A few of the women rose from their cushions and moved out of her path as she took her usual seat, at the farthest end of the table from Gülfem. Even in the sitting positions, Aleksandra had been assigned the least desirable, where most of the best food was gone by the time the platters reached her end of the table.

Midway up the table sat Verda. She watched Aleksandra, her eyes widened, her mouth opened in surprise.

Aleksandra said nothing. She simply sat on her cushion and stuck the snake into the center of the table from where she sat. The dagger pierced the wooden table, the hilt sticking up out of the snake's lifeless body.

Silence fell over the women as they stared at the snake in disbelief. Aleksandra didn't look at anyone; she simply filled her plate with pieces of fruit and round sweet cakes. Finding the jug of wine empty at her end of the table, she motioned for one of the eunuchs to bring a fresh jug.

It was Kaan who stepped forward. He brought the jug forward and poured the drink for her. Aleksandra took a long swallow, then started to eat. One by one, the women left the table, leaving the food on their plates untouched. Gülfem and her group were among the last to leave, but Aleksandra still didn't raise her head to acknowledge her as was the custom when the second wife left the room.

Aleksandra didn't know if she was hungrier than usual, but the food tasted delicious. Perhaps the little sleep she'd had somehow made her ravenous. From the corner of her eye, she saw Verda carefully wipe her mouth with a cloth, then rise to her feet. Verda walked around the table and stopped near Aleksandra. Placing her hand on her shoulder, she made an obvious display of comfort and support for Aleksandra in front of the entire harem court.

"I will order a latch secured to your bedchamber door so that you might lock it against intruders," Verda said.

Only at this moment, did Aleksandra raise her head and acknowledge Verda. "Thank you. Can you also arrange a meeting with the Master of the Girls? It's time we met."

Verda brought her hands together and gave a small bow. This was another signal to the harem women that Verda was acknowledging Aleksandra as a woman rising in rank. Verda was now taking orders from the foreign woman.

Finished eating, Aleksandra decided she'd better rest before such an important meeting. She set down her utensils, took a final swallow of wine, and rose to her feet. She brushed her hands over her intricately embroidered tunic. She was pleased to see Gülfem in a secluded corner of the room, keeping absolutely silent, watching Aleksandra. Let the woman witness Aleksandra's changing.

She pulled her knife out of the snake, then turned from the table, leaving the snake in its limp position on the table, and strode from the harem court. She had much to prepare before her introduction to the Master of the Girls.

❖ CHAPTER TWENTY-EIGHT ❖

ISTANBUL

The dead pig in the middle of the antiques shop didn't bother Omar, but the stink was unbearable, and the symbol of a dead pig in a Muslim shop was disturbing enough to make his stomach churn even more. Was it left there by Baris on purpose as a deterrent and a bad omen if someone tried to break into his shop? Or had someone else left the carcass as a warning to Baris? Great effort had obviously been made just to bring a pig into the country.

Omar had worked in putrid conditions before, but this smell was intolerable. He snatched a tapestry hanging from one of the walls, and told Mia, "Hold the back door open. I'll take it to the Dumpster."

Holding his breath, Omar used the tapestry to pick up the carcass and carry it outside. Mia followed, and he tossed in the pig along with the tapestry into the open Dumpster. Then made their way back to the shop.

"Do you think he's coming back?" Mia asked Omar as they entered the shop. The smell was still there, but fainter now, and knowing the carcass had been disposed of, Omar could automatically breathe easier.

"He left a lot of stuff here to never be coming back." Omar turned his cell phone light toward the interior of the store. "I'll start at the front, if you want to start here."

Mia tilted her head toward a door near the back register. "Storage room?"

"Sounds good." Omar walked around a grouping of bronzed chairs. He didn't take the time to stop and examine the chairs to determine their era. He was looking for things less tangible, like a hidden compartment behind a picture on the wall, or a rug that covered a small storage space. Places where Baris might hide purchase records or information about those he was working with or against.

Mia opened the storage room door and shined her light inside.

"See anything?" Omar asked as he removed a painting from the wall and felt along the plaster for any sudden hollowness.

"A table and few vases," Mia said. "The room is surprisingly empty."

Omar moved on to the next painting, not bothering to replace the first one. Covering his tracks would take too much time, and he didn't exactly want to keep his intrusion a secret.

As Mia came out of the storage room, Omar shined his light across the rest of the shop. It was artfully arranged, and he decided it was a good show place. Which probably meant that this was the part of the store Baris intended for customers to see.

"Check the register," Omar said.

She moved to the curtained off area and drew the curtain back all the way. Omar joined her, looking in the cupboards below the register counter. Then he lifted up the small rug. One of the floorboards was discolored—a paler color as if the wood were newer. "Shine your light down here," he said.

Mia crouched next to Omar, holding her light steady as he ran his fingers along the edges of the plank. Finally, he caught hold of the edge and was able to pry it up. Beneath was a pistol, and underneath that, a ledger. Omar lifted out the ledger after pocketing the gun. Before opening it, he said, "With all of our technology today, it seems that good old pen and paper trumps all."

Turning the ledger toward Mia's light, Omar opened the cover. A series of numbers was written neatly in the left column running down the page. In the right column were numbers that looked more like prices. Omar flipped the page to find two more columns of numbers, then he turned the page again.

"Are these SKUs?" he asked, trying to determine how hard it would be to match each inventory number SKU with its item. Were they legitimate purchases?

Mia moved closer, examining the columns of numbers. "I don't think they're SKUs," she said. "Or each number sequence would be the same length."

"So what do you think?"

"A code, maybe," Mia said. She tapped her finger on one of the number sequences. "See how some of them are grouped together, so that Baris could match the letters with numbers. We just have to figure out his code."

"How many languages does he speak?" Omar asked.

"Turkish and Arabic. Probably some English." Mia met his gaze over the cell phone light. "What are you thinking?"

Omar traced a finger along the same number sequence that Mia had pointed out. "If this one is a Turkish *A*, then this word would be . . ." He shook his head. "That doesn't make sense."

Mia nodded. "You're right. What about Arabic?"

"The numbers are English though." Omar ran through the English alphabet, matching the letters to the numbers on the ledger. "It seems to work. Ottoman gold urn, Abdullah . . . 1526. The last four numbers are supposed to be numbers—the death date of Abdullah? Whoever that is."

"The sultan's wife Roxelane had a child named Abdullah."

Omar stared at the codes on the ledger. "So Baris has the death urn of Abdullah. Or at least it passed through his hands."

Mia stood up and moved her light around the register counter. "We have this ledger, now what?"

Omar balanced his light and flipped pages. "We start doing Internet searches for these items and we track where they are now. One of these customers might lead us to Baris." He stopped and deciphered another number sequence. "Sultan Süleyman coronation robe, 1520."

She touched Omar's shoulder, and he looked up. "Do you think Baris would ever sell those in his shop to a customer off the street?"

"No," Omar conceded. "Especially if he's as fanatic as he's shown himself to be."

"That's what I'm thinking," she said. "If he was sensible, he'd sell it to a museum, or if he was feeling generous—"

"He'd gift it to a member of the Turkish Royalists," he cut in. "A bribe?"

"Maybe. Or maybe a security measure," Mia said. "The man he gives the coronation robe to will now have a priceless artifact in his possession. I'm sure it will bring him great pride and a deeper connection to the cause of the Royalists, but it will also put him in danger. My guess is that Baris might try to promise him protection, although the recipient is still caught up in a web of the black market, so he'll never really be protected."

Omar nodded. "Do you want to keep looking?"

"The storage room looks like it was recently cleaned out. I don't think Baris is storing anything he values from the Ottoman Empire here. At least not any longer."

Replacing the floorboard, but keeping the ledger, Omar said, "Let's get out of here then. A shower and a hotel bed are calling my name."

As they neared the back door, Mia said, "That wish might have to be delayed." She lifted her hand from the door as they heard the sound of a vehicle in the back alley.

Omar grabbed Mia's hand. "Come on," he said. There wasn't time to make it to the front of the shop if whoever had just arrived came inside. "We'll put that storage room to use."

They hurried through the darkness, and Omar pulled open the storage room door. Small dark rooms weren't his favorite places to exist, but he didn't see a better option right now. Mia went in first, and Omar stood by the door, his hand on the knob, keeping it turned so that it didn't latch.

The back door crashed open, and the first thing that went through Omar's mind was that whoever had entered the shop wasn't Baris. The man would have at least used a key.

Although Omar couldn't see Mia, he sensed that she was close to him. He grasped her arm, pulling her next to him so that he could whisper. "When I open this door, get out. I'll meet you on the other side of the street."

"Omar—"

"Just do it," he said, pressing the ledger in her hands. "If I'm not out in five minutes, then get out of the neighborhood, and I'll find you later."

She pulled back from him, and Omar knew she was about to protest again. He leaned down, and found her mouth with his, silencing her with a kiss. She clung to him for a second, then released him.

He gripped the door handle, tensing as he heard something crash to the floor. And then footsteps sounded right outside the storage room door. As the knob started to turn, Omar's pulse skyrocketed. He withdrew the gun from his pocket with his right hand, then with his left shoulder he shoved the door open, slamming it into whoever was on the other side.

A voice cried out in pained surprise.

"Go!" Omar barked at Mia. She slipped past him and ran for the back door.

Omar stepped around the door and trained the gun on the intruder. The man on the ground wasn't moving, but Omar kept his stance, waiting, and making sure Mia had a good head start.

When the man opened his eyes with a moan, Omar said, "I have a gun pointed at your head. It's in your best interest to stay on the ground and answer my questions."

The man didn't say anything for a moment, and when Omar shined his cell light into the man's face, he raised a hand to cover his eyes.

"Why did you break into this shop?" Omar asked.

The man lowered his hand, squinting against the light Omar held. "Don't shoot me. I am innocent."

Omar scoffed. "You just broke down the door of this shop. How is that innocent?"

"I was hired to mess up the place, that's all. I swear on my own life."

Omar crouched, keeping the gun in the man's line of vision. "Who hired you?"

"I don't know his name—"

"Don't lie to me," Omar said, cocking the pistol.

The man's Adam's apple bobbed. "It was the boss—he wanted the place to look like it was robbed."

"Baris Uzuner?" Omar asked.

"Yes," the man's voice was faint.

Omar straightened again. "Tell me what he said to you, exactly."

"He . . . he said that some of his goods were stolen, but the insurance would only cover the items if there was proof of a break-in." The man took a shaky breath.

Omar was surprised that Baris wouldn't hire someone more professional. His jaw tightened at the thought of the thug who'd harmed his mother. "How do you stay in contact with him?"

"Cell phone," the words were almost a whisper.

"Is he in Istanbul?" Omar asked.

The man hesitated. "I think so, but I'm not sure."

"Are you a member of the Turkish Royalists?"

"The . . . no," the man said, confusion lacing his voice. "Is that a club?"

"Something like that." Omar stepped back. "Stand up and put your cell phone on the counter."

The man scrambled to his feet, then reached into his pocket. He pulled out a cell phone and set it on the counter.

"And your keys," Omar said.

He released a sigh, then set his keys on the counter as well. "Baris is going to fire me."

"He should have never hired you," Omar said. He scooped up the phone on the counter, then hurried to the broken door and stepped over the debris into the back alley. A small truck that had seen much better days sat there. Omar didn't waste any time climbing in, and starting the engine. His eyes smarted at the thick scent of cigarette smoke, not that it bothered him. Quite the opposite. It only brought back the old cravings.

Within moments, he was driving onto the street, scanning the shadows for Mia. When he saw her petite form two buildings down, he pulled up to the curb and unrolled the window. "Need a ride somewhere?" he called out in a soft voice.

Mia stepped out of the shadows, the expression on her face amused. She slipped into the passenger side. "Is this the best you can do?"

"I'll find us something nicer later," Omar said with a laugh as he pulled out onto the street.

He handed over the confiscated cell phone. "Baris hired the guy to ransack his own shop. He's looking to capitalize with his insurance company. I thought we could use this."

Mia picked up the phone. "It might be of some use," she said, flashing Omar a smile.

◆ CHAPTER TWENTY-NINE ◆

CONSTANTINOPLE

AD 1521

Aleksandra wrote her name with a stylus on the thin piece of parchment she'd procured from Kaan. The eunuch had become a friend over the past week she'd been living at the harem court. In fact, he'd been her only friend besides Verda. With the other women not speaking to her, and possibly now petrified of a woman who brought a dead snake and stabbed it against the table, she'd be able to better focus on her goal: entering into the good graces of the sultan.

Other women before her had done it, and she knew she'd have to outwit the women who were trying to climb in rank now. They might think they knew her, but "foreigner" was only part of who she was. She'd had all of her hopes dashed, her entire life changed, and changed again. When she had spent time with the sultan, she'd felt valued and intelligent . . . appreciated. Here, in the harem court, she was like an unwanted insect, to be fed to a snake.

She let the ink of her name dry on the parchment for several moments. Staring at the neat letters, she thought of the evenings when her father had taught her letters after his work in the fields was done. And whenever he was called into battle, he'd bring her a scroll purchased from a traveling merchant, and ask her to copy it down.

She eyed the curve of the letters in her name, and knew this was the last time she'd allow herself to write her name or to think of herself as Aleksandra. The realization sent a dull ache through her. But then she remembered the cold, silent stares of the harem women, and the deadly snake that had been in her room. She rolled the vellum into a neat scroll and tied it closed with a piece of embroidery thread.

Verda had told her about the lives of some of the women in the harem. Most had been brought in as young, beautiful women, and only a handful had ever risen to concubine status. Two of them were now wives, but the rest of the women were simply elevated servants. One woman's entire existence was centered on putting away the sultan's clothing every morning after he left for his councils.

Another woman worked with the shoemakers to design and sew his shoes. Unless a woman was able to impress the Master of the Girls, she would remain doing remedial tasks the rest of her life.

Aleksandra was not interested in becoming a laundress or repairing shoes. If she had to do some of the things her mother had to survive, then she'd do so but she'd expect to be taken care of and protected in turn. If she could rise in status enough, then women like Gülfem wouldn't be able to touch her. She'd already been given a name by the sultan himself . . . he'd been grateful for her help in battle. She'd helped negotiate a peaceful passage through one of the villages. Surely he hadn't forgotten all of that. Aleksandra just had to get the Master of the Girls to agree to her cause.

One of her most pleasurable moments since being abducted was when the sultan read his poetry to her. Surely he hadn't done that without thought. Surely he would be pleased if she were to be assigned to serve him directly.

Taking on the new name from the sultan was the first step in turning the Master of the Girls' attention to her. Rising in rank would give her independence, protection, her own servants, and her own income.

But first, she had to become fully committed. She removed her tunic so that she only wore a shift, arms bare. She struck a piece of chert on the stone floor and set the spark to a small pile of dried grass she'd pulled from the courtyard. In moments, a tidy flame leaped up, and Aleksandra held her carefully rolled scroll over the flame.

"With this burning, I forever give up my name and my home." The parchment caught fire and burned slower than she anticipated. As the flames neared her fingers, she dropped the scroll onto the pile of grass and watched as the last bit turned to ash.

She crouched over the smoking heat until the ashes started to cool. She dipped a finger into the black and rubbed the ashes along the inside of her arms. And then she used the same ash to write out the letters, "Roxelane," across her floor. She stared at the letters, unblinking, until her eyes started to water.

She was Roxelane now, and she was prepared to meet the Master of the Girls.

Kaan waited for her outside her chamber where Roxelane had washed and dressed. If he noticed a difference in her countenance, he didn't say anything. He led the way along the corridor, taking her in the opposite direction from the harem court. They reached a narrow staircase and started up. The higher they climbed, the warmer the air became.

Roxelane lost count of the steps after a couple of dozen, and eventually at the next landing, they had two choices. Open the door or continue upward. Kaan put his hand on the door handle, and said, "Remember the Master of the Girls presides over the duties of the harem women, and he reports to the sultan's mother. Whatever impression you make, he will ultimately decide your fate."

She gave a small nod and said, "I understand."

Kaan opened the door and ushered Roxelane into a high-ceilinged room that was as elaborate as the harem court.

At the far end was a credenza, and behind it sat a tall dark-skinned man who looked as if he were sitting at a child's table.

He didn't look up as they entered, but two pale-skinned eunuchs stepped forward and greeted Kaan.

"I've brought Roxelane to meet with the Master."

The two men nodded and stepped back into their places.

The Master rose and Roxelane knew she'd been right. He was very tall and imposing. She didn't have to think twice before lowering her eyes and bowing. It seemed the most natural thing to do.

"There is no ceremony here," the Master said in a deep tone. His voice carried across the entire room, filling it with sound. "Tell me your name."

"Roxelane," she said, straightening, taking a deep breath so that she might meet the Master's gaze. "I've come to seek your counsel."

The Master took a few steps forward, literally peering down at her. "You are from the Kingdom of Poland?"

"I am from Constantinople now," she said, hoping he'd understand with just those few words what her commitment was.

His mouth straightened, and Roxelane didn't know how to interpret his expression.

"What do you have to recommend yourself?" he asked.

"I find that recommending myself is a boastful task," Roxelane said. "I've brought my friend, Kaan, to introduce me."

At that, the Master's eyebrows lifted, and his mouth seemed less stern. He stared at Roxelane, then said, "Will a *friend* make an honest recommendation?"

"Friend or no friend, Kaan is trustworthy to his core," she said.

The Master nodded. "I am acquainted with Kaan's attributes. What I'd like to know is what are yours?"

At that, Roxelane bowed her head again, and waited . . . waited for Kaan to speak. The warmth of relief passed through her as he began to tell the Master about her service as a slave. "She worked from morning until night, subsisting on a single bowl of gruel, while doing all her tasks with heavy shackles on her ankles."

"With no complaint and a smile, I gather?" the Master said.

"There was plenty of complaint," Roxelane said. "But that was when I was still a village girl. Now I am a member of the sultan's harem court."

Kaan described how Roxelane defended the harem women in the battle against the Polish soldiers.

"Hatice was killed," the Master pointed out.

"Her sacrifice will never be forgotten," Roxelane said. "It was in that battle that my heart was changed. I saw the Polish for what they were, attacking innocent women. I fought like a Turk on that day."

The Master smiled. "I've had the report from the sultan himself, and you are to be commended. Even though Hatice's life was lost, you saved all the other women."

Hope pulsed through Roxelane at the acknowledgement.

"What is it you want from me?" the Master asked.

She tried to keep her gaze at him as steady as possible. "I want a chance, that is all. I know more than one language. I can read and write. I am loyal to the people of Constantinople. I want to learn, and I want to serve the sultan."

"Roxelane is the name he gave you, is it not?"

She nodded, her mouth suddenly feeling dry.

"You know that in exchange for my services, you must give me something in return."

Her mind spun as she considered a myriad of possibilities. Was there an initiation? A servitude period? A terrible deed to perform? "Whatever you wish," she whispered.

He took a step closer, and the intensity of his gaze strengthened. "What is the name your father gave to you?"

She remembered Roma's words. *Never give them your name. It's the only thing they can't take from you.*

Her face burning, she hoped she wasn't about to throw everything away, and she said, "The only name I remember is Roxelane, the name the sultan gave me himself. It will be my name until the day I die and will be inscribed on my tombstone."

The room had been quiet before but now it was deathly silent. She could even sense Kaan holding his breath. Had she made a terrible error? Had she forever condemned herself to be a servant who might work in the cooking room or clean up after an elevated concubine?

The Master walked to where she was standing, barely holding herself erect. He placed a large hand on her shoulder and said, "Tonight, you will serve the wine at the sultan's banquet. He's invited his two wives and chief architect Sinan for a celebration meal. You will not speak, but if you are pleasing unto the sultan, you will be given another assignment."

She didn't ask what the next assignment would be, but she intended to serve the wine with the utmost care. Her hands wouldn't tremble, and she would not spill a drop. She would see the sultan's first wife at last, but more importantly, she would see the sultan himself.

Leaving the chamber with Kaan, Roxelane had no words. Questions tumbled about her mind, yes, but it didn't seem appropriate to ask them. She followed Kaan down the stairs, and when they reached the bottom, he turned in a different direction than they had come. Roxelane didn't question him, merely followed. When they stepped into a beautiful courtyard, Roxelane stared at the bubbling fountains and blooming flowers. It smelled like paradise.

But even more magnificent was that above the courtyard, Roxelane could see the dome and elegant spires of an elaborate mosque. And then she knew why Kaan had brought her here. She turned to him. "Are you Muslim?"

"Many who serve the sultan closely have converted," he said. "I converted because I wanted to understand the city I live in and the women I serve."

"Were you Christian?" she asked. At his nod, she said, "What about the other eunuchs? Did they convert too?"

"Most of them have converted," Kaan said. He tilted his head back to take in the full view of the towering mosque. "It is a requirement of the sultan's wives and concubines, though. As for me, I have not regretted it a day."

Roxelane let that settle in. She knew that Ibrahim had converted as well, but he'd worked closely with the sultan, so it seemed only natural.

"I know you want to rise in the hierarchy," Kaan said in a careful voice. "But you will have to change more than your name, and do more than forget your family and home. You will also have to forget your God and Savior."

Roxelane had known this on some level, but hearing the words spoken so plainly by Kaan, she felt as if she suddenly couldn't catch her breath. "Do those who convert truly forget their birth religion, or do they harbor both in their hearts?"

Kaan was silent for a moment, then he said, "There is a parable that no man can serve two masters. If you try, you will tear yourself in two."

"Tell me," she said in a quiet voice. "Tell me how you did it."

"I learned all I could about Islam," Kaan said. "It's a beautiful, peaceful religion, with many strict requirements. I found that I didn't disagree with any of them. But I also found that my soul was craving more—and that I couldn't deny that my Savior had lived and died for me." His voice cracked, and it took him a moment before he continued again.

Roxelane couldn't look at him, or her own eyes would fill with tears.

"But . . ." He released a breath. "I decided to turn my life over to God's hands. And once it was securely in His hands, I opened my mind to Allah. In the next life, I will once again be in the arms of God."

The breeze blew through the courtyard, surrounding her with the sweet fragrance of flowers. She thought about Kaan's words and what process he must have gone through to worship in another religion.

She turned to face him, then. "Tell me about Allah."

And he did. "First you need to understand that the word Islam means *surrender* or *submission*. When you accept Islam, it means you surrender to the will of Allah. Allah is the creator and restorer of the words. The prophet Muhammad was the last of the great prophets, and the will of Allah was revealed to Muhammad through the Koran."

She was quiet as he spoke, letting his words tumble into her mind before she formulated her questions.

"If I remain faithful, the discipline is more strict than I ever experienced as a Christian," Kaan continued. "Muslim duties include five daily prayers, the welfare tax and taking care of the poor, fasting during Ramadan, a profession of faith, and a pilgrimage to Mecca."

"The five pillars," she said. He'd explained the requirements well. But how did one reconcile with the belief when one's heart was not in it? Did one live with dual faith? She knew the story of Queen Esther, a woman who was Jewish and hid her religion from the Persian king, Xerxes. It wasn't until her people were to be annihilated that she confessed her deceit. The king forgave her and she remained his queen.

Was this the reason the sultan required those in his family and household to convert? It made sense on one hand, Roxelane realized, to have the people of the court of one mind, one faith.

Throughout Europe, battles were fought, kings and queens killed, as they debated over which religion their subjects should bow down to.

She thought of the way her father knelt on one knee and pled for deliverance and grace. The last time she remembered seeing him pray to God was before he left for his final battle. He'd been killed, hadn't returned to his family, despite his prayers.

And now . . . she was living in Constantinople and had taken on a new name, had forsaken her village and family and all that she'd left behind. If she were to rise in the hierarchy, she would have to convert.

She looked at Kaan and met his gaze. In that moment, she knew that she would do whatever it took. She would take ownership of her destiny even if it meant forever burying the religion of her father.

Somewhere, deep inside, it would coexist with her birth religion. But until the day she entered the gates of paradise, she would be Roxelane, a member of the Islam faith.

It was as if Kaan had read her thoughts. His hand touched her arm. "Tonight, you will serve the sultan and his wives. You will do so with impeccable grace and intelligence." He reached up and removed a pendant on a thin chain from around his neck. Lifting it from his tunic, she saw that it was a crescent moon and star. "Wear this, and the sultan will know your change of heart the moment he sees it."

Roxelane fastened the chain around her neck. For its thinness, the weight of it was surprisingly heavy. "Thank you," she said. "I will wear it with pride and appreciation." This time she couldn't stop the tears.

❖ CHAPTER THIRTY ❖

CONSTANTINOPLE

AD 1521

Roxelane stood in the sultan's cooking room with a dozen other female servants. The only thing that set her apart from them was her clothing. Verda had procured an intricately embroidered tunic for her in a lavender color, then spent nearly an hour braiding and twisting her hair, adding fresh flower buds to her upswept style.

Kaan had even been impressed when she'd left her chamber and stepped into the corridor. "If you don't spill any wine, you'll be a concubine soon."

Roxelane let out a nervous laugh. She knew it wasn't that simple, but she did feel beautiful. The sultan had to notice her—had to recognize her.

The head cook was a thin man, with an even thinner mustache. Roxelane soon learned that the man never sat down and never stopped throwing out commands. He might have been a head shorter than most of the female servants, but his presence was several heads taller.

"Hold the wine jug away from your body," the cook said, coming up to Roxelane.

It was full and heavy, so it was easier to cradle it in her arms. But she did as the cook instructed, and when he gave his approval, she set off down the short hallway to the banquet room. She'd been given a peek at it before the table was finished being laid with pure silver utensils, gold-cast plates, and gold-plated goblets. The image was bright and stunning, and Roxelane was grateful she was not just now seeing it for the first time.

As she entered, she realized the guests were still taking their seats. Gülfem spotted her immediately, and her eyes narrowed into a vicious slit. It was all Roxelane could do not to turn around and leave. She took a deep breath and glanced over at one of the other serving girls who carried a tray of baklava, a delicate, layered honeyed treat. Roxelane followed the girl as she started to place baklava on a gold plate.

Roxelane ignored the sharp looks from Gülfem and filled up the goblets with sweet wine as she walked around the table. The atmosphere changed to a hush when the sultan walked in. Although Roxelane had told herself not to stare at him, she couldn't help glancing over more than once as he greeted Gülfem, then another older woman who was wearing elaborate jewels. The woman had to be Mahidevran, the chief wife. She was older than Roxelane expected, but beautiful, curvy, with deep-set eyes the color of topaz. Her thick hair was threaded with gold embroidery thread, and her tunic was the color of an evening sunset. Walking beside her was a young boy whose facial features mimicked his mother's. He must be the sultan's son, Mustafa.

The sultan greeted each with a kiss on both cheeks, then motioned for them to take their seats. Next, a broad-shouldered man entered the room, bowing first to the sultan, and then to the wives. He had a quiet presence about him, as if he were willing to listen before speaking.

Roxelane moved around the table, out of the glaring sight of Gülfem, and took the opportunity to watch the sultan converse with the new man. He must be the chief architect that Kaan had told her about, which meant he was the one who'd designed and built most of the recent buildings in Constantinople, including the mosque Kaan had showed her.

The wine goblets filled, Roxelane now only had to stand to the side and wait until someone drank enough wine that she'd need to fill another goblet.

The sultan called for everyone's attention, and his rich deep voice brought back the memories of the caravan—their conversations and his kindness toward her.

She was lost in her thoughts when she felt his gaze. She couldn't explain it, but she knew the instant he noticed her standing by the sideboard. She turned her gaze and met his. Heat flushed her skin as his mouth lifted into a smile. He remembered her.

She wanted to smile back but in the same moment, both of his wives had followed the sultan's gaze. Gülfem's attention was the usual suspicious glare, whereas Mahidevran's seemed benign. At least Roxelane thought so at first, but then the woman's eyes shifted and there was an almost imperceptible straightening of her shoulders and lifting of her bosom.

The sultan's chief wife had definitely noticed her husband's attention toward Roxelane.

She lowered her gaze, her skin still warm with the sultan's attention, and now that she'd had it, there was nothing more she dared hope for.

If she had her way, she would speak to him, if only to ask how he was faring. If he was happy to be home. If he was in good health. If he'd been writing more poems. But even if he summoned her to his side, she couldn't ask any of these things in such a setting with his wives and children looking on. She would have more than a poisonous snake in her room to contend with.

"What a fortuitous evening," the sultan said. "Our architect is here to tell us of his plans for a new mosque, and we have Roxelane serving us."

"Roxelane?" the architect said, turning to look. "Has she brought her famous yataghan with her?"

The sultan laughed, and the wives smiled with tight lips.

The architect had heard about *her*? He rose to his feet and crossed to Roxelane. Her heart beat furiously as he grew closer. Then he bowed and said, "It's an honor to meet you."

Roxelane's mouth fell open, and she quickly recovered herself. "It's an honor to meet you as well. You and the sultan have built a magnificent city."

The architect gave her a slow wink. "That is why they call him Süleyman the Magnificent."

From the other side of the long table, the sultan laughed again.

She could almost feel the fury coming from his wives. They would never forget her now. But she wouldn't cower; she would look the architect in the eyes and speak to him.

She straightened her shoulders, still holding the jug of wine, and said, "It is no wonder so many Christians convert to Islam after arriving in Constantinople. The mosques are the most beautiful I have ever seen."

The architect gave her a benevolent smile. "Are there many mosques in the Kingdom of Poland?"

Everyone in the room had their eyes on her. "No," she said. "And the country is amiss for it."

"Excellent," the architect said, clapping his hands together. "Now tell me of your home."

The wives turned back to their food, but it was plain they were still listening. The sultan made no pretense of doing anything other than listen in on Roxelane's conversation.

"I live in a room in the north corridor of the Harem Court."

The architect shook his head, his mouth lifted in amusement. "I meant your home in Poland."

"I have a new home now," Roxelane said in a clear voice. She hoped the sultan would overhear and not mistake her words.

"Your loyalty is impressive," the architect said. "Have you learned to shoot the short bow yet?"

Roxelane looked at him with surprise. "I am not a warrior."

"I don't know about that," the architect said. "I've heard you called a warrior more than once. Did you not save the lives of a dozen harem women?"

"I . . ." she started, then glanced at the sultan. His gaze upon her was open and direct. "I fought along with all the other women."

"She is humble," the sultan said, rising to his feet. "And intelligent."

"And she is only serving you wine?" the architect said, thick brows raised. Was he teasing? Making a suggestion?

"I'm pleased that you have joined us tonight, Roxelane." As the sultan said her name, his tone sweetened.

And it was as if the others in the room faded into silence. The sultan walked toward her and lifted the wine jug from her hand. He moved it to the sideboard, then grasped her hand. Lifting her fingers to his lips, he said, "We would be honored if you'd sit with us as a guest tonight. Tell us of experiences in the harem court and what you think of our great city of Constantinople."

One of the women gasped, and Roxelane couldn't blame whoever it was. She wanted to gasp too. Everything was happening so quickly. She was being led by the sultan to the table, where he asked her to sit.

She settled onto a cushioned chair, and a plate and goblet were immediately set in front of her. The architect took a seat next to her, and although the sultan moved back to his place at the head of the table, he remained turned in her direction.

"I find it remarkable that you speak Turkish so well," the architect said.

Roxelane spoke softly. She wished that the sole attention wasn't on her. "Languages have come easily to me, and my father insisted that I learn Turkish."

The architect nodded. "Tell me about your father. Does he still live?"

Again her face warmed. "He died in battle against the Turks," she said. She didn't say it with malice, but she wanted her next words to be understood. "He was a farmer first, then a soldier. It was how he supported our family. But he respected other people enough to learn about their culture and languages."

"Remarkable," the architect said.

"I think he had a sense that the Ottoman Empire would spread across the continent and he would be better off if he could communicate."

The architect drank from his goblet. "Your father was a wise man. Tell me, do you have brothers?"

"Three younger brothers," Roxelane said. It was the first time since joining the caravan and leaving Roma that she'd spoken of them. It brought a new hollowness to her chest.

"And did your father teach them Turkish, as well?" he asked.

"No," Roxelane said. "They were quite young when my father died."

"It is hard to lose a parent, is it not?" the architect said. "What of your mother?"

Roxelane looked away from him now. She refused to speak of her mother in front of the other wives. She knew whatever she said would travel the harem like a fire spark.

"She still lives," Roxelane said. "May I fill your goblet with more wine?"

The architect chuckled. "You are a woman of duty. A woman I'm impressed with."

Roxelane interpreted that as agreement, and as she rose to fetch the wine jug, she saw a look pass between the architect and the sultan. She didn't know how to read their shared glance, but it sent her pulse into a frenzy. She was no longer among the hundreds of women at the palace, but one who stood out.

By the time she refilled the architect's wine goblet, he was speaking with the sultan, and anything about her had seemed to fade. She took her place by the sideboard again and remained as motionless as possible while the conversation rose and fell about her. Platter after platter was delivered, braised lamb shanks, steaming rice pilaf, stuffed eggplant, tabouleh salad, and flatbread with hummus.

At the end of the meal, Roxelane left with some of the other servants, not daring to look back to see if the sultan or his wives had noticed her exit.

By the time she returned to her chamber, she was ready to collapse into bed. But when she opened her door, she found an oil lamp burning and Kaan waiting for her. He stood near the window, his arms folded across his chest. Alarm shot through her, and she asked, "Is something the matter?"

Kaan grinned. "Everything is the matter, that's why I'm here. Your name is on every concubine and harem servant's lips tonight."

She crossed to the bed and sat down. "He spoke to me. I felt like I was in a dream. But his wives hate me more now than ever."

"He? Are you talking about the sultan?"

"Yes, who are you referring to?"

"The architect. One of the most powerful men in the court of Süleyman is enamored of you. There is already talk that he'll ask for you. Perhaps as a concubine, or perhaps as his fourth wife."

Roxelane's breath stopped in her throat. "The architect is older than my father. He can't possibly . . ." She had not intended to attract one of the men of the court, she had intended . . . even now that she thought about it, she realized how foolish she was. How could she, a Polish slave, think she could rise in the harem and become a concubine or wife to the sultan of the Ottoman Empire?

Doubt coursed through her as she reconsidered her brazen plan. Even with the Master of the Girls putting his confidence in her and allowing her to serve at the sultan's banquet, she had set something unexpected into motion.

"Don't you see, this is the best scenario that could have happened," Kaan said, crossing to Roxelane and standing near her.

She looked up at him. "What do you mean?"

"If the sultan is interested in elevating you, then he'll be pressed to act quickly if one of his chief advisors is also interested in you."

Roxelane considered this. How could she hope to have two powerful men in the Ottoman Empire vying for her?

Someone knocked on her door, then cracked it open. Verda stepped inside her room, then quickly closed the door. "I heard you returned. Tell me what happened. The rumors are growing wilder by the moment."

So Roxelane told Verda and Kaan about the conversation at the banquet, and how the sultan had led her by the hand to the table. Verda gave her a knowing smile. "I will not be surprised if he requests your presence in the coming weeks."

But Roxelane didn't have to wait weeks. Another knock sounded on the door.

When Kaan opened it, the Master of the Girls stood there. "The sultan has requested your presence."

❖ CHAPTER THIRTY-ONE ❖
BATA ISLAND

Leyla gazed at the men waiting on the tarmac as she followed Naim off the jet. One of the men looked as if he could lead a life in professional boxing. He stood a few feet behind the first man, and Leyla decided he was either a bodyguard to Mr. Bata or a vigilant employee. Next, her gaze shifted to the man standing closest to the jet.

He had to be Naim's father. Mr. Adem Bata had his arms folded over his chest and although his hair was peppered with white, his face was remarkably smooth, and there was a resemblance to his son. Mr. Bata was well dressed in a suit jacket and trousers. Leyla looked for any bit of softening as the man watched Naim. There was none. It was clear that Mr. Bata was not pleased to see his son.

Naim turned toward Leyla, slipped his hand in hers, then leaned toward her as if in affection, and whispered. "Smile and act like you love me."

Then he kissed her cheek.

She returned his smile, although she was filled with nervousness.

"Father!" Naim called out to be heard over the idling jet engine. "I didn't expect you to meet me at such a late hour."

Mr. Bata said nothing, just kept watching as they neared. Behind them, the jet turned and taxied to the end of the runway.

"Hello, Kerem," Naim said, stepping forward to shake the second man's hand.

The sound of the jet still made regular conversation difficult, but Naim pressed on, undeterred. Leyla noted that his palm had grown sweaty in her hand, although his voice was steady and cheerful.

"Father," Naim said, stopping before Mr. Bata, close enough that Leyla could see the men shared the same color of eyes, although Mr. Bata's were rounder, wider. And Mr. Bata's face was more narrow and angular than Naim's, giving him the look of a wolf.

"I'd like to introduce Leyla," Naim said. He released her hand, and wrapped his arm about her shoulders. "We've been dating, and when she was hired by Baris Uzuner, I had to come clean with her. And I decided it was time for her to meet the family."

Leyla's heart thumped in her ears, but she smiled at the formidable man before her and extended her hand.

He glanced at her, then back to Naim. Leyla kept her hand outstretched, determined to play her part, as if she really were meeting her boyfriend's family for the first time.

"Father, don't be rude," Naim said in a low voice.

Mr. Bata blinked, and seeming to remember himself, he looked back to Leyla and her outstretched hand. He grasped hers, albeit briefly, and gave it a shake. He released her hand almost before Leyla had time to process his firm grip.

"I need to speak to you alone," he said, directing his gaze at Naim.

Naim hesitated. "Let me get Leyla settled in, and then I'll meet you in your office."

His father seemed content with that. He even nodded to Leyla. "It's nice to meet a friend of my son's. What is your family name?"

Leyla glanced at Naim, not sure how to answer such a direct question.

"We'll worry about formalities later," Naim said. "Come, Leyla, let me show you around."

Without another comment to his father, Naim walked her to a two-seater Ranger parked by a small building that must have served as the airport controller center. "We're about a kilometer from the main house," he said, putting her bag behind the double seat.

As they drove, Leyla couldn't see much of the landscape in the dark, most of the lighting came from the Ranger's headlights. Naim turned off the road onto a lane, and a high wall came into view. Two massive metal doors were set into the wall, and a security post was stationed at the side.

A security guard stepped out as they drove up, and Naim slowed the Ranger down. "Hello, Talha," Naim said.

The guard didn't look surprised to see Naim. "Mr. Bata," he simply said. Then he stepped into the station, and the metal doors began to rotate inward, making a path wide enough for the vehicle.

Naim drove through the opening, and Leyla took in her surroundings. It was like entering a small city. An elaborate villa stood at the end of a short parking lot, along with other buildings that looked to be a mixture of small homes and shops.

Naim parked, climbed out, and grabbed their bags. "Welcome to my home," he said, flashing her a smile.

He guided Leyla toward a door to the side of the villa, and as Leyla walked she saw several more guards, at various posts, all of them well armed. She glanced behind her to see guards standing on top of the wall, as if keeping a lookout across the entire compound. Eyes seemed to be everywhere.

As they stepped into the cool interior, Leyla was immediately struck by the austerity of the villa. She didn't know what she'd expected, but it wasn't cold steel appliances in the kitchen, and black painted wood tables. They passed a lounge room with straight back chairs and a dark fireplace, then a conference room with multiple blank TV screens. Naim opened another door, and they stepped into an empty corridor. Empty except for the security cameras dotted along the ceiling.

"This is where the bedrooms are," Naim said in a low voice. "Fortunately, my father has his own bedroom suite near his offices." They passed several doors, when Naim finally stopped. He opened a door and led her into a spacious room. Flipping on the light, Leyla was surprised to see the room was actually cozy. Warm reds and soft browns made up the décor of the large bed and two overstuffed chairs. A mahogany desk stood in the corner surrounded by three book shelves.

"Is this your room?" Leyla asked in an equally quiet voice.

"Yes," Naim said, motioning for her to keep her voice down. "There might be security cameras in here." He crossed to the desk and powered on the computer atop it. "You'll be staying with me. I don't trust my father to not come up with some way to get you off the island." He turned to face her, pulling out his phone from his pocket. "Lock the door when I leave, although I won't be gone long."

"What do you want me to work on?" she whispered, glancing at the computer.

"I'm calling your phone, and leaving mine on so that we can stay connected in case something happens. Also, listen for anything that might be a clue as to where he's keeping the rest of the sultan's letters. If they're as valuable to him as I think they are, they're on the island somewhere."

"Are those buildings outside warehouses?"

"A couple of them are," Naim said. "But he's continually moving stuff around, and there are secured areas on the north side that even I'm not allowed to enter."

Leyla exhaled, trying to take it all in.

"Look," Naim said, crossing to her and stopping close. "I won't let anything happen to you, but we need to be smart. Until I speak with my father, I don't want you going anywhere alone. Wait for me here until I return."

"Of course," Leyla said.

"The bathroom's through there, and I'll bring us back something to eat," Naim said. His gaze held hers for a moment, and Leyla thought he might say something else. Instead, he walked to the door.

Her phone rang, and she clicked "Accept Call" knowing it would be Naim. He slipped his phone in his pocket, then gave her a nod, and stepped into the hallway.

She crossed to the door and turned the deadbolt, wondering why a bedroom door in this secure compound needed an extra level of security. Leaning against the door for a moment, she scanned the room. It might be Naim's bedroom in his home, but there was nothing personal about it. With him gone, it could have been any other room in the compound.

The sound of a whistle came from her cell phone, and she clicked on the speaker phone. The sound grew clearer accompanied by Naim's footsteps as he walked through the corridors. Leyla wondered what part of the house contained his father's office. She carried her phone to the desk and sat in the chair, setting the phone on the desk.

Moments later, a sharp knock sounded, and Naim's voice said, "I'm here."

His father must have invited him in, because a door opened, then shut.

Then came Mr. Bata's voice, more muffled than Leyla had liked, so she turned up the volume on her phone and listened carefully.

"Why the hell did you bring that woman here?" Mr. Bata said, his tone so fierce that it made Leyla flinch.

"I told you," Naim said, in a calm tone. "We decided it was time to meet each other's families."

"This is not the time, and you know it," Mr. Bata ground out. "Just the fact that she was hired by Baris Uzuner puts us in a precarious position and makes us a target for Baris. That man is a fool. I'd rather just send her somewhere with a security team if you're worried about protecting her. Anywhere but here."

"She stays with me," Naim said, his voice less calm, but still controlled. "I've finished at the university, and I've completed several successful transactions for you. Leyla and I are becoming serious. It's a natural progression of things, Father. The Baris incident was just an unfortunate detour."

"You know there's no room for a woman in your life right now," his father countered. "You're still training."

"I've finished training," Naim said, his tone gaining more steel. "I've been finished for months, and because you decide to have me tailed with every transaction doesn't mean that I'm not trained. It's you who are holding back, not me."

Silence filled the next few moments, then, "What's her family's name?"

"You're not doing a background check on her," Naim said.

"What are you hiding?"

"Nothing," Naim said, his voice back to steel. "When we leave tomorrow night, I'll give you her family's name, but not before. It shouldn't matter where she's from."

"You met her at the university?"

"Yes."

"What were her studies?"

"Political science with an emphasis in history."

When Mr. Bata spoke next, his voice was surprisingly softer. "What are you getting yourself into? You know the life your mother had to live. I tried to make her happy, but I know she had regrets."

There was no immediate response from Naim.

Leyla waited for his answer. She was becoming too involved in her role; it was as if she were waiting for Naim's declaration when he had nothing to truly declare.

"I've told her some things," Naim said. "And she understands the life Mother had to live, and the sacrifices she made."

"What does . . . Leyla think of the need to be constantly under guard?" Mr. Bata asked. "Does she understand that if the two of you marry, she'd be a target?"

I already am, Leyla thought. *And I'm not even Naim's girlfriend.*

"She has some sense of it, but I haven't explained it fully," Naim said. "I wanted her to see the compound, to meet you, and then I'll meet her family."

"It's a security breach to bring her here," Mr. Bata said, his voice growing hard.

"She can be trusted," Naim said. "She understands that she's never to speak of where she met my father."

Leyla sat back. This conversation was going better than she thought. Naim's father sounded truly concerned.

Then the tone changed once again. "Where are the records that you recovered from Baris?"

"In a secure place," Naim said.

"I want them returned to the compound."

"I'll get a courier assigned to the job right away," Naim said. "But for now, I'm tired, and I'm Leyla's host. Will you join us for dinner?"

"I don't eat dinner at midnight," his father stated.

Leyla smiled to herself.

"She can sleep in the blue room down the hall from yours," Mr. Bata said. "It's always kept ready."

Leyla wondered what the blue room was but Naim had made it clear she'd be staying in his room. Apparently he wasn't going to tell his father.

"Thank you," Naim's voice came through the phone. Moments later, she could hear him walking along the corridor again, then other noises that were probably from the kitchen. She propped her elbows on the desk and rubbed her neck.

By the time Naim returned and knocked on the door, she realized how hungry she was and how exhausted. She rose and unlocked the door, relieved to see him. She hadn't known what to expect with his conversation with his father. It was both more intense and more cordial than she expected.

Naim carried in some sandwiches and fruit and water bottles. As they ate at the desk, he asked, "Did you hear the conversation?"

"Yes," she said, trying not to gulp down the sandwich in just a couple of bites. "Your father's more patient than I thought he would be."

Naim grimaced as he removed the laptop from the desk and walked over to the bed, settling on the right side. "You're welcome to go to sleep if you're tired. I'm just going to check on some things."

Leyla hesitated, then decided she couldn't very well sleep in the desk chair, and the floor didn't look very appealing. She'd spent forty-eight hours with Naim, and so far he hadn't done more than kiss her cheek or hold her hand. Both of which she didn't mind at all.

She crossed to the other side of the bed, then kicked off her shoes. She settled on top of the covers and looked at the screen that Naim had pulled up.

"Inventory?" she whispered.

He nodded, but didn't say anything, just continued to scroll through list after list. She tried to keep her eyes open, but they kept closing of their own accord. When she heard Naim's sharp intake of breath, she opened her eyes. He was peering at the laptop screen. Leyla lifted her head and saw that the list was a series of Ottoman artifacts.

"What is it?" she asked.

"This is a division of the warehouse I haven't been to before," he said in a quiet voice. "I'm not even sure which building it's in, and I'll have to find a way to break in as it is. My father doesn't know that I've found a way to access this database." Naim tapped the screen. "By the dates of the receiving invoices, these are vases that were recently acquired. Didn't you say that Baris removed the letters from vases in his antiques shop in Istanbul?"

"Yes." Leyla was fully awake now. She sat up and moved closer to Naim to look at the list of items. The vases were described and catalogued with their date of discovery and location found.

"They were found beneath one of the ancient buildings connected to the Gülfem Hatun Mosque in the Üsküdar district," Leyla said.

"Is that significant?"

"Gülfem is the name of one of the sultan's wives. She's the one who commissioned the building."

"Do you think she knew about the plot to kill the heir?"

Leyla searched her memory for all she knew about Gülfem. "The woman tried to raise money to build the mosque, but she was not favored among the harem women. Very few of them would donate to her cause. Legend is that she wanted to impress the sultan with this mosque of hers. She became desperate, and one of the harem women said she'd give her money if Gülfem allowed her to go to the sultan's bed in Gülfem's place."

Naim nodded. "I think I remember reading about that."

"The sultan was furious and had her executed," Leyla said. "Although later he finished the mosque she'd started to build."

"He felt guilty, perhaps?"

"Possibly," Leyla said. "It would have been a pretty good hiding place for him, or for his chief wife Roxelane."

"Do you really think they hid the letters themselves? Or someone close to them, someone who wanted the truth to come out eventually?"

"Like an advisor or a servant?" Leyla suggested.

"Perhaps it was one of the other wives or concubines?" Naim said. "Roxelane couldn't have had too many fans in the harem. The women were very competitive."

Leyla thought for a moment. "Do you think those vases have the letters in them? Your father may not even know what he has."

"He knows," Naim said with surety. "I don't know how they fell into Baris's hands, but my father acted quickly to get them back."

Leyla exhaled. "So what can we do?"

Naim used his phone to snap a picture of the inventory list on the screen, then closed the laptop. "I don't profess to be perfect or to be a squeaky-clean citizen of Turkey, but my father has gone too far. Paying Baris to kill off the descendants of Sultan Süleyman is something I never thought my father capable of. If he had stuck with black market antiques, I could support this lifestyle, even though it turned my mother into a virtual prisoner." He looked around the room. "We need those letters, we need to find a way to stop whatever his plans are—and we need to check the vases first."

A faint click came from the other side of the door, and Naim froze, looking over at Leyla.

"What is it?" she mouthed.

He climbed off the bed and silently walked to the door. He unlocked the dead bolt, then tried the knob. It didn't budge. He turned to face Leyla, his face like stone.

"We're locked in. There's an electronic seal that can only be opened from the corridor."

Leyla didn't know what to think. It seemed impossible.

Naim ran his fingers through his hair. "I shouldn't have brought you. My father must be suspicious, thinks I know something. I thought—"

A blaring alarm sounded, and Leyla scrambled off the bed. "What's going on?" she called out to Naim.

"I don't know," Naim yelled over the sound of the alarm. He crossed to the windows and tried them both. "Electronically monitored," he said. "This is an all-new installation since I was here a few weeks ago." He hurried to the door and tried to open it, but it wouldn't budge. "This room is a fortress."

The alarm turned off, but it left Leyla's ears ringing.

"Text Omar," Naim told Leyla as he walked back to the windows on the other side of the room. "Tell him that we need a way off the island. He can track your phone to find us."

"Can he just show up?" Leyla asked, out of breath. "I mean your father barely let you into the compound."

"If it's possible, he'll find a way," Naim said, pulling up the blinds that covered the windows.

Outside, lights from the compound shone, casting small glowing circles about the open courtyard. Leyla knew if she stood by the window, she'd see ample evidence of guards. "I don't understand how Omar will—"

"Hurry, text him, and then we'll break out of this room."

Leyla had more questions, but Naim had started opening and shutting the drawers of the desk. Her fingers trembling, she typed out a text to the number Omar had given them both.

"Move to the right of the door, so that when it swings open, you'll be hidden," Naim said, holding something that looked like a small marble statue. "I'll break the window and activate the alarm again. When someone comes through the door, we'll wait until he's at the window then make our escape through the corridor."

Questions collided with panic in Leyla's mind, but Naim was waving her toward the door. He tossed his cell phone in one of the desk drawers, then shut it. Leyla hurried to her position by the door and held her breath while watching as Naim struck the window.

◆ CHAPTER THIRTY-TWO ◆
CONSTANTINOPLE

AD 1521

Roxelane hovered in the waiting chamber, knowing that with each passing moment, her tension increased. With the evening banquet long since over, she'd been led to the sultan's private quarters by the Master of the Girls.

Kaan had followed dutifully behind, but Roxelane could see that even he was at a loss for words of how to advise her.

The Master of the Girls had simply said before leaving her to wait, "If you are loyal, you'll have nothing to fear."

"Is this how the other women assigned as concubines met with the sultan?" she asked.

"Yes," the Master of the Girls said. "But first the women are inspected by the sultan's mother. This is an unusual time to request a harem servant's presence."

Roxelane nodded and continued to gaze about the waiting chamber. Plush chairs and divans outlined the room, and the walls were hung with intricately embroidered tapestries in rich colors of deep red, green, and blue. Some were scenes of battle, and for a moment, Roxelane wondered if she were going into a new type of battle.

And then a very white-skinned servant came out of one of the doors and said, "The sultan will see you now." He gave a half bow to Roxelane.

She looked from the servant to the men she'd come with; they both gave her encouraging nods. With a deep breath, she followed after the servant, stepping from the tapestry-filled room into an indoor courtyard of sorts. It felt like a garden, yet it was surrounded by high walls.

Trees, bushes, and beds of flowers grew inside, and torches were placed about the chamber, making it bright, chasing away the darkness of night.

Roxelane was struck by how quiet the garden was. She expected servants, advisors, or others to be milling about. Yet, on the far side, the sultan sat upon a bench, bent over a scroll, stylus suspended in the air.

The servant bowed to Roxelane, then scurried through another door.

Roxelane exhaled and kept her gaze on the sultan. He hadn't seemed to notice her presence yet, which was strange, since he was the one to request it. She looked around carefully, seeing paths, benches, and greenery.

It was an oasis of calm in the center of a busy palace.

A sound from one of the larger trees caught her attention, and she saw a bird perched there. She stepped closer, intrigued to see a bird this time of night.

And then the air surrounding her shifted, and she somehow knew that Süleyman was no longer sitting on the bench across the garden.

"Roxelane," his voice was low and honeyed.

She turned slowly.

Looking up into the sultan's brown eyes that were touched with green, and breathing in his spicy scent, and remembering the way he'd always spoken to her, made her realize she would do nearly anything to leave the harem court behind and become his.

"You have been generous in your attentions to me," she said quietly. If she spoke any louder, she wouldn't be able to hide the tremble.

"When I saw you at the banquet, I was struck with a new poem," he said. "It seems that you have inspired me yet again."

Roxelane was so startled that she stepped back with a gasp.

He only smiled and moved closer, taking her hand.

If she had been able to breathe, she might not catch any air.

Looking straight at her, he began to speak in poetry, and Roxelane knew it was about her. For who else would he call the *warrior slave*?

She closed her eyes as his words washed over her, filling her soul, and pushing thoughts of all else out of her mind. She could only think of this man—sultan or not, powerful or weak, married or unmarried.

Nothing else mattered except that he was speaking poetry to her in the stillness of a very dark night.

My pain for thee balm in my sight resembles
Thy face's beam the clear moonlight resembles.
Thy black hair spread across thy cheeks, the roses
O Liege, the garden's basil quite resembles.
Beside thy lip opened wide its mouth, the rosebud;
For shame it blushed, it blood outright resembles.
Thy mouth, a casket fair of Romas and rubies,
Thy teeth, Romas, thy lip coral bright resembles.

She was afraid to look at him, afraid of what he might see in her eyes as he spoke the words. So when he fell silent, she kept her eyes closed. But when she felt, rather than saw, him move closer, and his hand brushed her cheek, she opened her eyes to gaze at him.

His expression was serious, intent, and she didn't have to consider what it might mean before his fingers trailed along her jaw, then down along her neck to where her pulse beat rapidly.

"You are a beautiful woman, Roxelane," he said. "But that is not why I am so drawn to you."

She wanted him to pull her into his arms, to press his mouth against hers, to make her his, but this was a sultan. She couldn't ever make her needs known. He had to be the one to choose. So she kept her hands to her side and her body still.

"Tonight while you spoke with the architect, I saw how another man might see you," he said, his voice above a whisper. "Strong, beautiful, tempting."

Did this mean he thought all of these things about her too?

"To me you are all of these things."

Yes.

"Yet, you are so much more," the sultan said. "I value education and intelligence above all else."

"My mother selected my first wife for me," he said. "Mahidevran is a beautiful woman, but she is selfish in her intentions. If I were to ask her to listen to a poem, I'd only feel disdain radiating from her. And if she could, she'd tell me that writing poetry is a waste of time for someone like me."

He continued. "If I told my second wife, Gülfem, that I'd written a poem for her, she'd have it copied and sent to every woman in the harem for spite. To prove that I love her above all other women in the kingdom." He fell quiet, and Roxelane wished she could wrap her arms about his waist and lean against his chest.

"But you, Roxelane." His voice dropped to a whisper again. "You close your eyes and listen to my poems with every beat of your heart."

Roxelane stared into the sultan's eyes and saw something there that was only for her. Hope. Faith. "Your words transport me into a different place," she admitted. "I cannot put my thoughts into words as you do with your poetry. The poems you have shared with me somehow reach into my soul and hold on tight."

The sultan moved his hand along the soft cloth of her shoulder, then glided down her arm until his fingers wrapped about her wrist. He pulled her gently to him until their bodies touched. Then he lowered his head until she felt his breath on the side of her neck, and she knew that if she moved at all, his lips would touch her skin.

But she didn't move. She breathed in and out, her body aware of the contrasting hard planes of his chest against the curves of hers.

"Will you give up your god for Allah?" the sultan said in the quietest whisper.

The most delicious shiver began where his breath touched her neck and spread to her feet. The sultan had just requested *her*. Invited her to be with him. She was not sure if he intended to marry her, but she would have him in whatever way he allowed.

"Yes," she told Süleyman.

His hands slid up her arms, and rested on her shoulders as he drew back and gazed at her. She could remain here until paradise claimed her, looking into the depths of this man's eyes, making her heart trip.

She could see how he was able to command armies and countries, and how his perseverance had made him the ruler of the Ottomans. He was intelligent, powerful, and caring. She reached up and touched the side of his face. He inhaled as her fingers traced the warmth of his skin.

Süleyman turned his head slightly and kissed her fingers. She caught her breath.

"I was told about the snake in your room," he said in a low voice. "I promise that you'll not have to endure such danger again. You'll have bodyguards in your new quarters."

She stared at him. "I will be your concubine? With chambers of my own?"

His eyes were alert and his mouth soft when he said, "Does that please you?"

"It pleases me."

He gave a slight nod. Then he grasped her hand that still lingered on his face. "There will be much preparation and many changes. Once you are settled into your new rooms, I will send for you."

She considered what this would mean.

"You will meet my mother and be trained by her in the ways of the court," he said. "She will not be pleased that I have chosen a new concubine without her clearance. But she will agree to whom I choose."

How would Roxelane get along with the sultan's mother if he was already going against their tradition in order to select her for concubine status?

He seemed to understand her concern. "Do not worry," he said, squeezing her hand. "My mother will not defy me, and it will be in her best interest to make sure you are well prepared in all things."

Her face heated at the wonderment of what he meant by *all things*, but it wasn't something she could question him about.

A door opened at the far side of the courtyard, and Süleyman squeezed her hands a second time. "Soon, we'll be together." He released her hands and stepped back as a servant approached. He was the same white-skinned servant who'd led her inside.

The sultan nodded to him, then gave a small bow to Roxelane.

She was reluctant to leave his presence and return to the harem court where everyone would be watching her and wanting to ask questions.

Regardless, she followed the servant back into the waiting room where Kaan and the Master of the Girls stood. As soon as the servant left them alone, Roxelane told the men what had happened in the courtyard. Both of them smiled broadly. "I have not seen such favor bestowed on any other women of the harem," the Master of the Girls said.

"What about his wives?" Roxelane said.

"Both were selected by his mother," Kaan said. "*You*, Roxelane, were selected by the sultan himself."

She wanted to laugh and rejoice, but now she knew all too well that she'd become even more of a target.

Kaan was still smiling. "You will be selecting your own servants to establish a household." He lifted his brows, as if waiting for her pronouncement.

"You will come with me, of course," Roxelane said. "And Verda too."

The Master of the Girls nodded. "Both are wise choices; both are loyal to you and won't stand in your way."

"My way?" Roxelane asked.

"Of rising to chief wife."

It had been a dream of Roxelane's, but not until tonight, and not until the Master of the Girls spoke it aloud, did she dare to believe. "Do you think I can become a wife?"

The Master of the Girls and Kaan exchanged glances, then both said at the same time, "Yes."

Only then did Roxelane allow herself to smile. Soon she'd be living in her own chambers with her own household. And soon, the sultan would send for her. Could she dare dream that she would rise in status above the other women in the harem, and show them they were wrong for discounting her? She would gain power and wealth and become loyal to one man, all the things her mother hadn't been. And she would honor her father's memory by dedicating herself to learning.

The following morning started before dawn when Verda awakened Roxelane from a deep and dream-filled sleep. Roxelane had dreamed she'd failed her training with the sultan's mother, and she had sent her to live outside the palace in a hovel.

When she opened her eyes to see Verda, it was with great relief that her terrible dream hadn't been real.

"We must pack everything, and Kaan will personally oversee the delivery of your things to your new chamber," Verda said.

Roxelane climbed out of bed, taking a moment to orient herself. A sliver of light came from the window, telling her that dawn was on its way. "I am moving into my new chambers today?"

"Not so soon," Verda said. "You will sleep in my chamber tonight. Word has already spread through the harem, and there are many women who are very upset. You are not to be alone for one moment by yourself." She reached under Roxelane's pillow and withdrew the yataghan that Roxelane had used to spear the snake. "Strap this to your waist for all to see. It will be a useful warning."

Roxelane quickly dressed in her best tunic of deep blue, then strapped the yataghan securely to her waist. Verda worked to gather Roxelane's belongings and piled everything into the center of the bed. Then she tied the edges of the blanket together, creating one large bundle.

Between them, they carried the bundle to Verda's chamber that was in another corridor. The earliness of the morning meant they only encountered a few scurrying servants along the way. It was too early for even the most competitive harem woman to be awake. But still, rumor would travel with the servants who dutifully reported to their mistresses.

Once in Verda's room, with Roxelane's bundle of belongings set in a corner, Verda turned to Roxelane. "You will be nothing but obedient to the sultan's mother, Ayşe Hafsa. No matter her words, cruel or kind, you will not speak unless she asks you a direct question. As the sultan's mother, she has great power and acts as co-regent. She is the second most influential person in the Ottoman Empire."

"Is she so harsh?" Roxelane asked.

"She is strict and disciplined," Verda explained. "She will not like your appointment because it didn't come through her. She oversees all the goings-on of the harem court, and the Master of the Girls is to report everything to her. Undoubtedly she already knows who you are, and now she will be responsible for training you as concubine to her son."

Roxelane lowered her head. Doing the sultan's bidding would be no easy task, but it was what Roxelane wanted more than anything. "You will come with me?"

"As your lady servant, I will always be at your side," Verda said, her voice growing softer. "But you will have to pass the training and accomplish all that Hafsa asks of you. Only *you* can do that."

Roxelane nodded then she grasped Verda's hands. "Thank you for serving me as I begin my training. I will always take care of you, and I will always be in your debt."

Verda's smile was genuine. "When you first stepped into the harem tent on the battlefield of Poland, I knew there was something different about you. But it wasn't until I saw the way the sultan looked at you that I realized I wasn't the only one who noticed."

"I am far less beautiful than his wives," Roxelane said. "I do not understand why he is drawn to me."

"You are beautiful, Roxelane, in an innocent way," Verda said. "You are clever and intelligent. The sultan has shared two of his poems with you, which means you have become an inspiration to him."

Roxelane felt gratitude, as well as moisture collecting in her eyes. "You have helped me so much," she told Verda. "If it weren't for your counsel, I don't know where I'd be."

"Embrace your fate, and don't dwell on the past," Verda said.

A soft knock sounded at the door, and Kaan came in. "Ready?" he said, looking at Roxelane.

"I am," she breathed, although her hammering pulse made her want to stay and hide in Verda's chamber.

Instead, she followed Kaan out of the room, Verda joining her, and they made the trek to the sultan's mother's household.

❖ CHAPTER THIRTY-THREE ❖

ISTANBUL

The truck's brakes screeched every time Omar turned a corner or stopped at a red light. He cursed as he noticed other faulty things about the vehicle he'd stolen. The check engine light was on, as well as the check oil light.

Mia followed his gaze from her position in the passenger seat. "Top-notch transportation. There's nothing like it. Baris must be on a tight budget."

"Call him. Let's see if we can fake our way into a meeting," Omar said, glancing at the phone in her hand.

"He won't pick up," Mia said, as she pulled up the contact list and selected the number.

"Not the first time," Omar said. "But he will the second time."

Mia dialed and waited. "Nothing," she said. "Five rings, then nothing."

Omar nodded, slowing at a corner to wait for a car to turn in front of him. Omar's stomach grumbled with the scent of food wafting from the various restaurants they were unfortunately passing.

"Now he's bothered," Omar said. "Call again. See what happens."

Mia dialed and put it on speaker. A moment later, Omar heard a male voice answer the other end.

Speaking in Arabic, Mia said, "Good evening, sir. I've been given this number by one of your employees. I'm an antiques collector from Damascus."

"Where did you get the phone?" Baris's voice cut her off.

Mia glanced over at Omar and smiled. "I'm particularly interested in the letters that you have from Süleyman the Magnificent, written to his wife Roxelane."

There was a significant silence.

"Who do you work for?" Baris asked.

"Why, sir, I'm independent. You probably haven't heard of me because I deal mostly in Syria," Mia continued. "I've been building a significant collection of the Ottoman Empire. I have several clients who are very interested in the era."

More silence, then, "Who are your clients?"

Mia gave a tinkering laugh. "You know I can't breech client confidentiality, sir."

"Give me one name, and I will agree to meet you," Baris said, his voice clipped.

"Omar Zagouri," she said.

Omar's eyes flew to Mia. What was she doing? He felt as if he'd been punched in the stomach, and he could only imagine what Baris was thinking now.

Finally, the measured reply came. "That's impossible. Omar Zagouri is Israeli."

"Only on his mother's side," Mia said. "I suppose I have a bit of a reputation, so he contacted me. He was *very* eager to find these letters. I hadn't heard of them until he told me. And now, I must confess, I'm intrigued as well. Zagouri has promised to double my fee if I can find them soon."

"When did you last speak with Mr. Zagouri?" Baris asked, his tone interested, although it was clear he was trying to hide it.

"This morning," Mia said. "What does that have to do with any—"

"Was he in Israel?"

It was Mia's turn to go silent though she wasn't looking at Omar for help in what to say. "Sir, I just arrived in Istanbul and was hoping I could meet with you."

Baris didn't even hesitate. "Certainly. Hotel Amira. Thirty minutes."

"Thank you, sir, you won't regret this accommodation." She hung up the phone before Baris could reply one way or the other. Not surprisingly, the phone rang again, but Mia just turned it off.

"Well?" she said, placing her hand on Omar's arm. "You're about to meet Baris Uzuner. Won't he be surprised?"

Omar blew out a breath. "He's a fool, but that makes my job a lot easier."

While Mia pulled up the address of the hotel, Omar slowed in front of a food pushcart. He hopped out of the truck and bought two beef *içli köfte*. By the time he'd paid and was back inside the truck with the sandwiches, Mia had the hotel's address. "We're only a few minutes away."

"Good," Omar said. "That will give us plenty of time to check out the place before Baris arrives."

He ate the *içli köfte* with one hand and drove with the other. His stomach clashed with hunger and the introduction of new food and the thought of meeting Baris in person—the man who'd sent someone to torture his mother for information.

"Omar," Mia said, touching his arm. "I know that look. Maybe we'd better call the police, have them waiting in the wings."

"Baris's death won't be a benefit to me . . . yet. We need information from him. We need to find out the names of the other Royalist leaders."

"Omar," Mia said again in a warning tone.

Intimidating the guy wouldn't hurt anything, he decided. The hotel that loomed before them was a tall, white elegant building with ornate balcony rails on the upper levels. Omar bypassed the valet parking and drove down the adjacent ramp to the hotel to park. The underground parking lot was well lit, which Omar decided was to his advantage. He was out of the truck and opening Mia's door before she could open it herself.

"I'll push my hair behind my ears when I'm ready for you to make an appearance," Mia said. "You work on syncing his phone to yours and downloading his contacts and files."

"All right," Omar said. He didn't know how patient he could be. "I'll be the guy behind the potted plant."

Mia laughed and tugged Omar's hands toward her and wrapped them around her waist. "Relax, we're close."

Omar buried his face in her neck, breathing her in. "After this, I need to check in on my mother. See how she's doing."

"We will," Mia said. "Then we'll contact Naim and Leyla. Hopefully they're making progress."

Omar lifted his head and brushed a kiss against her lips. "As soon as I introduce myself to Baris, get hotel security. Find something to convince security to hold him until the police come. I don't want this guy sending out any warnings to Bata."

Mia nodded and squeezed Omar's hand, then released him and walked toward the hotel's side entrance. Omar waited a couple of seconds after she disappeared inside before he followed.

The scent of stale cigarettes and cool air greeted him as he stepped inside the hotel. Two hallways down from the entrance, and he reached the marbled tiles of the lobby. Clusters of chairs and, unsurprisingly, many potted plants in metal pots decorated the area. At the far end was a long reception desk with two dark-jacketed men manning the counter.

The lobby was surprisingly busy. Several groups of men stood or sat, drinking Turkish coffee and smoking e-cigarettes. It took only a moment for him to spot Mia approaching a man who stood before a marbled fireplace with his hands clasped behind his back. Omar moved behind the potted plant as the man turned at Mia's greeting.

Baris Uzuner was a tall man with hunched shoulders. His gray suit was rumpled, and the white turban he wore did nothing for his grayish complexion. The man did not look healthy, and something within Omar triumphed in that.

He wished he could overhear the conversation between Mia and Baris. She stood with him by the fireplace mantle, and Omar could only see her profile as Mia set to explaining something. Baris shook his head more than once, then Mia folded her arms. The side of his face reddened while Mia kept her stance.

Baris pulled out his cell phone, still shaking his head. He powered up the phone in response to something Mia said.

Omar quickly opened the app on his phone that would connect to Baris's phone and sync to it. As long as Baris's phone was active and in close range, Omar could download his contacts and sync with his email.

Whenever a password prompt came up, Omar would activate the administration override through the synching app. He loved technology.

Baris turned off his phone, and Omar released a breath, hoping he'd retrieved enough information to lock away the man for the rest of his life. If a handful of murders didn't do it, then perhaps conspiracy against the Turkish government would.

Abruptly Baris turned from Mia and hurried through the lobby, toward the back entrance that Omar had first come through. Mia's dark eyes searched out Omar's potted-plant hiding place, panic in her gaze. He stepped into view and gave her a nod, then followed after Baris's quick strides.

He'd detain Baris until Mia could get security alerted, but he wasn't promising to be nice about it.

By the time Baris pushed his way through the glass door leading to the parking lot, Omar had caught up with him. Baris must have sensed an angry man practically breathing down his neck because he looked behind him as he took his first step outside.

Omar didn't give Baris time to register who might or might not be following him. He threw a shoulder against Baris, knocking him off balance, and slamming him into the outside wall of the hotel. Omar gripped Baris's neck with his right hand and drew his pistol out with his left.

"Do I know you?" Baris said in a rasp, his eyes bulging in the garish lamplight.

"My name's Omar," he said. "But you can call me Mr. Zagouri."

The color drained from Baris's face. "I—I just spoke with your antiques dealer, and—"

"Shut up," Omar growled. "I know everything—about the men you are killing, about my name on your freakish genealogical chart, about the thug you sent to torture my mother. I've forgiven a lot of things in my life, but I can't forgive that."

Baris had the gall to try to twist out of Omar's grasp. Omar cocked the pistol, and Baris went absolutely still. "So you do value your life," Omar said, keeping a firm hold on Baris's throat. "I thought you had a death wish."

"Please . . . ," Baris said in a pathetic whine. "I can get you what you want for your collection."

Omar barked a laugh. "You think I'm a *collector* on the side? I work for the Israeli government putting away people like you. At least that's my day job." If possible, the man's eyes went even wider. Omar lifted the pistol so it was eye level with Baris. "My current night job is to avenge my mother." It would be so easy to crush this man's throat or to shoot him, to make him pay for what he'd done. Because of Baris, Omar's mother had almost died.

"I didn't—it wasn't supposed to—"

"You still don't have permission to speak," Omar ground out. "It's a shame we share relatives a few hundred years back, but that doesn't give you any claim to me now."

Baris blinked slowly, his eyes reddening. He let out a shuddering breath.

"The Turkish Royalists will be reduced to nothing more than a men's club who drink and gamble together, if there are any threads still left after I expose you," Omar said, thinking he could make this man suffer more this way, instead of a simple death. "It will be a pleasure to watch the media frenzy."

"You don't understand," Baris cut in.

Brave, thought Omar. Also, what was taking Mia so long?

"I made a mistake . . . please . . . we can do this together," Baris continued. "We can share in the triumph of bringing back our mother country to its rightful monarchy. We can rule together as brothers, as comrades. We can have all the power we've ever dreamed of."

"You're a sick man," Omar said, as if he'd ever team up with a man as despicable as Baris. He tightened his grip on Baris's neck, making his face flush red.

The back door to the hotel burst open, and two security guards ran out, Mia behind them.

"Omar," Mia said, and in that one word he heard relief and fear. He'd told her he wouldn't kill the man, so what was she afraid of?

"Are the police on their way?" he asked.

"They are," one of the security guards said, grasping Baris's arm while the other guard grabbed his other arm.

The man sucked in a desperate breath as Omar reluctantly removed his hand from his neck, then lowered his gun.

"He has some of my property," Mia said, stepping forward, and snatching the phone from Baris's pocket.

"There are no guns at the hotel," one of the security guards informed Omar.

"Good to know," Omar said simply, pocketing his gun. He exhaled slowly steadying his breath. "Search this man then."

Baris's gaze met Omar's, and Omar didn't know if he'd ever seen such a deep well of hatred directed at him. If he was to admit it to himself, it was a bit unnerving. But he could well match it. "How close are the police?" Omar asked Mia.

A siren sounded before Mia could answer, and moments later, three police cars pulled around the hotel. At least something had gone right tonight.

"I've got this," Mia said in a quiet voice, touching his arm. "I'll meet you at the truck."

She could read him like a neon sign, Omar decided. It was hard to just walk away, leave Baris to the cops, but he had no choice now. With a final look at Baris, he headed toward his truck, past the police who were rushing toward the security guards. Omar leaned against the passenger side of the truck until Mia finished writing up various charges for the police to look into. He was gratified when he saw the police handcuff Baris and lead him away.

It seemed they'd taken Mia seriously, and Omar would make sure his father was one of those who called the police department and filed more charges.

"You all right?" Mia asked, walking up to Omar.

One of the police cars had remained, while the other two left, one with Baris in the back seat.

"Yeah, you?"

"Let's get out of here," Mia said with a shiver. Her gaze said it all. She was worried about *him*.

Omar climbed in the truck and started the engine. "You think we could swap cars with that policeman?"

Mia leaned her head back on the seat and turned to look at him. "Let's just find a hotel . . . a different one, and crash." She looked over at him. "Talk to me."

He put the truck into gear and drove out of the parking lot. "I could have killed him with my bare hands," he said. "Didn't even need the gun."

She nodded. "I'm glad you didn't."

He slammed his palm against the steering wheel. "I'm not sure I am."

She scooted over and leaned her head on his shoulder. "You will be when this is all over. I hear Turkish prisons are a nightmare."

"Hm." Omar went quiet. A few moments later, Mia busied herself searching through Baris's phone.

Omar turned the next corner, cringing as the truck's brakes squealed. "I'll find a place to ditch this thing when we get a room." His phone buzzed, surprising him. Only his father and Mia had his number. And Naim.

He snatched the phone and held it in his line of vision. The text was longer than just a quick read and from a number he didn't recognize. "Here, read this," he told Mia.

She took the phone. "It's from Leyla."

Omar looked over at her. "What's going on?"

"*N's father has locked us in a room. We are breaking out, but we need to be picked up from the island. Track this number for our location. We're leaving N's phone behind —L*"

Omar slammed his palm on the steering wheel for the second time. "I should have never let Naim take that woman there. Now she's in danger. How do they expect me to get them out? It's a private island with more security than North Korea."

Mia scoffed, shaking her head. "I don't know."

"Can you trace her number?" Omar asked.

"Yep," Mia said, typing something in his phone.

Omar turned left at the next intersection, away from the approaching hotel. "It looks like we'll be taking this truck to the airport."

Mia's head snapped up. "We're going to the island, now?"

"I don't have much love for Naim, but I've started to respect him. And of course Leyla is an innocent. If anyone can bring down his father, it's Naim himself." He flashed a smile at Mia. "It might be a glorious thing to watch."

"Hm." Mia didn't seem too excited about a good old father-son showdown. Maybe Omar had watched too many American westerns.

"I guess you have your credit card with you if we're going to catch a flight?" she asked, finally returning her gaze to the road.

"Commercial jets don't fly to that island," Omar said. "We'll have to charter something. Did you bring a credit card by chance?"

"Yes, but both of our cards won't be enough."

"We just need a down payment," Omar said.

Mia pulled up the map icon on the phone. "The island is only a few miles off the coast, but a boat would give them too much warning."

"And it's practically hidden at night," Omar said. "Mr. Bata keeps few lights visible."

"Wow," Mia said, looking at Baris's phone. "He just got a text. From 'AB.'"

"What does it say?" Omar asked.

"*If you know the location of Omar Zagouri, contact me ASAP,*" Mia read. "Who do you think sent it?"

Omar went silent for a moment. "Naim's father is Adem Bata." He met Mia's gaze. "Do you think it's possible? If so, how are those two connected?"

"I think it's possible," Mia said. "How should I answer this *AB*? Omar's right next to me in this crappy truck?" Mia smiled. "Should I pretend to be Baris?"

"He'll find out soon enough about Baris's arrest. Throw him for a loop. Keep him guessing for a while."

Mia started typing, speaking aloud as she did. "*Baris was just arrested.*"

Omar turned off the main road onto the thoroughfare leading to the airport. "I wish I could see his expression right now."

The phone buzzed. "Ah." She opened the new text. "*Who is this?*"

"You could have a lot of fun with that," Omar said, glancing over at her.

Mia powered off the phone. "Maybe I can tell him when I meet him."

Omar was already shaking his head. "I'm going alone, Mia."

"Like hell you are," Mia said.

He wasn't surprised at her retort, but he'd made up his mind. He didn't have a good feeling about the Bata Island, and he wasn't entirely sure if he'd get off the island safely. "I'm going to need help from this side." He parked in short term parking and turned off the truck's engine. He handed the keys to Mia, who sat staring at him, her arms folded.

"I hate this over-protectiveness about you," Mia said. "You know I don't like being dictated to—I'm just as qualified and skilled as you are."

"I didn't say you weren't," Omar said. "I don't even know if I'll get Leyla out safely." He stared at her and she stared back.

Baris's phone buzzed, breaking up the tense moment between them.

Mia glanced down at it, her face paling. She turned the phone so that Omar could read the incoming text: *I just had an interesting conversation with my son. I think I know who you are now. You won't get away with this.*

Omar read the message twice. "Naim caved?"

"There has to be more to it than that."

Omar sent a text to Naim's phone. *What's going on?*

The reply came back seconds later. *Everything has changed. I need to get Leyla out of here asap.*

◆ CHAPTER THIRTY-FOUR ◆

CONSTANTINOPLE

AD 1521

Several female servants turned to watch as Roxelane entered with her small entourage. The Master of the Girls accompanied Roxelane, for he would be making introductions.

A couple of servant girls seemed openly curious while others turned away with feigned nonchalance. Roxelane knew they were watching her every move. She glanced around the waiting room to Ayşe Hafsa's inner chamber and took in its elegant water fountain and surrounding plants.

"Are we early?" Roxelane whispered to Verda.

"We could never be too early, but who knows how long we'll be kept waiting?" Verda motioned for Roxelane to take a seat on a nearby bench. The frame of the bench had been plated in gold and the cushion covered with silk damask.

There was no way she could relax, no matter how long she had to sit and wait. Kaan stood sentinel by the bench, and finally Verda sat as well.

The sun was well up in the sky and the room getting too warm, when the outer door finally opened. It was clear that the mistress had just arrived. All the female servants turned toward her and bowed.

Roxelane followed suit and rose from the bench, only to kneel and bow before the woman who'd entered the room. When at last Roxelane raised her eyes, she was surprised by the woman's beauty. Her cheekbones were high and her neck elegant and smooth. Her eyes were large, set beneath thinly arched brows which gave her face an open look. She wore a silk turban wrapped around her head, set back from the dark, curly hair framing her face and forehead.

The woman's gaze settled on Roxelane with indifference, or was she just controlling her true thoughts? She lifted a thin, honey-skinned, jeweled hand toward Roxelane, who understood she needed to cross to Hafsa and kiss her hand.

All eyes were on Roxelane as she walked across the floor, moved past the fountain, and bowed over the woman's extended hand.

"Ayşe Hafsa Sultan, it's an honor to meet you," Roxelane said, as she'd been coached by the Master of the Girls. She was not to speak to Hafsa after her initial greeting unless the woman asked her a direct question. "I am at your bidding."

The woman touched Roxelane's chin and raised it, turning her face to one side then the other as she studied her face.

Heat bloomed in Roxelane's cheeks, but she kept steady as she underwent inspection.

"You still have the sun's curse from the caravan journey," Hafsa said.

Roxelane knew enough not to reply until she was asked a question. She'd kept out of the sun as much as possible on the caravan, but it had been difficult to do so completely.

The woman grasped her arm and turned it over. "Your skin needs softening. Have you been bathing and using oils in the harem court?"

"A few times," Roxelane answered.

"We will put you through a twice daily regimen," Hafsa declared. And as if she'd given a command, two of the female servants scurried away. Hafsa reached for Roxelane's hair and unwound it from its twist. "The damaged ends will need to be cut off."

Roxelane hoped that would entail very little.

Hafsa released her hair and walked around Roxelane three times. Then she stopped in front of her and said, "Once we have your physical appearance corrected, we will teach you to read and write Turkish."

"I can already read and write Turkish."

Hafsa snapped her head up and stared into Roxelane's eyes.

Too late, Roxelane realized she'd spoken when not questioned. "I alone will determine when you can read and write Turkish satisfactorily. You will learn the laws of the government and the laws of the land. You will also learn how to aid the sultan in his needs."

Clearly, everyone in the room could see embarrassment staining her face.

"You are a virgin?" Hafsa asked.

It was a question, and Roxelane needed to answer it, but her breath was still short from her previous mistake. "I . . . I am a virgin," she affirmed.

She thought she heard one of the servant girls giggle. But Roxelane stood straight, knowing that her virgin status would be a very important attribute if she were to bear the sultan's children and not be questioned.

Hafsa's expression softened the smallest bit, although her gaze remained stoic. "No one enters the sultan's private chambers without my permission or knowledge. There are never any exceptions." She looked past Roxelane, then back to her, as if having just decided something. "You will abide by this rule or face execution."

Roxelane wanted to ask what would happen if the sultan sent for her, and Hafsa was not informed. Would she face the same judgment then? But she could not make another mistake. Not when the woman standing before her noticed every single thing.

"And now," Hafsa said, clapping her hands together. "We begin."

Roxelane was led from the waiting room, out of Hafsa's presence and into a private bathing chamber. Roxelane marveled at the exquisite stone columns that stretched from the steaming pool of water. Eunuchs were positioned around the pool, their eyes heavy as if they'd spent hour upon hour in the steamy interior, which perhaps they did.

Verda and one of Hafsa's servants undressed Roxelane, and she was instructed to walk into the water and soak.

It might have been relaxing had Roxelane not had an audience, and not worried about making another mistake. When the bathing ritual was over, she dressed in a soft linen robe and accepted tea brought by one of Hafsa's servants. Before she could take a sip, Verda said, "Let me taste it first to ensure that it's not poisoned."

Roxelane threw Verda a sharp glance. "Am I not safe in the sultan's mother's household?"

"Maybe less so than ever," Verda said in a low voice. She glanced at the servant, who was already walking away. "I will taste all of your food and drink until we know who we can trust."

Roxelane handed over the teacup to Verda, who took a careful sip. After a few moments, she said, "I've had no adverse effects. You may drink the tea."

It tasted of a woodsy herb that Roxelane was not familiar with. She drank the rest of the tea, then walked with Verda into a partitioned dressing room where she sat on a cushioned bench and Verda brushed her hair dry. The dressing room was bright with sunshine that spilled from high windows. Mirrors decorated the walls, and two small tables contained bottles of kohl.

Roxelane closed her eyes as Verda combed through her long hair, letting the motion soothe her unsteady nerves. Soon she'd be meeting with Hafsa again, and she would have to try to be perfect in every way. Kaan brought in a tunic made from the softest silk, dyed in blues and greens.

"It's beautiful," Roxelane told Kaan. "Where did it come from?"

"The sultan, of course," Kaan said with a wink. "You will have a wardrobe . . . fit for a queen."

Roxelane's face warmed at the implication. "You should not say such things here," she whispered. "We are never alone."

"Then I'll have to keep my predictions to a whisper."

As she dressed with the help of Kaan and Verda, he said in a quiet voice, "I have sent for the allamah. It's best that you go through your conversion as soon as possible. Then Hafsa can have no complaint if the sultan calls for you before you're trained."

Roxelane nodded. Inside, her emotions were spinning. She already knew she would have to convert, heart and soul to Islam, but to think it would be today . . . "Tell me of Islam, and tell me about the conversion ceremony."

Kaan spoke in low, soothing tones, telling her about the new commitments she'd be undertaking and explaining the five principles of Islam. She knew he was a convert, and it had enriched his life and enabled him to serve the sultan. Roxelane wanted the same for herself. Kaan placed a hand on her shoulder. "You are making the right decision. Embrace the good in Islam and you won't be led astray."

"Thank you," she whispered. She still had more to learn about the Islamic religion and what her duties would be, but if she was to rise in the sultan's estimation, this was a necessary step.

"Sit down, and I'll place your veil," Kaan said.

She sat on a plush chair, and her tunic fell in beautiful waves about her body. She watched her reflection in the mirror as Kaan tied a delicate blue scarf about her head, artfully arranging it so that the dark of her hair framed her face, the total effect haloed in blue.

"The veil brings focus to your eyes, and accentuates your cheeks," Verda said. "You make a very pretty Islamic concubine."

"Wife," Kaan whispered with a grin.

Roxelane gazed at her reflection and straightened her shoulders. By converting to Islam, she'd keep her head covered in public as well. Verda came to stand by her side, and together the two women gazed at their reflections.

"I am ready," Roxelane said.

Verda nodded and brushed at her eyes, then turned to Kaan. "You have been wise to call the allamah so early."

"Come, he should be here by now."

They walked together out of the dressing room, passed the bathing section, and walked back into the courtyard where Roxelane had first met Hafsa.

She was there, speaking to the Master of the Girls, along with a man dressed in a long robe and turban.

Roxelane realized he must be the allamah. His eyes moved to her as soon as she walked into the room. His gaze was sharp as he scanned her attire, then he gave a slight nod, and turned back to Hafsa.

Roxelane stood in the middle of the room, near the flowing fountain, as she waited for the allamah to approach her. At last, he turned from Hafsa and the Master of the Girls, and crossed the room. Again, Roxelane felt all eyes on her, but she kept her chin lifted, and her back straight.

"I am Allamah Polat," he said. "Are you ready?"

"Yes," Roxelane said.

Just before Allamah Polat started the ceremony, a door opened on the far side, and several male servants stepped inside, followed by the sultan.

Immediately, all those in the room dropped into bows. Roxelane followed suit, her heart thundering at the sultan's sudden presence. Did he come to speak with his mother? Did he know Roxelane was within these chambers?

As she came out of her bow, she discovered that his gaze was solely on her. She wasn't sure if she was breathing, and as he walked toward her, she was certain she was not.

"I have arrived just in time, I see," the sultan said, his gaze flickering toward Allamah Polat, then back to Roxelane, so she knew he was speaking to her.

"Yes," she said, wondering if her breathless excitement showed in her voice. Would the sultan's mother approve of her eagerness? Would she think she was only converting to be a part of the sultan's household?

It was true on the one hand, but on the other, Roxelane had forsaken her old life, her old name, and now her old religion. She would make the conversion complete today, and she would have to make it a true conversion in her heart, as well.

The sultan grasped her hand and brought it to his lips. Although not a sound was made by the other women in the room, Roxelane could hear their inward gasps. Then he stepped back and nodded to the allamah, who began the ceremony. Allamah Polat turned to Roxelane and said, "Do you believe in the principles of Islam?"

Roxelane nodded.

"Please state your beliefs."

Nerves thrummed through Roxelane as she began, repeating the words that Kaan had reviewed with her. "I believe that the Holy Quran is the literal word of God, revealed by Him. I believe that the Judgment Day is true and will come. I believe in the prophets that God sent and the books He revealed, and in His angels. I will worship only God."

"Do you accept Islam as your true religion?"

"I do," Roxelane said in a soft voice.

"Recite the Shahada, your testimony of faith," Allamah Polat said.

"I testify," Roxelane said, "there is no true god but Allah, and I testify that Muhammad is the messenger of Allah." She bowed to Allamah Polat, then couldn't help but look over at the sultan. He was smiling at her. In that smile, she saw more promise than she'd ever dare to hope for herself. It was as if everyone else in the room faded into the tapestries.

And then those assembled began to approach her and welcome her formally to Islam. She accepted their good wishes. It was a heady moment, almost as if they were a married couple receiving congratulations.

Hafsa approached with one of her servants and spoke with the sultan, then said to Roxelane, "Welcome to Islam." she leaned in and kissed Roxelane's cheek.

Past Hafsa, Roxelane caught a glimpse of Verda smiling. Roxelane knew the moment of triumph would last only a short time. She still had much to learn.

"Has Roxelane been shown her quarters?" the sultan asked his mother.

"She has only recently arrived; we will take her to them soon."

The sultan nodded and turned to speak with Allamah Polat.

Hafsa introduced the servant next to her. "I am assigning Tuana to you so that she might orient your servants in our ways. She'll keep you informed of your schedule, and she'll take you to your quarters."

The woman was perhaps Roxelane's age, and her eyes radiated intelligence. Tuana bowed to Roxelane. "I will take you there now if you'd like."

It was a relief, and Roxelane had much she needed to absorb. Since before the sun rose, she'd been making drastic changes.

She nodded to the sultan and thanked Hafsa before leaving, then with Verda and Kaan, she followed Tuana out of the courtyard. They walked along a series of corridors until they reached another courtyard. This courtyard was a smaller and plainer version of Hafsa's, and there was no fountain in the center of the room.

She pointed to the three doors on the other side of the room and said, "This courtyard and those three rooms belong to you. They are furnished, although there may be some dust."

Roxelane walked into the center of the courtyard, and plain as it might be, it was still extravagant to her. Most important, she had her own household.

"We must make a list of repairs," Verda said, as she walked around the outer edges of the room to inspect the walls, a couple of the tapestries, and one of the benches.

Kaan moved past the women and opened all three doors on the other side of the courtyard. Roxelane joined him, and standing in the doorway of the first room, she saw it was a bedchamber.

Dust or no dust, it was magnificent. The deep blue and gold damask covering on the large bed glittered in the sunlight that came from two huge windows on the east side of the room. Delicate sofas and tables were artfully arranged, and one set was situated before a fireplace.

Roxelane walked across the thick rugs to the windows that were taller than she. The view was breathtaking. The sultan's mosque dominated the view, and the crystal blue sky surrounding the elegant spires made the building look like the entrance to paradise. Something shifted in Roxelane as she realized she now belonged to the people who attended that mosque. She was now a part of Islam and would worship as they did.

The next room was a dining room. A table with six chairs sat in the middle. Plush chairs surrounded another fireplace. And a sideboard had been set with platters of food. The third room was a receiving room of sorts with a credenza and chair on one side, then more sofas and chairs arranged throughout.

"Here you'll meet with the tutor and learn to write Turkish," Tuana said, coming into the room after Roxelane.

"I will not attend lessons with the other harem women?" Roxelane asked. The Master of the Girls assigned certain harem women to the palace's university.

"In the beginning, no," Tuana said. "Her Highness wants you to become trained first so that you don't make foolish mistakes in front of others."

Roxelane decided not to take offense. If she had to take university lessons with the other harem women, then waiting might be a good thing.

"We will start to clean the rooms today," Tuana said with another bow. "We did not have much notice of your arrival."

"I understand," Roxelane said.

Tuana let a small smile appear. "But first we'll eat."

Roxelane could make no argument there, her hunger overrode any protest. Verda sat with her and tasted the food first. Rice pilaf and steaming eggplant were served, and as Roxelane finished her meal, Tuana brought in a young man wearing a white turban.

"This is Ali," Tuana announced. "He is your new tutor."

The young man seemed to be a few years younger than Tuana, and as he stepped forward to greet Roxelane, she noticed he dragged his left foot. He must have some sort of deformity or injury, she thought, but any concerns for his ability to teach were swept away from the moment he began to tell her of the history of the Turkish language.

He told her the origins of Turkish were thousands of years old, and the oldest written Turkish could be seen on stone monuments in Central Asia dating back more than two thousand years. The Turkish spoken in the Ottoman Empire had been refined by Sultan Valed and the famed poet Gulsehri.

Roxelane listened closely, interested that a poet had helped to develop Ottoman Turkish. When Ali finished reciting the language's history, Roxelane said, "I would like Verda to do our lesson along with me. That way I can make sure I'm practicing correctly."

Ali bowed his head. He brought out pieces of fine paper from his satchel and spread them on the desk, then set two inkpots and three quills on the table, as well. Ali sat at the table and proceeded to write the letters of the alphabet, and he asked Roxelane to repeat each letter as he went.

As they worked, several servants came in, introduced by Tuana as servants to her household. The women started to vigorously clean the room. As Ali worked with Roxelane, and Verda mimicked the lesson, Roxelane quickly realized she knew more than she thought.

Ali seemed pleased with her work and offered only a few corrections. "You have an artistic hand," he said. "Are you an artist?"

"No," Roxelane said, her face heating at the compliment. The people in her village didn't have time for luxuries such as drawing and painting. There was always a field to plow or a cow to milk.

By the time Ali concluded his lesson and was satisfied that Roxelane was writing each letter of the Turkish alphabet to perfection, he put the stoppers on the inkpots and straightened them. "Tomorrow, we'll copy some of the sultan's poems that he's had distributed to the public. I think that will please him if you are able to write his poems."

Roxelane warmed. It was as if Ali was trying to help her in more ways than just performing his job. "I would love that," she said sincerely.

Ali bowed to her, then made his exit.

"I like him," she said to Verda after he left.

Verda brought her finger to her lips, then cast a sideways glance at the three servant girls who were taking down tapestries in the room to be beaten with a dust paddle.

Roxelane gave a nod, then linked arms with Verda as they left the room. In the courtyard, Kaan was instructing some of the servants to clean the windows.

"Am I to be wary of Ali?" Roxelane asked Verda in a quiet voice.

"It's best to be wary of everyone," Verda said. "You are too generous with your trust and your words. Any of those servant girls could be eyes and ears for Hafsa, or even one of the other wives."

Roxelane felt the warmth drain from her face. "But they're assigned to my household, right?"

"Yes, but that doesn't mean they are loyal to *you*," Verda whispered. "At least not yet. It may change with time as you become more firmly established in the sultan's favor. Pretty soon, they might be spying for you."

"Spying?" Roxelane said, although she knew there would be a benefit to knowing the goings-on of the other women and their households. Perhaps if she'd had her own spies, the episode with the snake could have been averted.

"You have been elevated over many other beautiful women who have been vying for privileges long before you arrived."

"Will I always be the foreigner?" Roxelane asked.

Verda met her gaze, sure and true. "Yes. And now more so than ever. The women will use every argument they can to ostracize you and to influence the other wives against you. This will also extend to the sultan's mother."

"It seems no one commands Hafsa except for the sultan," Roxelane said in a thoughtful tone, looking around at the others milling about. She met Kaan's gaze from across the courtyard, and he started walking toward her.

"Exactly. And that is why we need to be very careful in what we say around the servants. Hafsa has immense power. And in some matters, she can wield great influence over the sultan—she will state her case as being for the good of the kingdom." Verda's voice lowered as Kaan neared them. "Remember, the sultan is married first to his country. Allegiance to his mother comes next, and you are down the list in priorities from there."

"What list of priorities?" Kaan said, coming to stand by them, having overheard Verda's last whispered sentence.

Verda blinked innocently at Kaan.

"You can't keep secrets from me, you know. Roxelane will just confess all when you're gone."

Roxelane laughed. "Verda was schooling me on keeping my opinions to myself at all times."

"And all comments and all thoughts," Verda said. "At least to others except for me and Kaan."

Kaan nodded, a smile quirking his face. "She's right." His expression grew sober. "We have come this high, which means there is a good ways to fall." As if on cue, the doors at the end of the courtyard opened, and Hafsa stepped inside.

Roxelane couldn't be more surprised, but then again, she shouldn't have been surprised at all. She'd completed the tutoring session, and Hafsa probably didn't want the new concubine spending a moment in rest.

The woman scanned the courtyard, before allowing her discerning gaze to settle on Roxelane.

Roxelane bowed before her and waited for the woman to speak.

"Ali reports that you are a swift learner and accomplished with the quill," Hafsa said. "Yet you have never drawn nor painted."

Roxelane detected a note of condescension. She waited for the question, but it never came. Only a command.

"This afternoon you will meet with an art instructor to begin drawing lessons."

The statement was so unexpected that Roxelane found herself looking over at Kaan and Verda. She immediately knew it was a mistake. A concubine, or a woman with her own household, never looked to servants for advice or approval.

Hafsa clearly noticed. Her eyes were like daggers, piercing Roxelane's very center.

"I will dismiss any servant who is afforded too many privileges. The sultan selects only the finest to serve in his household."

Roxelane nodded, because again, she had not been asked a question. Yet she'd been sufficiently warned.

Hafsa strode to the servants scrubbing the windows. "This place is shameful. It should not have been allowed to get so filthy." The servants shrank away from her words and only started scrubbing harder and faster.

She walked across the corridor and looked into each of the three rooms, calling out sharp commands to the servants who were cleaning within. Then she crossed to stand before Roxelane again. "You have much to do to clean up your slothfulness. Know that neither I nor the sultan will stand for anything less than perfection."

Roxelane could have argued with her, could have told her about the kindness her son had shown Roxelane when she was a shackled, rag-dressed slave. But she kept her thoughts wisely silent and only bowed before Hafsa—a woman Roxelane hoped would one day be her mother-in-law.

◆ CHAPTER THIRTY-FIVE ◆

BATA ISLAND

The door slammed open, and Leyla raised her hands to prevent the door from hitting her face. It drilled into her arms, but the pain didn't stop Leyla from running with Naim as he grabbed her hand and pulled her into the corridor.

The guard who'd enter the room spun on his heels and followed.

Leyla's stomach plummeted as a shot rang out, and she realized it had been directed at them. As they continued running down the corridor, Naim pointed his gun straight at the man and returned fire. She couldn't look at where the bullet had landed, but she heard the man's grunt and the thud when he hit the floor.

"In here," Naim hissed, opening another door. He practically shoved Leyla inside, and she stumbled against something in the dark room. It took her a moment to realize she was in a closet of sorts.

"Don't move," Naim said. "I'll be back to get you." And then he was gone.

When Leyla's breathing had finally steadied, she realized she hadn't heard any commotion for several moments, and her heartbeat seemed to tick down the seconds. She'd eventually be discovered, she knew. She could only speculate on what might be happening to Naim. Was he facing down his father right now? Or something worse? The guards had shot at them . . . as if they'd been intruders, not the son of Mr. Bata.

The ping of her cell phone startled her, and she looked at the glowing screen to see Omar's text. *I'm flying in to get you. Relocate to someplace near the runway. I won't be able to stay long enough to search. Naim is on his own. I'll be out of touch for about an hour, then look for me.*

The message shot daggers into her chest. How was she supposed to get to the runway, and how could she leave Naim on this island as a prisoner of his father?

She read the message from Omar again and knew she had to act soon. The island airport was a kilometer away, and Leyla wasn't sure how she'd get there without being captured. She let out a ragged breath and climbed to her feet. Using her phone light, she found the door knob and leaned against the door for a few moments. She couldn't hear anything in the hallway, but that didn't mean there wasn't a guard watching and waiting.

Slowly opening the door, she peered out in the hallway. The brightness surprised her since she hadn't seen light coming beneath the door. She looked toward one end of the hall and the door leading to the outside, and then down the other end in the direction of Naim's room.

Leyla exhaled, weighing her options. Surely the guards would see her as soon as she stepped through the exterior door. Maybe she could go into one of the bedrooms and escape out the window if they weren't all electronically locked. Naim had called his room a fortress, surprised at the security changes from his last visit. She blinked against her bleary eyes. They'd come all this way, taken all this risk, and Naim was probably being threatened by his father right now . . . They'd never get the letters, and Mr. Bata would continue pushing forward his agenda to overthrow the government. And all of that didn't take into account what would happen to her.

A thought pushed its way to the front of her mind. Words that Naim had spoken about the Ottoman vases being in a location he didn't recognize, and how his room had been turned into a fortress in his absence. His father's suggestion that Leyla stay in the blue room.

Leyla's breath came short as she turned over the possibility that Mr. Bata was storing the vases inside Naim's bedroom. Before Leyla could connect the thoughts spiraling in her mind, she set off down the hallway toward Naim's room. She knew that at any moment she could be seen, but she couldn't stay in a closet. The bedroom door was still open, and a breeze blew into the room from the window that Naim had broken.

She worked quickly, checking under the bed, pulling out the desk from the wall, running her hands along the bookshelves. Then she stopped. She hurried into the bathroom and opened the linen closet, then pushed aside the towels. Nothing. She thought through places that could act as a hiding location in a single bedroom. Her mind went to the blue room where she was supposed to stay. His father said it was down the hall from Naim's.

She exited Naim's room, looking down the corridor to make sure it was empty. Then she started trying one door after another. She found another closet and a guest bathroom, then opened the door to what was clearly the blue room. Even with the light coming in from the hallway, she saw that the carpet was a pale blue, and a floral blue bedspread covered the bed. Beyond the bed, it appeared that the curtains were blue as well.

Leyla stepped into the room and closed the door behind her, then turned on the light. She worked quickly, inspecting every part of the room just as she had Naim's. One addition this room had as opposed to Naim's was a thick headboard. She tugged the bed away from the wall, but it was too heavy to move very far. So she sat on the ground and used the strength of her legs to budge the bed, bit by bit. When it was about a foot away from the wall, she peered at the space between the wall and the headboard.

Her heart thumped at the sight. There was an open square, as if someone had cut away the plaster board. She positioned her legs again, and pushed with a groan, moving the bed more so that she had room to slide sideways through the space.

Her breath stuck in her throat as she reached into the opening of the wall and pulled out a black hard-sided suitcase. She set it on the floor. Popping the clasps, she lifted the lid to see three vases lined up in carved-out foam.

She lifted the first vase and slid out a set of rolled-up letters. She did the same with the next vase. The third vase was empty. Her hands went still as something sounded in the hall. She wasn't sure if it was a voice or other sounds, her heart had been beating so loud. She rolled all the letters together and put them back into one of the vases, then tucked the vase beneath her jacket, using her arm to anchor it close to her body. She'd come this far. She was either all in or all out.

She waited breathlessly, listening for more sounds in the hallway, but when all was silent, she opened the door. The hallway was empty, so she stole back into Naim's room.

Moments later, she'd tugged the bedspread from Naim's bed and set it over the jagged window sill. She climbed out the window and dropped to the ground in a crouch, keeping the vase hidden inside her jacket.

Her head pounded, her mouth was dry, and her legs were shaking, but she forced herself to scan the dark courtyard that was punctuated by the occasional light. She had to get out of the compound and back to the airport. As her breathing began to steady, she noticed more and more about the buildings surrounding her. Not all corners and alleys were lit, although she suspected there were plenty of motion detector lights. She would just have to move fast.

Leyla crept out from below the window sill and ran hunched over alongside the wall until she reached a pool of light that shone down from the corner of the building. The light edged a row of bushes, and

she took shelter behind them for several moments, watching and waiting. At the far end of the courtyard a guard stepped into view. The only
thing distinguishable about his dark form was the glow of a cigarette
butt hanging from his mouth.

"Where are you, Naim?" Leyla whispered to herself. When the
guard moved on, she did too. She rounded the building and was dis-
heartened to come face-to-face with a massive wall. Feeling along the
smooth stone grooves, she knew she'd never be able to find purchase,
even if she were a skilled rock climber. Returning the other way, she'd
risk being spotted by the guard.

She texted Omar, knowing he wouldn't get it right away. He was
probably flying in the skies right now. *I don't think I can get out of the
courtyard. It's only a matter of time before I'm discovered.*

Leyla huddled in the corner, wedging herself between the wall and
the building. She was literally at a dead end. Trapped until she was
spotted by a guard or the sun came up, putting her in plain view of the
entire compound.

She closed her eyes, thinking about her family. Her parents. Would
she ever see them again? She didn't know what the chances were of
Naim getting her out of this place safely, when he, himself, had been
captured.

Leyla didn't know if she'd fallen asleep, but she was startled to con-
sciousness when a low thrumming vibrated through her. She opened her
eyes, knowing something was different. Rising to her feet, and ignoring
the sharp ache in her knees and back from her huddled position, she
listened carefully.

It sounded like a helicopter, and the noise was getting louder.

Her stomach turned over, and her heart leapt in hope. As the noise
increased to an almost deafening sound, she covered her ears and gazed
up into the sky. Moments later, the black helicopter flew over the wall
she'd been leaning against. It veered right, then landed in the courtyard
beyond.

Leyla began to run toward it, not able to explain how she knew what she had to do.

The door of the chopper opened, and a figure in dark clothing stepped out. Leyla couldn't make out any features of the person with all the wild wind and noise. But he or she was motioning for her to get in. So she did. She climbed in, breathless, only to see Omar's smiling face looking at her from the pilot's seat.

"We've got another runner!" a woman's voice shouted. *Mia*, Leyla realized.

Leyla turned to look out the window to see a man running toward them. *Naim*.

And right behind him, two other men, closing in.

Leyla pressed her hand against the window and yelled, "Hurry! Run!"

"Buckle yourself in, Leyla," Omar shouted back at her. "It's going to be rough."

Naim practically dove into the helicopter, scurried toward her, and Mia slammed the passenger side door shut. The helicopter lifted then tilted hard, then lifted some more. Naim slid into Leyla, trying to right himself.

"Are you all right?" she asked him.

He looked up at her, breathing hard. One of his eyes was swollen shut. "When I heard the helicopter, I knew I had to try and make it too."

"Everyone hang on," Omar called out. The helicopter pitched sideways again, and Naim slid away from Leyla.

He scrambled for purchase, then strapped himself into the seat behind Omar. Finally, buckled in, Naim stopped sliding. He turned to Leyla and looked her over. "You're all right?"

"I am," she said. "I was worried about you."

Naim winced, and she didn't know if it was from her comment or because he was in pain.

The helicopter pitched again, and Leyla swayed against Naim. He grabbed her hand and squeezed. "I can't tell you how glad I am to see you."

Below them, gun fire erupted, and Leyla gasped.

"They're too far away," Mia said. "I'm surprised they didn't shoot earlier."

"Mr. Bata must not be ready to disown his son just yet," Omar said, glancing at them, then turning his focus back to flying the helicopter.

"Mr. Bata is definitely going to disown me," Naim said in a dry tone. He pointed to his swollen eye. "This is no love tap."

"Is that how you got away?" Leyla asked.

"No," Naim said. He went quiet for a moment as the helicopter buzzed over the trees of the island. "When I heard the helicopter, I . . . uh, took action against one of the guards. My father just stood there and watched. He didn't move, didn't say anything when I opened the door unimpeded. But . . . I've never seen such disappointment and hatred in someone's eyes."

"He let you walk out?" Mia asked, turning from her seat to look at Naim.

"I'm still his only heir," Naim said in a rapid voice, as if trying to keep all emotion out of it. "Tradition is important to my father, handing down the business from father to son . . . Which means I'm more valuable to him alive than dead. He might have let me leave the compound, but he's not finished with me."

"He's not finished with me, either," Omar said. "Your father was texting Baris, looking for me."

Naim exhaled heavily. "I have more to tell you, Omar. I discovered that my father's name, Adem Bata, has been an alias my entire life. His true name is Sehzade Mehmed. And now that we've discovered that my father is paying Baris to kill any royal descendants, it seems that my father is clearing the way for his own rise to power."

It didn't take long for Omar to say, "Ah, so your father is the lost descendant of Mustafa. Does Baris know this?"

"I don't think so," Naim said. "Baris thinks he's following his own agenda, but he's really following my father's to clear the way for my father's rise to the throne of Turkey. Baris just doesn't know it yet."

"Wow," Omar said. "So that's what you meant by *heir*. You weren't kidding."

Naim shook his head.

"So what are you going to do?" Mia asked. "Take over from your father? Join the Turkish Royalists?"

Naim rubbed his hand across his neck. Then, looking straight at Leyla, he said, "I'm going to bring my father down. I can't stand by while he funds an assassin. It's time to put a stop to Bata Enterprises."

Even though Leyla heard him saying the words, there was no joy, no relief, no accomplishment in his eyes. Only weariness and frustration.

"Any luck finding those letters?" Omar asked, as the coastal lights of Turkey came into view.

"Not yet," Naim said. "I'm going to meet with key government officials and persuade them to open an investigation."

Leyla leaned back and removed the letters she'd folded and slipped beneath her waistband. "I found the letters."

Mia snapped her head around. "What?"

Naim was staring at her, and Leyla had to smile. "In the blue room, behind the bed." She felt heat rising to her face.

"Well, read them to us," Naim said.

Leyla looked at the letters in her hands and laughed. "What if they aren't what we've been looking for?"

Mia turned and shone her phone light so that Leyla could read the script. It was the same beautiful script from the other letters—the same writer—Roxelane. Leyla took a deep breath and began to translate.

❖ CHAPTER THIRTY-SIX ❖

CONSTANTINOPLE

AD 1521

"The sultan will visit your quarters tonight," Hafsa announced, and the chatter of women in her courtyard stilled.

Roxelane said nothing. She could not, although her face had surely bloomed red at Hafsa's very public announcement. Over the past few weeks, Roxelane had hoped for this very occurrence, as she accustomed herself to her new activities and duties. Still, she wanted advice. She couldn't wait to be alone with Verda to ask what she should prepare for, what to expect.

But apparently, Hafsa had decided to give her that counsel herself, in front of any who happened to be in the courtyard at the present time. Surely within the hour, it would spread into the farthest reaches of the palace, that the sultan was visiting his new concubine for the first time.

Roxelane tried to breathe, but the air hovered just out of reach.

"He will not touch you tonight, but he will spend time with you. Relations only take place within his chamber so that the sultan can be fully protected by his guards, and no deceit occurs."

Roxelane wasn't sure what Hafsa meant by deceit.

"You are to please the sultan in everything that he wishes and desires," Hafsa continued in her firm clear voice that echoed down the corridors. "You are his concubine and have been groomed for his companionship and pleasure. The sultan is responsible for millions of people and vast amounts of land. He only has limited time to spend in these matters. It is your job to make sure his time is not wasted."

Finally, Hafsa took a breath.

Roxelane wondered if it was possible to melt straight into the tiled floor and disappear between the cracks, to forever be trodden upon by servants and royalty.

She bowed her head when it was apparent that Hafsa had completed her lecture, or was it a declaration? Surely everyone had heard it. Tonight Roxelane would be on their minds as they waited to see if the sultan left her chambers pleased.

Roxelane determined that he would be pleased.

When Hafsa finally dismissed her with the announcement that it was time to bathe before the sultan's visit, she had to stop herself from running along the corridors back to her own set of rooms.

Verda walked swiftly by her side, and Kaan followed close behind.

Once Roxelane reached the arched doorway leading to her small courtyard, she stopped, knowing that once they entered the courtyard, they'd again be surrounded by other people. "Tell me what I must do to please the sultan."

Verda gave her a reassuring smile. "Show him one of your paintings. You have improved greatly over the weeks, and it will impress him. Then if he asks to kiss you, allow him that."

A trembling started within Roxelane. "What if he wants to do more than kiss?"

"You are his concubine," Kaan whispered. "And you have been trained and groomed for many weeks now. You will obey him in all things."

"I want to obey him," Roxelane said. "But what if I make a mistake? What if he becomes upset with me?"

"That's not possible," Verda said, grasping her hand briefly, then letting go.

"Ask yourself these questions," Kaan began. "Are you stronger than he in battle?"

"Of course not," Roxelane said.

"Are you smarter than he in politics?" Kaan asked.

"No."

"Are you closer to his family than he is?"

She shook her head. "I am not."

"A man becomes softer when in the arms of a woman," Kaan said, and Verda nodded. "When a man is entranced, a woman has great power at her fingertips. If you use your power with the sultan wisely, he will desire you for a wife."

Roxelane was breathless at the very thought of it. But she did not want to seduce the sultan; she had to let him show his interest first.

It was as if Verda read her thoughts. "You are here for a reason, Roxelane. The sultan will expect to be enraptured by you, and you in turn should have your own wishes granted. This is not deception or betrayal, but an act of your love and loyalty to the sultan."

Kaan nodded and leaned in close. "In your red trunk, we have added some delicate and fine clothing that none of the servants know about. It should only be worn when you are alone with the sultan. Not even his mother should know about it."

Panic shot through Roxelane, but the footsteps of an approaching person could be heard coming down the corridor. "What is the clothing?"

"Intimates," Verda whispered, and opened the door to the courtyard.

Servants buzzed inside, cleaning the room from top to bottom.

Eyes watched her as she crossed through the courtyard, Verda and Kaan accompanying her to the bedchamber. She paused in the doorway, and Kaan said, "We'll leave you here. We don't want to be inside when the sultan arrives. It's best that he sees you alone and waiting."

Roxelane nodded and kept her hands at her sides, although she wanted to embrace them both. She stepped into her chamber and shut the door. She was alone, but she didn't know for how long. Her room had been transformed in the past few weeks, and it was as elegant as anything in Hafsa's chambers, albeit on a smaller scale.

Roxelane knew that she'd received special treatment for a concubine. Her quarters were just as nice as the rooms of the wives, and she had almost as many servants. She crossed to the painting that she'd covered and set in the corner of the room, next to a bureau. It was her first attempt at using colors on one of her drawings.

She lifted the linen covering and stood back to survey the work in the late afternoon light coming through the windows. She had painted the caravan that she'd traveled in to Constantinople. It was just before the battle had taken place, before Hatice had been killed. The colors were muted, but it was clear where the harem women were in the caravan.

Near the front, she'd painted the sultan upon his horse. It was a rough effort and missing the final details, but it was clear who the sultan was. Roxelane stared at the painting so long that she could almost smell the countryside and feel the heat of the sun on her back. Then, as her thoughts progressed, she remembered the absolute fear she'd felt and the knowledge that all men could be brutal, Polish and Turkish alike. They were all fighting for the same land, and women often got in the way. Like Hatice.

But a woman could make a difference. Roxelane had fought and had saved lives. She realized she would fight again, not with her yataghan, but in a different way. Especially for friends like Verda and Kaan.

So absorbed was she in her memories that she didn't hear the door slide open behind her, and she didn't hear the almost silent footsteps move toward her. It was only when she felt the air change about her that she realized someone had entered the room and now stood behind her.

"Are you the artist?" a man's voice.

The low tone washed over her like a caress, and Roxelane let it touch her skin, if only for a moment. She slowly turned. The sultan wore a dark robe of indigo, and he had a sword strapped to his waist. It reminded her of his appearance on the caravan, except his face was free from dirt and perspiration.

In the spill of afternoon light, his eyes appeared to be golden-green and burning with fire. Her breath stopped in her chest, and she finally remembered to bow. As she rose, she went through all the things she'd planned to say to him, but nothing would emerge from her lips. So she lowered her head and clasped her hands.

"The painting is very interesting," he said, as if not bothered by her sudden muteness. "Even though you travelled in the middle of the caravan, you've drawn an accurate depiction of the entire group."

Roxelane turned toward the painting again since it was easier to look at than to become lost in the sultan's burning gaze. "I wanted to remember Hatice before . . ." She stopped for a moment. "I thought it would be nice to have a tribute to her."

The sultan stepped closer to the painting and studied it quite thoroughly. Roxelane didn't know if that was a good thing. "You have a kind heart and a brave soul," he said at last. "Hatice would have liked to be remembered this way."

"It is only an elementary depiction, but I hope to become better with practice," she said. "I've only worked with the drawing master for a few weeks since being transferred to these chambers."

He didn't answer, just continued to study the painting. But then he turned and reached out his hand, running his fingers along her cheek. She was so startled that she dared not move.

"You are a treasure," he said, stepping even closer to her.

The warmth from his body seemed to reach across the space. She had to remain calm, she had to let him lead. But she wanted him to touch her more, to even kiss her. This was not like her village in the market square where she'd determined to flirt with the men to see which one she favored most. She already *knew* she favored Süleyman. The question was, did he favor her?

She was here, in these beautiful chambers, elevated to concubine status, being trained in arts and language . . . yet . . . Roxelane knew boldness could set her back, even have her dismissed. So she remained as still as she could.

"What do you think of your new quarters?" the sultan asked, as if they were complete equals.

She almost laughed. Looking into his eyes, she told him the truth. "It is beyond anything I could have ever dreamed of. But if you were not a part of this, it would not be my wish."

He held her gaze. "What if the King of England or the Prince of France were to offer you a place in his court as a concubine?"

A moment passed before she whispered, "I would say no."

His fingers touched her cheek again, and she couldn't help but lean toward him. Would he finally kiss her? Would he take her to his chamber and make her his true concubine?

"Roxelane," he said. "You've never told me your true name."

She closed her eyes and lowered her head, moving away from his touch. She had locked away her true name, forsaken it, and relegated it to the smallest part of her heart that she could never reopen.

Why did he want to know it? And why couldn't she tell it to him? But the words of her friend Roma returned, and Roxelane couldn't bring herself to utter her former name.

"The name you gave me is all I need," she whispered. She hoped the sultan would not press her further. She'd already committed all she could to him and wanted to keep this one thing to herself.

"The name I gave you pleases me," the sultan said, no malice in his voice. "I hope it pleases you."

"Yes," she said, looking at him again.

His eyes had deepened to bronze, and his gaze moved to her lips, then back up to her eyes. He raised his hands and slipped off the headdress she wore now because of her new Islamic faith. He cradled her face with both of his hands. The first brush of his lips could barely be considered a kiss, but it sent fire straight through her veins. The second kiss brought a gasp to her throat and made her legs tremble. This kiss was longer and filled with heat—commanding yet gentle.

The sultan's hands moved from her face to her shoulders, then down her arms. He drew her against him, and her arms rose of their own accord to wrap around his neck. Was she being too wanton? Was it because she'd thought of this moment over and over that her body responded so quickly?

In his arms, she felt something she'd never felt before—cherished, wanted. It was as if the palace intrigue beyond the walls of her bedchamber no longer mattered. Only this moment with Süleyman was real. She wasn't a mere concubine and he wasn't the most powerful man in the Ottoman Empire. They were each other's equals.

She kissed him back, unsure at first if she was doing it right, but his heart was beating as fast as hers. When he drew away, he stroked her face. "Come to my chamber tonight, Roxelane. I want you by my side."

Joy soared through her. The sultan had requested her and soon she'd be his true concubine. He might belong to the entire kingdom, but now she knew she had a place in his heart.

"I will come to you," she said, and he bent again and kissed her lightly, but it stole her breath away.

When the sultan left Roxelane's chamber, she crossed to her bed and sank onto it, thinking of all he'd said and done. Her skin still throbbed from his touch, and she could hardly believe he'd invited her to his room . . . tonight.

Tonight she'd cement her position as his official concubine. She watched the final rays of the sun fade as it disappeared beyond the horizon. It wasn't until the oranges of the sky changed to violet that her door slowly opened.

Roxelane blinked and turned her head toward Verda.

Her smile was broad as she crossed to Roxelane and grasped her hands. "So he has invited you to come to his chamber tonight."

Roxelane could only nod, her throat was too thick to speak.

"You will be a different woman when you return," Verda said, sitting next to her on the bed, and keeping their hands linked.

"I am already a different woman," Roxelane whispered. "Is it possible to be in love with a man who shares his life with other women?"

Verda was silent for a moment. "I am sure it has happened before. And, Roxelane, I believe the sultan has reserved part of his heart just for you."

Roxelane turned to her friend. "Do you think if I please him, he'll select me as his wife?"

"I think you have a very good chance," she said. "The sultan favors you highly and has brought you into his household for a reason. Is it so hard to believe that he wants you for a wife?"

Roxelane's thoughts soared at the idea—it seemed possible now more than ever. The door opened again. "It's time," Kaan said, coming into the room. "You will dine with the sultan, then spend the night in his chamber."

Inhaling slowly, Roxelane gripped Verda's hand for a moment, then rose from the bed. "We will walk you to the sultan's chambers," Verda said. "Although his mother will be accompanying us, as well."

"You also need to know that Hafsa will dine with you," Kaan added.

It was not ideal, Roxelane thought, especially considering how tight her nerves were and how close the memory of recently kissing the sultan. Would his mother be able to see her thoughts as they dined together? Surely it would be impossible to hide her emotions completely. Roxelane didn't want to make a mistake.

Verda helped her rearrange her headdress, and then she was ready to walk through the corridors to the sultan's chambers.

The corridor and the rooms they walked past changed from elegant to magnificent as they neared the sultan's inner quarters. Guards were positioned at every door, yataghans strapped to their waists. Their dark eyes followed Roxelane's every movement.

Kaan stopped at a set of massive doors, and when he announced who they were to the guards, one of them opened the door.

Inside was a smaller version of the banquet room where Roxelane had served wine. The table in the center had a dozen chairs about it, but the room had a more intimate feel as if the meals here were served just for family.

Only a couple of servants were inside, setting down platters of food and pouring wine. Neither the sultan nor his mother had arrived yet. The servants bowed to Roxelane and continued in their duties.

Then the door on the other side of the room opened, and Roxelane was surprised to see Ibrahim stride through it. He crossed to Roxelane and kissed her hand. "Welcome," he said, glancing at Verda and Kaan. "I am to entertain you until the sultan arrives. You may dismiss your servants."

Roxelane turned to Verda and Kaan and nodded to them, although she wished she could ask them if they thought Ibrahim's presence unusual. When her servants had left, she turned back to Ibrahim.

"Has the sultan been delayed?" she asked, not sure if she was being too presumptuous.

Ibrahim just smiled and said, "We will be patient." He led her to a seat and sat next to her.

"Tell me of your studies," he said. "I hear you have your own household now."

"I have a tutor in language and art," Roxelane said in a careful voice. She supposed she could trust Ibrahim. After all, he was close to the sultan and had been his childhood friend. But she felt exposed here in the sultan's private dining room. She would be cautious. "I have much to learn, but I have been fortunate."

"And your new faith?" Ibrahim asked.

This she felt more comfortable discussing. Ibrahim had been Christian once. "It is certainly a change," she said. "But there is much good in Islam to embrace."

"I have found that the case, as well," Ibrahim said. "It brings much peace to the kingdom when religious beliefs align."

"Yes," Roxelane said. "I often think of you and how you have lived a dedicated life to both the sultan and to Islam."

Ibrahim's mouth lifted into a smile. "You and I have much in common. It seems you are favored by the sultan."

Unbidden, heat rose to Roxelane's face. "He is generous with his attention."

He arched a brow. "Which brings you here tonight." He glanced at the servants, then leaned close to her and whispered, "The sultan has only one living male heir. That is not enough to keep a throne secure."

Roxelane opened her mouth, wanting to ask what he meant exactly, when the door opened again, and the sultan stepped through, followed by his mother.

Roxelane stood and bowed before them. Hafsa gave her a tight smile, then took her place to Roxelane's right and across from Ibrahim. The sultan greeted Ibrahim, then crossed to Roxelane and took her hand in his.

His touch and his gaze brought back the memory of him kissing her in her chamber. She was sure her breathing was too fast and her eyes too bright for everyone in the dining room not to notice. The sultan leaned in and kissed her gently on the cheek, and Roxelane felt her heart melt even more.

Once they were seated, the main meal was brought in, platter after platter of fresh salads, followed by courses of steaming lamb, cooked vegetables, and still-warm pastries. It was too much to eat, let alone take in with her eyes. For the most part, Roxelane remained silent as she took small bites of food, and listened to the sultan and his mother discuss politics with Ibrahim. Roxelane was impressed with the deference the sultan gave his mother on more than one issue. He even asked her to sign a few of the points into law.

It seemed he trusted her completely, although he'd made one exception, to choose Roxelane himself.

Roxelane was proud of the distinction between herself and the sultan's two wives, although she knew it didn't elevate her in the eyes of the other harem women.

Ibrahim drew her out in a conversation or two, but Roxelane was more than relieved when the dining portion had come to an end, and Hafsa took her leave. Roxelane continued to sit at her place while the sultan and Ibrahim discussed an upcoming meeting with officials.

This invitation to dine with the sultan, combined with Roxelane's anticipation of his visit to her chambers, was starting to accumulate into a dull throb in her head. She felt exhausted, and the evening wasn't even over yet. This evening was a precipice of her relationship with the sultan, and she couldn't afford to be weary.

At last, Ibrahim kissed Roxelane's hand in farewell and took his leave.

The hour was indeed late as the oil lamps had burned low. The sultan rose and crossed to Roxelane. He took her hand and drew her to her feet then he led her out of the dining room. They walked along a corridor she'd never walked through, past another set of guards, and then into what had to be his bedchamber.

The room was massive. Gold and blue tapestries decorated the walls. The heavy curtains had been drawn open, allowing waxing moonlight to spill into the room that glowed with several oil lamps set on small tables.

And it was just the two of them. No servants, no mother, no advisors.

The sultan shut the door and twisted the bolt, surprising Roxelane. She thought he wouldn't lock a door, in case there was an urgent matter at hand.

She walked to one of the high windows and gazed at the glittering beauty spread before her. Lights from torches and oil lamps flickered across the palace grounds as the moon seemed to smile benevolently upon all.

"This is beautiful," Roxelane said, her voice trembling.

The sultan came up behind her and slid his hands around her waist, pulling her back so that her head rested against his shoulder.

She released a sigh. It felt divine to have his arms around her, and she knew that of all men, he would be gentle as he initiated her into becoming his.

"I did not imagine you could be more beautiful than you are, Roxelane," he murmured against her neck, his warm breath raising goose pimples on her flesh. "But the moonlight turns you into a goddess."

She found herself smiling. "Do you believe in goddesses, then?"

"Tonight I find that I do," he whispered.

His mouth brushed her neck, sending sharp heat through her all at once, making her desire flare hotter than she could have imagined. She felt absolutely wanton, and for a small moment, she felt a kinship with her mother and what a man's touch must coerce her into doing. But she pushed that thought away. Surely this was different. She loved the sultan despite that he was a man loved by so many. What happened between them was unparalleled by the common man and woman spending a night together.

Roxelane turned in his arms, unable to bear being touched by him but not being kissed by him. His lips found hers, and she met his with urgency. It seemed he intended to be gentle in his approach, but her desire for him flared.

It didn't take long for him to slip off her clothes and carry her to his waiting bed. And it took even less time for him to transport her into a new paradise—one she never wanted to leave.

❖ CHAPTER THIRTY-SEVEN ❖

ISTANBUL

Omar landed the helicopter in the charter-aircraft sector of the Istanbul airport and turned to his passengers. "The sooner we're out of here, the better. I'm not sure if there was quite enough on our credit cards to pay for this. I gave them a forwarding address, but that might not satisfy the charter company, and we'll be caught in red tape."

As if the airline personnel had overheard Omar's comments, a man with thick glasses and thinning hair came out of the terminal and walked toward them, waving a piece of paper.

"Too late," Mia said with a grimace.

Omar and the others climbed out while the man striding forward adjusted his glasses at the sight of Naim's face, but then continued toward Omar.

"How much do I owe you?" Omar asked.

The man's stern expression didn't soften. "Your combined cards cleared only half the amount needed."

It was Naim who now fished around in his pocket and drew out a rather worn wallet. "This should cover the rest," he said, handing over a credit card.

The man looked down at the platinum card with a raised eyebrow. "Thank you, Mr. Bata." His gaze lifted to Naim's face. It was clear the employee knew the Bata name.

"You're welcome. And now we need a private car," Naim said.

"Of course," the man said. "I'll make the arrangements."

The man made a couple of phone calls as they walked, and Omar refrained from rolling his eyes as he and the women followed Naim. They entered one of the terminals, then through an employee door, and after a trek down a bland hallway, the employee showed them into a small parking garage.

A black sedan was parked. "Perfect," Naim said, motioning for the others to climb inside.

Naim thanked the airport employee and sat in the driver's seat, then started the engine. They drove out of the parking garage and after several turns, emerged onto a road leading away from the airport.

"I guess you'll be missing all these benefits," Omar said, relaxing back onto the leather upholstery.

"While we've been driving," Mia said, "I've had an idea." She pulled out the phone confiscated from Baris. "While Omar has been busy flying helicopters and the two of you running about an island, I've unencrypted Baris's phone, and found several links that I explored. One led to a database of the Turkish Royalists membership. After cross-referencing the names, I've singled out seven men who are working for the Turkish government, a direct conflict of interest to their Royalist agenda. I also did general searches on those seven, and there is no mention of their names in the media, which means they've kept their memberships secret. Any protests they've conducted or petitions they've filed haven't been signed by any individuals."

Omar leaned closer to Mia to see the list she pulled up. He recognized two of the names, but wasn't entirely sure which departments they were in.

"So what's your idea?" Leyla asked from the front seat, her voice eager.

"We put together an emergency Royalists leadership meeting and tell them that an important investor will be in attendance who will help determine their future growth," Mia said. "All seven of these men will be invited. We'll bring in undercover police and present the evidence of the Royalists' crimes. The police officers can take it from there."

"I like it," Omar said, "but how will we pull it off?"

Naim scoffed, glancing back at Omar. "You think I can convince the Royalists to listen to me? I might be the son of Adem Bata, but I have no political influence. It has to be someone else."

"Someone trusted from *within* the Royalist organization," Leyla said.

"Exactly," Naim said. "But how?"

"You're onto something, Leyla," Omar said with a smile. "It looks like we're going to have to bust Baris out of prison. He'll organize the meeting, and invite the anonymous investor."

Naim's jaw clenched. "My father will never come. He'll smell a trap all the way from his island."

Omar's voice remained calm. "Then we'll have to come up with an offer he can't refuse." He could see Naim's interest in the set of his shoulders as he turned off the highway onto a boulevard.

"Such as?" Mia prompted.

Omar folded his arms, giving her a sideways glance. "What do you think would persuade Mr. Bata of Bata Enterprises to leave his island?"

"His son?" Leyla asked.

"Possibly," Mia answered. "Or better yet, the promise of the president of Turkey being willing to enter into a negotiation. Through my research, I read some of their petitions to the government—one of them was to make select descendants of the Ottoman Empire into ambassadors of the country, and give them more prominent roles in the communities, in essence, return some of their 'dignity.'"

"Convincing the president to come sounds impossible," Naim said. He slowed the car as they approached a stoplight.

"The president doesn't actually have to come," Mia said. "At least your father won't know until it's too late."

"But the president should be there," Omar cut in. "He, of all people, needs to see the evidence against the Royalists and the list of crimes which we'll be bringing against them."

"What do you think, Naim?"

He was silent. Omar wondered what he'd do if he were in Naim's position with such a father.

"It's the right thing, as painful as it might be," Naim finally said. "Let's do it."

When Naim met Omar's glance in the rearview mirror, Omar saw the determination there. And it was good.

❖ CHAPTER THIRTY-EIGHT ❖

CONSTANTINOPLE

AD 1522

Roxelane's stomach clenched in warning, and she grabbed for the copper basin that Verda had set by her bed. For five days, she'd awakened feeling like hell was battling inside her. For five days, she'd wondered, hoped, and now, it could only be true.

"Should I send for the physician?" Verda asked, her voice quiet and anxious, although Roxelane knew she, too, was hoping for good news.

In the past three months, Roxelane had spent many nights in the sultan's bedchamber. Nights she treasured, but even more, if she was pregnant, then her place in the palace would be more secure. And more threatening to others.

As Verda hurried from the room, Roxelane crouched for the second time that morning over the copper basin. Her stomach seized, and she released the sickness. Remarkably, she soon felt better and was able to sip some water.

While waiting for the physician, she crossed to the windows and paced in front of them. She felt too ill to sit or lie down comfortably. Only pacing seemed to help. When Verda arrived with the physician, Roxelane was sure that everyone in her household had figured out what was going on.

The physician took one look at her and said, "You should be resting."

"Walking helps to relax my stomach," she said. But she was obedient anyway and let the physician direct her to the bed.

The first thing he did was ask her about the times of day she was the most nauseated and how long were the episodes. He checked her heartbeat, and pressed his fingers gently about her stomach. Then he asked when her last menses was. He seemed satisfied with her answer and said, "You will deliver a child in seven months, Allah willing."

Roxelane kept her expression serene until the physician left. Then the tears started, and Verda was at her side in moments.

"I need to tell the sultan," Roxelane said. "If he sends for me tonight, I'll tell him the news."

Kaan came into the room, carrying a tray of food, none of which Roxelane would be able to eat. "The news will spread to the sultan long before tonight," he said, smiling.

Roxelane reached over and hugged him after he set the tray down. Unconventional, she knew.

She was still buzzing with excitement when her tutor arrived in the receiving room to go over her writings. She dressed and prepared to meet him, but he stopped inside the doorway. "I was told that you would be kept resting in your rooms. I was going to gather the inkpots so they wouldn't dry out."

"What were you told?" she asked.

His face flushed, making it quite obvious that he'd heard the news about her pregnancy.

"I'll continue lessons for now," Roxelane said. "It will not hurt my health."

"For a normal woman, no," Ali said. "But a woman carrying the sultan's child—nothing must be risked."

"I will be fine," Roxelane insisted, but Ali wouldn't be swayed. He gathered up his inkpots and exited the room.

Roxelane knew she must speak with Hafsa in order to have her lessons restored. She didn't want to bother the sultan with something so mundane. And she didn't know what his reaction would be to the news about her pregnancy. Would he turn to one of his other wives or choose another concubine while she was in confinement?

She rose to her feet determined to seek out Kaan and perhaps request to speak to the Master of the Girls. How was she supposed to run her household if she spent most of her time resting?

But before she reached the door of the receiving room, the atmosphere in the courtyard changed. Everyone paused in their tasks. Had Hafsa arrived?

Roxelane walked to the door, and much to her surprise, the sultan entered the courtyard. His gaze met hers as she stood in the doorway, and she knew he'd heard of her condition. He didn't break his stride as he headed straight for her. Ibrahim walked with him, as well as several bodyguards.

When the sultan stopped before her, he said, "Is it true you are with child?"

"Yes," she said in a tremulous voice, aware of Ibrahim's gaze.

"Tell me what the physician said," the sultan said, passing her and stepping into the receiving room, then drawing her with him by her hand. It wasn't completely private with the door still open, and Ibrahim watching from the doorway, but at least they were away from most of the eyes.

"The physician confirmed my pregnancy and said I should deliver within seven months."

The sultan's mouth softened into a smile. "Truly?"

"Truly," she said. She held her breath, not knowing how he would react. But the fact that he was here, questioning her, told her he was pleased. At least she hoped so.

And then he sank to his knees. He grasped her waist and leaned forward and kissed her stomach.

Tears pricked Roxelane's eyes at the tender gesture. Then he rose and took both of her hands. "Marry me, Roxelane," he said in a soft voice. "It is no secret that I favor you above all other women in the empire. Become my chief wife and my queen, and we will raise this child and many more together."

She threw her arms around his neck, despite the public setting. "Yes," she said, tears in her eyes, and laughter bubbling up. "I will be honored to marry you."

His arms pulled her close as he laughed, then he drew away and cradled her face with both of his hands. Then, in front of Ibrahim, the bodyguards, and all the servants beyond in the courtyard, the sultan kissed her on the mouth.

Three days before the marriage of Roxelane to Sultan Süleyman, she underwent a series of rigorous cleansing rituals. Bathed and oiled, Roxelane lay on a mat while Verda and three other servants used *band andazi* to remove all of Roxelane's facial and leg hair. They continued along the rest of her body, working the fine threads to pull the hair from Roxelane's body from the roots, including the hair from her stomach, back, and under her arms.

The pain of the hair removal distracted her from the nausea in her stomach. The sultan had scheduled the marriage ceremony for the afternoon so that Roxelane would be feeling her best. The rest of the days leading up to the marriage, Verda continued to massage oils into her skin and hair.

Roxelane's servants had brought in a clothing artist from the city, who had an entire crew of women to embroider the white gown she'd wear. When Roxelane was presented with the dress, she nearly cried. It was exquisitely sewn, with emeralds stitched into the neckline, as well as the headdress.

And finally, it was time. Verda and Kaan fussed over Roxelane as she was dressed by the servants and her face was painted and her hair twisted so that it fell neatly beneath the headdress. Verda stepped back to admire Roxelane. "You are more beautiful than any goddess an artist could dream up." Tears coursed down her cheeks, which made Roxelane want to cry.

"I could not have made this journey without you," Roxelane said, leaning forward and kissing Verda on each cheek. The two women embraced lightly so as not to disturb the creation Roxelane had become.

Kaan grasped Roxelane's hand and gave her the barest of kisses on the cheek. "You have made us proud since the day you arrived in Constantinople."

"Thank you," Roxelane whispered, her voice too full of emotion to say much else.

Hafsa came into Roxelane's bedchamber to give her approval. Hafsa did the final honor of lowering Roxelane's sheer veil.

The Master of the Girls arrived to escort Roxelane to the sultan's throne room, and they made quite an entourage as they walked through the corridors. Every room they passed was decorated in celebration of the marriage with hanging vines intertwined with flowers.

As they entered the courtyard leading to the throne room, the gathered assembly of courtiers and harem women turned their eyes upon Roxelane. She'd never felt so privileged, yet so nervous at the same time. It was as if everyone could see right through the veil.

She knew the sultan's other wives and children were in the gathering, but she didn't allow herself to seek them out. As she walked through the courtyard, arm in arm with the Master of the Girls, Roxelane took a deep breath. The massive doors to the throne room stood open. She'd never been inside, and as she walked in, the first thing that struck her was the sight of the throne on a dais at the far side of the room.

Süleyman was sitting there in his splendid white wedding clothes, and when he saw Roxelane, he rose to his feet. Everything else in the room fell away—the courtiers lining the walls, the marble pillars reaching the sky, the expanse of the mosaic tiled floor, the painted ceilings and the intricate tapestries upon the wall—all seemed to fade as Roxelane held the sultan's gaze.

The night when he'd come to her hiding place and pulled the knife out of her fingers, she couldn't have ever dreamed of this event, not in a hundred lifetimes.

With each step toward the dais and the sultan, the people in the room slowly came back into focus. They were of all different shades of skin tones, wearing various clothing pieces from their different lands, and all of them were paying deference to her.

Süleyman watched her, his hands clasped in front of him, his stance wide, his gaze steady. A flower garland hung across his shoulders. As she passed the guests, one by one they bowed, just as if she were the sultan herself.

And today she would be made wife to the sultan and queen of the Ottoman Empire.

Roxelane reached the steps, and holding onto the Master of the Girls' hand, she ascended the steps until she reached Süleyman's outstretched hand. It was then that she was led by the sultan to the top of the dais where she stood in front of the throne before hundreds of people.

Her breath expanded at the sight of masses of bowed heads, not only bowing to the sultan, but to her, as well. Her Polish village and her family seemed far away, another lifetime, and she wondered if she had ever truly been a village girl turned slave.

She felt Süleyman's gaze upon her, and she turned to look at him. He smiled at her, squeezing her hand, and she wondered if any other feeling in the world could be as exquisite as what she was feeling now. Even if she hadn't been standing on the dais, she knew she'd feel like she was floating above the earth.

This man was the most powerful ruler on earth, and he was gazing down at her with a smile, about to take marriage vows with her. All the same, she knew Süleyman belonged first to the empire, second to his people, and somewhere down the line, to her. She had shared him ever since the day she met him, and she would share him with others the rest of her life. She could never expect that he'd be hers alone. And now the child growing within her belly also had claim upon him, but it would be all hers too.

Her hands began to tremble as a group of Magi walked into the room, wearing official robes of red. The ceremony was about to begin. One Magus carried a loaf of bread, another a goblet of wine. When the Magus with the bread approached the dais and climbed the steps, Roxelane sank to her knees before the sultan and bowed her head. The sultan took her hands in his and kissed each one. Then he lifted her hands upward, pulling her to her feet.

He led Roxelane to the smaller throne chair beside his. Then he said in a quiet voice so that only those closest could hear. "Roxelane, sit beside me and help me guide our people."

Roxelane sank into the throne chair, hardly daring to believe she was sitting at the sultan's side before all of these people. The Magus with the loaf of bread stepped forward. The sultan stood and withdrew a sword from his belt. Then he lifted the sword and sliced the bread in one swift stroke.

The sultan replaced his sword, then took both pieces of bread from the Magus and handed one to Roxelane. She lifted her veil a little and took a bite from it, and the sultan did, as well. The second Magus stepped forward with the goblet of wine and offered it to the sultan. He took a sip of the amber liquid, then handed the goblet to Roxelane. She lifted her veil again and swallowed the wine, the sweet fruitiness only adding to the surreal moment.

Roxelane handed the goblet back to the Magus.

The Magus turned to the sultan. "Do you take Roxelane as your wife and queen?"

"Yes," the sultan said, his warm voice rushing through Roxelane in its confidence.

Then the Magus turned to Roxelane. "Roxelane, do you take Sultan Süleyman as your husband and sultan?"

She did not reply. She'd been instructed to wait for the Magus to ask the same question three times. On the third inquiry she said, "Yes."

The sultan smiled as he drew her hand into his and kissed it. He leaned close and said, "You are now officially my wife. Kneel and I will crown you queen."

Roxelane rose from the throne, then sank to her knees in front of the sultan. He bent to lift her veil. The touch of the air against her face brought fresh tingles to her skin, and then the sultan placed the crown on her head.

Somewhere in the courtyard, musicians began to play drums, accompanied by the sweet melody of a lone flute. The sultan drew her to her feet and stood before the crowd in the throne room, clasping tight her hand.

The weight of the crown was a solid thing, but the sultan's hand in hers as they stood before the people of the empire felt more solid than the heaviest of gold. The musicians in the courtyard added tambourines to their retinue, and as Roxelane stood side by side with the sultan, she felt tears start.

Group by group, viziers, dignitaries, courtiers, and others came forward and offered their well wishes. Many of them presented gifts that began to accumulate quickly on the dais. Jewelry boxes, necklaces, bolts of silk, lengths of fur, and heavy rings were only some of the gifts set before them. The sultan graciously accepted each gift and introduced Roxelane to each person.

Her mind spun with all of the introductions, and she marveled that the sultan had such a keen memory. After the gifts had been presented, they moved into the courtyard where banquet tables had been set up. The crowd had thinned, but there were still hundreds of people in attendance at the banquet.

The sultan stood at the head of the table and called for quiet, then thanked all of the guests and family members for coming. Sitting on his right, it was the first chance Roxelane had the opportunity to really see all who were in attendance. Of course the sultan's mother was there, his siblings and their spouses and children, the sultan's other two wives. Everyone was all smiles, some more genuine than others, but Roxelane also felt an undercurrent of anticipation.

The sultan had declared her his favorite wife and had crowned her as queen. She knew this was a threat to his first two wives. It meant he favored her over them, and now the jostling would start all over again. The sultan took his place, and the feasting and entertainment commenced. Platters piled high with meats, fruit, vegetables, pastries, breads, and cheeses were brought in, and the flow of tea and wine never seemed to stop.

One dancing troupe after another performed for the guests, from acrobats, to belly dancers, to fire dancers, to jokers and snake charmers. The entertainment didn't miss a beat as the sun dipped below the horizon, and dozens of torches were lit and placed around the courtyard.

Roxelane found herself laughing and cheering along with the other guests at the end of the performances. More than once, she felt the sultan's adoring gaze on her. She had not thought it possible to be so supremely happy.

She ate sparingly, unsure of the reaction from her unpredictable stomach, and she drank very little wine. As the hours marched forward, fatigue tinged Roxelane's enjoyment. She wanted nothing more than to spend the rest of the evening alone with the sultan in his bedchamber, away from all the chatter, laughter, and curious eyes.

"Are you well?" the sultan asked quietly, leaning toward her.

She smiled at him, for she knew others were watching. "I am well," she confirmed.

"Is the child giving you trouble?"

She flushed, sure that at least a few people had overheard him, especially his mother who sat just to the side of the sultan. "He is tired."

The sultan gave her a slight nod, then straightened. Turning to his mother, he said, "You will continue on as host in my absence. I will take my new wife back to the royal chambers."

If Hafsa was bothered by the request from her son, no one would have known it by her smooth, compliant features.

"I will remain until the last guest has departed," Hafsa said, in a clear, regal voice.

The sultan thanked her, then stood, and a hush fell across the table. "This day will always be remembered as a favorite of mine. You have all been more than generous. My mother will continue as your host, so please enjoy yourselves. I will retire now with my new wife."

Smiles met him, and a few people even cheered. The sultan returned their smiles indulgently, then reached for Roxelane's hand.

She set her hand securely into his and rose to her feet, finding that she felt more achy and tired than she'd first thought. The guests bowed as she and the sultan walked past them and out of the courtyard.

Out of the milling servants, Verda appeared along with Kaan. They took up the entourage with the sultan's bodyguards, and Roxelane found that she was breathing more freely than she had sitting so close to Hafsa and the sultan's other two wives.

The walk back to the royal chambers was quiet, and the sultan simply held her hand. As they reached the bedchamber, he dismissed everyone. A look of surprise crossed over Verda's face to be dismissed before helping Roxelane change out of her gown, but no one dared to argue with the sultan.

Roxelane followed him into the bedchamber and found it a complete contrast to the crowds and entertainment in the courtyard. Her head buzzed with the quiet. A servant had lit several oil lamps in the darkened room, and the dancing light moved against the golden walls.

The sultan shut the doors firmly, then turned to Roxelane.

"How are you really feeling?"

She smiled at him, feeling her heart expand with even more love, if that were possible. "I am filled with gratitude."

He leaned down and kissed her forehead. "You are too generous. As the woman carrying my child, you must be tired. We have been celebrating all day."

She lifted up on her toes to wrap her arms about his neck. "I will be celebrating the rest of my life having been chosen as your wife."

He kissed her cheek, then he kissed her jaw, and was soon trailing kisses down her neck. If she had been weary at the banquet, thoughts of exhaustion soon fled her mind.

"Turn around," he said, and she obeyed.

Slowly, he began to unfasten the back of her dress. She had spent the night with the sultan many times in his chamber, but tonight was different. She was with her husband for the very first time. As the sultan slid the gown from her shoulders, she closed her eyes, reveling in the sensation of his fingers on her bare skin.

Next he worked on her undergarments, removing them one by one, piece by piece, until she finally stood before him with only her head-dress remaining. He moved around her, his fingers still trailing along her skin and she could feel the intensity of his gaze. Her body broke out into goose bumps, and when he brushed against her to remove the final thing she wore—her headdress—she shivered in anticipation.

"You are beautiful, my wife," Süleyman whispered.

She waited for him to kiss her first. And when he did, she grasped at his shoulders to pull him closer. He laughed softly against her mouth, then intensified his kiss. She was already swept away, and he was fully clothed. By the time he carried her to her marriage bed, she knew she would do anything . . . anything at all to ensure this man's happiness.

He was her world, her everything. And nothing and no one would ever stand between her and granting him his every desire.

◆ CHAPTER THIRTY-NINE ◆

ISTANBUL

"It's not every day you get to meet with the President of Turkey," Mia said. She adjusted Omar's tie.

"Too tight," he said, reaching up to loosen the knot.

But Mia stopped his hand. "It's perfect. You need to look professional, you know."

Omar shook his head. "You should come with me," he said.

She only laughed. "Make up your mind. You can't have it both ways. First you don't want me on the helicopter, and now you want me with you."

Omar grabbed her waist and pulled her close. "I always want you with me." He held her gaze until she finally lifted her face and pressed a kiss against his mouth.

"I know, babe." She smiled but said nothing more.

Omar released her and checked his appearance in the mirror. "Where will you be stationed?"

"There's a restaurant across the street, down a little ways. I'll be there with Leyla," Mia said.

"Celebration drinks after?" Omar looked at her through the mirror. "I hope so."

He kissed her cheek, then left the hotel room. He hoped they'd have something to celebrate and that they hadn't just spent the past four days working twenty-four-seven putting together the coup they were about to pull off.

"Going to a wedding?" Omar asked when he saw Naim emerge from the elevators of the hotel where he and Mia, and Naim and Leyla had booked rooms. The man wore a dark suit with a small rose pinned to his lapel.

Naim's mouth turned up. "You could be a groom yourself."

The comment wasn't as funny to Omar as Naim might have intended it. "Where is Baris?" Omar asked Naim.

They hadn't had to break Baris out of jail after all. Naim had found a much more civilized approach that involved the cooperation of the police and didn't involve any getaway cars.

"He's in the lobby with the detective."

"How did the briefing go?" Omar asked.

"Baris is a puppet, whether he's ours or someone else's, he'll do what it takes for a plea bargain." Naim crossed the sidewalk with Omar and pushed through the hotel doors. "For now, he's our puppet, especially since we informed him who his anonymous donor is. Baris sees prison as protecting him from my father's retaliation."

Omar scanned the lobby, spotting Baris sitting in a corner chair, with two men flanking him. Omar could only assume the men were the undercover police they'd be working with. The sight of Baris in a hotel with no handcuffs made Omar feel agitated. Thankfully it was only temporary.

"Before we join up with Baris, tell me about what you have on the first Royalist? Calling him Man 1, right? Mia told me she briefed you," Omar asked, turning to Naim.

"Department of Economics. Married, two children, vacations in England. Sister lives there with her husband. His mother was a Christian, converted to Islam before marrying. Man 1 is allergic to nuts."

"Is he wealthy?" Omar asked.

"Very."

"Man 2? Anything more than we knew before?"

"Moved departments six months ago," Naim said. "Estranged marriage. Wife lives near London. Oldest two sons are at the university there. Two of the men are cousins." Omar nodded, glancing over at Baris again. The man was staring at something on the floor and hadn't appeared to notice Omar and Naim across the lobby.

"Man 3 and Man 4. Both studied in London, paid for by a British benefactor," Naim continued.

Omar's interest was piqued. "What's the name of the benefactor?"

Naim grinned. "Thought you might ask that. Leyla found this." He reached into his pocket and pulled out a flier that looked as if it had been scanned several times over. The type was too dark in some places, and barely readable in others.

"Turkish Citizen Club Meeting," read the bold typeface. Omar scanned the rest of the contents. "Reconnect with other Turkish students on campus. Food, discussions, events." He looked over at Naim. "A recruiting club?"

"A good place to start," Naim said. "Leyla sent an e-mail to the one listed at the bottom of the flier. She said she was working on a highlight feature for the campus paper about the various clubs for university students. She asked if she could get a list of other members." He pulled a phone out from his pocket and powered it on. After he opened one of his emails, he turned the screen toward Omar.

It took only moments for Omar to make the connections of three of the last names to the list of seven government officials. "Sons? Relatives?"

"Leyla's working on it," Naim said. "But it's my guess this club is a feeder for new members of the Turkish Royalists."

Omar nodded. "The membership database link that Mia found encrypted on Baris's phone has a couple thousand names on it. Not enough for a revolt, unless each of the members also connects to support groups."

Naim nodded. "Do you have the letters?"

"I do," Omar said. He nodded toward Baris and the officers. "Let's go. We don't want to be late."

They walked to where Baris was waiting, and Naim spoke with the officers. Baris's face paled when he saw Omar. Omar just smiled and held the man's gaze. They would talk later.

The group left the hotel by way of the rear entrance where the officers had an unmarked sedan waiting. Omar stayed quiet, keeping his focus on Baris's profile and Naim continued to speak with the officers, giving them instructions in Turkish until the car pulled to a stop. The high-rise in front of them stood white against the pale blue sky of the morning, the country's flags billowing above, creating a sharp red color against the vast blue.

Just as one of the officers popped open his door, Naim said, "Wait."

The officer paused and turned to look at Naim.

"It's my father," Naim said.

A limo pulled up behind them, and when the door was opened by the driver, none other than Mr. Bata stepped out.

Omar slunk down in his seat although the windows of the sedan were plenty dark.

"We'll wait a few minutes," Naim told Omar. "He can't see us together before the meeting. My father's late, which means he'll be the last one at the meeting with the exception of Baris here."

Omar was struck with the similarities between father and son, although Naim didn't have the same hardened edges in his face as his father. Omar could only imagine the emotions that were hitting Naim right now. He was about to witness his father's arrest. That was, if everything went as planned.

"Ready?" Naim finally said.

The officer opened his door, and soon, the group of men were walking toward the building, Baris wedged between the two officers. After clearing the security checkpoint, a receptionist ushered them up to the third floor.

"Open the app where you can watch the action," Naim told Omar, as they reached the conference room door.

Omar wouldn't be entering at first, not until Naim started the presentation. Baris was to pretend he and Naim had been working together to translate Roxelane's letters, and then Baris would report on his assassinations. This was where it would get tricky. Baris had to convince Mr. Bata and the other men to confess their parts, while everything was being recorded by the hidden camera system. Once the confessions were flowing, Omar would enter with police officers and the arrests would start.

Until then, Omar's hands were tied as he watched and waited. He pulled his phone out of his pocket and opened the app where he'd see and hear everything that Naim did.

"Good luck," Omar told Naim. Then to Baris, he said, "One mistake, and there will be no life in prison. Your sentence will change to capital punishment." Omar hadn't predicted Baris's reaction. Instead of looking worried or anxious, his gaze was hard when he looked back at Omar.

"Wait," Omar started to tell Naim, but he'd already opened the conference room door, and Omar had to move out of the line of vision from those inside.

Naim and Baris disappeared through the door, and Omar was left in the corridor with the officers. A door at the far end of the corridor opened and more than a dozen police officers entered the hallway. They moved silently toward Omar and positioned themselves close to the door to wait for their signal. It was a little disconcerting that there was only one way in and out of the conference room.

Omar turned his attention to his phone and watched the events unfolding through Naim's hidden camera.

A total of fifteen men were gathered, and it seemed the introductions were over, if there had been any. The men were looking at Naim with interest—and several of them kept glancing over at Naim's father. Omar suspected that a few of them didn't know who he was.

Omar's attention was distracted once again as the door at the end of the hallway opened and the president of Turkey walked through the door, accompanied by four men, most likely bodyguards.

"Omar Zagouri?" the president said as he approached Omar.

Omar shook the man's hand. "Thank you for your cooperation on all of this," he replied in Turkish, letting the president know he spoke the language.

Then the voices that came through Omar's phone turned angry.

The president peered down at the phone with Omar, and they both listened as Mr. Bata rose to his feet, demanding to know where the president was.

Naim lifted his hands and told his father to be patient, they needed to hear Baris's confidential report before the president arrived, and negotiations began.

"Baris will explain an important discovery first," Naim told the group. "In fifteen minutes, the president will be here to review your petitions."

Mr. Bata seemed pacified for the moment and retook his seat.

Naim powered on his laptop and brought up a PowerPoint of the letters. Various lines were highlighted.

"We've discovered a series of letters written between Sultan Süleyman and his chief wife, Roxelane, that will further the cause of the Royalists and attract new members to our group. Four hundred years ago, Süleyman and Roxelane gave birth to their first son, followed by five more children over the years. Süleyman had two other wives at the time, and Mustafa was the sultan's oldest son, born to his wife Mahidevran," Naim said. "As with many monarchs, to be born a prince or princess meant that your life was constantly in danger. Sometimes by your own family members. History demonstrates that brothers killed brothers, nephews killed uncles, and fathers killed sons."

Omar watched his phone as Naim paused and looked around the room. His father's eyes were trained on Naim.

"A few days ago I discovered that Baris Uzuner was planning to kill a man named Omar Zagouri," Naim continued, "a man who's been a nemesis of Bata Enterprises."

Omar could see that Baris went stiff in his chair as the men around the table looked at him.

"You know Baris as the director of your organization," Naim said, "but this meeting is not only about a new archaeological find and a meeting with the Turkish president, but to inform you that your director has been assassinating descendants of the Ottoman royals one by one over the past six months."

Baris's face paled, but he kept his gaze trained on Naim, a hardness in his eyes.

A hardness that made Omar nervous as he watched the action play out on his phone. The tension in the room had doubled, and Naim's father rose to his feet again, a fight-or-flight expression on his face. Omar guessed the man would try to exit as soon as possible. It wouldn't be long before Bata realized he'd been set up.

"And now," Naim said. "We'd like to welcome our president as we reveal the most interesting finds in the newly discovered letters of the Ottoman Empire. We are hoping to impress our president enough to begin negotiations on the Royalists' petitions." Naim looked directly at the door, and Omar nodded to the president. This was their cue.

Omar followed the president inside the conference room as the police officers filed in after them.

Mr. Bata stared at the procession, a stunned look on his face. Omar met his gaze and held it. He didn't bother to notice the reactions of the other Royalists.

Naim greeted the president, then returned to his presentation. This time as he spoke, the room went dead silent as the Royalists watched the police officers.

"Mr. President," Naim said. "I'd like to introduce you to Baris Uzuner, a local antiques dealer."

The president nodded at Baris, but didn't say anything.

"The reason why we invited you here today," Naim continued, "is that he's the director of a private organization called the Turkish Royalists. For decades, they've been recruiting faithful members, collecting Ottoman artifacts, raising money, and placing their members into governmental and other influential positions throughout the country of Turkey. Many petitions have crossed your desk over the years, requesting that direct descendants of the Ottoman Empire be given civil and government positions honoring their royal heritage. We hope today to fulfill some of those petitioned requests."

The president's attention was completely focused. Not one person in the room moved or spoke.

Naim handed the PowerPoint clicker to Omar, and he stepped forward as Naim moved to the side. Omar zoomed in on the PowerPoint slide. "But first, we need to establish the true royal line to the sultan. A recent archaeological find was this set of letters, written in the early 1550s between Queen Roxelane to the sultan. I've added the translation of the old Turkish next to the lines. As you can see on this first image, she is keeping the sultan informed about his son Mustafa's activities and whereabouts." Naim let everyone read the translations for themselves, then he said, "Is she playing the role of the concerned stepparent? Or is she planning something sinister?"

The Royalists were riveted to the words on the screen, and Mr. Bata's narrowed gaze was focused on Omar.

"Mr. Baris Uzuner is not alone in his excitement over this set of letters," Naim said. He motioned to Omar to advance to the next picture. "This sentence tells us of Roxelane's displeasure over Mustafa's wife, Rümeysa. This is just a small example, and it seems that with each letter, the details about Mustafa grow more defined. Roxelane had four sons, two of them healthy, at the time of these letters. She'd lost Mehmed at the age of twenty-two, and her youngest son had been born physically malformed and was exempt from rule because of that."

Omar jumped in. "Roxelane's healthy sons were Selim and Bayezid. She wanted them on the throne." He lowered his voice. "At all costs." He advanced to the next slide. "In this letter we learn that Mustafa insisted on putting together an expedition against the Mongols, in addition to the army Selim had already raised. From history we know that Mustafa had been arguing military strategy with Selim. Selim wanted Mustafa sent to Amasya to be kept out of the way."

Omar clicked to the next slide. "You can see the translation of this next letter. Roxelane indicates that Selim has been honorable in every way, whereas she questions Mustafa's loyalty to the throne." Another slide. "This letter is perhaps the most damning. Roxelane states that Mustafa has gone too far, that he 'must be stopped.'"

No one spoke for a moment.

"What is the connection you are driving at?" the president broke in with a steely tone. "These letters were written hundreds of years ago by long-gone members of the monarchy. What does that have to do with Turkey today?"

"We'll answer your question shortly, Mr. President." The next picture that Omar showed on the PowerPoint was a rendition of the genealogy chart of Roxelane's line. "Do you see my name highlighted in yellow near the bottom?" The president nodded. "On my mother's side, I'm a descendant of Roxelane."

As Omar advanced to the next picture, Naim crossed to near where the president sat and all eyes turned to him. "That is my father's name highlighted in yellow, listed as Sehzade Mehmed, named after his ancestor, and his true name before he changed it to Adem Bata."

Naim's father's face drained of color, and Omar felt a bit of triumph.

"Mr. President," Naim continued. "To the left you'll see Mr. Uzuner's name. Both men are descended from Mustafa. And both men are current members of the Turkish Royalists. As you know, the Turkish Royalists have mostly been a peaceful organization with the occasional rally. You've seen their petitions, and they have so far been denied. But what you may not know is that in recent months they have grown to an organization several thousand strong, with one mission in mind—to restore the monarchy to Turkey."

The president placed his hands on the conference table. "I have a committee that monitors and prosecutes such organizations if they start riots or otherwise interfere with daily public life. I'll have them look more closely at the Turkish Royalists."

"If it were so simple," Omar began, "we would have called that committee. But I'm afraid that this threat to Turkey is very real. The roots run extremely deep, and the following men have been killed during the past six months simply because they are the descendants of Roxelane and the sultan." Out of the corner of his eye, Omar saw Mr. Bata start to rise to his feet, but an officer moved closer to him, and Bata sat down again. The other men in the room had noticed the change in the meeting's agenda, as well, and sent furtive glances toward each other. Omar clicked on the next picture, and a list of names and coordinating photos popped up on the screen.

The men started to whisper among themselves, but Omar's gaze was trained on the president as his eyes scanned the pictures, then stopped at the most recent death. That of Muhammed Emir.

"Muhammed," the president said. "He was murdered because of . . ."

"All the men in this room belong to the organization led by the Director of the Royalists. Their leader ordered the slaughter of Muhammed and the others," Naim said. "Even worse, each of the men here hold influential government positions, and when the time is right, plan to use their influence and connections to rebel against the Republic of Turkey and turn this country's leadership upside down."

Omar watched as the seven principals shifted in their seats. Almost as one, their gaze moved from panic to outright fear and disbelief. One man pulled out his phone, keeping it under the table and started to text. Another man scooted his chair out from the table, his gaze flitting to the door. Two other men shared glances.

The president was the one to rise to his feet now. "Is this true?"

Omar clicked to the next picture on the PowerPoint. Seven names and seven pictures appeared. "I present to you, Mr. President, the names of the traitors to your government." Omar clicked once more, and an eighth picture showed up, that of Mr. Bata. "And this man is the one funding the assassinations, paying Mr. Baris Uzuner twenty thousand dollars for each hit."

Silence seeped into every being and every corner of the room, and then one of the men started yelling. Nerves shot through Omar and he moved toward the yelling man. On the same side of the table as Omar, two men bolted for the door, trying to push past the policemen. Omar blocked their way, and blocked a punch coming from one of the men. Then he grabbed the man's arm and twisted it sharply and held it in place, giving a police officer enough time to slide handcuffs on. Omar gripped the handcuffed man's collar and forced him to face the wall. "Don't move," he hissed. "The guns will come out next."

But when he turned to face the rest of the room, the guns had already come out. Several of the police officers had their guns trained on the Royalists, and others were busy handcuffing the men. Naim had pulled out a gun too, aiming it straight at his father. Surprise jolted through Omar. Naim should have known better than to bring a gun into this room. The officers were running the show now.

"Hold up, Naim," Omar said, crossing to where Mr. Bata had pressed his back against a wall. To his credit, his face was pale as he stared at the gun his own son had trained on him.

"No son of mine will ever point a gun at me," Mr. Bata growled.

Omar didn't like the way Naim's hand was shaking as he held the gun. A nervous assailant was a sloppy assailant, and the room was full of criminals and policemen. "Naim, don't do something you'll regret," Omar said, and when Naim finally looked at him, Omar held out his hand.

Naim's face was the same pale color as his father's.

From the corner of his eye, Omar could see that several of the officers had escorted the other Royalists out, leaving just three officers, Baris Uzuner, Bata, the president, and his bodyguards behind. Cursing and shouting echoed down the outside hallway as the men were led away.

Omar kept his hand extended until Naim handed over the gun. And then before Mr. Bata could move, Omar turned, keeping the gun trained on Mr. Bata. "I'm not your son, Mr. Bata," Omar said in a steady voice. "So you can't threaten me."

Bata's eyes grew a shade darker.

"Turn around with your hands up," Omar commanded.

Bata's gaze slid to Naim's, and Omar wondered what he might have done if he'd been in the same situation with his own father. Any reunion between these two would never be cordial.

Bata slowly turned, keeping his head high and his jaw set firm. Omar called over one of the officers and within moments, Bata was handcuffed.

"We saved you for last, Father," Naim said in a sharp voice.

A shudder went through Omar as Mr. Bata turned his gaze again upon his son. The look of hatred was palpable, and Omar knew it was something that neither he nor Naim would ever forget.

"You have no proof that I'm involved in any of the deaths," Mr. Bata said. "Yes, I am a descendent of the Ottoman royals, and so are you, but I would never do something so foolhardy as getting mixed up with Baris Uzuner. You can't arrest me."

"They have copies of the bank transfers," Baris said, the first words that Omar had heard from him.

Mr. Bata looked over at Baris, and his lips thinned, almost a sneer. "Impossible."

Omar pocketed Naim's gun and walked over to the projector. He clicked to the next slide, displaying the scan that Simon Greif had e-mailed.

Bata's expression slackened as he stared in disbelief at the screen. "How—" he started, then checked himself. He lifted his cuffed hands. "Release me now, or you'll be facing a lawsuit."

"I'm afraid you're under arrest," the police officer said.

Bata released a short laugh. "A slide presentation is not enough to arrest me. Like I said, contact my attorney."

"You can call him from the police station," the officer said, and a second officer joined him, grasping Bata's arm.

Bata looked directly at Naim. "I don't know where you've found your information, son, but if you don't put a stop to this, you will regret it for every day of the rest of your life."

Naim stared at his father, but didn't say anything.

Bata's gaze went from determination to disbelief to anger. Then he cast a final, murderous look at Baris. The officers urged Bata out of the room, and when the door shut behind him, Naim sank into a chair, looking defeated and exhausted. Omar placed a hand on Naim's shoulder, thinking it had been foolish for him to draw a gun on his father, but Omar didn't entirely blame Naim.

"We're done here," Omar told the remaining officers, glancing over at Baris across the table. "You can return Mr. Uzuner to his cell."

Baris suddenly lunged toward one of the officers and grabbed for his firearm. The move surprised the officer enough that Baris secured the gun and aimed it at his own head. Baris's fear of Mr. Bata must be greater than his fear of prison.

"Don't touch me," Baris said. "I'm not going back to prison. Ever."

But Omar wouldn't let Baris take the easy way out. While the officers glanced at each other, Omar decided not to wait another moment. He dove at Baris before he could pull the trigger, and knocked the gun from his hand, landing on top of the man. They went down hard together, and Baris let out a cry of pain. Omar knew he'd have bruises later, but for now he concentrated on pinning Baris down so that he couldn't reach the gun.

"Get the gun," Omar shouted just as one of the officers hurried to retrieve it. Then Omar looked at Baris. "You're not taking the coward's way out. You'll cooperate with the authorities or you'll never walk free again."

"Let me end it!" Baris pleaded, his eyes wild, as he strained against Omar's grip. "I'm a dead man anyway. Let me out of prison, and Bata will take me down. But I'd rather be dead than in prison."

"That's not a choice you get to make," Omar said, taking one of Baris's arms while an officer grabbed the other one. They wrenched Baris's hands behind his back so that the officer could handcuff him. Omar climbed to his feet, and the officer hoisted Baris up. Baris hung his head, his chest shuddering with sobs as two of the officers led him out of the room. Omar didn't think he'd ever seen a man cry so openly.

His pitiful pleas continued to echo down the corridor even after the door had shut behind him.

Omar stared at the door for a few moments after Baris left.

"Are you all right?" Naim's voice cut into Omar's thoughts.

He turned slowly to face Naim. Omar should be asking Naim how he was doing, not the other way around. "I'm fine. There've been enough deaths," Omar said, rubbing his shoulder where he'd hit the ground when falling with Baris. "How are you?"

"I've been better," Naim said, giving Omar a half smile, although no part of it reached his eyes. "Thanks for helping me come to my senses. No matter what my father does in this life, I don't know if I want his death on my conscience."

Omar nodded. He understood.

The president took out his phone and made a call to security. "We'll need to make sure you men are able to leave here safely."

Only two police officers remained, along with the president's bodyguards.

"There's more work to be done," Omar said. He picked up the files next to the projector and handed them to the president. "These spreadsheets contain the names of the members of the Turkish Royalists. Citizens who would like nothing better than to see your government crumble and fail."

The president took the papers and leafed through them, his eyes wide as he scanned the columns of names.

"You will see that Mr. Adem Bata was involved every step of the way, funding Baris Uzuner and using him as a pawn." Omar paused and lowered his voice. "Naim has exposed his father at great risk to himself."

"We have been trying to shut down Bata Enterprises for years," the president said. He looked over at Naim. "Thank you for coming forward. We can offer you protection."

Naim gave a short nod of appreciation, his jaw clenched.

"What about you, Mr. Zagouri?" the president asked. "How can we thank you for your service to our country?"

"My thanks will come in other ways," Omar said, shaking the man's hand. "We'll be sending all of the documentation from Baris Uzuner to your committee. You will also find there are many connections to England that will need to be explored."

The president's eyebrows arched.

The door opened and a woman walked in. "Naim?" Leyla said. She was all cleaned up and professionally dressed. "Are you all right? I saw them leading Baris away—he seemed pretty upset."

"Thanks to Omar, Baris will be returning to prison alive." Naim looked relieved to see Leyla. He crossed to her, taking her hand in his. He walked her straight to the president. "Mr. President. I'd like to introduce Leyla Kaplan. She recently graduated in political science from Istanbul University, with an emphasis in Ottoman studies. She has been integral in helping with this investigation. I'd like to recommend that she serve on your committee to filter out the rest of the Turkish Royalists." His gaze was on her, affectionate and grateful. "The country will be safer in her hands."

The president extended his hand and shook Leyla's. It took him only a moment to say, "With such a recommendation, I'd be honored to appoint you to the committee."

Leyla gave Naim a bright smile, then turned to the president. "I accept."

Omar rocked back on his heels. Who would have thought?

The president clapped a hand on Naim's shoulder. "Maybe when the dust has settled, Naim will consider joining the task force as well."

Naim shook the president's hand. "Thank you, sir."

"Security will escort you to your new location," the president said.

Naim nodded to the waiting security guard, then turned to Leyla, his gaze shifting to the door, then back again. "I'm afraid I won't be walking out of this building with you. My father's connections have a broad reach, and he won't stay docile, not even in prison . . ." He shoved his hand through his hair.

Leyla reached for his hand the same time Naim reached for hers.

"I'll be in touch soon," Naim said. "I'll be in a witness protection program for a few months."

Leyla nodded, although Omar spotted a storm of emotions crossing her face. She stepped closer to Naim and kissed his cheek. He pulled her into a fierce, brief hug, then he turned to the waiting guard, and the two men left the room together.

Leyla turned toward the president, her smile tremulous.

He nodded to her. "Welcome aboard."

It was over. At least it was out of Omar's hands. He made his farewells to the president and Leyla, and exited. The corridor was quiet now, devoid of police officers and Baris's screaming.

Omar was looking forward to leaving this building once and for all, intent on meeting Mia at that restaurant. He wondered if she was still there since Leyla was supposed to be with her.

Once outside, Omar strode briskly down the sidewalk until he reached the next intersection, then crossed at the light. The restaurant had outside café tables, and although the woman's back was toward him, Omar knew Mia when he saw her short dark curls. He entered the restaurant, told the hostess he was meeting someone on the patio.

She let him through, and he stepped out onto the terrace in the dappled shade created by the tall, thin trees surrounding the patio.

Mia heard his footstep and turned. Smiled.

"It went well?" she said, rising to be enfolded in Omar's embrace.

"You already heard?"

She drew away and looked at him. "I can see it in your eyes."

"Adem Bata was arrested, and Baris is back in prison. Naim is going into witness protection, and Leyla is the newest member of the president's investigative committee."

Mia lifted a single brow, as if she weren't surprised in the least. "And you . . . where are *you* going?"

"Home," he said, then pulled her close and kissed her.

She twined her arms about his neck and melted into him, which Omar didn't mind at all. Perhaps when they returned to Tel Aviv, he would bring up the subject of his marriage proposal again. But for now, for this moment, he was content to hold her in his arms, warm and safe.

His cell phone buzzed, but he ignored it. After the third buzz, Mia broke away from his kiss. "You know it drives me crazy when you ignore your phone."

"I'll turn it off then."

She narrowed her eyes, and Omar said, "All right." He released her and pulled out his phone. "It's my father."

He met Mia's gaze and saw the anticipation in her eyes, matching the thudding of his heart. "Hello," he said, a lump already growing in his throat before he even heard anyone speak.

"Omar?"

"Mother?" He looked at Mia, who smiled at him. "How are you? It's good to hear your voice."

"I need a vacation," she said, her voice sounding light. "Your father's hovering too much and driving me crazy. How many rooms does your apartment have?"

The words sung through Omar, and he sat on the chair next to the table that Mia had occupied. Relief shot from his fingers to his toes, and he blinked back emotion. "You're coming to Tel Aviv?"

"Isn't that where you live?"

Omar laughed. "That's where Mia and I live. There are two bedrooms, and one is all yours."

"Oh, wonderful," she said. "I suppose your father will be coming with me—fussy man that he is. And I'm so looking forward to meeting your sweetheart when I can actually walk and have a conversation. Does Friday work?"

Omar's gaze found Mia's across the table. Her elbows were propped up on the table, her chin resting in her hands, as she smiled at him.

"You'll love her," Omar said into the phone. "And Friday is perfect."

❖ CHAPTER FORTY ❖

CONSTANTINOPLE

AD 1522

"The child is a boy, delivered early this morning," Roxelane heard the Master of the Girls announce to those who waited outside her bedchamber.

She'd been in labor for nearly two days, and once that announcement was made, she finally allowed herself to close her eyes in exhaustion. She had yet to speak to the sultan about the son she'd just delivered, but that would all come in due time. First, she must recover her strength as the servants around her cleaned up the sweat-soaked and bloodstained bedding, and the physician instructed the two nurses in how to care for her in the coming weeks.

A cry sounded from the next chamber over, and Roxelane's eyes immediately opened. "Bring me my son," she said, her voice a rasp.

The physician's face came into view. "We are examining him, and then we'll bring in the wet nurse."

"I will take him to my own breast."

The physician bowed his head and said, "You are the sultan's chief wife, and you are needed to rule at his side in all things. Not stay hidden in your chamber while you feed a lusty boy. That is a job for the wet nurse."

"Bring him in, so that he might know his mother."

The physician bowed again, and within moments, one of the servants brought the babe in, and Roxelane immediately reached for him. She put him to her breast and let the child fall asleep. Soon she fell asleep too, and when she next opened her eyes, the sultan was sitting next to her on the bed, stroking her hair.

"You are here," she said with a tired smile.

"I am." He leaned forward and kissed her. Then he kissed the babe in her arms. "We have a son." His fingers trailed along the child's full cheeks and soft neck.

Despite her exhaustion, Roxelane felt exhilaration shoot through her. They were a family, a real family. Süleyman was her husband and this infant boy her son. "What will we name him?"

The sultan went still for a moment, gazing at her, then at the infant. "Mehmed."

Roxelane nodded. "Mehmed. I can think of no greater honor for our son." *Someday,* she thought, *someday he'll rule the Ottoman Empire after his father and his grandfather.* "He is part of a grand legacy. And it will only become grander because I plan to give you more sons."

Süleyman smiled and grasped her hand. "You have given me so much. Love. Happiness. And now a son."

"An heir," she whispered.

The sultan did not flinch at the suggestion. Instead, he stroked the infant's head. For the moment, Roxelane knew she'd entered true paradise. The adoration in her husband's eyes brought her joy, and the sweet body of her newborn child in her arms filled every part of her soul with light.

The door of her chamber opened again, and two young men stepped inside, wearing the royal guard clothing, yataghans strapped to their sides. Roxelane looked at the sultan in surprise. Why were these guards in her private bedchamber?

The sultan rose and greeted the guards as they bowed to him. Then Süleyman turned to Roxelane. "These are bodyguards for our son. They will spend every moment watching over him. The only time they are to be out of the room he is in, is at your request."

"Our son is but an infant," Roxelane said, not wanting her privacy further invaded. "He will be surrounded by my own women and my own guards."

Süleyman's expression stiffened.

"What is it?" Roxelane said. "Has something happened? A threat against our son?"

"He will live a life full of threats against his life," Süleyman said. "He is the son of a sultan." There was no humor in his voice as he spoke.

Roxelane looked from her husband to the two new guards. If the sultan felt this much caution was necessary, then she would support it, but she wanted to know what threats had come in. "Tell me," she said.

Süleyman settled next to her again and took her hand. "When I was born, my father assigned me bodyguards and sent me to another place away from him to be raised."

What her husband was implying slowly dawned on Roxelane. "I don't want to send our son away. I couldn't bear it."

"You will not be made to bear it," he said. "But we will have to provide the utmost security for him, however inconvenient that might be for you."

"Mehmed's safety is the most important thing in the world to me," Roxelane said.

"And to me," Süleyman said, his voice finally softening. "Sometimes the worst threats come from the ones closest to you."

Roxelane stared at him, unsure what he meant. "Who?"

He gave her a faint smile. "Those who can truly be trusted grow fewer. With the birth of Mehmed, the politics of the palace have shifted."

"Has Gülfem spoken against our son?" she whispered.

When Süleyman shook his head, Roxelane knew. Mahidevran. Her son was the oldest and recognized heir to the throne of the Ottoman Empire. Roxelane looked down at the precious features of her newborn son. A fierce burning began in her chest and spread through her limbs. This child of hers would become the true heir to the throne. Süleyman loved her and had made her chief wife, and to Roxelane, that meant her son deserved all honors and privileges due a first son.

"What has she said?" Roxelane asked, desperate to know if Mahidevran could be accused and tried.

"No one has come forward with a confession," the sultan said. "Which is what I expect. But all rumors have been reported to me." He tilted his head toward the bodyguards. "These men are loyal and will protect our son."

In that moment, Roxelane vowed that nothing would ever come between her son and her husband. Nothing would take away her son's divine rights as witnessed under Allah. Roxelane would do anything and everything in her power to make sure her son received his full rights.

The following days were filled with visitors and gifts and congratulations given over the tiny infant. Hafsa hovered in Roxelane's chambers, seemingly ever present as she oversaw the household. A cradle had been built for Mehmed, and the visitors dropped coins and jewelry inside it as they passed, with the two royal bodyguards watching over the child

On the fourth day, Mahidevran and her son Mustafa visited. Roxelane had been expecting the woman for some time, but when she finally arrived, Roxelane was stunned by the anger that shot through her veins upon sight of the woman. Mahidevran wore her most elaborate clothing, and Mustafa seemed a younger version of the sultan, even stopping to bestow a benevolent smile upon the servants who rushed about the room, doing Roxelane's and Hafsa's bidding. For once, Roxelane was grateful for Hafsa's presence. It probably prevented Roxelane from making verbal accusations against Mahidevran.

The room felt cold as they approached, and Roxelane found herself glancing toward Hafsa to see what her mother-in-law's reaction was. Surely Hafsa had heard the rumors of Mahidevran's poisonous words against the new babe as well. Hafsa was smiling at the sultan's other wife and son, greeting them as if she was very pleased to see them. They surrounded Mehmed's cradle for so long that Roxelane rose from her reclining chair and crossed the room to join them.

"You shouldn't walk so far," Verda murmured, but Roxelane ignored her.

She didn't like Mahidevran or Mustafa spending so much time looking at Mehmed. Despite the fact that Mustafa was a mere boy of seven years, Roxelane had no doubt that it wouldn't be long before his mother had already told him that this new baby was a competitor to the throne. Roxelane stood near them and gazed down at the small child. Everything about him was perfect. From his fingers to his fine black hair to his dark lashes that lay upon his healthy cheeks.

"You have a beautiful son," Mahidevran said in her imperial tone.

Roxelane didn't miss the layer of disdain beneath her tone. The boy Mustafa stepped closer to the cradle, peering into it.

"This is your half brother," Hafsa said. "You will grow up to be great friends."

None of the women spoke in answer, although Mustafa said after a moment, "Can I hold the baby?"

Mahidevran might as well have gasped by the jerk of her body at her son's question.

"When he is a bit older," Hafsa said with a sweet smile.

Roxelane wanted to shoo the mother and son out of her chamber as quickly as possible. She wanted to take her child to her breast, feed and nourish him herself, and protect him from any threats to his inheritance.

She wanted to lock him away from the world and any prying eyes and plotting minds.

When Mahidevran and her son left, it wasn't soon enough. It had been seven years since Mahidevran had borne a son to the sultan. Roxelane didn't plan to wait that long to bear her next son. She'd give him a dozen if she could. She'd create a strong lineage for her children so that they would overshadow the sons of the other wives.

Verda came to stand by her. "You need to rest," she said in a soft voice.

Roxelane turned to her trusted friend and servant. "I am too angry to rest. Why did that woman have to come?"

"She had to see for herself who threatens her son," Verda whispered.

Roxelane exhaled. "I cannot stand the thought of anything happening to my Mehmed."

"We will keep him safe, always," Verda said. "You have a loyal household, and you are the favored wife of the sultan, and you have now borne him a healthy and strong son."

She let her friend's words settle into her heart and soothe her. "I will not stop with one son," she vowed. "I will provide the sultan with many sons that he can be proud of. That he can put on the throne." She grasped Verda's hand in hers and clung tightly. "Will you help me?"

Verda smiled and leaned close. "Always."

Roxelane moved back to where her son lay. His eyes had fluttered shut in sleep and his long lashes lay softly against his healthy cheeks. She ran her finger gently along his sweet face, and in her heart she made an unbreakable vow to her first son. *As long as I live, nothing will stand between you and your destiny, my Mehmed. No cost will ever be too great to ensure you one day inherit all that your father has.*

author's notes

Süleyman the Magnificent was the only son of Selim I. In 1520, at the age of twenty-six, Süleyman became the tenth sultan of the Ottoman Empire where he ruled for forty-six years. After multiple battles, including capturing Belgrade, Rhodes, and Transylvania, his domain extended into Egypt and Persia, and he controlled the Red Sea and most of the Mediterranean. Süleyman was a poet, writing under the name Muhibbi, and the poetry quoted in this book is the English translation of Süleyman's original work. The sultan was also known as an accomplished goldsmith. He also directed architectural masterpieces with the renowned architect Sinan.

Süleyman's favorite wife, Hürrem Sultan, or Roxelane, was originally a foreigner named Aleksandra Lisowska, from Rohatyn of the Kingdom of Poland (Ukraine). She was abducted as a slave girl after one of Süleyman's expeditions in the 1520s. Finding favor in the sultan's eyes, she outmatched the other harem women for his affections, and they married.

The Ottoman harem was referred to as the Golden Cage. It wasn't a harem as one might think of one today, but a residence where the women who had been abducted or assigned to the harem lived and were educated. Some of them never even saw the sultan. The sultan's mother was the one to approve whether a harem woman could share her son's bed. The women were educated and trained to serve in the palace. The competition was fierce, and deception was around every corner. Specific rooms were reserved for the sultan's mother, his wives, his concubines, and his children. The highest number of women recorded at one time topped at 474. The women were served by black eunuchs, usually from the Sudan. The head eunuch position was prestigious, second only to the sultan's chief vizier.

At any given time, there were seven hundred to eight hundred residents at the sultan's Topkapi palace, rising to five thousand residents at its peak. The later years of Süleyman's life were conflicted with trouble between his sons. The sultan had his oldest son Mustafa executed in 1553 because of believed disaffection. Some historians allege that his favorite wife, Roxelane, orchestrated the events leading to his death in order to make room for her own son, Selim. Another conflict arose between the princes Selim and Bayezid, which led to the execution of Bayezid, and Selim's rise to the throne in 1566.

The Ottoman Empire began its teetering fall with the Treaty of Kucuk Kaynarca in 1774, and finally the empire collapsed in 1918 with World War I. In 1920, even before the Treaty of Sèvres was signed, the Turkish national government and assembly formed in Ankara. The nationalists defied the authority of the sultan and entered into a treaty of friendship with the Soviet Union. By 1922, the Turks had regained Izmir and routed out all the Greeks. On November 1, 1922, the Ankara assembly declared the sultan deposed. Turkey was formally declared a republic in October, 1923, with Kemal Atatürkas its first president.

In 2009, Osman Ertugrul, the last of the Turkish royals, passed away in Istanbul.

acknowledgments

In a recent interview, I was asked who my writing mentor was, and I realized that the answer comprised a whole list of people. When I started writing my first novel in 2001, I soon learned that I had a lot to learn about the craft of writing. When Annette Lyon invited me into her critique group, I had no idea the journey that I'd be led on. Critique members came and went, and I'd like to thank all of them for shaping me in one way or another: Michele Holmes, Lynda Keith, Jeff Savage, Annette Lyon, Robison Wells, James Dashner, Stephanni Myers, Lu Ann Staheli, and Sarah Eden.

I'd also like to thank the ladies who I meet with a few times a month for a write-in: Julie Daines, Taffy Lovell, and Jaime Theler. Writing is a solitary job for the most part, so it's nice to feel a part of something bigger than just myself. Many thanks as well to my beta readers for *Slave Queen*, including my parents Kent Brown and Gayle Brown, who were my "Turkey" experts since they are currently living in Izmir. And thank you to Susan Aylworth, whose critiques are always invaluable and who's willing to work with my breakneck deadlines.

Many thanks to my agent Jane Dystel who has been a great champion of my work, and thanks as well to Miriam Goderich for her behind-the-scenes help.

I'm especially grateful for my publisher Thomas & Mercer and their team of professionals. I've been privileged to work with outstanding editor Charlotte Herscher for the Omar Zagouri thrillers, and it's been a pleasure to work with managing editor Grace Doyle on *Slave Queen* as we prepare the book for publication. I appreciate her confidence in my books. Additional thanks to the Thomas & Mercer PR team and author relations manager Sarah Shaw. Thanks as well to copyeditor Dan Born, proofreader Rick Edmisten, map designer Don Larson, and cover designer M.S. Corley. Cleaning up the finer points makes a book shine. It takes a village to raise a writer, but it takes a city to transform a manuscript into a book and present it to readers.

Finally, I'd like to thank my family, my husband and our four children, and my father-in-law Les Moore, who have all been supportive of my work from day one.

about the author

H.B. Moore is the award-winning and *USA Today* bestselling author of more than a dozen historical novels set in ancient Arabia and Mesoamerica. She attended the Cairo American College in Egypt and the Anglican International School in Jerusalem and received her bachelor of science degree from Brigham Young University. She writes historical novels and thrillers under the pen name H.B. Moore. She also writes inspirational nonfiction, women's fiction, and romance, including *Heart of the Ocean*, A Timeless Romance Anthology series, and *Love Is Come*, under Heather B. Moore. Her kids just call her *Mom*. Join her newsletter list for updates at www.hbmoore.com/contact.